PRAISE FOR

*Leah's Choice*

"I loved *Leah's Choice* by Marta Perry! More than just a sweet Amish love story, it is a complex mix of volatile relationships and hard choices. I couldn't put it down. I highly recommend it!"

—Colleen Coble, author of *The Lightkeeper's Daughter*

"*Leah's Choice* is a wonderful, fresh addition to the growing collection of novels about the Amish life. Marta Perry has created characters that I came to care for deeply and a plot that kept me guessing at every turn."

—Deborah Raney, author of *Above All Things* and the Hanover Falls novels

"*Leah's Choice* captured me on the first page—complex characters, unexpected conflicts, and deep emotion. Make the right choice. Savor this special book."

—Lyn Cote, author of the Texas Star of Destiny series

"What a joy it is to read Marta Perry's novels! *Leah's Choice* has everything a reader could want—strong, well-defined characters; beautiful, realistic settings; and a thought-provoking plot. Readers of Amish fiction will surely be waiting anxiously for her next book." —Shelley Shepard Gray, author of the Sisters of the Heart series

*continued . . .*

"*Leah's Choice* by Marta Perry is a knowing and careful look into Amish culture and faith. A truly enjoyable reading experience."

—Angela Hunt, author of *Let Darkness Come*

"I was moved and challenged by Leah's honest questioning, her difficult choices, and most of all by the strength of her love and faith. *Leah's Choice* is a lovely book. Simply lovely."

—Linda Goodnight, author of *Finding Her Way Home*

"*Leah's Choice* takes us into the heart of Amish country and the Pennsylvania Dutch, and shows us the struggles of the Amish community as the outside world continues to clash with the Plain ways. This is a story of grace and servitude as well as a story of difficult choices and heartbreaking realities. It touched my heart. I think the world of Amish fiction has found a new champion."

—Lenora Worth, author of *The Perfect Gift*

# RACHEL'S GARDEN

*Pleasant Valley*

BOOK TWO

MARTA PERRY

BERKLEY BOOKS, NEW YORK

**THE BERKLEY PUBLISHING GROUP**
**Published by the Penguin Group**
**Penguin Group (USA) Inc.**
**375 Hudson Street, New York, New York 10014, USA**
Penguin Group (Canada), 90 Eglinton Avenue East, Suite 700, Toronto, Ontario M4P 2Y3, Canada
(a division of Pearson Penguin Canada Inc.)
Penguin Books Ltd., 80 Strand, London WC2R 0RL, England
Penguin Group Ireland, 25 St. Stephen's Green, Dublin 2, Ireland (a division of Penguin Books Ltd.)
Penguin Group (Australia), 250 Camberwell Road, Camberwell, Victoria 3124, Australia
(a division of Pearson Australia Group Pty. Ltd.)
Penguin Books India Pvt. Ltd., 11 Community Centre, Panchsheel Park, New Delhi—110 017, India
Penguin Group (NZ), 67 Apollo Drive, Rosedale, North Shore 0632, New Zealand
(a division of Pearson New Zealand Ltd.)
Penguin Books (South Africa) (Pty.) Ltd., 24 Sturdee Avenue, Rosebank, Johannesburg 2196,
South Africa

Penguin Books Ltd., Registered Offices: 80 Strand, London WC2R 0RL, England

This is an original publication of The Berkley Publishing Group.


Cover art by Shane Rebenschied.
Cover design by Annette Fiore DeFex.
Text design by Tiffany Estreicher.



PRINTING HISTORY
Berkley trade paperback edition / March 2010

Library of Congress Cataloging-in-Publication Data

Perry, Marta.
Rachel's garden / Marta Perry.—Berkley trade paperback ed.
p. cm.—(Pleasant Valley; bk. 2)
ISBN 978-0-425-23236-1
1. Amish—Fiction. 2. Lancaster County (Pa.)—Fiction. I. Title.
PS3616.E7933R33 2010
813'.6—dc22

2009047800

PRINTED IN THE UNITED STATES OF AMERICA

10 9 8 7 6 5 4 3 2 1

*This story is dedicated to my husband, Brian, with all my heart. Without your unflagging support and belief in me, it would never have happened.*

# Acknowledgments

I'd like to express my gratitude to those whose expertise, patience, and generosity helped me in the writing of this book: to Erik Wesner, whose *Amish America* newsletters are enormously helpful in visualizing aspects of daily life; to Donald Kraybill and John Hostetler, whose books are the definitive works on Amish life; to Louise Stoltzfus, Lovina Eicher, and numerous others who've shared what it means to be Amish; to the unnamed Plain People whose insights have enriched my life; and most of all to my family, for giving me a rich heritage upon which to draw.

# Chapter One

A flicker of movement from the lane beyond the kitchen window of the old farmhouse caught Rachel Brand's eye as she leaned against the sink, washing up the bowl she'd used to make a batch of snickerdoodles. A buggy—ja, it must be Leah Glick, already bringing home Rachel's two older kinder from the birthday party for their teacher.

Quickly she set the bowl down and splashed cold water on her eyes. It wouldn't do to let her young ones suspect that their mamm had been crying while she baked. Smoothing her hair back under her kapp and arranging a smile on her lips, she went to the back door.

But the visitor was not Leah. It was a man, alone, driving the buggy.

Shock shattered her curiosity when she recognized the strong face under the brim of the black Amish hat. Gideon Zook. Her fingers clenched, wrinkling the fabric of her dark apron. What did he want from her?

She stood motionless for a moment, her left hand tight on the door frame. Then she grabbed the black wool shawl that hung by the door, threw it around her shoulders, and stepped outside.

The cold air sent a shiver through her. It was mid-March already, but winter had not released its grip on Pleasant Valley, Pennsylvania. The snowdrops she had planted last fall quivered against the back step, their white cups a mute testimony that spring would come eventually. Everything else was as brown and barren as her heart felt these days.

A fierce longing for spring swept through her as she crossed the still-hard ground. If she could be in the midst of growing things, planting and nurturing her beloved garden—ach, there she might find the peace she longed for.

Everything was too quiet on the farm now. Even the barn was empty, the dairy cows already moved to the far field, taken care of by her young brother-in-law William in the early morning hours.

The Belgian draft horses Ezra had been so pleased to be able to buy were spending the winter at the farm of his oldest brother, Isaac. Only Dolly, six-year-old Joseph's pet goat, bleated forlornly from her pen, protesting his absence.

Gideon had tethered his horse to the hitching post. Removing something from his buggy, he began pacing across the lawn, as if he measured something.

Then he saw her. He stopped, waiting. His hat was pushed back, and he lifted his face slightly, as if in appreciation of the watery sunshine. But Gideon's broad shoulders were stiff under his black jacket, his eyes wary, and his mouth set above his beard.

Reluctance slowed her steps. Perhaps Gideon felt that same reluctance. Aside from the formal words of condolence he'd spoken to her once he was well enough to be out again after the accident, she and Gideon had managed to avoid talking to each other for months. That was no easy thing in a tight-knit Amish community.

She forced a smile. "Gideon, wilkom. I didn't expect to be seeing you today."

*What are you doing here?* That was what she really wanted to say.

"Rachel." He inclined his head slightly, studying her face as if trying to read her feelings.

His own face gave little away—all strong planes and straight lines, like the wood he worked with in his carpentry business. Lines of tension radiated from his brown eyes, making him look older than the thirty-two she knew him to be. His work-hardened hands tightened on the objects he grasped—small wooden stakes, sharpened to points.

He cleared his throat, as if not sure what to say to her now that they were face-to-face. "How are you? And the young ones?"

"I'm well." Except that her heart twisted with pain at the sight of him, at the reminder he brought of all she had lost. "The kinder also. Mary is napping, and Leah Glick took Joseph and Becky to a birthday luncheon the scholars are having for Mary Yoder."

"Gut, gut."

He moved a step closer to her, and she realized that his left leg was still stiff—a daily reminder for him, probably, of the accident.

For an instant the scene she'd imagined so many times flashed yet again through her mind, stealing her breath away. She seemed to see Ezra, high in the rafters of a barn, Gideon below him, the old timbers creaking, then breaking, Ezra falling as the barn collapsed like a house of cards . . .

She gasped a strangled breath, like a fish struggling on the bank of the pond. Revulsion wrung her stomach, and she slammed the door shut on her imagination.

She could not let herself think about that, not now. It was not Gideon's fault that she couldn't see him without imagining the accident that had taken Ezra away from them. She had to talk to him sensibly, had to find out what had brought him here. And how she could get him to go away again.

She clutched the shawl tighter around her. "Is there something I can do for you, Gideon?"

"I am here to measure for the greenhouse."

She could only stare at him, her mind fumbling to process his words. The greenhouse—the greenhouse Ezra had promised her as a birthday present. That had to be what Gideon meant.

"How do you know about the greenhouse?"

The words came out unexpectedly harsh. Ezra was gone, and plans for the greenhouse had slipped away, too, swamped in the struggle just to get through the days.

He blinked, apparently surprised. "You didn't know? Ezra and I went together to buy the materials for your greenhouse. He asked me to build it for you. Now I'm here to start on the work."

The revulsion that swept through her was so strong she could barely prevent it from showing on her face.

Perhaps he knew anyway. The fine lines around his eyes deepened. "Is there a problem with that?"

"No—I mean, I didn't realize that he had asked you. Ezra never said so."

"Perhaps he thought there was no need. I always helped him with carpentry projects."

True enough. It wasn't that Ezra couldn't build things with his own hands, but he was far more interested in the crops and the animals. Since his childhood friend Gideon was a carpenter, specializing in building the windmills that had begun to dot the valley, Ezra had depended on him.

But that was before. Now . . .

Now the thought of having Gideon around for days while he built the greenhouse that was to have been a gift of love from her husband—

No, she couldn't handle that. She couldn't. It was, no doubt about it, a failure on her part, one that she should be taking to the Lord in prayer.

"Rachel?" She had been silent too long, and Gideon studied her face with concern. "Was ist letz? What's the matter?"

"Nothing," she said quickly. "Nothing at all. It's just that I hadn't thought about the greenhouse in months." Her voice thickened—she couldn't help that.

Gideon heard it, of course. A spasm of something that might have been pain crossed his face.

"It gave Ezra great pleasure to think about giving it to you." His deep voice seemed choked.

She blinked, focusing her gaze on the barn beyond him, willing herself to be calm. Think. What could she say that would not hurt Gideon, but would get him to go away?

"I haven't—I haven't decided what to do about the greenhouse." As she hadn't decided so many things in the past few months, lost as she'd been in grief. "Will you give me a little time to think?"

"Of course."

But his voice had cooled, as if he knew something of what she was feeling. His gaze was intent on her face, probing for the truth, and all she could think was that she wanted him to leave so that she didn't have to talk about the bittersweet nature of Ezra's last gift to her.

The creak of an approaching buggy broke the awkward silence between them. She glanced toward the lane.

"Here is Leah, back with the children." She probably sounded too relieved as she turned back to him. "Perhaps we could talk about this some other day."

His expression still grave, Gideon nodded. "Ja, another time, then." He turned away, but then glanced back over his shoulder. "I promised Ezra, ain't so? I have to keep that promise."

He walked toward his waiting buggy, back stiff.

Leah shook her head, cradling between her hands the mug of tea Rachel had given her. "I don't understand. Why are you so ferhoodled at the idea of Gideon putting up the greenhouse for you? He'd do a good job, that's certain sure."

"Ja, he would." She couldn't argue with that. Everyone knew how skilled a carpenter Gideon was. "I just . . . it makes me feel . . . makes me remember . . ." Her voice trailed off.

Leah reached across the scrubbed pine kitchen table to cover Rachel's hand with her own. "It's hard, I know. I'm sorry."

"Ach, I'm being foolish." She shook her head, determined not to slide into burdening Leah with her sorrow and her worries. She'd done that enough lately. She freed her hand and stood. "I think I'd best take a look out at those children. I haven't heard any noise from them in a while."

Three-year-old Mary, building a house with her favorite blocks in the corner of the kitchen, chose that moment to knock it over, chortling when the blocks crashed to the floor. Leah laughed, and Rachel shook her head.

"Plenty of noise in here, though. Mary, pick those up, please. It'll be time to help with supper soon."

"I set the table," Mary announced, and began to pick up the blocks, putting them in her wagon.

Rachel leaned against the sink to peer out the window over the plants that crowded the sill. Her daughter Becky and Leah's stepdaughter, Elizabeth, seemed to be in a deep conversation, side by side on the wide swing that hung from the willow tree. Her first-grader Joseph and Leah's Jonah, who was a year older, were romping with Dolly, the nanny goat.

"All seems well at the moment." She sat down again, pushing the plate of snickerdoodles toward Leah.

"That's usually when they're the most ready to get into mischief," Leah said. She took another cookie, sighing a little. "I shouldn't eat this, but it tastes like more. Since the morning sickness finally went away, I've been eating everything in sight."

Rachel studied Leah's glowing face. "Being pregnant agrees with you, for sure. I've never seen you look better."

Leah shook her head, smiling a little, and patted her rounded belly. "I look like a hippo."

"I'll bet Daniel doesn't think so."

Leah's cheeks grew pink, but instead of answering, she shoved the plate of cookies back toward Rachel. "You have another. You need all the energy you can get."

Leah undoubtedly thought she had grown too thin in the past months, just as her mamm did, but Leah was too kind to say so outright.

It was strange, how much their situations had changed. A year ago Leah had been the devoted teacher at the Amish school, single and content to remain so, while Rachel had been completely occupied as a wife and mother, helping Ezra to run the farm, far too busy to think about anything else.

Now they'd switched places, it seemed. Leah was happily married to Daniel Glick, instant mother to his three children, and glowing with the joy of her pregnancy.

As for her—Ezra was gone, and she struggled to raise their children without him, caught in a web of indecision about the future.

Leah must have guessed at her thoughts, because her green eyes darkened with concern as she leaned toward Rachel. "Are you all right? Are you getting enough help? Daniel would be glad to come over, or we could send Matthew to do chores."

"That's gut of you, but we are managing to get everything done. There's not so much this time of the year. William comes every day to deal with the milking, and he's so willing to do anything he can. I think it helps him with his grief, knowing that he's doing what Ezra would have wanted."

She didn't need to explain further. They both knew how Ezra's shy younger brother had loved him.

"He's probably glad to get out from under Isaac's thumb a couple of times a day," Leah said, her tone tart.

Rachel had to hesitate for a moment to think of something positive to say about Ezra's oldest brother. "Isaac means well, I'm sure. He just believes he's the head of the family now, and so everyone should heed what he says."

"I'm convinced William's stuttering wouldn't be nearly so bad if Isaac listened and encouraged him instead of snapping orders at him." Leah spoke like the teacher she had been for so many years.

"I try to do as you suggested, listening to him and making him feel comfortable, and I do think he speaks more when he's here with us."

"That's good. I'm glad it's helping. I used to get so frustrated when he was one of my scholars and I'd see his sisters speaking for him, instead of helping him try." For a moment she studied Rachel's face, as if she hadn't been distracted from her concern by the talk of William. "Still, you will let us pitch in, any way we can."

"I will." Rachel could feel her forehead wrinkling into the frown that came too often these days, and she tried to smooth it out. "The real problem is that I can't seem to make up my mind about anything. I was spoiled."

"Spoiled?" Leah's eyebrows lifted. "That's silly."

"I was. My life went so smoothly. You know that. I loved Ezra and he loved me, we were able to buy the farm from my aunt and uncle, the children came along easy and healthy—everything went the way I wanted it to. Until the day Ezra and Gideon went off to look at that barn." Her hands clenched so tightly that her knuckles were white.

Leah put her hand gently over Rachel's. "Is that why you don't want Gideon to build the greenhouse? Because you blame him for Ezra's accident?"

Rachel shook her head, tears choking her throat. "I don't know. Forgive, that's what God commands. Besides, it was an accident, no one's fault. Everyone knows that. But when I see him—"

She broke off. She couldn't explain to Leah. She couldn't even explain to herself.

"Forgiveness is only right, but our Father must know it is hard. But Ezra and Gideon were as close friends as you and I are," Leah said, her voice gentle. "You know he wouldn't want you to hold Gideon at fault."

That hit home, and her heart clenched in her chest. Ezra had loved Gideon like a brother. But how could she look at Gideon and not feel the pain of Ezra's loss?

She took a deep breath, forcing her hands to relax. "I know," she murmured.

Leah patted her again, seeming reassured. "Just think how much you'd enjoy having a greenhouse." She nodded toward the windowsills, crowded with the plants Rachel had started from seed. "By the looks of those windows, your plants will be pushing you out of the kitchen soon."

She managed a smile. "True enough. But I'll be selling them at the Mud Sale next Saturday, so that will clear off my windowsills."

Leah had a point, though. With a greenhouse, she'd be able to produce many more plants for sale.

"Ach, I'd best be getting along home." Leah seemed satisfied that she'd made her point. "I'll see you at the sale, if not before."

She rose, but stopped partway up, her breath catching as she clutched her belly.

Rachel was beside her in an instant, fear shooting through her. "Leah, was ist letz? Are you all right?"

"Ja." Leah laughed a little as she straightened. "Just a muscle spasm, I think. All the books say to expect them."

"You and your books," Rachel teased, reassured by the laugh. "I think you have a book about everything, ain't so?"

"You can never have enough books," Leah said. "Anyway, I have you to ask for advice when it comes to being pregnant."

Rachel put her arm around Leah as they walked toward the door. "That's right. That's the only subject on which I'm the expert, instead of you."

Over the years she'd turned to Teacher Leah and her books whenever she'd had a question, and Leah had usually found the answer. For the first time in their relationship, she was the knowledgeable one, and it was gut, knowing she could help Leah.

They hadn't yet reached the door when it burst open. Becky and Elizabeth surged inside. Elizabeth looked to be on the verge of tears, but Becky wore the rebellious pout that Rachel had seen on her face too often lately. Her heart sank. What now?

"Mammi, my shoes are all wet," Elizabeth wailed.

Exchanging an understanding look with Rachel, Leah went to her. "Well, that's not so bad. Sit up here on the chair, and let's see how wet they are."

Rachel focused on her daughter, knowing perfectly well that if anyone had instigated mischief, it would have been Becky. "Becky, how did this happen?"

Becky's lower lip came out, her gaze sliding away from Rachel's.

"I'm waiting, Rebecca."

The pout deepened, and Becky shrugged her shoulders. "I wanted to see if the ice is melting on the pond. That's all. Elizabeth didn't have to follow me."

Unfortunately they all knew that where Becky led, Elizabeth would follow.

"You know you are not allowed on the ice without a grown-up there. Go find some dry stockings for Elizabeth to wear home. You will go to bed early tonight so that you'll have time to think about being disobedient."

"But, Mammi—"

The pout melted into the threat of tears, and Rachel had to force herself to remain unmoved. "Now, Rebecca."

Becky scurried out of the room. Leah, having soothed away Elizabeth's tears, was scolding her gently for being so foolish. "Run along with Becky and get something dry to wear home."

She gave her stepdaughter a little shove. Her face brightening, Elizabeth hurried after Becky toward the stairs.

"I'm sorry—" Rachel began.

"Don't be silly," Leah said quickly. "It's not your fault. I'm sure we did much worse when we were their age."

Had they? Those days seemed very far away just now.

"I don't think either of us was quite so gut at leading others into trouble as Becky is. And it seems to be getting worse, not better."

"She's had a lot to handle since last year." Leah's voice was soft. "I'm sure that's all it is."

She nodded, because she didn't want Leah to have another cause to worry about her.

But the truth was that she was no longer so sure that she was the gut mother she'd always thought she was. What if it had really been Ezra's influence that ensured the children's obedience and happiness? What if she couldn't do it on her own?

Loneliness swept over her—loneliness mixed with longing for something she'd never have again.

"*Don't* you have any snapdragons?" The English woman leaned across the stand at the Mud Sale on Saturday afternoon, peering at Rachel's remaining plants and seeming to dismiss them at a glance.

Only the success of the sales she'd made already gave Rachel the confidence to speak up.

"It's too early to plant snapdragons here. You won't want to set those out until the danger of frost is past. What about some of these nice pansies?"

The woman eyed the cheerful faces of the pansies. "I suppose they'll do. Do you have two dozen of them?"

Taken slightly aback by the sudden agreement, Rachel did a quick count. "Ja, I can just manage that."

Exultant, she began putting the plants into the boxes she'd brought for the purpose. This sale cleaned her out, and it was only two o'clock.

Leah had been right. If she'd had the greenhouse already, she could have made two or three times the money today.

She couldn't go back. She accepted the money and thanked the woman. But she could go forward.

She glanced down the row of booths that had been built for the sale in the field adjoining the township fire house. True to its name, the Mud Sale had turned the field into a sea of mud, with furrows filling with moisture where pickup trucks and buggies had made their way.

Mud Sales were a rite of spring in Pleasant Valley, and probably folks—Amish and English alike—enjoyed them so much because their appearance meant winter was over. People who hadn't seen much of their neighbors for months were visiting even more than they were buying, it seemed, at the couple of dozen booths that had been set up.

A few booths down, she could see her daadi, buying bags of popcorn for his grandchildren. She could only hope the kinder hadn't been eating junk food since he'd taken them off her hands an hour ago.

"Rachel, are your plants all gone so soon?" Her mother, who was sharing the booth with Rachel, looked as pleased as if she had just sold all her jams and jellies. "That is wonderful gut, that is."

"Ja. It makes me feel . . ." She paused, searching for the word. "Hopeful, I guess." Her mood seemed to have flipped around in the week since she'd talked to Gideon.

She studied her mother's kindly, lined face, knowing every wrinkle had been honestly earned. Mamm's hair might be snowy white now and her vision starting to fail, but the sweetness in her face would always make her beautiful.

"Mamm, is that the way of grieving? To be weak and doubting one day and then confident and hopeful the next?"

Her mother's faded blue eyes seemed to be looking at something in the distance. "Ja, you have it right. That's the way of it." She patted Rachel's arm. "It will get better. You'll see."

Rachel clasped her mother's hand in hers. "I'm sorry. I've made you think of Johnny, haven't I?"

A kind of longing crossed Mamm's face. "I never stop thinking of him, Rachel. Just as I never stop praying that one day I'll see him again."

"If Daadi would change his mind—"

Her mother shook her head. "Don't, Rachel. It's not your daadi's fault. He's only trying to do what's right. You know that."

*No matter how much it hurt.* Rachel finished the thought for her. Daad held hard to the letter and spirit of the Ordnung, the rules by which the Amish lived. Some might choose to bend the rules, but not Amos Kile.

A customer approached Mamm's side of the stand, and she moved away quickly, as if relieved to be distracted from thoughts of her only son, gone nearly eleven years now.

It had been hard for Rachel, too—terribly hard—to lose her twin when Johnny deserted his family to go English. Still, even a twin brother wasn't so close as a husband, and Johnny hadn't died.

She'd even seen Johnny a number of times in the past year, thanks to Leah's intervention. Leah understood too well herself the grief of having a beloved sibling go English, since her younger sister, Anna, had jumped the fence.

Rachel leaned against the counter, watching her mother wait on the customer. She should have thought twice before she'd asked her mother that question. With no other children but her and Johnny, the loss of him weighed heavily on her parents.

Daadi hadn't seemed able to reconcile himself to the truth—Johnny was never going to come back to the church. So he clung to the bann, refusing to see Johnny, even though it hurt him and Mammi more than it did Johnny, busy and happy with his work at the medical research clinic.

Her parents were growing older, more frail it seemed, with each passing month. Daad wanted so badly to help her with the farm since Ezra's passing, but his health just wasn't good enough. She knew it was a constant worry to him.

Mamm, having sold three jars of her raspberry jam, came back to her, studying Rachel closely. "You've been fratched about something. I can see it in your face. Is it too much for you, trying to keep the farm going?"

She shook her head, suspecting she knew the direction of her mother's thoughts. "I'm doing all right. William helps a lot."

"Still—" Mamm put her hand on Rachel's arm. "Won't you think about your daadi's idea? Sell the farm and move home with us. We'd love to have you and the kinder living with us. You know that."

"I know, Mamm," she said gently. "I just can't bring myself

to do that. The farm was Ezra's dream. It's what he had to leave to his children. How can I let him down?"

Mamm's eyes clouded with concern. "You can't run a dairy farm alone. Who knows how long Ezra's brothers can continue to do so much? If you sold, you'd maybe get enough to start a small business of some kind. Wouldn't that be better?"

It was tempting, so tempting. To be back under her parents' roof, having them share the responsibility for the kinder. Being able to lean on them when things got difficult. But—

"I can't, Mamm. I just can't make up my mind to that. Not yet, anyway."

But she had to, didn't she? She had to stop drifting along and make some definite decisions about their future, hers and the children's.

Isaac and William, Ezra's brothers, came up to the stand just then, relieving her of the need to keep talking about it, even if she couldn't dismiss it from her thoughts.

"How are your sales today, Rachel? Gut, I hope." Isaac, bluff and hearty, his beard almost completely gray now, stopped in front of her counter.

"They're all gone." She swept her hand along the empty countertop.

"Gut, gut," he said, and William nodded in agreement, giving her a shy smile.

The nearly twenty years between the oldest of Ezra's siblings and the youngest accented the many other differences between them. Isaac was stout and graying, with an assured manner that seemed to have grown since the death of their father had left him the head, as he thought, of the family.

William, just turned eighteen, hung back, shy as always. He

had huge brown eyes that reminded Rachel of a frightened deer and blond hair so light it was nearly white. He seemed always on the verge of growing right out of his clothes.

"Are you having a pleasant day at the sale?" The guilt she felt over her uncharitable thoughts toward Isaac made her voice warm with interest.

"Ja. For sure. Made a couple of deals and have a line on someone who has a fine colt for sale." He gave William a hearty slap on the shoulder. "Maybe I'll let William train this one."

Not sure what William felt about that, she could only smile. But for the most part, William did what Isaac said without questioning, as far as she could tell.

"By the way, Rachel, I found a buyer for those greenhouse supplies you've got in the barn," he went on. "You won't want it now. I'll come by and pick those materials up on Tuesday."

For a moment Rachel could only gape at him. Slowly, the temper she rarely felt began to rise. Not only did Isaac assume he knew what she should do—he thought he had the right to make decisions for her.

Forcing down the anger, she managed a smile. "That is kind of you to go to so much trouble. But I don't wish to sell."

He blinked. "Not sell?" His voice rose in surprise. "But what will you do with all that lumber and glass?"

"Build a greenhouse." The words came out almost before she thought what she'd say. She'd been having such difficulty in making decisions, and suddenly she'd made one on the spur of the moment. Yet Isaac had pushed her into this one.

Annoyance flared in Isaac's face, quickly masked by an air of concern. "Ach, Rachel, don't be so foolish. The money will be of much more use to you than a greenhouse."

"Ezra gave it to me for my birthday. I don't want to sell his gift. I want to use it the way he intended."

"Ezra would want you to do the sensible thing." Clearly the sensible thing, according to Isaac, was to listen to him.

The smile was so tight it felt her face would split with it. She shook her head. "I appreciate the trouble you've taken, but I've made up my mind."

Temper flared in his eyes, and his fist clenched on the counter. "How do you expect to get a greenhouse built? I don't have time to do it for you. And you certainly can't do it yourself."

"I w-w-want t-t-t—"

William didn't get any further before Isaac turned on him. "Forget that idea. I need you at the farm. You'll have no time to indulge this whim of Rachel's."

Her teeth gritted at the way Isaac disregarded William's wishes. Just because it took the boy a long time to say something didn't mean he couldn't have an opinion.

But that was how most of the family treated him, finishing his thoughts for him instead of having enough patience to hear him out.

"If that is indeed what William intended to say, it is very kind of him." She smiled at him, and he blushed to the tips of his ears.

"William is not available." Isaac ground out the words.

William's jaw clenched as if, for once in his life, he might go against Isaac's wishes. But she couldn't let the boy get into trouble on her account.

"I can't take him away from his work—he does so much for me already. I'll manage."

"How do you plan to do that?" Isaac's face darkened to a deep red, and he looked dangerously close to an explosion.

It seemed she didn't even consider the words before they were out of her mouth.

"Gideon Zook is going to build the greenhouse for me."

She caught a glimpse of movement from the corner of her eye. Gideon was standing there, watching them, close enough to hear every word.

## Chapter Two

*Gideon* winced inwardly as the expression on Rachel's face hit him. She'd just announced that he was going to build the greenhouse for her. But as soon as she'd seen him, she'd regretted her hasty words.

He hadn't been listening intentionally. He'd just noticed that her stand didn't seem to be busy at the moment, and he'd thought this might be a good opportunity to see if she'd made up her mind about the building.

Well, now he knew. She had, and if he wasn't mistaken, she'd been driven to that by Isaac's attempts to boss her around.

Ezra had always said his eldest brother was a little too fond of giving people orders. Even when they were boys together, he remembered Isaac trying to rule the roost. But Ezra had been a peaceable person. He'd listened politely to what Isaac advised, and then he'd gone his own way.

The surprise was Rachel. Who would have thought that someone who seemed as soft and gentle as Rachel would display such a stubborn streak when she was pushed?

Isaac, apparently following the direction of Rachel's gaze, turned and saw him. His face darkened a little.

"Gideon." He jerked his head in greeting. "Is this true, what Rachel is telling us?"

"Ja."

Sometimes the less said the better, and Isaac, though a good enough man in his way, had an uncertain temper to go with his bossy ways.

Isaac hesitated, and his expression said he was trying to adjust his attitude. "That's kind of you." It sounded as if he had to push the words out. "Still, Rachel's family is well able to help her."

It didn't seem the moment to point out that he'd just refused to do that very thing. "It makes no trouble. I promised Ezra that I would build the greenhouse if he got the materials." He kept his voice even with an effort, Ezra's face filling his mind, head thrown back, laughing as he'd done so easily. "I want to fulfill that promise."

Isaac's jaw hardened at the words, his eyes narrowing. He'd probably be surprised to know that Rachel had reacted much the same way.

And neither of them would ever know that his determination to do this thing went far beyond a matter of wanting to fulfill a promise to a dead friend.

A fresh spasm of pain went through him. He would do this because Ezra had been closer than a brother, and because he owed it to him. Ezra was dead, and he was alive. The pain deepened.

"Ja, well . . ." Isaac's words trailed off. "We can talk about it more later, when Rachel has thought this whole thing through."

When Rachel had come to her senses, Isaac clearly meant. His piece said, Isaac nodded to Rachel's mother, then turned and walked away. William, with a slightly apologetic smile directed toward Rachel, followed him.

Gideon watched the brothers walk down the now-muddy stretch between the rows of booths. He hesitated for a moment. The expression on Rachel's face wasn't very encouraging.

Still, since she'd committed herself openly to the project, he'd best nail it down before she had any more regrets than she already did. He approached the stand and leaned against the waist-high wooden counter.

"It looks as if you had a fine sale day, Rachel." He gestured to the flats that had been filled with blooming plants when he'd passed by her stand earlier. He'd not only taken note of them—he'd directed several people to her stand for flowers.

"Ja." She glanced at the counter, as if surprised to find it empty. "It's the first Mud Sale of the year, so everyone's eager to get something blooming, they are."

"We've had a wonderful fine turnout today, with the sun finally shining. The fire company will have a nice profit when all's said and done."

Mud Sale season would run for a few more weeks, probably, but their township volunteer fire company liked to be the first, especially this year, with the fund drive for a new fire engine. He'd been a fire company volunteer for years, and even though he and the other Amish couldn't drive the fire truck, they knew well how important it was to have up-to-date equipment.

"Ser gut." Rachel seemed to relax a little with the conversation safely off her own affairs.

He couldn't leave it at that, or she'd be backing out again. "You'll be able to grow a lot more plants for sale once you have your greenhouse up and running."

"I guess so." Her gaze evaded his, and she began stacking the flats, as if she wanted to keep her hands busy. "About the greenhouse. I—well, I spoke hastily. You don't have to feel obligated to do the building."

He studied her downcast face for a moment. Rachel had always been a pretty girl back when they were in school together, with those big blue eyes and the light brown hair that curled rebelliously out of her braids. She had become thinner since Ezra's passing, and dealing with loss had given a new maturity to her face.

Why did she dislike the idea of his helping her so much?

He brushed bits of potting soil off the counter's surface, trying to find a way to bring her to acceptance. It was strange, in a way, that he knew so little of how Rachel's mind worked, when Ezra had been his lifelong friend. Somehow his relationship with Rachel had always been a tenuous thing. Ezra had been the focal point, and with Ezra gone, he wasn't sure how to talk to her.

But he had to try.

"You know, it's more than a year ago now since Ezra showed me the sketch you made of the greenhouse you'd been dreaming about. He said he'd had to sneak it out when you weren't looking, trying to keep it secret until he was sure we could do it. I used that sketch to work up the plan and figure the materials."

She looked at him then, her face suddenly soft. "Really? Ezra started planning it that long ago?"

He nodded, glad that he'd been able to bring some pleasure to her. He remembered that day so clearly, hearing the love in Ezra's voice when he talked about his wife. "He knew we wouldn't get around to building it for a bit, but he was wonderful happy to find a gift you'd like."

"He knew how much I love growing things." Her fingers toyed with a leaf that lay on the counter.

"Ja." Memory blossomed in his mind. "He told me once that you had such a green thumb that you could put a stick in the ground and it would grow a flower."

Her eyes were wet suddenly. Maybe his were, too, as Ezra's words brought him back in the minds of the two who'd loved him.

He had to clear his throat before he could speak. "There's something I've been wanting to say to you. I had a lot of time to think about this while I was laid up."

After the accident. He sensed her withdrawal. Was she shying away because she didn't want to think about Ezra's death? Or was it because she blamed him?

If she did, that seemed only fitting, since he blamed himself.

She started to turn away, as if to end the conversation, and he touched her sleeve to halt her. She froze instantly.

"I need to get this said once, and then I'll never mention it again." His voice thickened, and he fought to control it. He'd be fortunate to get the words out once, with the pain and guilt riding him constantly. "I couldn't make any sense out of the fact that the Lord let me live when Ezra died."

His throat tightened at the thought of the other, older pain that was so similar, hovering over him, darkening his life. With Ezra's death the darkness might never leave, and then how would he keep going? He pushed the thought back and concentrated on saying what he had to.

"It seems to me the only reason I survived was so I could help Ezra's family." Surely she could hear the truth of it in his voice. "And that's what I plan to do, God willing."

. . .

It had been raining nearly every day since the sale, and the well-trodden paths where the cows approached the barn were a sea of mud. Rachel peered out the kitchen window, streaked with the latest shower. William was working in the barn. She must catch him and give him a cup of coffee when he finished.

She hadn't seen Gideon since the day of the sale. He'd probably been kept away by the rain. At least that would stop him from doing anything more about the greenhouse.

Just as well. She hadn't figured out yet how to deal with him. Most of the time, she didn't even want to try. That moment when they'd seemed to share their grief—that had unsettled her, shifting her perception of him, she supposed.

He grieved for his friend. Somehow she had too easily forgetten that. She'd been so absorbed in her feelings that she hadn't made room in her heart to remember that he suffered, too.

The barn door moved, and William came out. Thankful to be distracted from the difficult thoughts, she hurried to the back door and waved at him.

"Komm out of the wet and have something hot already," she called.

He hesitated a moment, then nodded and started across the expanse of wet grass that seemed to be greening more and more by the day, maybe even the hour.

By the time William had removed his boots and reached the kitchen, she had a mug of coffee poured for him and had set a plate of cinnamon rolls within reach.

"Sit down. What are you working on so hard out there?"

William sat and took a gulp of the steaming coffee, then grabbed the largest of the cinnamon rolls.

She smiled. At eighteen, William was still growing.

"B-b-broken b-b-board," he said briefly. He always found the shortest way of answering any question, having learned the hard way that most people didn't like waiting around for an answer.

"That's kind of you," she said. "I didn't even realize anything was broken. I guess I haven't been out there in several days." She spoke casually, busying herself with the coffeepot. Given a little time and acceptance, William's stammer improved remarkably. "You've been taking care of things so well that I haven't had to."

He nodded, taking a huge bite of the roll and speaking around it. "Okay n-n-now."

He was relaxing already, she could see. Filling her own mug, she sat down opposite him. If only there was a way to make it easier for him to communicate. He suffered so, locked out of the easy talk that should flow between him and his friends.

"I w-w-anted to d-do the greenhouse for you." He blurted the words out, his hand tightening on his mug.

"I know you did, William." She hurried to assure him. "It's all right. I understand that your work for Isaac has to come first."

"Not just that. We should d-d-do it, not Gid." He frowned, his mouth setting in a firm line.

William took his responsibilities seriously—too seriously, maybe. He was still a boy who should be enjoying his rumspringa, his running-around time, instead of trying to take care of her.

"I know what you feel," she said carefully, not wanting to make it seem that she was angry with Gideon. "I didn't want

Gideon to do it either, at first. But he was Ezra's good friend. It's only natural that he wants to keep his promise."

A red flush ran up William's face to the roots of his straw-colored hair. He clutched the edge of the table. "It's not r-r-right. That he lived when Ezra d-d-died."

The words caught her on the raw, and it was a moment before she could respond. "Du muscht schtobbe. You must stop thinking that. If we want God to forgive us, we must forgive others."

She patted his hand, taut on the table's edge. It was big and rawboned, the wrist protruding a little from his shirt—the hand of a boy still growing into a man.

William shouldn't be angry that Gideon survived when Ezra died. That was wrong. And yet, didn't she sometimes feel that herself, despite all her prayers to forgive?

She wasn't alone in feeling it. Gideon himself felt it, judging by his words to her.

"I sh-should help you."

"You do." She was comforting him as she'd comfort one of the children. "You help every day, me and the children."

"I'm g-g-glad to." He flushed a little, his gaze almost too intense for comfort.

Maybe it was time to change the subject. "Speaking of the kinder, is Joseph still out in the barn?"

Becky would rather stay in and read when it was raining, but Joseph had hurried out as soon as he spotted William coming.

He nodded, his face breaking into a grin. "W-w-wants me to make a b-bed for the goat."

She shook her head, smiling in return. "He treats that goat better than he does his little sister. What Ezra would think about that, I don't know. He never believed in making a pet out of a farm animal." Her smile faded. "Still, Joseph seems to get comfort out of it. I don't have the heart to discourage him."

They were silent for a moment, and she knew they were both thinking of what Joseph had lost.

"I'll d-do it."

"You're a gut onkel," she said, her voice filling with affection for him. "I don't know how we'd get along without you."

William flushed again. "I been thinking about th-that. You n-n-need someone to take c-c-care of you." He seemed to be growing nervous, the stammer increasing.

"The family already does that."

"N-not enough." He leaned toward her, his face suddenly filled with intensity. "R-Rachel, will you marry me?" He said the words as formally as if in worship.

For a moment she thought she'd misunderstood him, but a look at his face told her he was serious. The boy actually felt so strongly about taking care of them that he'd propose marriage to a woman old enough to be . . . well, not his mother, but certainly his big sister.

She didn't know what to say. Whatever it was, she couldn't let him think she was laughing at him. He was so young, so vulnerable already because of his stammer.

*Please, Lord, give me the right words to do this without hurting him.*

"William, that's so kind of you." She infused the words with caring for the little brother Ezra had loved. "I know you want to help us, but that's not the way."

His lips trembled, and he pressed them together for a moment. "You're s-s-saying no."

It was kinder, surely, to make this clear. "I'm saying no. You're my bruder, William. That's how I've always seen you, and you're very dear to me."

He was only doing this for Ezra's sake, she was sure. But still, he would be hurt by the rejection.

"D-dumb idea." Tears welled in his eyes, and he knuckled them away like a child would.

"Not dumb. Just very kind." She smiled at him. "I'm too old for you, William, and that's the truth. I can't take you away from the sweet girl God has planned for you."

"N-nobody w-w-would have m-m-me." He turned away, face sulky, his ears red with embarrassment.

"Someone will love you for the gut person you are. I promise." She patted his hand. She felt about a hundred and two in comparison to him, and in a moment she'd start to laugh hysterically. "Why don't you go on out and give Joseph a hand before he tears down Dolly's pen?"

He jerked a nod, shoved himself to his feet, and rushed out the back door, letting it slam behind him.

She could laugh now, but somehow the impulse had left. Poor William, thinking he could make up for Ezra's death that way. Thinking that marriage to him would solve her problems.

*Bless him, dear Lord. He has such a gut heart. Surely You have a girl in mind who will love him for that and will set him free to love her, too.*

Rachel drove her buggy down the road that led to Daniel and Leah's farm a few days later. Brownie, her mare, could probably take her there and back home again without any guidance, they'd made the trip so often.

Letting the lines lie slack in her hands, Rachel glanced down at the boxful of baby things at her feet. She'd had a gut clearing out and packed up things that Leah might need for her little one. Smiling and sometimes tearing up a bit while she did it, for sure. It seemed incredible that lively Mary had ever been small enough to fit in those clothes.

She tilted her face up so that the sun's warm rays reached beneath the brim of the black bonnet she wore for traveling. Her daffodils grew so fast now that it seemed she could almost see them moving, and even the green spikes of the tulips stood taller each day. Spring was nearly here, and with its coming her spirits lifted.

At worship yesterday it had felt as if everyone seated on the backless benches in the Millers' barn had shared her feelings. Except, possibly, for William.

Her fingers tightened on the lines, and Brownie glanced back over her shoulder, as if to ask what was wrong. Brownie couldn't offer her any advice about the boy, but Leah could. And that was another reason for coming here today.

Brownie turned in at the lane, and in a few minutes the mare stopped at the back porch, lowering her head immediately to snatch a mouthful of grass. Leah, not even bothering with a shawl, came to the door, smiling.

"Wilkom, komm in. I'm wonderful-glad to see you today."

Rachel slid down and pulled the box of baby clothes out. "You'll be even happier when you see what I've brought. Mary's outgrown things for the boppli."

"Ach, how kind of you. It'll be another six weeks before I'm needing them, if the doctor is right." She held the door to let Rachel into the spotless kitchen. "And where is Mary? You didn't bring her with you?"

"Her grossmutter wanted to spend time with her this morning."

She set the box on the table and gave Leah a hug. "That was gut, because I wanted to spend some time with you. And it's never too soon to get the swaddling clothes ready. Your little boppli might surprise you by coming early."

Leah patted her belly, laughing. "Not a bad idea. I can barely get close enough to the stove to cook now. Sit. I have coffee ready, and I think the young ones have left some of the apple kuchen my mamm brought yesterday."

"Sounds gut."

Rachel settled down, nearly as comfortable in the Glick kitchen as she was in her own. Leah hadn't moved far when she married, only to the farm next to the one where she'd grown up, where her parents still lived.

While Leah busied herself at the stove, Rachel began sorting the baby things she'd brought, laying them in rows on the pine tabletop. She unfolded a gown so tiny it seemed hardly likely it would fit a baby doll, let alone Mary. Her fingertips smoothed the fine stitches her mamm had sewn into the soft fabric—smoothed and clung, reluctant to let go. Reluctant to think that Mary would be the last boppli she'd have.

Leah brought the coffee and apple kuchen, leaning over to touch a baby shawl, letting it run through her fingers. "Your mamm made this, didn't she? Maybe you'd rather keep it for—" She stopped, biting her lip. "I'm sorry. I shouldn't have said that."

"It's all right, Leah. Really. I'm not upset at that."

Leah eyed her, still looking a little flushed at her mistake. "If not at that, then at something. Are you still concerned about Gideon Zook and the greenhouse?"

"No. Well, maybe a little," she said, trying to be honest. "But I'm as sure as I can be that going ahead with it is the only choice.

He's coming over later this afternoon to go over the plans with me."

"No regrets at standing up to Isaac?"

She shook her head. "I surprised myself, I did. But Ezra never let Isaac make decisions for him. And if I once start, I don't know where it would stop."

"You might be like William, afraid to do anything unless Isaac approves," Leah suggested.

"William can be surprising, too." She blew out a frustrated breath. "You wouldn't believe what he said to me the other day."

Leah's hands paused on the tiny nightgown she was folding. "Tell me."

"He offered to marry me, that's what." She could feel the color come up in her cheeks at the thought of it. "Oh, it was kindly meant, I know. He thinks that with Ezra gone, I need someone to take care of me. And since he loved Ezra, I suppose he feels it's his duty. I turned him down as gently as possible, hoping he would understand."

"Did he?"

"I thought so. But then at the Millers' yesterday for church, he wouldn't even look at me—just scuttled off every time he saw me heading his way." She shook her head, still upset when she thought of it. "It has me downright ferhoodled, trying to see how to deal with William, and Isaac, and my folks pressing me to sell the farm and move back home with them. To say nothing of Gideon, all set on helping us whether we want it or not."

Leah leaned across the table to clasp her hand. "It sounds as if you have too many people thinking they know what's best for you."

"That's it exactly." She could count on Leah to understand. "Ezra always said you couldn't hurt Isaac's feelings with a two-by-four, but William is a different story. He's so self-conscious about his stuttering, anyway. Ach, I must have handled it badly, for him to be that eager to avoid me yesterday."

"I don't know what you could do other than make it clear to him." Leah's tone was practical. "You certain sure don't want William walking around imagining that you're going to marry him. You're old enough to be his—"

"Don't you dare say I'm old enough to be his mamm." She smiled, realizing she felt better about it already. "Big sister, maybe."

"Maybe. But I think you've missed something about him. Don't you know that William is stuck on you?"

She stared at Leah as her words penetrated. "William? Me? That's silly. He only did it because of Ezra, because he thought Ezra would want him to. He doesn't—"

"He does." Leah shook her head, lips quirking a little. "Do you really not know that?"

"No, and I don't believe it." But the words didn't come out sounding as convinced as she expected.

"That's because you don't see his expression when he watches you, times you're not looking at him."

She still shook her head. But if Leah was right—

"Leah, what am I going to do?" She nearly wailed the words. This was the last thing she'd expected to have to cope with. "It's impossible."

"Why is it impossible? William is at the age of looking around for someone to love, and he sees how lovable you are."

Her stomach twisted in protest, and she pressed one hand against her middle. "I'm not. I mean—of course Ezra loved me, but I've never thought of anyone else . . ." Her voice trailed off.

"If you haven't thought of it, you should. It'll soon be a year since Ezra passed, and folks are already thinking to match you up with someone. I bet more than one man has been looking your way, and you haven't even noticed."

"I don't believe it. You're making that up. No one is thinking about that at all."

Leah shook her head, green eyes dancing. "Ach, Rachel, you are ferhoodled for sure. Don't you remember how set you were on matching me up with Daniel when he came to the valley? Well, now it's your turn to feel like the target."

She stared at Leah, sure that the consternation she felt was written on her face.

Chuckling a little, Leah started to get up. "If you could see your face right now—" She broke off with a gasp, clutching the chair, and doubled over.

"Leah!" Rachel was there in an instant, putting her arms around her friend, her heart beating a wild rhythm of love and fear as she helped her sit down again. "Are you all right? Is this happening often?"

Leah gasped a little, leaning back in the chair, her face taut with pain. "Not—not too often. That was the worst one yet. But all the books say—"

"I don't care what the books say." Now it was her turn to be the practical one. "If you have a pain bad enough to make you turn white and double up with it, you need to talk to the doctor. Where's Daniel?"

"In the barn, I think. I'm sure I'm all right. It's just a muscle spasm."

"Maybe so. I hope so. But Daniel had best take you to the doctor now, and I'm going to tell him so."

Without waiting for an argument, she hurried across the kitchen and out the back door, her heart pounding in time with her feet.

*Please, Lord, please. Let it be nothing at all. Let Leah and her babe be safe. Please.*

# Chapter Three

*Anyway,* the doctor says that Leah and the boppli are both all right, but she has to start taking it easy, getting off her feet more every day if she doesn't want to be stuck on complete bed rest."

Rachel's brother, Johnny, looking out of place sitting at Rachel's kitchen table in his buttoned-down shirt and khaki pants, stirred his coffee with an absent frown. "If I know Leah, she won't like that. She always has to be up and doing."

"This time she'll do as she's told. Daniel and I made a pact to see to that."

She had gone to the doctor's office with Leah and Daniel, knowing that her mother wouldn't mind staying with Mary, and feeling that her friend needed her support. Daniel had been as happy at her presence as Leah. There were times when only another woman would do.

"I'm glad she's going to be all right." Johnny's voice had a strained note, and he bent his head over the tax forms she'd asked him to look at for her, as if to avoid the subject.

When Johnny had come back to Pleasant Valley a year ago to work at the medical research clinic, he'd tried to renew his friendship with Leah, the girl he'd promised to wed before he'd run off to turn English. He'd ended up imagining himself to be in love with her again, but Leah had chosen to marry Daniel.

Johnny seemed to have adjusted to that, but Rachel wasn't sure how much it bothered him. Once she'd have said that she knew her twin's every feeling, but that had been a long time ago. Now she was just happy to have a relationship with him, knowing they could never go back to what they'd been.

When Leah had first helped bring them together, they'd met once in a while on neutral territory, usually at the home of a friend who understood. Ezra, seeing how important it was to her, had encouraged her to talk the whole situation over with their bishop, Mose Yoder.

Bishop Mose, who saw those kinds of situations more and more as the years went on, had been helpful. As long as she kept to the letter of the bann, not eating at the same table with Johnny, not taking food from his hand, not riding in a car he was driving, the bishop saw no problem.

The outside world probably thought their rules silly. But the rules, the Ordnung, agreed to by every baptized member, spelled out how they remained Amish. How they lived in the world but not of the world.

Rachel's gaze lingered with affection on the dark gold of Johnny's hair as he bent over the papers. It was such a joy to be in the same room with him after all those years apart. And how much Mammi must long to see him, touch him.

For just an instant she toyed with the idea of setting up an "accidental" meeting. But that would be foolish, causing more harm, putting her mother in a position of choosing between husband

and son. As long as Daadi held to his determination not to see Johnny, she could do nothing.

Johnny finally pushed the forms back and tapped the yellow pad on which he'd been figuring. He looked up at her, shaking his head a little. "Almost anyone would probably do this better than I can, Rach. I do my own taxes, sure, but a dairy farm is a different matter." A smile flickered across his face. "Would you believe that some people think the Amish don't pay taxes, just because they rely on themselves instead of the government?"

"I hope you straighten people out if they say that to you. 'Render unto Caesar . . .'" She didn't finish the Scripture, because Johnny would know it as well as she did.

He shrugged slightly, as if to evade answering the implied question. She didn't press him. Maybe not correcting people's misconceptions was one of the compromises he made to live English.

"Even if you can just give me a rough figure," she said, "that will help me to plan."

"I might be missing something important. Why don't you have Daad do it?"

"He would, for sure. But I'm trying not to depend on Daad and Mammi too much. If he knew, he'd insist on paying the taxes for me. As it is, he and Mamm are pushing me to sell the farm and move back in with them."

Johnny turned to face her more fully, his face grave. "Nobody knows better than I do how stiff-necked Daad can be, but maybe he's right about that. How long can you keep on trying to run a dairy farm with people volunteering to help you?"

If Johnny was telling her to take Daad's advice, the tax news must be bad. She clasped her hands together. "How much do I owe?"

"I could be wrong. Probably am. Why don't I take these to a regular tax preparer for you?"

He was being kind, but his kindness just seemed to make things worse.

She took a breath, steeling herself for the worst. "I'll need to do that, I guess. But first I want to have at least an idea of what I'm getting into. I won't hold you to it, Johnny, but tell me what you think."

His blue eyes, so like hers, darkened with concern. "Okay. It looks to me as if you're going to owe around ten thousand, give or take a thousand."

She leaned back against the counter. "That much."

"I'm sorry." He pressed his fingers to his forehead, massaging, as if his head ached over giving her such bad news. "Look, I could be wrong. I might be missing some big deductions. Maybe it's not as bad as that."

"Maybe it's worse." She forced herself to be practical. It wouldn't do to let Johnny see how upset she was. "Don't worry. I do have money in the bank. Probably enough to make the payment."

"And then what will you have to live on?"

"We'll manage."

They could manage on very little, living as they did. Johnny, with his English standards, had probably forgotten that.

Still, she would find it difficult, just keeping up with the normal expenses of the farm. If she could find some additional source of income . . .

Or maybe everyone else was right. Maybe she was making things harder by clinging to the farm, not just for herself but for everyone who helped her.

"I don't make much money as a research assistant, but I can

get by on a couple hundred less a month. Let me give you that much."

Her heart was touched. But it was impossible; surely he saw that.

"I can't. Thank you for offering. It is so kind."

He moved back, his face tightening. "You mean you won't accept it because I'm under the bann."

"I love you for offering to help me, but I need to do this on my own."

"Don't try to sugarcoat your answer for me, Rachel." His tone hardened. "I'm not one of your children. You're willing to see me, but you won't take money from me no matter how much you need it."

Johnny was getting that mulish look that meant he had his back up, and she knew only too well how that would end. As dearly as she loved him, she wasn't blind to his faults.

She took a breath, trying to be patient. "You know I love you. But keeping my covenant with the church is important. Don't ask me to do something that would cause problems for me with the other people I love."

He shrugged, reaching for his jacket. "Some things never change, do they? I'd better get out of here before I say something I'll regret."

It seemed to her that he already had, but she wouldn't make things worse by telling him so.

"Denke for helping with the taxes. Komm again soon."

He gave her a quick peck on the cheek. "I'll see," he muttered. "We're pretty busy at the clinic just now."

Rachel watched him leave, trying not to feel upset. Johnny's attitude would be understandable if he really was English, but after eighteen years of being Amish, he ought to know better.

The truth was that he and Daadi were too much alike—both too stubborn and too proud to see beyond their own opinions.

Rachel dug her hand spade deep into the moist earth, loosening the roots of the weed that was already taller than the thyme uncurling its leaves delicately in the herb garden. This end of the bed was shady and moist, and the mint loved it here. She was eager to see how the variety of lemon thyme she'd planted last year had survived the winter.

"Weed, Mammi."

She grabbed Mary's hand just before her daughter could uproot the tiny plant. "Not that one, Mary. See, look for ones like this."

She showed her the weed she'd just removed, and Mary nodded solemnly, intent on doing it right. If taking pleasure in digging in the dirt was any sign, little Mary would turn into the gardener of the family.

The air was still chilly, but the sun felt warm on Rachel's back. Already the rhythmic movements and the scent of fresh-turned earth relaxed her. She might be tired and aching after her first hours in the garden, but it would be a happy tired. She glanced at Mary, smiling at her daughter's intent face as she worked away with her own little spade.

Rachel's heart warmed with the sun. This was what she'd longed for throughout the long, lonely winter. This was where healing would come for her.

*I know You love gardens, Lord. I feel as close to You here as I do when we're in worship. That's not wrong, is it?*

The bucket of weeds was nearly full when Mary sat back on her heels. "Look, Mammi. Onkel Isaac."

She followed the direction her daughter pointed, and her

peace fled. Sure enough, it was Isaac, walking across the field that separated their farm from his.

It was unkind to feel that his coming tore up her peace as surely as she had torn the weeds from her garden.

*Forgive me, Father. Help me to be patient with him and to remember his good heart.*

Even as she prayed, she couldn't help hoping that Isaac would conclude his business quickly. Gideon was supposed to stop by with the final plans for the greenhouse, and life with Isaac would go more smoothly if he were not reminded of that.

Besides, she found the whole business stressful enough, without having Isaac there looking on while she tried to arrive at some conclusion with Gideon.

She rose as Isaac approached, brushing the earth from her hands and shaking out her apron. "Wilkom, Isaac."

"Onkel Isaac." Mary, seldom shy, threw herself at his knees.

He caught the child, lifting her skyward, and tossed her in the air. His stern face softened into a smile at her giggles.

Warmth flooded Rachel's heart at the sight. Isaac, having only sons, had always had a soft spot for her two girls. Whenever she became exasperated at his bossiness, she should remind herself of how kind he was to her children.

"There, now, little Mary, that's enough flying for today." He set her on her feet and patted her head gently.

"I'm afraid she'll never think it's enough." Rachel steered her daughter back to her spade before she could demand more. "You know she loves it when you play with her."

"Ja." Isaac's face was soft as he watched her daughter. "She's a gut child." He turned to her. "And how is Leah Glick? We heard she's been ailing."

"Doing much better." The relief she felt sounded in her voice. "I went over this morning to help a bit with the kinder and make sure she's resting."

"Gut, gut," he said, a bit absently. He gazed past her, toward the barn, as if his mind were elsewhere.

"Did you want to talk with me?" she nudged, mindful that Gideon could show up at any minute.

"Just wanted to check on you and the little ones."

"That's kind of you. We're doing all right, thanks to everyone's help."

He nodded. "I didn't want to bring this up until after you'd had some time to get used to the way things are now, but have you been giving thought to the future?"

*The way things are now.* He meant her life without Ezra, but he was making an effort to be considerate.

"I think about it all the time. Making decisions, that's the difficult part."

"Ja. Ezra always took gut care of you. It's hard, a woman on her own."

Tension crept back along her nerves. Surely Isaac wasn't suggesting that she remarry, was he?

"I've been considering the situation. You know, Caleb's nearly nineteen now."

Caleb, Isaac's oldest, was actually a month older than his Onkel William, a thing that wasn't so surprising when families were large and spread out in age.

"He hasn't given you much worry during his rumspringa, has he?" Some youngsters did, especially the boys, taking their freedom to extremes, but Caleb had always seemed too serious and responsible for that.

"No, no, he's too wise for that. Thing is, he's ready to take a wife."

A suggestion that she consider marriage to Caleb, coming after William's proposal, would drive her to hysteria. "Is he?" Her voice sounded strangled.

"Ja, ja. He and Ellen Stoltzfus have decided between them, and we're agreeable, though we're not telling anyone but family yet, of course."

She could breathe again. Really, she was being ridiculous, having such thoughts. "I'm happy for them."

"Ja, so are we, but having five boys to get settled isn't an easy thing, you know. In the normal way of things, Caleb would take over my farm, but I'm nowhere near ready to move to the grossdaadi haus."

He chuckled, to show that was a joke. Naturally Isaac wouldn't want to give up the reins yet.

"I'm sure Caleb is willing to wait until you're ready." That seemed the proper answer, although she had no idea why Isaac would be talking to her about it.

"Well, and that's just what we don't want him to do. A young couple like that, just starting out, it's a gut thing to have their own place. Helps them to be steady-like, knowing what they're working toward."

"I see." She was beginning to, actually. "Are you talking about my farm?"

He looked a little nettled, as if he didn't care to be rushed toward the point he wanted to make, but then his face smoothed out into a determined smile.

"Don't hurry into answering me. I just want you to think about this. Seems it would be the best solution all around. Ezra's farm would go to his kin, as I'm sure he'd want, and we'd pay you a fair market price. Set it up any way you want, with monthly payments or a lump sum."

Ezra's farm, he'd said. Of course that was the way he'd see it, conveniently forgetting that the farm had come to them from her aunt and uncle. Childless themselves, they'd made it easy for their favorite niece and her husband to buy their place.

That didn't really matter, did it? The point was that if she was going to have to sell, it would be better to sell to family, as Isaac said.

The familiar indecision settled on her. "I'm not sure . . ."

"What aren't you sure about?" His voice sharpened. "You can't run a dairy farm on your own. You must be sure of that much. It was hard enough for Ezra, with the children not old enough to help yet."

Ezra had worked too hard, tried to do too much, but he'd loved it. No matter how tired he was, he always had a smile and a dream for the future. That was what he'd been working for—to have the right life for their family.

"You have to think about the children's future," Isaac said, gesturing toward Mary, who'd begun arranging pebbles around the edge of the bed. "Suppose you try to hang on to the farm and you fail. You could get into trouble with the taxes and end up losing everything Ezra worked so hard for. Better to make the decision now, while it's yours to make."

He made it all sound so sensible. It was sensible, she supposed. It just seemed wrong, somehow. This wasn't the way Ezra's dream was supposed to end.

"I . . . I'll think about it." Her voice sounded weak and indecisive, even to herself, and she hated that. Had she really been so dependent on Ezra that she couldn't make up her own mind?

"Gut, gut." Isaac rocked back on his heels, smiling. "You think on it. Pray on it. I know you'll decide right."

It was easy for Isaac to say. He wasn't the one who'd have to live with the results.

*Gideon's* hands tightened on the lines as his buggy rolled down the lane to the Brand farm. That was Isaac Brand he'd spotted, heading back across the fields to his adjoining farm.

Judging by what he'd seen of Rachel's relationship with her brother-in-law, he probably wouldn't find her in a tranquil temper after a visit from Isaac. That didn't bode well for the success of his mission today.

He'd have to be persistent, that was all. He'd been trying for well over a week to get Rachel's final approval on the plans for the greenhouse. He'd figured that once she'd committed herself to letting him build it, that would be the end of the discussion, and he could get on with it.

But each time he'd tried to pin her down, Rachel had found yet another reason to avoid giving him the final go-ahead. At first he'd thought she just couldn't figure out what she wanted. Now he was beginning to wonder if she still thought she'd find a way to get out of it entirely.

He didn't have all summer to get this job finished, not without having it affect the other projects he'd committed to. After the months of recuperation that he'd begun to think would never end, his shattered leg was finally healing. He might not be ready to climb on any scaffolding yet, but a small job like the greenhouse was the perfect place to start.

His hands tightened in the frustration that was becoming too familiar a companion. Orders for the windmills that were his specialty were stacking up. If he didn't start filling them soon, he risked losing the business to someone else.

Folks had been willing to wait for him so far, some because they were Amish and so were brethren, others because they wanted the skill he provided.

But they wouldn't wait forever. The doctors kept saying he had to be patient, that he'd regain much of his mobility in time. Unfortunately, patience was not something he'd ever had in great supply. Maybe that was why God had sent him this particular trial—so that he could practice developing it.

Truth was, he'd almost welcomed the pain of his injuries. The guilt he carried every day demanded some penalty. "Survivor guilt," the doctor had called it. Having a name didn't help him cope with it.

He stopped at the hitching rail, making an effort not to favor his left leg as he climbed down. Acting as if he were whole must be a step to getting there, he'd think.

Rachel had obviously seen him coming. She stood waiting for him by the herb garden near the back porch, with little Mary digging in the bed next to her. Motionless, she looked oddly forlorn in the slanting rays of the early spring sunshine.

Maybe she saw that he was watching her, because she squared her shoulders and smiled. He thought it took an effort. Her hands weren't gathered into fists, so apparently her encounter with Isaac hadn't made her angry, but it had had some sort of effect on her.

"I hope I'm not coming too late, Rachel. Mary, how are you?" He smiled down at the little girl. So like her mother, she was, her blue eyes fixed on him in an unwavering stare.

"No, it's fine. We're finished here." Rachel glanced at her daughter. "Mary, what are you doing?"

Mary had come over to him. She tugged on his pants leg, and then she linked her fingers together in a rocking motion.

"It's all right." He grinned at the child. "She remembers that I made her a cradle from my handkerchief once. That's been over a year ago. Think of her still remembering that."

Mary tugged at his pants leg again.

"Persistent, aren't you?" Chuckling a little, he pulled out his handkerchief. He folded it into a triangle and then did the double roll and twist that transformed a handkerchief into a cradle with a baby in it, if you had the imagination of a child. He rocked it once between his fingers and then handed it to Mary.

She laughed and swung it back and forth. "Schloofe, boppli. Schloofe."

Rachel was staring at him, and he couldn't read her expression. "You're very talented," she said.

He shrugged. "I have nieces and nephews who sometimes need distracting."

"When did you do this for Mary?" Her voice seemed to have cooled.

He didn't care much for the disapproval he sensed in her. She'd never really liked the time Ezra had spent with him, it seemed. Had it been jealousy of their close friendship? Or resentment that he took Ezra away from family sometimes? She certainly couldn't imagine he was leading Ezra into mischief. During their rumspringa, it had been Ezra who always came up with that.

"When she went with Ezra and me to an auction, I think." He held up the plans he'd tucked under his arm. "Are you ready to take a look at these?"

She blinked at the abrupt change of subject. He could see her scrambling to come up with an answer.

"I . . . I was thinking that maybe it doesn't make so much sense to start the greenhouse right now. I mean, the frost danger will be over in another month, and I probably wouldn't get much use from it for a while. If you have other projects to do first—"

He kept a rein on his temper. Rachel had been a pliant girl, and she'd always seemed eager to do as Ezra wanted. Now it seemed she didn't want to be told what to do, and he wouldn't fall into the same mistake that Isaac made in dealing with her.

"Now is the perfect time to get on with the greenhouse. My leg's not up to the high work on windmills yet, but I can certainly handle a greenhouse."

He wasn't going to tell her the rest of it—his sense that if only he could start doing something for her and her kinder, he'd ease the weight of responsibility that he felt each time he thought of Ezra.

Her face had tightened with the reminder of his injury, but she gave a jerky nod. "Makes sense, I guess. It's getting chilly. Komm inside. We can work there."

Success, of a sort, he supposed. He followed her into the haus, and Mary trailed after them, crooning a soft lullaby to her imaginary infant.

Obeying Rachel's gesture, he spread the plan out on the table, smoothing it down, while she poured coffee from the ever-present pot on the stove. She carried two mugs to the table, handing one to him, and stood for a moment staring down at the simple plan.

"You're right," she said. "I've hesitated about this long enough. If this is a gut time for you, let's go ahead already."

"Fine." He kept it matter-of-fact and leaned over, tracing the shape with his finger. "Here's the area we talked about adding along the side. It'll make the greenhouse a bit bigger than the original plan, but it'll give you more light, especially early in the spring."

She bent over the plan next to him, studying it. "I didn't think about it being bigger—will we need more materials, then?"

He heard a trace of anxiety in her voice, making him wonder if the cost was an issue. "I don't think so."

And if they did, he'd take care of that himself. She need never know.

"That's gut." Her fingertips glided over the outline almost lovingly. "I was just thinking that— " She hesitated, as if reluctant to voice the thought.

"What?"

"Well, it could be a little extra income for me, ain't so? Growing the plants and selling them. If I had more, I could maybe go to all the spring Mud Sales, even the farmer's market, ferleicht."

"No 'perhaps' about it. You could do that."

Now it was his turn to hesitate. Had Ezra not left her provided for? He'd always assumed this was a prosperous farm, but Rachel sounded as if finances were a worry.

He had been Ezra's closest friend. He had the responsibility to ask. "Is the money a problem? I thought the dairy herd brought in a gut income."

Rachel sighed, a little catch of breath that brushed his heart. With her eyes fixed on the plan she wasn't looking at him, and his gaze traced the clear line of her profile. She stood very close, and the air around them was so still it seemed even the room held its breath.

"I never had to worry about it when Ezra was taking care of things." She stopped, shaking her head. "But with Isaac and

William doing all the work for the dairy herd, it's only fair that they share the money from the milk."

His own breath seemed to be strangling him. Fair? Well, they deserved something for their work, but—

"How big a share?"

She didn't have to answer, but he hoped she would.

"We go halves." She glanced at him then, troubled. "That's only right."

"Does Isaac also pay half the expenses—the feed, the taxes?" Because it would be Isaac who expected the payment. He felt sure that young William was doing this because he had a gut heart and because he'd loved Ezra.

"Well, no. I mean, it's not his farm."

No, it wasn't. And if anyone accused Isaac of taking advantage of his widowed sister-in-law, all he'd have to say was that she'd pay as much or more if she had to hire the work done.

And saying anything to Isaac would only cause trouble in the family and dissension in the church. It was better, much better, to keep his opinions of Isaac's doings to himself and find some other way to help Rachel.

"I think your plans for the greenhouse are very sound. You might go a little further, if you wanted."

"Further?"

"Fresh flowers for the farmer's market, say. My brother Aaron and his wife go twice a week in the growing season. I'm sure he'd be willing to take them for you. And if you potted up some of the perennials you grow, that would be another thing to sell."

His enthusiasm for the idea built as he talked. A fine gardener like Rachel had plenty to offer that folks, especially the English, would pay for.

"Those herbs of yours, too," he added. "You might even go into growing some ornamental shrubs and raspberry or blackberry bushes and such-like for sale."

Rachel's eyes had widened, as if she could see all the possibilities. For a moment her face lit with enthusiasm, but then the light went out like a snuffed candle.

"There would be expenses. And besides, I don't know anything about running a business."

"I can help you with that."

He saw in an instant that he should have stopped at offering the ideas. Those she might take. Actual assistance, at least from him—that she didn't want. She was only accepting it with the greenhouse because she couldn't find a way out.

She pulled away from the table. "That's kind of you, Gideon. But I can't let you do anything else for me."

"Can't?" If he didn't do some plain speaking, this would always stand between them. "Or won't, because you don't forgive me for Isaac's death?" There. It was out, though his heart hurt with it.

Her face blanched. "It was an accident. You're not to blame. And even if you were, I would forgive."

It was the Amish way. They both knew that. Forgive as you would be forgiven. God didn't offer His forgiveness on any easier terms, no matter how much His children might want it.

"Forgiveness is more than words." He paused, but maybe it was best to say the rest of it. "The truth is that you didn't like my friendship with Ezra long before the accident. Every time he went off with me, I could see it in your face."

"No."

He ignored the denial, because they both knew what he said was true. "You resented our friendship. I never really understood why. And now you resent it that I'm still alive." The face of his dead wife flickered through his mind. Ja, he was still alive, for a reason only God understood.

He took a harsh breath. "I loved him, too, Rachel. I mourn for him. And I am going to do everything I can to help you and his children, so I hope you can find a way to live with that."

# Chapter Four

Folks in the outside world probably had people they went to when they had a problem. Doctors and other advisors, Rachel shouldn't wonder. When the Leit, the Amish of Pleasant Valley, needed someone to talk to, they went to Bishop Mose. So that was where she was headed today.

The weather had turned gray and chill again, as the end of March often did, and the wind had whipped at the brim of her bonnet as Brownie clip-clopped along the narrow blacktop road to town. If March was going to go out like a lamb, it had best start warming up. But she was here now, and Mose's workshop would be warm.

She swung down from the buggy seat and fastened the lines to the hitching rail. She reached back under the buggy seat for the piece of harness with the loose buckle. That needed mending anyway, so it gave her a good reason for coming to Mose Yoder's harness shop, just in case her courage failed her and she couldn't bring up the thing she wanted to talk with him about.

Bishop Mose, like all ministers and bishops among the Amish, worked at his trade as the apostle Paul had, accepting their Christian duties in addition.

There were two steps up to the little wooden porch, hollowed with the passage of many feet over the years. The glass-paneled door bore a hand-lettered sign. *Horse People Only, No Tourists,* it read. Beneath those directions Mose had added, in firm black-marker letters, *No Picture-Taking.*

She smiled a little. Once, the signs wouldn't have been necessary, but in recent years tourists had discovered the Amish of Pleasant Valley. Bishop Mose did business with the English horse-owners in the area, some even coming from as far away as Mifflinburg to get good handcrafted tack. But he could do without the tourists.

She opened the door, the bell jangling, and stepped inside. Bishop Mose stood behind the cash register, busy with a customer, but he gave her a quick, welcoming smile. Since the customer was English and not anyone she knew, she moved to the side counter, keeping her gaze politely averted from the business they were transacting.

The rich scents of leather and oil transported her back through the years. She'd been coming to Mose's harness shop since her father brought her and Johnny when they were little more than Mary's age. The shop fascinated her—the harness and tack hanging from pegs and lining shelves up to the ceiling; the mysterious, to her child's mind, machinery that Mose used on the leather; and most especially Bishop Mose Yoder himself.

She slid a sideways glance as he bent over the counter, listening courteously to some story the Englischer was telling. As always, Mose wore a heavy apron over his black trousers and blue shirt to protect them from his work.

Had he really not aged since she was a child? Somehow she'd

always thought him old, with his long beard and hair a snowy white and his face a patchwork of tiny wrinkles, much like a piece of his own leather.

Running her fingers along a fine Western saddle with elaborate leatherwork, she tried to figure out how old Mose must be. Close to eighty, surely, wasn't he? An Amish bishop was a bishop for life, just as the ministers were, chosen by lot through God's guidance. Had Mose started out looking like a patriarch of the Old Testament, or had the look grown on him as he ministered to his flock?

The customer finally headed for the door, apparently satisfied with the new bridle he had slung over his shoulder. He gave her a polite nod as he passed.

The door closed behind him, and Mose turned to her.

"Rachel. It's fine to see you today. How are you? And the kinder?"

"We're all well." Now that she faced his keen gaze, she was doubly grateful she'd brought the harness. She handed it across the counter to him. "I hoped you might have time to fix the buckle on this for me."

"Ach, I always have time for you, ain't so?" He took the harness, running it through his hands as if he saw with them, as well as with his eyes. "I mind when I made this for Ezra. Five years ago, it must have been, at least."

"About that."

She glanced past him, toward the alcove behind the counter where the big sewing machines sat, all connected to a massive belt that ran through a hole in the floor to a generator in the cellar. Sometimes Mose had several men helping him there, when he was especially busy, but today all was quiet.

She was alone with him in the shop. She wouldn't find a better opportunity to ask for his advice, if she could just get the words out.

Mose adjusted his glasses and began picking out the loose stitches that held the buckle, staying at the counter probably because he guessed that she wanted to talk.

She felt tongue-tied. How could she just come out with her mixed-up feelings about Gideon?

"Have you seen anything of John lately?" Mose gave her a keen glance, as if to assess whether her English brother was the source of her worry.

"A few nights ago." She remembered too well Johnny's annoyance at her for keeping to the Ordnung. "He is doing well, I think. I just wish—"

She paused, but Mose probably knew the rest of that thought.

"Your daad still refuses to see him?"

She nodded. "I don't bring it up much, because it upsets Mamm. Even though Daadi knows other Amish parents find a way to have a relationship with their children who have jumped the fence, he won't consider it."

"Ach, your daad always was one to do everything the hard way. No doubt he still hopes being cut off from his family will push Johnny into coming back to the church."

"It won't." Once she might have hoped that, too, but she'd seen enough of her brother in recent months to know the truth. He was committed to the English world and to the work that seemed so important. He would never come back.

"No. I never thought he would return." Mose's face showed regret and acceptance. "Some just aren't a fit for the life, even when they're born to it."

She'd never thought of it that way, exactly, but Bishop Mose was right. "From the time we were little, Johnny was always restless, always wanting more. Impatient."

He nodded. "I think— "

The bell over the door rang. Mose glanced that way, and his face stiffened. "No tourists," he said.

She darted a quick look. A man and woman, both with cameras hanging from their necks, had just come in. Surely they couldn't have missed the sign on the door.

"We just want to look around." The woman lifted her camera. "Just take a few pictures."

"No pictures. No tourists." Mose's tone was polite but firm. "That's what the sign says. I ask you please to leave."

Rachel stole another glance. The man's face had reddened. "Listen, if you people want to have any tourist trade in this town, you'd better be a little nicer when folks come in here."

"My harness shop is a business. Not a tourist attraction." Mose's face was as stony as Moses's must have been when he'd broken the stone tablets.

"Come on, Hal." It sounded as if the woman was tugging her husband toward the door, but Rachel didn't turn around again to see, wary of the camera the woman still held up. The brim of her bonnet cut them off very nicely. "There's a cute quilt shop down the street. I'm crazy about Amish quilts."

The door slammed, and footsteps thudded on the wooden steps. Rachel glanced around, just as the woman raised her camera to the glass and snapped a picture. Then, smiling in satisfaction, she went off down the street.

Mose grunted. "It spites me when they do that. Some folks don't have the sense the Lord gave a chipmunk. Can't they read?"

The flash of the camera had unsettled her, but she tried to

shake it off. "They think they're the exception to the rule. If they try that on Ruth Stoltzfus at the quilt shop, she'll chase them out with a broom."

Mose chuckled, his good humor quickly restored. "I'd like to see that, I would."

"So would I." She smiled, picturing plump, irascible Ruth's reaction.

"Now, then." Mose returned to the buckle, but his wise old eyes surveyed her over the rims of his glasses. "I think you did not come all the way to town today just to have this buckle replaced or to talk about the ways of tourists. Or even of your brother."

"No, I guess not." How to say this? "I . . . I'm concerned about something." She took a breath and plunged in. "It's Gideon Zook. You've maybe heard that he insists on building the greenhouse that Ezra promised me for my birthday?"

He nodded. Of course he'd have heard. The Amish might not have telephones in their homes, but they had a very efficient grapevine that passed on all the news.

"I know Gideon is not to blame for the accident." She said the words she'd been repeating to herself, staring down at Bishop Mose's weathered hands, darkened by the stain he used on the leather. "It was an accident, just that."

"But?" His voice was gentle.

"But when I see him, I feel resentment. It's as if I blame him for being alive when Ezra is gone." She clasped her hands together. "That's wrong. I know it. I have prayed to be able to forgive, to stop thinking this way, but God hasn't taken the feelings away."

"We forgive, as God forgives us," Mose said. "But God is God. We are not so gut at it as He is."

"I must forgive." She could hear the desperation in her voice. "I can't go on feeling this every time I see him."

"Rachel, child, when we suffer a great loss, as you have, we start by saying the words. That is gut, but we still have to go through all the grieving." His voice had thickened, as if he thought of his own losses—a son gone in an accident when a car hit his buggy, his wife dying of a stroke a few years after that.

Other people lost those they loved. Other people found a way to forgive and go on with their lives. Why not her?

"Gideon says that I never liked his friendship with Ezra." The words burst out of her. She'd been denying them for days, and that had made her no gut at all.

"Is he right?" Mose's voice didn't condemn. It just asked the question.

"I don't know." Her fingers twisted together, as if they fought it out. "I hope not. But maybe—well, since Gideon didn't have a wife, I guess it seemed like he was freer than Ezra. When the two of them went off together, even if it was just to an auction, it was like they were still having their rumspringa."

The words that came out of her mouth surprised her. Had she really felt that? She stared at Mose, longing to hear him say she was wrong. He didn't speak. He waited.

"Gideon was right, then." She said the words softly, almost to herself. "I did feel that."

"Rachel, Rachel," he said. "That's natural enough already. For sure a young frau wants to have her husband to herself. When there's a boppli, she wants him home with her."

Guilt was a rock in her chest. "Ezra worked so hard. I shouldn't have questioned it if he wanted to go off to do something with Gideon."

"Ach, child," he chided gently. "Don't start fretting about that, now. It's foolish. You were a gut wife to Ezra, and he loved you. Don't worry that you weren't perfect. We're not meant to be perfect this side of Heaven."

"But what do I do?" Her throat was tight. "I have to make it right. I shouldn't feel this way."

"The Lord calls us to obedience, not feelings."

"I don't understand."

His face hinted at a smile. "You try so hard, Rachel. Too hard, maybe. Just think about what you would do if you truly had forgiven. Then go and do that. Du Herr will take care of the feelings in His own gut time. Ja?"

She nodded slowly. *Think what you would do if you had truly forgiven, and then do it.* That was simple enough in one way.

And in another, given Gideon's determination to be involved in her life, it was not simple at all.

"*What* are you doing?"

Gideon looked up at the question to find Ezra's young son staring at him, his expression open and curious.

He set aside the trowel he'd been using to smooth the wet cement for the floor of the greenhouse. Squatting, he propped his elbows on his knees to pay attention to the boy. "This will be your mammi's new greenhouse. Today I am making the floor."

Joseph nodded. "Daadi gave the greenhouse to her for her birthday. I remember."

"You have a wonderful-gut memory, then. Do you think she'll like it?"

"It's a nice floor," the boy said, maybe wondering if that was all.

Gideon smiled. Young Joseph was a lot like Ezra had been at

that age in looks, but not in character. Somehow he didn't think Joseph was as daring as Ezra, who'd found far too many ways to get into mischief, usually dragging Gideon along with him.

"The floor is just the beginning. I still have to put up the walls and all the glass. And maybe build some tables for your mamm to put her plants on. It will take me a few days to finish it."

"I could help you. I helped Daadi a lot." Joseph's eyes clouded a little, as if the memory grieved him.

Gideon hesitated, not because he wouldn't be happy to have Joseph around, no matter how little help he was, but because he wasn't sure how Rachel would feel about that.

"You'd best go and ask your Mammi first. She might have some other chores for you to do."

Joseph considered that for a moment. Then he nodded and scampered off toward the kitchen door.

Maybe Rachel would have no objection. She had seemed welcoming enough when he'd turned up today. She'd even brought him out coffee and offered to make lunch for him. But that might be nothing more than a temporary truce.

He didn't know whether to apologize for what he'd said about her attitude toward his friendship with Ezra or let it be. Not that he'd changed his mind. But just because something was true didn't mean a person had to say it.

In a way, he could understand why she'd felt as she did. Young married couples usually had best friends who were in the same situation. If Naomi had lived, they'd have been friends as couples, sharing each other's lives as the children came along.

But Naomi hadn't lived. The baby hadn't. Even after all these years, letting himself think of that was looking into a bottomless pit.

Ezra had talked to him, just once, about remarrying. "Naomi wouldn't expect you to live your life alone, Gid." Ezra's normally merry face had been solemn as he leaned against the wagon they'd been fixing. "Everyone thinks it's time you were looking around for a wife."

He expected it from everyone else. Not from Ezra. He thought Ezra understood. The wrench he held clanged against the wheel rim.

"I can't." His voice rasped, and he forced the words past suddenly numb lips. "I let Naomi and the babe die." He saw the argument forming on Ezra's face. He didn't want to hear it. "Don't, Ezra. No matter what anyone thinks, I'll not be marrying again. I won't take responsibility for another life. I can't."

The back door banged, forcing him back to the present. Joseph raced across the lawn, his face alight with eagerness. "Mammi says yes, but I shouldn't be a nuisance, and I have to give water to my goat first, and keep her penned up so she doesn't get in the way."

It sounded as if he quoted Rachel. "Fine, do that."

The boy spun toward the barn, then paused, darting a measuring look toward Gideon. "Do you want to see my goat?"

Something in Joseph's expression said that this was a rare treat, so he got up from his knees. "I'd like that."

He followed the boy across the backyard toward the barn. The light breeze ruffled the boy's hair as he raced ahead.

Joseph ran the last few steps to a pen attached to the barn. A small Nubian nanny stood at the door, bawling for the boy as if he were her kid. Joseph opened the pen door and slipped inside, fending off the goat's attempt to get out.

"You must stay in now. Later I'll take you for a walk."

The little Nubian wore a collar, as if she were a dog instead of a goat. Her coat was glossy from much brushing. She was a beloved pet, obviously.

Joseph kept his arm around her neck and smiled proudly. "This is Dolly. She's beautiful, ain't so?"

"Ja, she is." Ezra's son might look like him, but he had Rachel's smile. Not that he'd seen much smiling from her lately, but he remembered the look.

"She's going to have a kid. Maybe two. Onkel William says that it might be twins. I'd like it if she had twins. Don't you think that would be nice?"

Gideon nodded. If his boppli had lived, he'd be a bit older than Joseph. They would have been friends. His heart twisted in his chest.

Joseph patted the little nanny's side. "I don't see how she's going to know what to do when the babies come, with no other goats around to show her."

"I'm sure it's in her nature."

"Maybe." Joseph didn't look reassured by the glib answer.

"I tell you what. I'll ask my brother Aaron about it, if you want. He raises goats, so he'll know. Then I can tell you what he says the next time I come."

"Would you?" Joseph's smile blossomed.

"Ja. Now, what do you say we get some work done?"

"I'm ready."

With a final pat for the goat, Joseph hurried out, fastening the pen door carefully. Then he darted across the yard toward the construction.

Gideon followed more slowly. He was a fine boy, this son of Ezra's. Rachel was doing a gut job with him, and it couldn't be easy for her, bringing up a boy without a man in the house.

He spotted her then—coming out on the back porch to shake out a rag rug. She paused, glancing from Joseph to him.

Taking that as an indication she wanted to say something, he detoured by the porch.

"Don't let him be a pest, now," she said.

"He's not. He was just showing me his goat, and now we're going to get down to work."

"That goat." She shook her head. "Ezra wouldn't approve of Joseph treating her as if she were a pet, but it's hatt."

Hard, ja, it was hard for Joseph. For all of them. "Ezra would have been happy the boy found comfort. You must stop worrying about it, because that I'm certain sure of."

There it was, then—that smile that softened her cheeks and warmed her eyes. Just like Joseph's.

But Rachel's smile was having a funny effect on him, and he wasn't sure he liked that. Or at least, not sure that he should.

*"Stretch* your hand out, now."

Rachel watched as Gideon helped little Mary press her palm into the still-damp cement floor for the new greenhouse. Mary giggled a bit, but her tiny handprint took its place next to those of Joseph and Becky, marking the spot that would be the entrance.

Joseph leaned over Gideon's shoulder, looking at them. "My hand is bigger than Mary's," he observed.

"But mine is the biggest," Becky said quickly.

"It's not a contest to see whose is biggest." Gideon lifted Mary back away from the floor. "We put your handprints there so that years from now, when you're all grown, you'll look at them and see how small you were the day we started the greenhouse."

Rachel had a lump in her throat already, and that comment

just made it worse. Panic gripped her for an instant. Where would they be, years from now? What if Isaac was right? If she couldn't keep the farm, someone else might be looking at the handprints, wondering at them.

The moment Gideon released her, Mary made an instinctive move to wipe her sticky hand on her dress. Rachel grabbed her just in time to avert disaster.

"Ach, no, Mary. Becky, please take Mary and wash her hands at the pump—real gut, now. Joseph, you go, too."

She kept her face turned away from Gideon, hoping he wouldn't see that she was upset. Or at least, that if he did see, he'd respect her privacy and not question it.

"Rachel?" He rose to his feet, brushing off the knees of his broadfall trousers. "Was ist letz? What's wrong?"

"Nothing." Despite her efforts, her voice didn't sound quite natural.

"Something, I think, or you would not have tears in your eyes." He stood, waiting, as solid and immovable as one of the sturdy maples that had been here since before there was a farm on this spot.

"I hope . . ." She had to stop. Start again. "I hope the children are still living here when they are grown."

"Why wouldn't they be?" His tone sharpened.

"If I have to sell the farm, it won't be the same." Even if she sold to family, and she and the children came back often, they wouldn't really belong here.

"You're not going to sell the farm." He reached out, as if to grasp her arm, but stopped, his hand falling back to his side. "You can't just give up."

"Give up?" Anger spurted through her, surprising her. "Do you think it's easy, trying to run the farm on my own?"

"No, I don't think that. But you have Ezra's brothers helping you with the dairy herd."

"There's more to it than that."

He didn't understand the constant worry. He couldn't. He was responsible for no one but himself. How long could she hold on? Even if she did start making money from her plants, would it be enough?

"Rachel, the farm was Ezra's dream." He did take her wrist then, holding it lightly in the circle of his fingers as if to keep her from walking away until he had the answers he wanted. "He wouldn't want you to give that up already."

"You make the same arguments as Isaac does. But to a different end."

He frowned. "What are you talking about? What arguments?"

She didn't want to tell him, but she seemed pinned to the spot by the intensity of his frowning gaze.

"Isaac wants me to sell the farm to him, for his oldest boy. He says that way it would go to Ezra's kin and still be in the family." Her fingers clenched. "He says that's what Ezra would want. You say Ezra would want me to keep the farm. The truth is that neither of you really knows what he would want."

"Maybe that's so." Gideon spoke slowly, his gaze intent on her face. "Maybe it's wrong to try to judge what Ezra would want. I don't know what Isaac is going on, but I'm saying it because I heard Ezra talk about his dreams for this place. About how it would be his legacy to his children, how one day Joseph would be running it, and you'd be adding on a grossdaadi haus for the two of you."

She seemed to hear Ezra's laughing voice, talking about the two of them growing old together in the grossdaadi haus he'd build. Her throat choked with tears.

"Do you think I don't know that?" She fought to speak around the tightness. "A wife knows her husband's hopes better than a friend, no matter how close he is. I lived the struggle to get established here. Even with the help my aunt and uncle gave us in buying the place, it wasn't easy."

His lips parted as if he'd speak, but she swept on, determined to have her say.

"This was our dream, but we never imagined that I'd be running it alone. I can't do it. If I didn't have Isaac and William's help, I'd be done. What if Isaac were no longer willing to help with the herd? What would I do then?"

"Isaac surely has not threatened to do that." His fingers tightened on her wrist.

"No. He seems willing to wait for my answer." She straightened, pulling her hand away, and he let her go instantly. "And it will be my answer, no one else's. I am the one with the kinder to raise, and I must decide what is best for them."

It sounded lonely. It *was* lonely, but it was also true.

For a long moment, Gideon stood looking at her. Finally he nodded. "I'm sorry if I spoke out of turn. You're right—the young ones must come first."

He turned, picking up the tarp that lay folded on the grass. He began to spread it over the cement.

She picked up an edge and helped him cover the new floor. The tarp slid over the small handprints, hiding them from her sight.

He fastened the corners with stones and then straightened, looking at her for the space of a heartbeat, his face very grave.

"I hope you will not have to leave, Rachel. But if you do, I'll make sure that every part of the greenhouse can easily move with you, except for the floor."

The tension that had been holding her up went out of her like a balloon deflating, and she felt flat and tired. "That's kind of you, Gideon. I don't know what the future will hold. Maybe that's for the best."

"Maybe so." His mouth closed firmly on the words, as if he wanted to say something else but was afraid to upset her.

She couldn't help smiling. She'd grown to know Gideon better in the past few days than she had in all the years before.

"You may as well go on. There is something more you want to say, so just say it."

He didn't quite smile in response, but his mouth seemed to gentle, somehow. "Just this. Ezra heard a lot of advice from Isaac all his life. He listened, but he always made his own decisions, whatever Isaac said." He paused, surveying her gravely. "I hope that you will do the same."

# Chapter Five

*Becky!"* Rachel called her daughter's name for the third or fourth time, still with no answer.

She could guess where Becky was. William had brought Ben and Bess, the Belgian draft horses, back from Isaac's this morning, intending to do the plowing. Becky, as fascinated as her father had been by the massive, gentle creatures, had raced for the barn the moment she got home. She was probably still there.

Grabbing her shawl, Rachel wrapped it around her as she hurried off the porch. Fickle April had turned cold after a few days that tempted with a promise of warmth.

Still, the ground was soft underfoot. William would be able to plow tomorrow. Perhaps she ought to have him add a strip or two to the kitchen garden, so that she could grow extra vegetables for market. And maybe some small shrubs, as Gideon had suggested.

She glanced toward the greenhouse. The uprights were in place now, so that she could visualize the completed project. It would be near as big as her kitchen, which made sense since she'd rather garden than cook.

Gideon hadn't come today—off to bid on another job. Just as well. She'd felt awkward with him since the day he'd helped put the handprints in the greenhouse.

Annoyance flickered through her. Gideon didn't understand how dependent she was on Isaac's goodwill. Without William here to handle the draft horses and do the plowing, she didn't see how she'd manage.

She'd try if she had to, but she shuddered at the thought. Ezra had teased her, but she'd always been in awe of the massive beasts, gentle as they were.

All Gideon could think about was what he imagined Ezra would want. Well, that was what she wanted, too, wasn't it? Why did it annoy her so much when Gideon voiced it?

*I'm not making sense, even to myself, Father. Please help me to know what Your will is for our future, because I do not see the path clearly just now.*

She reached the barn door, which stood ajar, and shoved it wider so that she could enter. She stepped inside and stopped, shock freezing her to the spot.

Becky—Becky was in the stall with Ben. The giant draft horse stood, perhaps dozing, facing away from the front. Becky looked like a doll next to him as she tugged at a hind leg the girth of a young tree.

Terror stifled the cry that rose to Rachel's lips. She mustn't do anything that would startle the animal. He was a gentle creature, but his sheer size made him a danger. The step of one of those dinner-plate-sized feet could break a bone, and the horse probably didn't even realize Becky was there.

She took a cautious step. "Becky." She fought to keep her voice soft when she wanted to scream. "Komm schnell."

Becky's face swiveled toward her. Her lower lip pouted, as if she were about to argue. A thud resounded from the loft overhead, reverberating through the barn.

Ben threw his head up, massive body shifting. Before she could breathe, Becky had disappeared, caught between the horse and the wall.

"Becky!" Rachel flung herself toward the stall, heart pounding in her ears, terror speeding her feet.

*Becky, Becky, Dear Father, protect her . . .*

She heard pounding boots above her, and then William dropped straight down from the hayloft. He vaulted into the stall, shoving at the horse's hindquarters. In an instant he lifted Becky over the stall door and into Rachel's arms.

"Are you all right?" She knelt, holding her, running her hands quickly along Becky's limbs.

"I'm fine, Mammi." Becky's voice trembled a bit, and her face was white. "Ben didn't hurt me. He wouldn't."

"N-n-no." William climbed out of the stall more slowly than he had gone in, and the horse stamped a giant foot as if to emphasize the word. "He w-w-wouldn't hurt you on purpose. He d-d-didn't know you w-were there."

"Are you sure you're okay?" Rachel smoothed Becky's fine hair back into its braid.

Becky pulled away, her lower lip coming out. "Don't fuss."

Fear slid easily into anger, fueled by the guilt she always felt when one of the children was in danger.

"That is no way to speak to your mother. What were you doing in that stall? You know better than to go in there."

Becky's gaze slid away from hers, a sure sign she knew she was in the wrong. "Daadi always checked the horses' hooves to be sure they hadn't picked up a stone. He showed me how to do it. I did it just like he did."

The picture filled her mind—Ezra bending over the horse's leg, knowing just where to pinch so that Ben would lift his hoof for checking, explaining it all in his confident voice to his small daughter.

She had to swallow before she could speak. "I'm sure Daadi didn't mean for you to do so now. When you are bigger, you will, when a grown-up is there to watch."

Becky's face turned sullen. "I'm big enough."

"No, you are not!" She was on the verge of losing patience with the child, and that was surely a failure on her part.

"B-Ben would squash you like a bug and n-n-not know he did," William said.

"But Daadi said—"

"Enough." Her voice was sharper than she intended. "Onkel William knows well how to take care of the animals. He will do it."

"Ja, I will, for sure." William tugged on Becky's kapp string. "D-Don't worry."

"Tell Onkel William denke for taking care of you."

"Denke," Becky whispered.

"Ja, it's okay."

"Go to the haus." Rachel gave her a little shove toward the door. "I'll be right in."

She gave Becky a moment to get out of earshot before she turned to William, because she knew that her voice was going to betray her.

"Denke, William." She clutched both his hands in hers. "If you hadn't been here—" Tears overwhelmed her.

"Ach, it was n-nothing." He flushed to his ears. "I sh-sh-should have been w-watching her better."

"That is not your job. It's mine." She brushed away the tears impatiently with the back of her hand. She was embarrassing William, and that wasn't fair to him. "I'm so grateful to you. I don't know what we would do without you."

His flush deepened, and his blue eyes seemed to darken with emotion. "I w-would do anything for you and the ch-ch-children. Anything."

Leah's idea that William had feelings for her forced its way into her head. Here she stood alone in the barn with him, their hands clasped.

Carefully she drew her hands away. "We're very grateful. Now I must go and find some suitable punishment to keep Becky from being so foolish another time."

It was on the tip of her tongue to tell him to come in for coffee when he'd finished, but Leah's words had made her wary of doing so. That was foolish, wasn't it?

Still, she turned and walked quickly back toward the house. It *was* silly, she was sure of it. She'd let Leah's comments change the way she reacted with William.

William had been upset, maybe a little emotional, too, just as she had been. But that was because he loved Becky. It couldn't possibly be anything else.

*"They'll* be opening the doors soon." Aaron Zook, Gideon's brother, gave Rachel a reassuring smile. "Are you ready?"

"Ach, she's been ready this past hour." Lovina, Aaron's wife, turned from arranging the loaves of bread she'd placed in a large basket on the counter of their stall at the farmer's market in Petersburg. "This is Rachel's first Saturday at market, so she hasn't been running around being a blabbermaul to the neighbors like me." Lovina chuckled, her round form jiggling.

"It is so kind of both of you to share your stall."

Gideon had arranged it, of course—Rachel had no doubt of that, even though it was Lovina who had come to see her a few days earlier with the suggestion.

Her plants—pansies and a variety of potted mints, basil, rosemary, and dill—were ready on the end of the counter they had given her. She had hung bunches of dried herbs from the overhead rack. There weren't many of those, because when she'd dried them last fall she hadn't been thinking of bringing them to market. This year she would do more, if this effort proved successful.

Lovina had been right. She had never even visited the market before, let alone been part of it. The rectangular brick building in the center of town was crowded with vendors of all sorts, some Amish, some English, all of them calling to each other in cheerful, familiar tones.

Lovina and Aaron participated with the ease of long practice. Had being out among the English ever seemed as strange and scary to them as it did to her?

Aaron, four or five years older than Gideon, shared a strong family resemblance with him, although Aaron's beard held a few traces of silver. Perhaps, if Gideon had not had so much sorrow in his life, he'd also share Aaron's jovial good humor and ready laugh.

Aaron had chosen a mate who matched him. Lovina had a round, merry face, snapping brown eyes, and a laugh that came often. She was spreading comfortably into middle age and ruled her large family with cheerfulness unimpaired by the mischief their four boys and three girls seemed to get up to, judging by the stories she'd told on the drive to town. Since they'd started out at five this morning, there had been plenty of time for talk.

"Here they come," Aaron said.

Rachel's gaze shot to the doors, and her breath caught in her throat. People poured through the openings, spreading out into streams that flowed down each of the aisles in the long building. The noise bounced from the high ceiling, and she feared she'd drown in the hubbub.

Lovina pressed her hand in a quick squeeze. "Don't fret. You'll soon get used to it."

She doubted that, but she managed to return Lovina's smile. Then those leading the stream of people reached them, and Lovina turned with a smile to her customers.

Folks headed toward the baked goods and Aaron's cheeses first, giving her a chance to watch the two of them in action. When customers approached her end of the counter, she knew what to do.

After she'd waited on a few people, her tension began to slip away. This wasn't that different from the Mud Sale, except that she'd known most of the people there.

Finally, the initial rush slacked off. "There now," Aaron said, grinning, "that wasn't so bad, was it?"

She shook her head. "I guess not. Is it over?"

"Ach, no." Lovina brushed up the crumbs that had fallen on the countertop. "This is just the lull. There's always those who think they have to be here right when we open. Then it settles down. It'll get real busy again around noon, probably. Meantime, I'll go and get us all some coffee. You'll mind my baked goods, ja?"

"Sure thing." Coffee would taste good about now. And Aaron was there to be sure she didn't make any mistakes while Lovina was gone.

No sooner had Lovina left than a woman appeared at Rachel's end of the counter, looking at the potted herbs with a faintly disdainful air. She carried a large basket that already held several bunches of dried flowers.

"May I help you?" Rachel asked, echoing the way she'd heard Lovina do it.

"Is this price correct?" The woman flicked at the small tag Rachel had attached to the dill.

Rachel took a second look. "Ja, that's right." Lovina had helped her price things, and Lovina knew what was right to charge.

"It's too high. I'm certainly not going to pay that." The woman glared as if Rachel had offered her an insult.

Taken aback, Rachel could only gape. "I'm sorry—"

Someone elbowed her lightly to the side. She glanced up and blinked. Not Aaron, as she supposed, but Gideon. Where had he come from?

She couldn't ask, since he was already dealing with the customer. He consulted the price tag gravely.

"That's the price for one," he said, as if they were his plants, not hers. "If you wanted a half dozen, we'd be glad to bring it down to six plants for five dollars."

Rachel opened her mouth to speak, and then shut it again as the woman scrutinized the plants.

"Hmm . . . don't know that I want that many. How about three for two-fifty?"

"You won't find finer herbs anywhere you look," Gideon said, his tone persuasive. "Our Rachel grows nothing but the best. Take six, and you can make it a mixed batch—say two each of three varieties. That's the best we can do."

For a moment she thought the woman would turn and walk away. Then, meek as a lamb, she picked out six of the potted herbs and handed over the money.

When the woman had moved on to another stall, Gideon shot a look at her, as if to assess her reaction. What he saw on her face must have reassured him, because his mouth relaxed into a smile.

"D'you mind my butting in on your business?"

"Not when you can sell the customer six plants instead of one. But how did you know how to deal with that woman? And what are you doing here?"

She thought, too late, that the question was rude, but Gideon didn't seem to mind. He rested one elbow on the counter.

"I usually stop by on Aaron and Lovina's market days unless I have a job. I spell them so they can take a break. But I guess you're taking over that job today."

"Lovina went for coffee."

Aaron was busy with a customer at the other end of the counter, but otherwise all seemed quiet enough for the moment. She could ask the question that bothered her.

"But you didn't explain—how did you know what to say to that woman?" She had stood there like a dummy, not knowing how to respond to what had seemed an insult.

He shrugged, seeming at ease in this situation. "Experience, that's all. When someone starts out by saying your price is too high, that usually means they want to haggle. It makes them feel gut to bargain over something they're going to buy anyway." He grinned. "No one ever outsmarted a Dutchman when it comes to a bargain."

True enough. She'd seen her daad and Ezra haggle over price. But she'd never been the seller, out among the English this way. "I don't think I can do it."

"It just takes a little practice. And a little nerve."

"Maybe I don't have that." She concentrated on the remaining plants, pushing them around to show them to their best advantage. "I never worked outside. Not like girls who work at the shops or restaurants until they marry."

If she had, maybe she'd have been better prepared for the life she had now.

"Why was that?" Gideon leaned his elbows on the counter as if he had all the time in the world to listen.

"My folks didn't want me to take a job." She said it slowly, seeing the situation more clearly now, looking back. "Daad said there was enough to do at home, and that I'd be better off learning what Mamm could teach me. But I suppose it was really because of Johnny."

"They held you closer because they'd lost him." Gideon's voice was a low rumble under the background noises of the crowd.

"That, I guess. And maybe also they didn't want me to be out among the English so much. Afraid I'd do what Johnny did. Not that I would have." She glanced at him, seeing the understanding in his face. "I mean, Ezra and I knew we'd marry from the time we went to a singing when we were sixteen. I didn't need to prepare for any other life."

He nodded, the lines of his face seeming to deepen, as if he looked at the naive youngsters they'd been and found it sad. "We don't know what tomorrow will bring." He echoed what she'd said to him. "That's just as well."

She didn't want to talk about the spouses they'd lost. "Anyway, I didn't want my folks to worry. They'd had enough of that with Johnny."

"How is he? Ezra said you were seeing him again."

She studied Gideon for a second, but she didn't find any condemnation in his face. "Since he came back to the valley I see him now and again. He's busy with his new life. Happy, I guess, in his work. It wonders me though . . ."

She let that trail off, but he picked up on it.

"What? If he'll come back?"

"No, I'm sure he won't." The familiar worry sounded in her voice. "I just wish Daad could accept that. Make it easier for Mamm to see Johnny again. Like I said, he's happy with his work. But for all he's changed, I don't think he really fits in the English world, either."

"You want to make it better for all of them." Gideon sounded almost surprised.

"Ach, for sure I do. But Johnny and Daad are cut from the same cloth—both too stubborn for their own gut."

"Families are like that. Drive you crazy sometimes, but you can't do without them." He glanced toward his brother as he spoke, and affection was written in his face and voice.

"Aaron and Lovina have been so kind to include me." She hesitated, but she might as well say it. "I know this was your doing, Gideon, and I appreciate it."

"All I did was to mention it to them. Then Lovina took over." He smiled. "That's what she does best. And here she comes now with the coffee, and none for me."

Lovina bustled up to the counter, shoving a steaming cup at Rachel. "If I'd known you'd be here, I'd have brought some for you. You go get your own, and bring back some crullers from Ida Mae's stand already. We could use a little something before the next rush."

Holding up his hands in surrender, Gideon pushed open the half-door that was built into the counter. "See, what did I tell you? Lovina's the boss, and it's just as well to do what she says to begin with. It saves arguing."

He moved off, and Lovina took his place behind the counter, clucking a little. "That Gid—he's a caution. He has a gut heart, he does." She slanted a glance at Rachel. "It's time he should be forgetting the past and having a family of his own."

A warning tingle slid down Rachel's spine. Was that aimed at her? Leah said folks were already talking about when and who she'd marry.

She couldn't very well say anything to Lovina, but if that was her idea, this was one time when she wouldn't get her way. Gideon had no intention of marrying again, according to what Ezra, who would have known, had told her.

And she—well, she wasn't ready to marry again, either. She didn't know if she ever would be.

But if she were, it certainly wouldn't be to a man who would be forever tied in her mind to Ezra's death.

*Two* English women in the booth opposite them stared avidly at the four figures in Amish dress when they stopped at their favorite restaurant for supper after market. They didn't bother Gideon, and Aaron and Lovina were used to it. Stopping here for supper was a tradition, and if the tourists wanted to stare, they were welcome to it.

He glanced at Rachel, sitting next to him on the padded bench, hands in her lap, eyes downcast. She wasn't so used to being the target of curious gazes. He wanted to wipe the strain from her face, but he didn't know how.

Rachel had had little experience with the English world. Now her situation forced her to deal with it.

It wasn't easy to live in the world, but not of it. Some found it simpler, but Rachel wasn't one of those.

He wasn't, either, but he'd had to adjust to it once he'd started his business. Now—well, he'd just as soon be dealing with Amish customers, because he understood them. But the English were gut customers, too, and becoming friends as well, some of them.

He let Lovina's stream of chatter about the success of market flow past him. It was a balancing act, to be Amish in twenty-first-century America. Rachel would face plenty of challenges, trying to hang on to the farm without Ezra.

She'd been right to flare up at him about that. He'd been thinking only of Ezra's dreams, instead of what was best for Rachel and the children without him.

Still, how could he dismiss Ezra's plans for his family? From the time they were boys, Ezra had talked about the dairy farm he'd have one day, even knowing that his daad's place would go to Isaac. Gideon had lent a hand with the milking now and then, and Ezra liked to lean his head against the cow's warm side and talk about running his farm. Wouldn't he expect Gid to help Rachel stay?

"Gid, did you hear me?" Lovina's voice sounded as if she might have asked the same thing several times.

"He tunes you out," Aaron teased, sopping up the last of his beef gravy with his bread. "He's so used to your gabble that he doesn't listen."

"Sorry, Lovina." He brought his thoughts back to the bright restaurant, the clatter of dishes, and the buzz of English conversation. "My mind was wandering."

"Your mind and Rachel's, too, I'd say," Lovina said. "Rachel, what deep thoughts are going through your head to make you stare so intently at your plate?"

Rachel's cheeks grew pink. "Just that this is nice, is all. Do you always stop here for supper on a market day?"

"Just about," Lovina said. "I'm certain sure I don't want to go home and start cooking." She chuckled. "It's a little treat we give ourselves without the kinder along. Much as we love them, we like some time apart."

"It's a nice place, anyway." Aaron glanced around the brightly lit dining room, with its painted versions of Pennsylvania Dutch art on the walls. "Gut food. Not so gut as Lovina's, but okay."

"Nice big servings, you mean," Gideon said. He smiled at Rachel, hoping to put her at ease. "Aaron wants to feel like he's got his money's worth when he eats out."

"Nothing wrong with that," Aaron said. "We worked hard, up since before dawn. We need a gut meal."

"And to take time to enjoy our profit," Lovina added.

"Speaking of that, here is your share, Rachel." Aaron pulled an envelope from his pocket, double-checked it, and shoved it across the checked tablecloth to Rachel.

Rachel opened the envelope, riffling through the bills, and her gaze widened. "But—this is too much. My plants didn't bring in this much, I'm sure of it."

She tried to push the money to Aaron, but he shoved it back. "It's a mite extra," he said. "It's only what's fair. You helped Lovina with her sales, so you deserve a cut."

"But it's your booth." Rachel paled a little. "I can't take money for helping when you are letting me use your booth."

Aaron shot Gideon a look, as if to ask for help in handling such a stubborn woman. "Your plants and dried flowers drew more people to the stand, and then they bought from us, too. So we benefit from having you there."

"Besides," Lovina cut in, her tone firmly practical, "we need the extra help. Having you there lets me do some other things besides standing in the booth all day already. We'd have to pay anyone else who helped out."

"You wouldn't have to pay Gideon," Rachel said, giving a sidelong glance at him.

"Oh, Gideon." Lovina's tone dismissed him. "He's a help, sure enough, when he's there, but lots of times he's not. We need to have someone we can rely on, like you."

She patted Rachel's hand and pushed the envelope into her lap. "Let's hear no more about it. We'd be grateful if you come along as often as you can, even if you don't have much to sell. We can use the help and the company."

Rachel didn't look entirely convinced, but she gave in, curling her fingers around the envelope of cash.

"I've been thinking on that," she said. "I can pot up more herbs, and there'll be perennials ready to go soon." Her eyes lit with enthusiasm.

Gideon liked seeing her that way, with the tiredness and grief erased for the moment. "You should find lots of buyers for your perennials," he said.

"When the greenhouse is ready, I can start petunias, marigolds, cosmos, and such from seed, without waiting until after the last frost." Her smile flickered. "I won't have to crowd my windowsills with pots."

"Gut idea." Lovina glanced toward the dessert buffet. "And that double chocolate cake looks gut, too." She slid out of the booth, nudging Gideon. "You heard what Rachel said. You work a bit faster on that greenhouse, so Rachel can get her seedlings started. What's taking you so long?"

"The job takes as long as it takes," he said mildly. "I don't tell you how to bake bread, so don't you be telling me how to build a greenhouse."

Lovina laughed. "You're just spinning it out so you can spend more time with Rachel. You can't fool me."

She walked off, still chuckling, before Gideon could think up a suitable retort.

But he'd have to come up with something. He couldn't have Lovina imagining there was going to be something between him and Rachel when there wasn't.

He glanced at Aaron, hoping to read some evidence of support in his brother's face, but Aaron's gaze evaded his.

"Guess I'll go take a look at those desserts myself," Aaron said, pushing himself out of his chair.

So they were both thinking that. He'd have to do some straight talking to the two of them. It'd be embarrassing all around, but most of all for Rachel, if they started in on matchmaking that was bound to fail.

Aaron and Lovina knew, better than anyone, why he'd avoided involvement with any woman since Naomi's death. To be the only one left when his wife and baby died had made him shutter his heart for so long that he didn't think it could open again. And if he had begun to change, Ezra's death had ended it. He couldn't take responsibility for the life of someone he loved. What if he let them down, too?

Rachel moved slightly, clasping her hands in her lap, the fingers twining together. He met her gaze, to find her regarding him with worry darkening the vivid blue of her eyes.

The color came up in her cheeks a bit. "Was ist letz, Gideon?"

He shoved away the unwelcome thoughts. Better to keep them safely buried, he knew.

"Nothing's wrong." He tried to smile.

"Maybe you're thinking that I should not have taken that extra money that Aaron insisted on giving me. I didn't want to, but it seemed so hard to keep on refusing—"

"Ach, no." This was what came of letting the dark memories out. "Aaron was right. You were a great help."

"But really, I didn't do much." Her face was still clouded, faintly troubled.

He wanted to put his hand over hers, to stop her fingers from straining together that way. But it would be too familiar a gesture and embarrassing besides, here in a public place. He contented himself with leaning a little closer as he searched for the words that would convince her to accept what they offered.

"You did plenty. Aaron worries that Lovina does too much, pushes herself too hard with the children and the house and the farm, besides all the baking she does to get ready for market day. If she'll accept help from you, Aaron is only too glad. Please don't back out now."

He did touch her hand then, very lightly. The warmth of her skin made him want to linger, which was all the more reason to snatch his fingers away quickly.

There was a bit of a stir as the English women who'd been watching them slid out of their booth, dropping shopping bags in the process and exclaiming as they picked up their belongings. It distracted Rachel, which was just as well, and her face relaxed in a small smile.

The women had themselves together at last and started toward the door. A high-pitched voice came floating back over the shoulder of one as she stole a last look at them.

"Aren't they just the cutest couple you ever saw? They're like those Amish dolls we were looking at in that shop this afternoon."

Color flew into Rachel's cheeks again. Gideon spared an uncharitable thought for the tourists while he tried to think of some way to ease the situation for her.

"Like those Amish dolls," he mimicked. "How would they like it if we were buying dolls dressed like them?"

She managed a smile, but it didn't reach her eyes. He could see her distress, and he couldn't do anything about it.

Except leave her alone. The thought occurred to him, and his negative reaction to that startled him.

He couldn't leave her alone. This wasn't just about fulfilling his promise to Ezra any longer. It was all tangled up with Rachel's valiant efforts to do her best for the children and with his instinctive need to help her, regardless of the cost.

# Chapter Six

The final slow hymn had been sung, and Bishop Mose stood to pray. His gentle face radiated love as he blessed the people. Rachel's heart warmed with it. Tired as she had been after the long day at market yesterday, worship had rejuvenated her.

Talk rustled through the Stoltzfus farmhouse as the service ended. "Mammi, can we go outside?" Becky tugged on her arm.

"Ja, but walk out nicely with your grossmutter." She knew her mamm found it a joy to greet her friends with her grandchildren by her side. "I must speak with Leah."

Mamm, hearing her words, nodded and took Joseph's hand. "We will save a place at the table."

Daadi stood, cradling a sleeping Mary against his shoulder. "You go, and give our best to Leah. Maybe this one will sleep a little longer."

Rachel made her way between the rows of backless benches, heading for the spot where Leah sat with Elizabeth snuggled close to her side. She liked seeing the bond Leah had formed with her stepdaughter.

She didn't like the fact that Leah had come to worship today. Nearly four hours on a backless bench wasn't her idea of the rest the doctor had ordered.

She moved along the row, exchanging greetings with those on the women's side of the worship area. The Stoltzfus place was ideal for worship, built so that the living room and dining room opened into each other, giving plenty of space for the service.

House worship was held every other Sunday, rotating among the members. Depending on whose turn it was, they might be in a house one time, in someone's basement the next, and in a barn the following one. When she and Ezra had hosted worship, they'd spent a week cleaning out the barn beforehand.

She had to see if there was anything she could do to help Leah. And then she'd tell Leah of her plans for the greenhouse. The ideas had been bubbling since she got home, tired but satisfied, from market yesterday. It would be gut to hear Leah's words of encouragement.

Some of the men had already begun removing the benches, carrying them outside for the lunch that would follow worship. She skirted past them, smiling and nodding, and fetched up beside Leah, bending over to enfold her in a warm embrace.

"What are you doing here? I'm sure the doctor wouldn't approve of this."

Leah rose, leaning a bit heavily on Rachel's arm. "I asked and he said it was all right." She winced, rubbing the small of her back. "Of course, he probably doesn't know how long our service is."

"Ja, that's for certain sure." Leah's mother, who'd been seated on the other side of her, ran a soothing hand along her daughter's back. "You go along with Rachel and have a nice visit. Elizabeth and I will see if we can help with the food, won't we, Elizabeth?"

"Oh, ja." Elizabeth's eyes filled with love when she gazed at her adopted grandmother. "We'll help."

"Wish I had a daughter so eager to help," Rachel said once Leah's mother and daughter had left. "My Becky is probably getting into mischief already, if Mamm has let her go off."

"I'd be pleased if Elizabeth felt secure enough to seek out some mischief." Leah's smile lit her face. "Sounds like we're always wishing for something we don't have."

"I guess so." Her arm around Leah's expanding waist to support her, Rachel led the way toward the door. "Let's find a real chair for you to sit in, and I'll get you a cool drink. It feels like summer in here already."

"It does at that."

They worked their way toward the door that stood open to the sunshine. Folks still stood in small knots, talking. Judging by the grave faces, Rachel knew the topic of conversation.

"Bad news about Eli Fisher," she said. "Everyone's upset to think he'll not be with us much longer."

Leah nodded. "He's a gut man and a gut minister. It sounds as if the Lord has need of him in Heaven."

"And that means we'll be praying on who will be the next minister."

"It's a weighty decision, to think of the name you wish to whisper to the bishop." Leah grasped the porch banister to help her descend the two steps. "At least we know that the final decision will be made by the Lord."

The Biblical tradition of choosing the new minister by lot from among those recommended by the people of the congregation meant that everyone accepted the decision with gratitude for God's guidance. Still, Rachel had to confess that she had not been overjoyed when Ezra's name had been put forward the last time there had been an opening.

Had the lot fallen on him, their lives would have changed in ways she couldn't even imagine. A minister had to continue with the work he already had, tend his own family, and still find time to minister to his flock and preach on Sunday.

The lot hadn't fallen on him, but their lives had changed anyway. *It was God's will,* she murmured to herself, hoping that one day she'd think those words and really mean them.

Betty Stoltzfus saw them coming toward the picnic tables. "Wait, wait." She hurried to drag a padded rocking chair from the porch to the end of one of the long tables. "Sit down and be comfortable." She patted the chair.

Rachel helped Leah to sit, concerned about how cautiously Leah lowered herself. "Are you having pain?"

"Not much. I'm all right, Rachel. Don't fuss so."

Rachel and Betty exchanged glances over Leah's head—the look of women who'd already had children and knew how uncomfortable the final month could be.

"You sit, too, Rachel, and keep Leah company. I have some lemonade ready to come out." Betty bustled away toward the kitchen.

Leah glanced at Rachel, looking a little embarrassed. "I'm sorry I snapped. Daniel said coming to worship would be too much, and he was right, but I'm trying to keep things as normal as possible. Anyway, there was something I wanted to speak to you about, and I knew I'd have a chance here."

"I would come to you, anytime." Rachel was assailed by guilt. "I'm sorry I didn't get over this week." She'd been busy, but that was no excuse to ignore Leah.

"I was fine." Leah patted her arm. "Mamm has been coming by every day, and folks have brought food. With the children in school, there's not enough for me to do."

"Get plenty of rest and enjoy it," Rachel said promptly. She didn't have to think twice about that. "Once the baby comes, you'll be only too busy. But what did you want to talk to me about?"

Something about babies, she'd guess. It was hard for Leah to think of anything else right now.

"It's Anna." Leah's voice dropped on the word, as if she didn't want anyone to hear the name of her young sister, who'd run off to the English world nearly a year earlier. "I've heard from her."

The smile slid from Rachel's face. "Oh, Leah."

Rachel clutched her friend's hand, not sure whether to be happy or not. She knew how much suffering accompanied the loss of a beloved sibling. And as the elder, Leah had felt guilty, too, as if she somehow could have prevented it. "How is she? Is she all right?"

Leah nodded, tears sparkling. "She seems to be, though whether things are as rosy as she pretends, I don't know."

"Where is she? Did she tell you?"

"She didn't say, but the envelope was postmarked a town in Illinois." Leah sighed a little. "I don't know why she feels she has to hide. She knows we accepted her decision."

"Maybe she's not so sure of it herself."

Leah swallowed, probably because of the tears that clogged her throat. "She's not with that boy anymore. I never thought that would last. But she has a job and a room to live in. She says she's gotten her GED, and she's even planning to take some college courses in the fall." She sighed. "It seems wrong to be hoping that she'd find things difficult out there."

Out there among the English. Rachel knew what Leah was feeling, because she'd been there herself—almost longing for Johnny to fail, if that was what it took to bring him back to them.

"I'm sorry," she said softly.

"I know." Leah squeezed her hand. "It's funny. It almost seems as if Anna and I have traded places. Imagine our Anna actually wanting more learning."

"Maybe she's grown up some since she's been away."

"That was what I always wished for. I just never thought it would come this way." Leah sighed. "Anyway, I wanted you to know about it, because you understand."

"Ja, I do. I know what it is to feel helpless to make things better. But at least you've heard from her. You know she's well and taking care of herself. That's better than wondering. Imagining."

"My imagination is too gut, that's for sure. But I trust that God is watching over her, and now I can picture her life."

Rachel's throat tightened, remembering all the times she'd struggled to picture what Johnny was doing, how he was, during those years when they hadn't been in touch.

Leah must have known what she was thinking, because she touched her hand lightly. "Enough worry about things we can't affect. Tell me how it went for you at market yesterday."

"Ach, better than I ever imagined." She couldn't stop the smile that bloomed on her face. "Leah, I made more money in a day than I've ever made before in my life. It felt so gut to be earning for my children."

"That's wonderful-gut news. I'm happy for you."

Rachel glanced toward where the children played, but instead of their running forms, she was seeing rows of flowers and shrubs, blooming in her garden.

"If I can just get seedlings started in the greenhouse, I'll have plenty of plants to take to market every week. And I was thinking that I would put in more perennials and even some small shrubs and trees. I could have a regular nursery business if I work at it."

She turned to Leah. But instead of the enthusiasm she expected, there was a look of caution on Leah's face.

"Are you sure that's a gut idea? I mean, won't it be a lot of work?"

"For sure, it will be work. But if I can make enough to provide for the young ones without selling the farm, that will be worth any amount of labor."

"It will take so much of your time. And then there's the bookkeeping you'd have to do if you actually started a business. And the taxes, and . . ."

"You think I can't do it." A chill settled around Rachel's heart. Leah was her best friend, the person who knew her better than anyone, and Leah thought she wasn't capable of this project.

"It's not that," Leah said, but her voice betrayed the truth. "I just feel you ought to think on it more. Talk to your parents."

"I know what they think without talking to them. They think I should sell the farm and move in with them."

Leah leaned forward, putting her hand over Rachel's. "I don't want to discourage you. I just think you have to be careful, that's all. You understand, don't you?"

"Ja. I understand." She tried to keep the flatness she felt out of her voice. She'd thought she'd known what to expect from her friend. It seemed she was mistaken.

"Rachel . . ."

"Ach, there's Becky, halfway up the apple tree." She didn't

know when she'd been so glad to see her daughter getting into mischief. "I'd best go and see to her." She hurried off before she could let Leah see how disappointed she was.

"Becky is all right, ja?"

Mary Yoder, their schoolteacher, watched as Becky scurried off to her grossdaadi once Rachel had gotten her down from the tree. She'd approached while Rachel was still looking up at her errant daughter. Maybe it was the presence of her teacher that had cut short Becky's complaints.

"She's fine, though I sometimes wonder why." Rachel made an effort not to let her frustration show in her voice as she smiled at the young woman. "She's far too daring, that's what she is. Takes after her daadi in that."

Mary nodded, but she didn't smile in return, and that set off all Rachel's maternal alarms.

"Mary? Is there some problem with Becky in school?"

"She's a fine scholar," Mary said, almost too quickly. "I've just been thinking—well, perhaps I could come by the house sometime this week to talk. Would that be all right?"

Rachel opened her mouth to ask the questions that flooded her mind and then shut it again. Obviously Mary didn't want to talk about school issues at the after-church meal.

She took a breath and tried to erase the worry from her face. "I'll be happy to have a chance to talk. Stop by any afternoon, whenever it suits you."

Teacher Mary moved off toward the picnic table, leaving Rachel with more questions than answers. It wasn't unusual for the teacher to come calling, but it hadn't happened before with Becky.

*Am I making mistakes with the children, Father? I want so much to do that right. Please, guide me and grant me patience and humility.*

"And how was your day at market, Rachel? You didn't find it too tiring?"

Isaac had come up behind her, and she was uneasily aware that he might have overheard her conversation with Mary. Still, what difference did it make if he had? Isaac was family.

"It was a long day, but very gut." The enthusiasm she'd felt when she talked about market with Leah had disappeared, and she tried to regain it. "Everything I took with me sold, so I'm thankful for that."

"Gut, gut." But Isaac didn't sound convinced, and his gaze avoided hers.

Her heart sank. Isaac no doubt intended to say something she didn't want to hear—probably more about selling him the farm. She'd hoped he'd respect her request for time to consider.

"About this business of going to market. Do you really think that's appropriate, with you widowed not even a year already?"

For a moment she couldn't answer. *Widowed not even a year.* The words sank into her heart. Soon it would be a year since the morning Ezra had driven off in Gideon's buggy. Would things be better once that terrible landmark passed? She didn't know.

But Isaac was still waiting for an answer.

She cleared her throat, so that she could reply gently, quietly, as was the Amish way. "I don't think anyone could complain about my behavior in trying to support my children as best I can."

"Not that, for sure, but in such a public place, among all them English."

"I was well-chaperoned by Aaron and Lovina, if that's what you're thinking." She reminded herself that Isaac meant well.

"They're gut folks, but they're not family. You should be relying on family just now."

"Isaac, I do. You should know how much I rely on you and the rest of the family." Was he thinking that it was a slight to him that she turned to others? "The children and I couldn't get along without your help, that's certain sure. You know how much we appreciate all that you do, don't you?"

"Ach, there's no need for thanks." He patted her hand. "Now, I won't talk business on the Sabbath, but I want to be sure you're thinking about my offer."

There it was, just the subject she didn't want to discuss. "You're right, Isaac. We shouldn't talk business on the Sabbath."

He looked a little disconcerted at having his words turned back to him that way. "I see your mamm and daad coming to collect you for the meal, so I won't say more. Just . . . don't let this business with your little greenhouse affect your decision."

Sure enough, her mother and father approached, Mary awake but clinging to her grossdaadi's hand. If Rachel asked them, they'd no doubt agree with Isaac and take the opportunity to urge her to move back home with them.

No one, it seemed, thought her plan at all reasonable. Well, except maybe Gideon, and Gideon was convinced, no matter what he said to the contrary, that she should do what Ezra would want.

*Guide me, Lord.* Her heart whispered the prayer as Mary rushed to grab her skirt. *I need to know what is right to do.*

*It* had been two days since that Sabbath meal, but Rachel still struggled with the opinions that had buffeted her. Most of all, she hadn't been able to reconcile herself to Leah's negative reaction.

Was Leah's approval really that important to her? Apparently so.

She'd been trying not to think about it, but this quiet moment at the end of the day, cleaning up the kitchen as she glanced through the window over the sink at the slow settling of dusk on the farm, seemed to let the concern slip back in.

She'd turned that conversation every which way in her mind. She'd told herself that Leah had just been tired, or was feeling overly cautious because of her pregnancy.

But the end result was the same. Leah didn't support her plan. She didn't think Rachel was capable of doing it.

Rachel hung the dish cloth on the drying rack and then grasped the edge of the sink with both hands, bowing her head in the stillness. She could hear the children's voices, coming softly from upstairs as Becky helped Mary get ready for bed. Otherwise, the farmhouse was quiet with the end-of-day serenity.

*Dear Father, I confess that I have been annoyed with Sister Leah over her lack of support for my plans. Please, Lord, if she is right about this, help me to see that clearly. And if she is wrong, if this is the right step for me and the children, please help me to rid myself of these feelings.*

She seemed to be praying the same prayer over and over these days, first for her feelings toward Gideon, now for those she harbored toward Leah. The advice Bishop Mose had given her was harder to follow than she'd thought it would be.

The soft voices from upstairs were suddenly no longer so quiet. She straightened, appalled to hear Becky practically shouting at her little sister. Hurrying toward the stairs, she tried to quell the frustration that rose in her.

Ezra used to joke that this was the time of day when even gut children turned into little monsters. How she missed his steady hand with them!

She reached the door of the bedroom Becky and Mary shared to find Mary sitting on her bed in her white nightgown, tears running down her cheeks. Becky stood in the center of the hooked rug between the beds, her hands clenched and her face red.

Joseph, who'd probably been drawn by the noise, slipped past Rachel and out of the room, obviously having no desire to get into this, whatever it was.

"Hush, Mary, hush." First things first. Rachel sat down on the bed and drew the little one into her arms. "Quietly, now. It's all right. Mammi is here."

Mary clung to her, burying her face in Rachel's shoulder, her sobs lessening already. Rachel stroked her, murmuring softly, until they calmed into little hiccupping sounds.

"Now, then." She kept her voice low as she focused on Becky. "Tell me what has Mary so upset. And you also, I think."

For a moment Becky didn't speak. Her fists were clenched tightly against her apron, and strong emotion twisted her lips.

"She doesn't remember!" The words exploded from her. "Mary says she doesn't remember what Daadi looks like!"

That brought a fresh outburst of tears from Mary. Rachel held her close, murmuring to her, patting her back. Poor Mary, who probably didn't even understand what was happening, only that Becky was angry with her.

And poor Becky, too. Rachel understood what Becky felt, because her own heart was sore at just hearing the words.

Could Mary have forgotten Ezra so soon? If so, it was her fault. She should have talked about him more, made sure his image was fresh in the children's minds. Without photographs, words and memories were all they had.

"Hush, little girl." As Mary's sobs lessened again, she tilted the small face up so that she could see it. It was blotched red with tears, and just the look of it wrenched her heart. "It's all right. You remember Daadi. You remember how he used to lift you high in the air, so high that you touched the ceiling, and you loved it. You'd say, 'Again, again!' to him."

Mary nodded, wiping the tears away with the back of her hand.

She must tell the child more, say the words that would bring Ezra clearly back into her memories. But panic swept through her like a cold wind. Ezra's image, his dear face, the sound of his laugh, the look in his eyes—they were fading, all fading.

Rachel was terrified at the thought of losing him, but even more terrified at letting the children know how she felt.

*Please, help me, dear Father.*

"His beard tickled you and made you laugh." Somehow the words came, as if the Lord had heard. "And his eyes were so blue—just as blue as yours are. He was strong, so strong he could lift all three of you children up at the same time. Remember? Remember how he'd make a Mary sandwich, with you in the middle?"

"I remember." Mary smiled at that, the tears banished. "I remember Daadi."

"Of course you do." She put Mary down on the bed, pulling her quilt up and tucking it around her. "You remember, and if you start to forget, we'll all help you remember."

She glanced at Becky. "Come and kiss your baby sister, and tell her how sorry you are that you made her cry."

Becky, looking on the verge of tears herself, crawled up on

the bed and wrapped her arms around Mary, kissing her cheek. "I'm sorry," she whispered. "I love you."

Mary clutched her in a throttling embrace. "I love you, Becky."

"Now is time for sleep." Rachel kissed Mary, holding her close for a moment. "Good night, my little one."

Mary snuggled down under the quilt, turning her face to the side as she always did for sleep. Rachel slid off the bed and put one hand on Becky's shoulder to shepherd her out of the room. She pulled the door to, leaving it a few inches ajar as she always did, so that she could hear if one of them cried in the night.

"Komm," she said to Becky. "Sit down here on the steps and let's talk."

She sat on the top step, trying to push away the weariness and the tears that would come too easily if she let them. Becky sat down next to her, her face downcast, the nape of her neck so exposed and vulnerable-looking that Rachel's heart twisted again.

"Mary is still a boppli in some ways, ja?" She put her arm around Becky. "She was only two when Daadi went to Heaven. She doesn't have as many memories as you do of Daadi, because she didn't get to be with him as long."

Becky nodded. "I'm sorry, Mammi," she whispered.

"It's forgiven and forgotten." She hugged her close. "We will keep Daadi alive in Mary's heart by our love for him and by our stories about him. Ja?"

"Ja, we will." Becky tilted her head up so that Rachel could see her face. The tears still lingered in her eyes, but she was smiling.

Rachel pressed a kiss to her forehead. If only she could always solve her children's problems with a little talk and a lot of love.

"Why don't you read for a bit before bedtime," she suggested. "I'd best see to Joseph."

Becky, nodding, went down the steps. Her book would be tucked under the cushion of the small rocking chair that her grossdaadi had made for her, and she'd lose herself in the story for a while.

The door to Joseph's room stood open, but he was not there. Rachel glanced quickly into her bedroom and the spare room before hurrying down the stairs, hand running along the wood rubbed smooth by generations.

She glanced into the living room, where Becky had lit one of the lamps. "Have you seen your brother?"

"No, Mammi." Becky slid off the chair, her finger marking her place in the book. "Do you want me to look for him?"

"I'll do it." She walked through the dining room, peeked into the pantry. Empty.

The kitchen had grown dark since she'd been upstairs. She lit the ceiling lamp that hung over the table, its yellow glow banishing the shadows. "Joseph?"

No answer, but the back door stood open. Hurrying, a nameless fear clutching her, she rushed onto the porch.

All was still quiet. But the barn door, which should have been closed, was open, a yawning dark rectangle. Before she could gather breath to call again, a massive dark shape erupted from the barn.

## Chapter Seven

Rachel's heart nearly failed her until she heard Joseph's panicked voice.

"Mammi! Wo bist du?"

"Here! I'm here, Joseph!" She jumped down the steps and ran toward the sound of his voice. "Are you all right?"

Joseph barreled into her, and she clutched him, torn between thanks and fear.

"Was ist letz? What's the matter?"

"The draft horses—one of them got out." He sounded close to tears. "I'm sorry, Mammi. I'm sorry. I didn't mean to do it."

"We'll talk about it later." Her eyes were adjusting to the light now, and she could see his face—a pale, anxious oval. She grasped his hand. "You must stay up here on the porch, you understand? Don't come off the porch."

She waited for his nod, and then she patted his shoulder. "It will be all right. Just let me get the lantern, and then I'll put the horse back in the stall."

He nodded again, which she hoped meant she sounded more

confident than she felt. She reached inside the door for the battery lantern that hung there on a hook. Lighting it, she managed a smile that seemed to chase the worry from Joseph's face.

"Stay here," she repeated, and stepped off the porch.

Luckily the horse didn't seem to have any immediate plan to run off—Ben, she saw now, the more skittish of the two. He'd dropped his head and was cropping the grass next to the lilac bush. If he went a little farther, he'd be munching on her tulips.

Well, he wouldn't have the chance. She went forward, repressing the butterflies that danced in her stomach. Stupid, to be so nervous of the animal. If only it were Brownie, her buggy mare—Brownie would come right to her when called. The big geldings were another story.

"There now, Ben." She spoke as soothingly as if she were talking to one of the children. "This isn't where you belong. What are you doing out here at night?"

And why on earth had Joseph let him out? That seemed to be what he had been saying, but it made no sense.

"Let's get you back in the barn where you belong." She was almost to the animal. She reached out gingerly for his halter.

Ben flung up his head and danced away from her, his eyes rolling so nervously that she could see the whites even in the glow of the lantern.

The lantern—that must be what had frightened him. She set it on the grass. She didn't really need the light it provided. The western sky was still streaked with purple, and night hadn't quite claimed the farm yet.

She had to quiet her own nerves before she could proceed. She tried to picture Ezra in this situation. He would probably walk right up to the gelding and grasp the halter, wouldn't he? Then that was what she should do.

Except that Ezra seemed very far away, and she did not feel very brave. *Please, Father.*

Ben had settled back to his eating. She moved closer, reached out, and patted his shoulder. His skin rippled as if she were a pesky fly, but he didn't move. More confident, she reached for the halter. She almost had him—

The door banged, the sound like a shot in the still night. Ben shied away from her. He wheeled, his huge hooves coming dangerously close to her legs, and ran straight for the road.

She spared one quick glance toward the house as she ran after him. Becky had come onto the porch, probably looking for them. Her mouth was a round O of surprise.

"Stay there!" Rachel ordered, sprinting after the animal. "Stay there."

They would obey, wouldn't they? The last thing she needed was to have them to worry about, in addition to the horse. If Ben got out onto the road—

She didn't want to think of that. Too often animals were hit, and a car or pickup coming fast along the narrow road wouldn't have a chance of stopping in time.

That pair of Belgian draft horses were one of the farm's biggest assets. She couldn't afford to lose Ben.

She pressed her hand against the stitch in her side and ran on down the lane. How far would he go? Surely, after he got over his initial fright, he'd stop to eat the lush grass along the side of the lane, wouldn't he?

But Ezra always said that horses were not the most sensible creatures, as apt to take fright at a blowing paper as at an oncoming freight truck.

Rachel rounded the slight bend in the lane. She could see the road now. Could see, too, the pair of headlights that pierced the darkness. A car was coming. If the horse ran out onto the road, what was the chance the driver would be able to stop?

She forced herself on, too breathless to cry out, not that it would have helped her anyway. *Please, God, please, God.* The words kept time with her running feet.

A dark shape loomed ahead of her on the lane. Then, coming closer, it separated itself, and she could see. The gelding, not free any longer, plodded toward her, his halter in the hand of a man who also led a horse pulling a buggy. Something about the size and shape of the lanky figure identified him.

"William! You caught him."

"Ja."

William was close enough now that she could see his grin. All the tension went out of her in a whoosh of relief.

"G-gut thing I was on my way home chust n-n-now."

"A very gut thing." Thankfulness swept over her. "I was afraid he'd run onto the road and be hit." The car swept past the lane, accentuating her words.

"He's s-safe now." William fell into step with her. "Don't you worry."

"Denke, William. I don't know what I'd do without you." She seemed to be saying that too often lately.

"I'll p-put him in the barn."

Nodding, she took the buggy horse from him, leading it to the hitching rail as William led the gelding on toward the barn.

She tied his horse to the rail, thankful that William hadn't repeated what he'd said the last time she'd had cause to be grateful to him. Maybe he realized that his words then had made her uncomfortable.

She crossed to the porch, almost too tired to put one foot in front of the other. When she sank down on the step, Joseph and Becky threw their arms around her.

"There, now, it's all right." Somehow she found the strength to comfort them. "Uncle William is putting foolish Ben back in the stall where he belongs. There's no need for tears."

Although she had to admit, she felt like shedding a few herself.

"I'm sorry, Mammi. I shouldn't have slammed the door." Becky hugged her, arms tight around her neck.

"It's no matter." Rachel turned to her son. "Joseph, how did this happen? How did Ben get out?"

Joseph sniffled a little. "I went to check Dolly, because she was bawling. She must have tipped her water bowl over, 'cause it was empty, and I filled it before supper, I really did."

"I'm sure you did." Joseph would no more neglect his precious goat than miss his own supper. "Why did you go in the barn?"

"I heard something moving inside. I could tell it was one of the draft horses, 'cause it was so loud. It sounded like he was out of his stall, so I thought I'd better check." He hung his head. "I should have come to tell you."

"Ja, you should." She ruffled his hair. "You will next time. So Ben was out of his stall?"

He nodded. "When I opened the door, he ran right out the barn door. I couldn't stop him. I'm sorry, Mammi."

"I know you are." She drew him closer, a chill running through her. If he hadn't gotten out of the way of the animal—

She suppressed that line of thought, looking up as William approached.

He stopped at the foot of the steps. "Everything else is all r-right."

"Ser gut. But how did he get out of the stall?"

William glanced at Joseph. "J-Joseph d-d-didn't let him out?"

"No!" Joseph looked up at his uncle. "Honest, Onkel William, I didn't. He was already out when I opened the barn door."

William shrugged. "Don't know. He was in and s-settled when I l-left."

It was troublesome, to say the least. Rachel couldn't doubt William's word. He wasn't careless. But Joseph's story had the ring of truth, too.

"No harm was done, thanks to you." She smiled at William, giving the children another hug. "Now I must get my little schnickelfritzes to bed. Say good night to Onkel William."

She kept a calm smile pinned to her face while the children bade William good night. It wouldn't do to let them know she was worried.

But how had the horse gotten out? She'd give a gut deal to know the answer to that.

*Gideon* stood back, hands on his hips, to survey the panel of glass he'd just set into place. He was close to putting the finishing touches to the greenhouse.

Rachel must surely be itching to move her plants in as soon as he pronounced it done. The chilly weather of the past couple of days had reminded everyone that the valleys of central Pennsylvania couldn't count on frost-free nights until about the middle of May, at least.

Some folks put their plants in early, if they felt reckless, but then ended up having to cover them or lose them.

Truth to tell, he'd be sorry when the day came that he'd be finished. He wouldn't have a reason then to come to Rachel's as often, and he'd have to think of some other way to help Ezra's family.

Rachel would continue going to market, surely. Aaron and Lovina would do their best to see to that. The problem might be to keep Lovina from being too enthusiastic in her pushing.

Joseph came running across the yard toward him, and Gideon's face relaxed into a smile. One of the best things about being here every day was getting to know Ezra's small son. He'd come to count on the boy rushing to help him the moment he got home from school. Nothing compared with working together to build a bond between them.

"You put the first glass in!" Joseph skidded to a halt. "Can I help? Can I?"

"Sure thing. I'm planning on you holding the panels for me while I put the putty in already."

"I *told* Mammi you'd need me to help you."

Gideon paused in lifting the next pane. "You're not skipping other chores to do this, are you? That wouldn't be right, with your mammi counting on you and all."

Joseph shook his head, his fine blond hair bouncing on his rounded forehead. "I have some watering to do, but Mammi said I can do it later."

"Gut." He lifted the pane of glass into place, letting the boy steady it while he tapped in the metal glazing points that would hold the pane even without Joseph's small hands on the glass.

This was how children learned to do the things they'd eventually need to do as adults. He hadn't given that much thought before he'd begun coming here. Joseph, with his father gone, would absorb what it meant to be an Amish man from his grandfather, his uncles, and maybe even a little from him, if the gut Lord willed.

"Did Mammi tell you about the horse getting out last night?" Joseph frowned at the pane, his palms flat against it.

"No, she didn't." He glanced toward the house. He hadn't seen much of Rachel today, as a matter of fact.

Joseph stared fixedly at the pane. "I didn't mean to let it happen."

"I'm sure you didn't." He smoothed the putty into place, his voice calm.

"I was checking on Dolly. I could hear that one of the horses was out of his stall. You know how their hooves go clump-clump on the boards?"

He nodded. The sound was different, more hollow when it wasn't muffled by the straw in the stall.

"I thought I could get him back in by myself." Joseph's voice trembled a little.

"You wanted to help Mammi." He certainly understood that feeling. He wanted to help Rachel, too. "Which horse was it?"

"Ben. He's the big draft horse. He ran right out when I opened the door."

"That must have been scary." And dangerous, but he figured Rachel had already pointed that out to the boy.

"Ja." His eyes met Gideon's then, and Gideon saw how troubled the boy was. "I wanted to help, but Mammi said to stay on the porch with Becky. And then Ben ran toward the road, and Mammi ran after him."

Joseph didn't need to say how frightening that had been. It was written on his face.

"You did what your mother said?"

He nodded.

"Well, then, you did the right thing."

"I wanted to help," he repeated, his voice shaking. "But Mammi couldn't get him either. Gut thing that Uncle William came by then. He brought him back."

"That was fortunate." William was a kindhearted lad, obviously willing to do anything he could for Rachel. Or maybe more accurately, anything that Isaac would let him do. "And you did the right thing by listening."

Joseph nodded again, but his forehead was still knotted with worry. Gideon thought he knew why. Joseph was trying hard to fill his father's shoes. That was natural enough, but those shoes were much too big for any six-year-old boy.

All three of the children had to be affected by the loss of their father. Mary seemed the least bothered, young as she was.

As for Becky—well, at the moment Becky had been dispatched to take the clothes down from the clothesline. Instead, the basket lay forgotten on the grass while Becky shinnied up the clothes pole.

He had to smile. Ezra had been like that as a boy—always willing to try anything, and like as not, leading Gideon into trouble, too. Ezra would know how to deal with that tendency in his daughter, having been that way himself. Gideon wasn't sure that Rachel did.

But here came Rachel now, crossing the lawn toward Becky, the breeze sending the strings of her prayer covering streaming out behind her. She said something to Becky—he couldn't hear what—and Becky slid down the pole and picked up the basket.

Rachel glanced his way, hesitated a moment, and then came toward him, pressing the skirt of her dress down with one hand when it flapped in the wind.

"You are making wonderful-gut progress," she said. "The windows going in already!"

"Thanks to my fine helper." He smiled at Joseph.

"I don't want to take him away when he's working, but Dolly is bawling, and no one will do for the silly creature but Joseph."

"She's not silly," Joseph said loyally. "She's going to have her babies soon, and that makes her nervous, ain't so?" He appealed to Gideon.

"That could be. Why don't you take a break from this and see to her? I can manage until you do that."

"I'll come right back," Joseph said, and sprinted across the yard toward the goat's pen.

"How long do you think it will take to finish the work?" Rachel was obviously counting the moments until she could put her plants in her new greenhouse.

"I should finish up in a day or two, if all goes well." He picked up the next pane. "I hear you had some trouble here last night."

"Joseph told you?" Her smooth brow furrowed with concern. "He shouldn't have opened the barn door, of course. But how did Ben get out of the stall? That's what worries me. I'm sure William wouldn't make such a mistake."

Without seeming to think about it, she moved around so that she could take Joseph's place holding the pane. Now it was her palms that pressed against the glass instead of the child's.

"William's the careful sort, I'd say." It was odd. And dangerous to the animal even if he hadn't gotten out of the barn.

"That's what makes it so puzzling." She shook her head, her face troubled. "Joseph shouldn't have been out there alone that late anyway. If it hadn't been for—" She stopped.

"Hadn't been for what?" Gideon prompted.

A small sigh passed her lips. "Becky was upset with Mary. And Joseph hates any rumpus, so he went outside to get away from it. For him, that was just a short step to going to check on Dolly."

She tried to smile, but he could see that she was bothered by more than just the boy being outside that late.

"What was going on between Becky and Mary? They always look as if they get along pretty well."

"They do. But apparently Mary didn't remember something about her daadi that Becky thought she should, and Becky got upset. She just doesn't understand that it's natural Mary isn't going to remember much about Ezra."

"That's too bad." He hated the thought that Ezra's youngest wouldn't have memories to keep him alive in her thoughts.

"Ja. Sometimes I almost wish we could have photographs, so we'd have an image of him. But I know the Scripture says not to make graven images." She shook her head. "And I suppose maybe if we had one, we'd make too much of the picture, instead of using our hearts to remember him."

Gideon's heart ached, just listening to her. If he could make the grief better—but he knew from his own loss that that was something no one else could do for you.

"Seeing so much of the children has made me think about Ezra a lot," he said. "They're each like him, but in different ways."

Now Rachel's smile chased the sorrow from her face. "That is what I think, too. Mary has his smile, but Joseph looks the most like him. And Becky—well, Becky has his manner, sometimes."

"His daring, too. She's like Ezra was as a boy." He glanced toward the clothesline, but Becky was doing her chore now without looking for mischief.

"Always getting into trouble. I know." Rachel seemed to look back through the years, but they were happy memories, he could tell.

"We did a lot together when we were boys," he said. "If you wanted it, I could talk to the children about him."

He sensed her immediate withdrawal. If she hadn't been holding the glass, she'd have moved away from him.

"I—I'll think about it."

But her voice was strained, and he could already tell what her answer would be. It seemed they hadn't moved as far as he'd been hoping they had.

Rachel washed the dishes, lingering over the job as she gazed out the window over the sink. As Gideon had said yesterday, the greenhouse was nearly done. Her last gift from Ezra would soon be a reality.

Gideon had done a wonderful-gut job. Everyone knew that he was a fine carpenter, none better. He worked steadily now, his movements deft and calm.

He'd gotten stronger over the course of building the greenhouse. She could see that now as she studied him. His leg wasn't so stiff as it had been that first day he'd come, and he moved more easily and more surely.

He turned from the greenhouse, glancing toward the window where she stood watching. Heat flew into her cheeks. What must he think of her staring at him?

Looking down at the pot she held, she scrubbed so vigorously that she was in danger of rubbing through the metal. She hadn't been admiring him. Of course she hadn't. He couldn't think that. She just liked watching anyone who did a gut job of something, like Mamma with her jams and jellies. Ja, that was all.

Once the pot was dry, she bent to put it in its proper place and walked across the kitchen to hang the towel on the wooden drying rack. She glanced out the side window. From here, she could see the schoolhouse, nestled in its little hollow. The scholars were coming out the door now, so Becky and Joseph would soon come running across the field.

And if Mary Yoder intended to come today, she'd soon be here, as well. Rachel's fingers tightened on the drying rack. She hadn't told the children that she expected a visit from their teacher. And she hadn't attempted to find out from them why Mary Yoder was concerned about them.

No, not them. Becky. Rachel had been able to read that much in Mary Yoder's face.

Well, she would find out when Teacher Mary came. And then she'd deal with it, whatever it was.

As Rachel turned away from the window, movement caught her eye. She swung back, leaning over to peer down the lane. Something came, all right, but it wasn't a buggy. It was a car.

Johnny? She tidied her hair automatically. She wasn't expecting him, but it was typical of her brother's impatience that he would come rather than sending a note through the mail.

But when she stepped out onto the back porch, she could see immediately that it wasn't John. She recognized the Englischer, though—Thomas Carver, it was. Mr. Carver owned the dairy that bought the milk from them.

Had he come with a problem? Her nerves tightened with dismay. William did everything just the way Ezra always had, so surely it wasn't that. But the man had never come to the farm before, not in all the years since Ezra had signed on with him.

She smoothed her apron down and stepped off the porch as Mr. Carver got out of the car. Middle-aged and balding, he wore the blue jeans and plaid flannel shirt over a white T-shirt that was the common dress among the English farmers in the valley.

"Mrs. Brand. Nice to see you." He approached, starting to extend his hand and then seeming to think the better of it.

"Mr. Carver." She nodded politely. "It's kind of you to call."

Her hands pressed against her sides, hidden by the folds of her skirt, as she waited for him to go on. It wouldn't be polite to ask what he was doing here when he'd never come before.

"Yes, well, I had a little business I wanted to talk over with you." He glanced toward Gideon. "Mind if we go inside and have a chat about it?"

He moved toward the step. She held her ground. He may be a perfectly nice man, but she'd feel more comfortable talking with him here, rather than in the house.

"It's a pleasant day. Perhaps we could talk here."

His face seemed to tighten. "Yeah, sure. I guess maybe you people wouldn't think it right for a widow to be alone in the house with a man who isn't Amish."

Since there was no reasonable answer she could give to that, she didn't try, but just waited.

"Guess this is fine." He leaned forward to rest his hand on the porch railing, bringing him uncomfortably close to her. "No need for you to be worried about the milk. Young William is doing fine with that. I got no complaints."

"This is gut." So what did he want, in that case?

"Still, it has to be rough for you, running a place this size without a husband."

He was trying to be kind, she supposed. "We are doing all right. The family has been taking care of things."

"Sure, I know how you Amish stick together. One for all and all for one, huh? Though I guess you wouldn't say it that way."

Again, there seemed no proper response, so she just inclined her head in a nod.

"Yes, well, anyway, I figured things might be getting a little difficult for you by now, without your man. Thought I'd stop by with a business proposition for you."

He was talking in circles. Maybe she could move him on toward a conclusion.

"And what is this business proposition?"

"Right to the point." He chuckled. "I like that in a woman. Well, see, it's this way. I hear tell you don't want to sell the farm, but you're having a tough time making a go of it."

Her stomach lurched. How could this Englischer know that about her? How could he know anything about her?

"Maybe there's a way you don't have to sell, but you can still make a decent living off the place. And you wouldn't even have to give up the house or that little greenhouse you've got going there."

"And what is that way?"

A year ago she wouldn't have been capable of having a business discussion with anyone, let alone an Englischer. But then, a year ago she wouldn't have had to. Maybe her introduction to bargaining at the market helped.

"I'd be interested in buying the dairy herd from you." He must have seen that she was about to say no, because he held up his hand to stop her. "Now, just hear me out. What I propose is buying the herd and just leasing the barn and the pastures from you."

"I don't think— " she began.

"See, that way you don't have to let the farm go." He rolled on as if he hadn't heard her. "You have a nice steady income coming in, and you get to stay in your house." He cocked an eyebrow at her. "Pretty good deal, don't you think?"

She took a breath, trying to steady herself. Coming out of the blue as it did, the idea had her brain spinning.

"I appreciate your offer, Mr. Carver. But I don't think that's the right thing for me to do."

"Now, you haven't considered it yet." He moved uncomfortably closer. "You have to stop and think a bit."

She tried to step back, but she was against the steps, and there was nowhere to go. "I'm sorry—"

"This is the perfect answer for you. Don't you want to be able to take care of your kids and keep them in this house? Trust me, you're not going to do any better than this. I wouldn't cheat you."

He was right in her face, and she felt his insistence pushing at her. "I don't—"

"Rachel, was ist letz?" The quiet question, coming in dialect, seemed to go right to the heart of her tension, soothing away her nerves.

Thomas Carver turned to stare at Gideon, and she took advantage of the opportunity to put some space between them.

"I'm fine." She answered in English, so that Carver would understand. "My business with Mr. Carver is finished."

Carver's smile was a mere twitch of the lips. "Not finished, Mrs. Brand. You think about what I said. I'll be in touch."

Gideon stood beside her while Carver got into his car. The man turned in the narrow lane, spraying gravel and clipping one of her rose bushes, and drove off toward the main road.

"What's wrong?" Gideon repeated his question as soon as the man pulled away. "You didn't look fine. Was it bad news about the dairy's deal with you?"

"No, nothing like that." She managed a smile. "He wanted . . ."

Did she really want to discuss that with Gideon? Maybe not. After all, Gideon had his own ideas of what she should do with the farm.

"Well, it was nothing important." She phrased her words carefully, intent on not telling a falsehood. "He wanted to talk to me about my arrangements for the dairy herd. If they'd be continuing the way they are."

Gideon's mouth firmed. He knew she wasn't telling him all of it, she supposed, but it would have to do.

She stared past him—toward the fine barn that had been in her family for generations, toward the pastures lush with spring growth. Sell? Lease? It seemed much the same to her. It meant someone else would be tending the farm that Ezra had loved.

She was being offered too many chances to do something she didn't want to do at all.

# Chapter Eight

Rachel had been standing in the backyard for several minutes, watching him put the finishing touches to the greenhouse while Mary trotted around, busy with her little bucket and shovel. But Gideon could see that Rachel's mind was far away.

Probably she was still caught up in that conversation she'd had with Thomas Carver, the Englischer. He didn't for a minute think that she'd told him everything about it.

Why should she? He frowned at the latch he was screwing into place. He didn't have the right to expect that. Her business with the dairy was just that, hers. And Isaac's and William's, he supposed, in a certain sense.

Still, in that moment when he'd seen her pull back as if she were intimidated by the man—well, his instinctive reaction was nothing to be proud of. For himself, he'd long since learned to turn the other cheek, as the Lord taught. For Rachel—he couldn't deny the bone-deep need he'd felt to protect her, not that she'd wanted or would welcome his protection.

Rachel had made that clear time and again. He was the one who didn't seem to be getting it.

"Becky and Joseph are coming." He nodded toward the two scholars as they raced across the lane on their way home from school, detouring to drop their books on the back porch.

"Ja." Rachel's solemn look disappeared into a smile when she saw the children. She seemed to dismiss whatever had been troubling her, or, most likely, put it away to think about later. "Mary, look." She turned the little girl with a light touch on the shoulder. "Here they are."

Mary's short legs churned as she hurried to meet her brother and sister.

Gideon dropped his screwdriver back into his toolbox. "Maybe you'd like for the young ones to help set up your greenhouse."

Rachel's breath caught. "Now?"

He nodded. "It is finished at last."

"Wonderful gut." She clasped her hands together, her face lighting up with pleasure at the thought. "Children, come see. The greenhouse is ready."

All three of them swarmed over the greenhouse, opening and closing the door. The girls darted inside and out again as if it were a toy house just for them.

After a quick inspection, Joseph came to stand next to him, surveying the greenhouse much as he did. He could sense the pleasure the boy felt at having been a part of the building.

He rested his hand on Joseph's shoulder. "Gut job we did here, ja?"

"Ja." Joseph leaned against him for a moment. A hand seemed to reach out and grasp Gideon's heart, squeezing it.

Before he could come to terms with the feeling, Joseph had

darted off to his mother. "Can we bring the plants out and set them up on the tables? Can we?"

"Let's do that." Rachel's gaze met Gideon's, and hers brimmed with happiness. "Komm, everyone help."

They all seemed to figure he'd help, too, so he followed Rachel into the house. Pots of seedlings that she had started perched on every sunny windowsill.

"I didn't know you had so many. You have been busy."

She pulled trays from the cabinet under the sink and began putting the tiny pots on it. "Ach, I love to do it. My mamm used to say that I was never so happy as when I had my hands in the dirt. I'm sure Daad was sorry it was his daughter with the green thumb instead of his son."

A shadow dimmed her face on the words, and he knew she was thinking about her brother.

"How is Johnny?" He wouldn't let her feel that she had to be wary of discussing John with him. "Have you seen him lately?"

"Not for a while. He came over one night to help me with the tax forms."

That seemed to make the shadows deepen in her face, unfortunately. He took another tray and began to fill it with the contents of the windowsill above the sink. "He's well?"

"Ja." She sighed. The children's voices echoed from the living room as they apparently divided up the plants to carry out. "He was unhappy with me because I wouldn't take money from him. I wish he'd understand about that."

Gideon nodded. "Not so easy to balance between him and your daad, I guess."

"They're both too stubborn." Her mouth set.

"That trait didn't pass you by, either, I think."

Her gaze met his, startled. "I'm not stubborn." A faint color came up in her cheeks, and she focused on the plants. "Well, only about some things."

Some things that included him, he suspected.

"These are ready," he said, as the children marched through the kitchen, each carrying a share of the plants. Mary had one grasped in each chubby fist, and she frowned as if daring them to fall. "I'll hold the door."

Coming along behind Rachel and her children as they crossed the lawn to the greenhouse, he felt a sense of—what was it? Belonging?

Not that, maybe, but as if for this moment, anyway, he could share in their happiness. He'd fulfilled his promise to Ezra, and he'd made things a little better for Rachel and the young ones. That should be enough for him.

Just ahead of him, Mary reached the very entrance to the greenhouse before she stumbled, the plants waving wildly as she tried to save them. Balancing his tray with one hand, Gideon scooped her up with the other, setting her on her feet before she lost her cargo.

Mary tilted her face up toward his, leaning against him confidingly. "Denke, Gideon," she whispered.

The small warm body in his grasp seemed to set something echoing through him, as if the door of his heart, long since closed, creaked ajar. First Joseph and now Mary, making him feel again.

No. He could not let that happen. He would help them, would try to do what he could for Ezra's sake, but he could not let himself care. His faith would never survive another loss, and the only way to prevent the pain was not to risk his heart again.

He set his mind to helping them arrange the plants on the

plank tables he'd built for the greenhouse. The children, enthusiastic at first, lost interest quickly, and Rachel sent them off to the kitchen, putting Becky in charge of getting them a snack.

It soon became clear that Rachel had her own definite opinions as to what should go where. Her face wore a serene expression as her hands busied themselves with her plants. She'd forgotten he was there. He had no gut reason to stay longer, so he began gathering up his tools.

"Ach, let me help you get your things together." Rachel shook her head. "Forgive me. I'm so eager to work on my plants that I haven't even told you how much I appreciate your kindness."

"Not necessary." He opened the lid of his toolbox. "Seeing your pleasure in the greenhouse is thanks enough."

"My last gift from Ezra." Her voice had grown soft. "It would have been treasured, whatever it was, but especially so since the greenhouse will help me support the children."

"You'll be going back to market again?"

"Ja. And this time with many more plants to sell, thanks to your help."

He shook his head. "I told you—"

She put her hand on his arm, the touch of it startling him into silence.

"I know. You did it because you promised Ezra. But I can still appreciate your actions, can't I?" Color flooded her cheeks. "Especially after the way I behaved that first day you brought it up. I'm still embarrassed to think about that."

"That's of no matter," he said carefully, wary of trying to press too far into her confidence. "Then, you couldn't see me without being reminded of Ezra's passing. It was only natural for you to blame me."

"I didn't. I don't. I know the accident wasn't your fault." She lifted her face to his, and she was so near he could almost feel her breath on his skin as she spoke. "You must accept that, too, Gideon. It would not be right to blame yourself for something that was in the hands of God."

She was too close, and he was far too aware of her. But he couldn't bring himself to move away.

Maybe she felt that, too. Her breath seemed to quicken, her eyes to widen.

And then suddenly she was looking down at the toolbox, as if searching for something to distract her. Or him.

"Is this a design for one of the windmills you'll be building this summer?" She touched the sketch he had tucked into the lid of the toolbox.

"Not exactly." He forced himself to focus on the paper, instead of on the curve of her cheek. He spread it flat. "I was playing around with an idea for a model windmill—something that folks might want to buy to put in their garden. It was just a thought I had when I was laid up. Don't suppose it amounts to much."

"Don't say that. I think it's a wonderful-gut idea. Think of all the ornaments the English like to put on their lawns and in their flower beds. I bet you could sell those easy. When are you going to make one?"

He folded the sketch and tucked it back into the box. "I'll tell you what. I'll make some when I get time, if you'll sell them along with your plants. That would be a gut deal."

He was only joking, of course. But he'd like it fine if he could make it come true.

*Rachel* tucked another marigold seedling into its own peat pot. The seedlings should be a nice size by the time frost danger was past. She stood back a little from the trestle table, admiring the lineup of plants. Ser gut. She'd have plenty to sell when the time came.

Picking up a water bottle, she began spraying the seedlings with a fine mist. Only a day had passed since the greenhouse was completed, and already it felt as familiar to her as her own bedroom.

Not only that—it had given her courage, it seemed. She'd asked William to help prepare an addition to the garden for some more ambitious plantings. Lavender would be simple to grow, and folks liked that. She'd put in a variety of small shrubs, maybe even some dogwood trees if she could afford them. She could get young plants cheap and bring them along until they were ready for sale.

Thanks to Ezra's gift, she had hope for the future. She and the children didn't need much, after all—just enough added income to make up for the portion of the milk money that went to Isaac. She wouldn't have to sell, and the children would have the security that went with a gut farm.

Thanks to Gideon, as well. She couldn't forget that. If he hadn't made her dream about the greenhouse again, with his insistence on fulfilling his promise to Ezra, she might never have pursued it.

Gideon had become close to them in the past few weeks—closer than she'd have imagined possible. Her hands stilled on the sprayer.

*Forgive me, Father, for my attitude toward Gideon. I'm trying to do better. Please help me.*

A shadow fell across the tray of seedlings in front of her. She looked up, startled, to find Isaac standing there, staring in through the glass at her.

Her stomach tightened even as she smiled at him. In her enthusiasm, she had forgotten that Isaac had his own idea of what should happen to the farm.

She put the sprayer back on its shelf and took a last look around the greenhouse, soaking in its peace. Then she opened the door and stepped outside.

Isaac's expression didn't give anything away as he surveyed the completed greenhouse, but that very lack of expression told her he wasn't pleased.

"See Gideon got it finished at last." He tapped on the framing around the door.

"Ja, just yesterday. It turned out nice, I think. I'm very grateful to him."

He peered through the glass at her tables, his forehead creasing in a frown. "You got a mighty big lot of plants in there. More than you can use yourself, I'd guess."

"They're to sell," she said, schooling her voice to patience. "I'll take them to the farmer's market, alongside Aaron and Lovina's things."

He grunted a response that might have meant anything and turned away from the greenhouse. He seemed to transfer his gaze to her newly plowed garden. "William told me you're talking about putting in a bunch of new things this year, bushes and whatnot."

This was what bothered him, she could see. She should have realized that he'd disapprove of those plans. The greenhouse he could rationalize moving to a new location, but if she started something bigger, like an actual nursery garden, he'd know she was determined to stay put.

"I'm hoping to grow enough to make a little income from it. For the children, you know."

"Is this your idea? Or did Gideon Zook come up with it?"

She blinked at the hardness of his tone. "Mine. Well, I did talk to Gideon about it, maybe."

"It seems to me you'd want to talk to family about this idea first, instead of an outsider."

"Gideon isn't an outsider."

"Not English, no, but he's not a member of your family, either. Just because he was Ezra's friend doesn't give him the right to interfere."

"He's not—" She stopped herself. The only way to deal with Isaac in this mood was to be patient with him. And he was right, in a sense. It would have been proper to discuss it with Isaac ahead of time. "I'm sorry I didn't talk with you about it first. I'm sure you'd have had some gut advice for me about what to plant."

"There's no reason for you to be planting anything. I told you that. Caleb will be glad to take over the farm, and then you won't have to worry about such things."

So this wasn't about her failure to talk to the family about her plans. It was about *his* plans—his plans to wipe out Ezra's dreams as if they'd never existed.

She actually felt a flicker of anger. She'd deferred to her father and to Ezra when it was needful. They'd had the right to be concerned with what she did, and they'd always wanted the best for her.

But Isaac—it seemed that Isaac wanted what was best for him and for Caleb.

She took a deep breath, quenching the anger before it could grow into a flame. Impossible to come to an actual breach with Isaac. He was family, he was one of the brethren, and she counted on his help.

But it was equally impossible just to cave in to him.

*Please, Father. Give me the right words.*

"I know you feel it's for the best that Caleb takes over the farm," she said carefully. "But I'm not sure that's what Ezra would want me to do. Isn't it my duty to carry out what I believe are his wishes in the matter?"

For a long moment Isaac just stared at her, as if he were measuring the extent of her stubbornness. Then he shrugged.

"Maybe you're right, but maybe not. I guess we can't say for certain, since Ezra is not here to speak for himself. But I do know he wouldn't want you to start in on something risky without thinking it through."

"What is risky about putting in a few more plants and shrubs? I'm able to take care of them, and the older children are big enough to help me."

"It would be risky if you invested money in them and didn't have enough water to keep them going over the summer."

She blinked. It took a moment to understand his meaning, and then her hands tightened into fists that pressed against her skirt. "Why would I not have enough water?" If he was going to threaten her, he'd better come right out with it.

"When your well has run low in the past, our spring has always had plenty of water to share." He hesitated, and she thought he was wondering just how far he wanted to go. Then his face tightened. "Could be that this summer we'll need all that we have."

"I see." She stared at him steadily, and his gaze shifted away from hers.

"Think about it." He turned away, his movements jerky. "I'm sure you'll see that my plan is best for everyone."

He walked away, leaving her fighting down unaccustomed anger.

*I'm sorry, Lord. I must not be angry with a brother. But what am I to do?*

"*Ach,* they're having a gut game, they are." Lovina Zook leaned back in the lawn chair she had dragged over to the edge of the field at the Zook farm.

"They are that." Rachel relaxed in the seat next to her.

Lovina and Aaron had invited her to come to supper and bring the children. She'd thought perhaps Lovina wanted to talk about plans for market, but so far Lovina seemed more concerned with making sure everyone had enough to eat. Their four boys and three girls made for a hungry, cheerful group around the supper table, especially with her three added.

And Gideon, of course.

His presence was only natural, since he lived here and had his shop in an old barn on his brother's farm. He and Aaron had organized an after-supper ball game.

At the moment Gideon was pitching, sending an easy ball toward Becky. Aaron seemed to be coaching her on how to hold the bat.

"I hear tell when the English play ball, there's lots of yelling and cheering, even loud teasing." Lovina smiled fondly at her brood. "Sounds funny, ain't so?"

"Maybe they'd think we're funny," Rachel suggested. "Playing a game so quiet-like." The more she saw of the outside world, the more she realized how strange Amish ways would be to them.

"There's no need to make a lot of ruckus to have a gut time. I'd say Aaron and Gideon enjoy it as much as the children."

"Ja. It's nice to see how well your family works and plays

together. You and Aaron must be doing a fine job, with raising seven of them."

The bat cracked, and they both leaned forward to watch Becky race for first base, apron fluttering, a huge grin on her face.

"A big hit for such a little girl." Lovina glanced at Rachel, her usually merry face turning serious for once. "I'd guess that being around other families makes you miss Ezra more sometimes, ja?"

"I guess it does." Rachel hadn't thought about it that way, but Lovina had a point. "I don't begrudge others their happiness, you understand. But Ezra was such a gut father. And husband. I miss that feeling that there's someone who's always there to help and support me."

She'd felt that keenly when she'd heard what Teacher Mary had to say about Becky. The young teacher's eyes had been filled with concern when she talked about how daring Becky had become—challenging even the older boys to climb higher or run faster at recess. Teacher Mary had been forced to discipline her more than once.

Ezra would have known what to do. Rachel didn't.

Lovina nodded. "I plain don't know how I'd deal with my seven if I didn't have Aaron," she said, an echo of Rachel's thoughts.

Somehow it was easier to talk about it with Lovina, who wasn't family. Rachel's mamm would listen, but she wanted so much to help that it almost hurt to talk to her.

"It's hardest when the children worry me." *Like Becky.* "I think about how it felt to be able to share it all with him."

"Ja." Lovina reached over and patted her knee. "But you're still a young woman, Rachel. Losing Ezra doesn't mean that you can't ever have that kind of partnership with a man again."

Rachel realized she must be healing, since that comment didn't pain her as much as the implication usually did. "I don't know. I guess I can't imagine loving anyone else the way I loved Ezra."

"Well, of course not." Lovina's tone was one of brisk common sense. "I mean, it stands to reason you're not going to love someone the same way when you're thirty as you did when you were sixteen."

"No, but—" It was certain sure that her love for Ezra had changed and deepened over time.

"I figure it's like loving your children." Lovina's gaze followed her oldest girl, chasing a fly ball. "They're all different, so you love them in different ways, but you don't love one more than another."

Rachel wasn't sure that applied to loving a man, but she did understand what Lovina meant about the children. "It is a challenge, knowing what each of them needs. My three are all so different."

Her gaze sought them. Mary, safely out in right field, was picking dandelions with Lovina's youngest. Becky danced off third base, daring Gideon to try to pick her off. And Joseph was at bat, his small face intent and serious.

"Imagine what it's like with seven." Lovina chuckled. "Course, we've had Gid around a lot of the time. He's a gut onkel, he is, in spite of having lost his own wife and the boppli. It helps having him here, but I'd sacrifice that gladly to see him married again."

Rachel wasn't sure what to say to that. Was it a hint?

"It's been a long time since the accident. I'm sure he's had plenty of chances to marry, if he wanted to."

Lovina shrugged ample shoulders, as if in agreement. "Has he maybe talked to you about it?"

"No."

That probably came out too sharp, but she couldn't seem to help it. Her mind had suddenly filled with an image of Ezra talking about Gideon. Explaining why it had been important for him to go off and do something with his friend on one particular day.

Rachel's cheeks flushed, just thinking about it. Had she been petty, nagging, wanting him to stay home with her?

*It's the anniversary of losing his wife and boppli, Rachel.* In her mind's eye, Ezra frowned at her in disappointment at her attitude. *I couldn't leave him alone today. He'll never talk about it, but he needs a friend right now.*

She'd been embarrassed, of course. Apologetic. But she'd still probably harbored a little resentment.

*Maybe it's time he started looking for someone else.*

At the memory of her words she cringed. She hadn't understood, then, the power that grief could wield.

*I don't think he can.* Ezra's eyes had gone dark with pain for his friend. *I don't think he ever will.*

"Aaron says I'm too eager to manage everyone else's business." Lovina's cheerful voice interrupted Rachel's thoughts. "And maybe he's right, but I don't like to see anyone alone. It's not what the gut Lord intends for us, to my way of thinking."

Joseph hit the ball at that moment, saving Rachel the difficulty of answering. The boy just stood looking at it in astonishment until Gideon called to him to run. Then he scrambled toward first base.

The hit was an easy fly ball that Aaron unaccountably failed to catch. That gave Becky the chance to score. Laughing, Aaron declared it was time for a snack, and the game was over.

The players flooded toward the picnic table, where Lovina had put out a pitcher of lemonade and a platter of cookies. Joseph ran to Rachel, his face lit up.

"Mammi, did you see? I hit the ball."

"I saw." She gave him a quick hug. "Go and have your lemonade and cookies now. It'll soon be time for us to head home."

"Not yet," he said, dancing with impatience. "Gideon promised to show me Aaron's goats first."

She'd like to get started before the sun set, but there was still time. And she couldn't deprive him of something that was so obviously important to him. "Go along then, but don't pester Gideon, all right?"

Joseph nodded and ran off.

"Ach, don't let that fret you." Lovina grasped the chair arms and shoved herself up. "Gideon is always talking about that *bu* of yours. He's very fond of Joseph and happy to show him the goats. I'm surprised Aaron's not going along, too. He's so pleased with those creatures that he loves the chance to show them off. Komm, let's have some cookies and lemonade, too."

Rachel followed Lovina toward the picnic table, wrestling with the thought. Gideon was fond of Joseph, always talking about him, according to Lovina. Well, that was a gut thing, she supposed. A child couldn't have too much love, and Joseph needed a man to look up to.

She just wasn't sure that Gideon was the man for the job.

Becky was full of herself over having scored the winning run, and Rachel sat on the picnic bench, listening to it twice over. Mary crawled up on the bench next to her, settling down with a cookie in each hand. In only a moment she was leaning against Rachel's shoulder.

Rachel patted her. "We'd best think about getting along home."

"Not yet, Mammi," Becky protested.

"Soon," she said, getting off the bench. "You finish your treats, and I'll go and see if Joseph is finished looking at the goats. Then we must be leaving."

She crossed toward the fenced area next to the barn. Aaron's herd of goats was larger than she'd expected. He must be having good luck with the goat cheese he sold at the market.

Gideon and Joseph leaned on the fence watching them, their backs toward her. The goats clustered close to them. Gideon had probably let her son hand-feed them, or they wouldn't be so eager to be petted.

She drew closer, her sneakers making little sound on the grass. Gideon and Joseph seemed so intent on whatever they were saying to each other that she hated to interrupt them.

". . . Becky says it's silly to have a goat for a pet. She says goats are farm animals, not pets." Joseph's voice reached Rachel clearly. "I guess Aaron's goats aren't pets, are they?"

"I guess not, but Aaron is a farmer." Gideon sounded as if he were torn between saying what was true and reassuring her son.

"I'm going to be a farmer, too, when I'm bigger." Joseph's profile tilted toward Gideon. "But Dolly—" He stopped.

Gideon put his hand on Joseph's shoulder. "Dolly is special to you, isn't she?"

"My daadi gave her to me, for my very own."

Rachel's heart twisted. Why hadn't she seen that? The greenhouse was important because it was Ezra's gift to her, and Joseph loved that goat for the same reason.

"Well, then, if you're asking me what I think, I'd say that Becky is wrong."

"Wrong?" Joseph's eyes widened, as if that thought hadn't occurred to him.

"Not about other things, mind. But about this."

The boy reached between the rails to scratch the muzzle of a persistent little goat. "But you said Aaron doesn't think his goats are pets, either."

Joseph, like the little goat, was persistent. She should intercede, but somehow she wanted to hear how Gideon would answer that.

He hesitated for a moment. "You know, I remember another boy who had a pet most people would think was silly. He was just about your age at the time, too."

"Who?"

"Your daadi."

"He did?" Joseph breathed the words. "What was it?"

Rachel's breath caught. Gideon had said he'd wait for her permission before talking to her children about Ezra as a boy. Now, it appeared he was about to do exactly that.

"A duckling."

"A duckling?" Joseph blinked. "But that's silly."

"Maybe so, but that's what it was." Gideon seemed to be looking back through time, and his face softened into a smile that made him look younger. "The little thing hatched out when its mammi wasn't there. I guess it thought your daadi was a gut substitute. It used to follow him around, quacking."

"Did folks laugh at him?" There was a world of feeling in Joseph's words.

"They did. But he never let that bother him, not one little bit. He figured they could think what they wanted to, but that little duck depended on him, and he wouldn't let it down."

Joseph seemed to mull that over for a moment, and then he gave a decided nod. "My daadi was right." He stood a little straighter. "I want to be just like him."

Tears choked Rachel's throat and blurred her vision. Gideon had just given her son a gift that she'd been unable, or unwilling, to give. She stifled a sob.

# Chapter Nine

A soft sound behind him had Gideon turning. Rachel stood there. She'd obviously been listening, and her blue eyes were bright with tears.

Regret pierced him. He shouldn't have spoken to Joseph about his father. That was Rachel's responsibility, and the one time he'd brought it up, she'd evaded the subject. She hadn't wanted this, and now he'd done it anyway.

Still, even though it was wrong to talk to the boy without his mother's permission, the idea itself wasn't wrong. He'd be sorry to face Rachel's anger about this, and sorrier still that he'd caused her more pain.

But he felt as sure of this as he'd been of anything in his life. All three children needed to have stories of their father to remember, but Joseph needed it most of all, because those stories would help him grow into a man like Ezra.

Rachel came toward them, not looking at him, all her attention on her son. "Here you are, Joseph. Have you seen all of Aaron's goats already?"

"Ja, Mammi." Joseph hurried to her, his face lit with excitement. "Aaron has a fine herd, but he doesn't have any Nubians like Dolly. He said I could come another time with Gideon and learn how he makes the cheese, if you say it's all right."

If Rachel objected, she wasn't letting it show on her face. Her smile for the boy was gentle. "We'll talk about it," she said. "But now I need you to run back to the table. Tell your sisters I'll be there in a moment."

She waited while the boy hustled across the yard, her face turned away from Gideon so that he saw only the curve of her cheek. He stiffened, preparing himself to bear the brunt of her anger, preparing to tell her—

The child out of earshot, Rachel turned toward him. A single tear glistened on her cheek, and the sight of it wiped away everything he'd thought he'd say to her.

"Don't, Rachel." He longed to smooth the tear away, but he didn't dare. "I'm sorry. Don't mind so much."

She dashed the tear away herself with an impatient gesture. "No, I'm the one to be sorry. I didn't understand." She took a step toward the fence, grasping the rail with her hands and looking at the goats without, he thought, really seeing them.

He studied what he could see of her averted face. The line of her profile was as sweet and innocent as that of one of the children. She wasn't angry, it seemed, but he couldn't be sure just what she was feeling.

"I'm sorry," he said again, figuring that, at least, was safe. "I should not have spoken with Joseph about his father before asking you if it was all right."

She shook her head, still not looking at him. "I'm glad you didn't wait." She swallowed, the muscles of her neck working as if it took an effort. "Joseph came to you with a problem. I might wish he'd come to me instead, but maybe this was for the best. You gave him an answer that will help him much more than whatever I would have said."

"If you truly feel that, then I'm glad, too."

Rachel's eyes glistened with the tears she didn't want to shed. "You're a gut man, Gideon Zook. My children and I are fortunate to have you as a friend."

She was setting the boundary for him, and it was one he should be happy to accept.

He nodded. "Denke, Rachel. It is my pleasure."

For a moment they stood there, hands close on the fence rail, looking at each other. If Lovina was watching, she probably thought her matchmaking efforts were bearing fruit. She couldn't know how far from that they were.

He cleared his throat. "Are you ready to go to market again on Saturday?"

"Ja." She frowned slightly, but then seemed to chase the expression away. "My parents are so happy to have the children for the day that it makes it easy for me to go."

"Lovina will be pleased to have your company." He would, as well. He knew without even thinking about it that he'd show up, because it would mean a little extra time with her. And he'd keep talking about it at the moment for the very same reason. "You have many plants ready to take?"

"Ja. I think I will take some of the marigold and snapdragon seedlings, even though it's early for them. Some folks might want to risk putting them in."

He forced himself to concentrate on her plans for the flowers instead of on the play of expressions that crossed her face. "Did William get the soil ready for the other things you want to put in your garden?"

"He did." She stopped, but her troubled frown told him there was more to it. "He must have mentioned it to Isaac, because Isaac came to see me about it. Not that I would try to keep a secret from him, in any case."

Judging by the look on her face, he thought she might be wishing that she could.

"What does Isaac have to do with your plans for planting?" He tried to keep his voice neutral, even though the question itself probably announced how he felt about Isaac's actions in regard to his brother's widow and children.

"Isaac is family, after all." She sounded as if she were making excuses for him, which must mean that Isaac had not approved of her plans. "And he's still hoping that I will decide to sell the farm to Caleb. He probably thinks that the more I become involved in the nursery business, the less chance there is that I'll sell." She shrugged. "And that's true, of course."

"As Ezra's brother, he should be happy that you're doing what Ezra would want."

"He doesn't see it that way. And I suppose he's right when he says that we none of us really know what Ezra would advise."

He bit back the impulse to say that he knew. That wasn't helpful to Rachel right now, with her brother-in-law being difficult. And this was about Rachel's needs, not about his own feelings.

"I know you want to keep peace in the family," he said carefully, not sure how far he could go. "But I would hate to see you give up things that are important to you and the children because they might upset Isaac."

"No, but— " Her hands twisted together, as if they were fighting with each other. "I depend on him, you see."

"I know William does all the work with the dairy herd, but you're paying for that, ain't so?"

"It's more than just that." Her forehead furrowed. "Ezra was always going to work on the well. Maybe even put in a new one or pipe water from the spring. But there was always so much else to spend the money on, and . . ."

"I'd forgotten. Ezra piped water down from Isaac's place in dry weather." Now he frowned, too. "Isaac wouldn't deny you the water just because he wants you to sell the farm to his boy."

Her mouth tightened. "Maybe, if it came down to it, he wouldn't. But he hinted at it pretty strongly."

That was so wrong that Gideon wasn't sure what to say. Not just wrong as a family member, but contrary to everything the church taught about supporting each other.

Words sprang to his lips, but he held them back. Better to be slow to speak and be sure that what he said made things better, not worse. "Maybe it would be gut to take this to Bishop Mose . . ."

"No." Something that might have been panic whitened her face. "Not that. I won't be the one to make a breach in the family known to the whole church."

"Bishop Mose could talk to Isaac. Make him see how wrong that would be. Other people don't need to know about it."

She shook her head. They both knew that if a dispute among the brethren could not be resolved by a private talk with the bishop, he would take it to the church.

"I won't do that," she repeated. "I'll have to find another way. Maybe it will be a wet summer."

"Maybe," he agreed, mind busy with possible answers to the problem. "But maybe you need to think about something else."

"Like what?" Her face flushed with exasperation. "I can't afford to have another well dug."

"No. But it could be that a windmill would give you the power to pump enough water from your existing well."

For an instant, hope dawned in her face, but it faded just as quickly as it had come. "I can't afford a windmill, either."

"I'd be glad to build one—"

She cut him off with a quick gesture. "Building windmills is your livelihood. The greenhouse was one thing, a promise you made to Ezra. But a windmill is totally different. I couldn't let you do that unless I could pay for it, same as anyone else would."

Maybe she didn't need to know what he would charge anyone else. "The cost wouldn't be near as much as having a well drilled."

"By the time I pay the taxes, I'll have barely enough to keep us going until the next payment from the dairy comes in." She shook her head. "No, Gideon. I know what you're going to say, but there's no point in discussing it. Unless I can pay for having a windmill put up, it's out of the question."

He nodded in seeming agreement. But he wasn't done with the subject, not yet. Let her think about it for a time. Let her mull over how gut it would feel not to be dependent on Isaac's generosity.

Obviously she didn't want to depend on his generosity either. She wouldn't let him build the windmill unless she could pay for it. So he'd have to find some way to make sure she could do just that.

"*Mammi,* please can we have some? Please?" Becky tugged on Rachel's arm, pointing to the popcorn stand at the firemen's carnival.

The mingled aromas of popcorn, cotton candy, sausage sandwiches, pizza, and who-knew-what other treats were beginning to be overwhelming. "Becky, we have popcorn at home. Why—"

"Ach, let the little ones have popcorn if they want." Her father was already reaching for his wallet. "The carnival is a special event, ain't so?"

Rachel shook her head, smiling in surrender. "It'll be even more special if they end up with tummy aches from all the junk food they're eating."

But Daadi had already stepped up to the stand, Becky and Joseph on either side of him, ready to supervise the purchase. Mary clung to Rachel's hand, and already she drooped a little from all the excitement. Rachel exchanged looks with her mother.

"Let him do it," her mother said. "They won't suffer from having a few extra treats, and it gives your daadi pleasure to do things for his grandchildren."

"You do so much for us already." Rachel pressed her mother's hand. "You know how grateful I am."

Her mother dismissed it with a quick shake of her head. "It's nothing." She touched Mary's hair gently. "We'll be able to do more once you move back home with us. Daad and I were just talking about it last night. He's thinking he'll add on another room to give everyone a bit more space with growing children in the house."

"Mamm—" The sinking feeling in her stomach had nothing to do with eating junk food. "You know I don't want to give up the farm."

"Chust think about it already. Think about how much easier it will be on everyone."

There didn't seem to be any doubt in her mother's mind that

sooner or later Rachel would be moving in. That made it all the more difficult to bring up the subject she'd been circling around since her parents had picked them up for this outing.

Should she ask them for the money to build the windmill? And if she did, what would they say?

She'd had a successful day at market on Saturday, even better than the first time, building her confidence that she could actually do it. But whether her parents would agree—whether they'd even consider it when they were so firm in their notion that she and the children move in with them—well, that was another thing entirely.

The popcorn bought, they started moving along the row of stands, the children's gazes darting from one unfamiliar sight to another. Rachel let Becky and Joseph go ahead with their grossdaadi while she and her mother lagged behind, suiting their steps to Mary's.

Mary's small bag of popcorn tipped, spilling onto the sawdust pathway. Rachel grabbed it before it could all go.

Her mother's eyes twinkled. "I know what you are thinking chust now, my Rachel."

"You do?" Whatever Mamm imagined, it certainly wouldn't be that her daughter's mind was caught up in the subject of windmills. That even her dreams had been filled lately with their paddles spinning against a clear blue sky.

"You are thinking that your daadi didn't spoil you and Johnny the way he wants to spoil your young ones."

It took an effort to conceal her surprise at her mother's bringing up Johnny's name. "That's certain sure. Though Johnny did a pretty gut job of wheedling."

"Ach, that was his way. That boy could charm the birds out of the trees when he wanted to." Mamm glanced down at Mary, who was staring openmouthed at a clown on stilts. "We know that you see him, Rachel." Her voice grew soft on the words. "Even if your daad will never willingly mention it."

She'd been reluctant to bring it up, telling herself she didn't want to cause more pain. Maybe she'd just been a coward. "Does that upset you, my seeing him?"

"No, no. Don't think that. I'm glad that he has you. I chust wish . . ."

She let that trail off, but Rachel could figure out the rest of it. Mamm would never go against what Daad said, but she longed to see Johnny for herself.

Rachel squeezed her mother's hand. "I know. I wish it, too."

"Look, Mammi. It's Elizabeth." Becky darted away from her grandfather to greet her friend, while the rest of them followed a little more slowly.

"Daniel, it's gut to see all of you." Rachel smiled at Daniel Glick and the three young ones. "Leah is home resting, I hope?"

"Ja." Daniel grinned. "And complaining all the time about it, too. I had to promise to bring her a caramel apple when we return."

"That was always her favorite treat, even when we were your size." She tapped the brim of young Jonah's straw hat, and the seven-year-old gave her a gap-toothed grin.

"We appreciated the food you brought on Thursday," Daniel said. "That was kind of you. Cheered Leah up, it did."

Rachel nodded, hoping he was right. She saw Leah just as often as ever, of course, maybe more often, as she tried to help at this difficult time. On the surface, things were the same between them, but the truth was that she'd felt a constraint since the day she'd told Leah her plans and come away shaken by her lack of support.

"Can Elizabeth walk around with us, Mammi?" Becky held hands with her friend.

Rachel glanced at Daniel, but he shook his head. "Not this time. We're going to pick out desserts for everyone and then be on our way home."

"Ja, we'll be going soon as well. I have one almost asleep on her feet already." She patted Mary's shoulder as she smiled at Elizabeth. "Maybe you can come to spend the afternoon sometime soon, ja? We'd like that."

Becky and Elizabeth brightened immediately, the hint of a pout vanishing from Becky's face. "Soon, Mammi?" She obviously wanted to nail it down.

"As soon as Elizabeth's daadi and mammi say it's a gut day." She glanced at Daniel. "Just let me know. Anytime. And give our love to Leah."

He nodded. "We will." He raised his hand in farewell and shepherded his children away.

"Leah is doing all right?" Mamm asked as they moved on.

"The midwife is happy with her progress, she says. But Leah frets at having to be off her feet so much, wanting to tend to the family herself."

"Well, she'd best listen. It's no easy thing to have a first boppli at her age."

"She's just as old as I am," Rachel protested.

"But you've already had three. That makes it easier. If you were to marry again . . ." Her mother darted a look at her, as if waiting for a reaction.

Rachel did her best to keep her face from expressing anything at all. If she were to marry again. Everyone seemed to have ideas about that. Everyone but her.

"Rachel?" Her mother's voice was questioning.

"We'll have to wait and see what the future holds," she said. Mary stumbled, and Rachel bent and lifted her into her arms. "And right now, I think the future must hold bedtime for this little girl."

"Ja, you're right about that. I'll tell your daadi that we're ready to go."

Mamm moved forward briskly to intercept Daad and the children, who'd gotten a few yards ahead of them while they'd talked. Rachel stood where she was, Mary heavy in her arms, and suddenly found her breath catching in her throat.

Johnny. Johnny came toward them, walking with an English woman, carrying a paper plate of funnel cakes in his hand. His head was bent toward the woman as she talked, and he didn't see them until he was almost upon them.

He stopped. Daad stopped. For a moment Daad's face softened, as if he would reach out, would say something.

And then Daad turned sharply away, muttering, "Komm," over his shoulder. Mamm sent Johnny one pleading, loving glance before clutching Joseph and Becky by the hands and following.

Rachel reached her brother in a few steps. "I'm sorry," she said softly.

"Don't be." Johnny's face hardened until he no longer resembled the brother she loved. "I didn't expect anything else." Taking his friend by the arm, he walked off.

Rachel made her way toward the buggy, her heart as heavy as the child asleep in her arms. Was there no possibility of peace between them?

She already knew the answer to that, didn't she? As long as Daadi believed there was a chance to bring Johnny back to the fold by his attitude, he'd continue, no matter how much it hurt.

Maybe that was the answer when it came to asking Daadi to

fund the building of the windmill. She'd be asking him to pay for something that allowed her to continue on a path he didn't approve. Whether he said yes or no, it would create tension between them.

And tension was something they already had in abundance. There had to be another way. She'd just have to find it.

*Gideon* settled on the polished bench in the hallway of the medical clinic, his hat on his knees. The English woman behind the reception desk had given him an odd look when he asked for John Kile, as if that was an unusual request.

Well, it most likely was, at least coming from an Amishman. Every Amish person in Pleasant Valley knew that John was under the bann, even those who weren't members of his former church district. They wouldn't willingly seek him out. But Gideon had to.

He'd been turning Rachel's problem over and over in his mind for the past few days, methodically considering all the possibilities for a solution. Ezra had often chided him for his slowness in coming to a conclusion about things, but he wasn't inclined to change now, and the situation between Rachel and Isaac was too delicate for any rash solutions.

Rachel certainly knew that Bishop Mose would intercede if she took the problem to him. Isaac would not be acting in accordance with Scripture or the Ordnung if he went so far as to cut off Rachel's water, and Gideon doubted that any member of the church would support his action.

But the decision wasn't up to him; it was up to Rachel, and he understood why she'd long for just about any solution that would avoid such an open breach in the family. To take her late husband's brother to the judgment of the community—such a thing could not be undertaken lightly.

Indeed, he wondered how serious Isaac's threat was. Would he actually follow through with it, knowing it could bring the condemnation of the community? Or did he hope to bend Rachel to his will without the need to carry it out?

Gideon frowned down at the brim of his hat, considering, and then quickly changed the frown to a smile when he realized he was being watched by an Amish mother and child from the waiting room. The little boy, probably not more than four or five, had the golden skin and yellowed eyes that marked children who suffered from Crigler-Najjar syndrome.

Gideon didn't know this family, which told him they weren't from the valley, but Dr. Brandenmyer's work with the genetic diseases that afflicted the Amish was widely known. This family might have come from as far away as Ohio or Indiana to seek out his help.

The door beside him opened, and John Kile came through with a quick, businesslike stride. He glanced around, and his face registered surprise when he saw who waited for him.

"Gideon?"

Gideon rose. "John. You look well."

Actually he was nearly unrecognizable. The Amish boy Gideon had once known seemed present only in the shape of his features. His hair was a bit darker now, and cut so short that it appeared even darker. He wore a pale blue shirt with a pair of tan pants, topped by the sort of loose coat doctors wore. If Gideon had passed him in a crowd of English, he wouldn't have known him.

"Gideon Zook." John said the name slowly, his eyes narrowing a bit. "When the receptionist told me an Amishman was waiting to see me, I found it hard to believe."

Would Johnny have thought—or hoped—that it would be his father? Everyone knew how strict Amos Kile was when it came to holding to the bann. And Gideon knew how much that situation was hurting Rachel and her mother.

"I'm sorry to interrupt your work. I'd like a few minutes of your time, if you can spare it."

John's jaw tightened. "Aren't you afraid someone will see you talking to me?"

Natural, maybe, for John to be less than friendly. It couldn't be easy for him to be back in the valley and have folks avoid him. Still, leaving had been his choice. As had coming back.

"I wouldn't be here if I were worried about that. We need to talk about Rachel."

John just stared at him for a moment, and Gideon couldn't begin to guess his thoughts. Then he held open the door he'd come through. "Come on back. We'll find someplace private to talk."

Nodding, Gideon followed him.

This side of the building was entirely different from the ordinary medical clinic that occupied the opposite side. He glanced into the rooms they passed as they walked along a hallway that seemed to run the depth of the building. Medical labs and computer rooms lined the hall—the tools of Dr. Brandenmyer's trade, he supposed. And John's now, as well.

They passed a door marked Conference Room and came to an outside door, which John pushed wide. "Come out on the porch. Nobody will bother us back here."

The porch was furnished with a small table and a couple of chairs, and some cartons were stacked at one end, as if a delivery hadn't been put away yet. A driveway curved around the building, and beyond it pasture stretched all the way to the distant line of trees. A hitching post had been conveniently placed under the shade provided by a couple of maples.

It was a pleasant spot; some would probably say a funny spot for a medical research laboratory. Dr. Brandenmyer had been smart enough to know that he'd have to go to the Amish if he wanted to study their diseases.

John leaned against the porch railing, as if he didn't expect to prolong this visit. "What brings you to visit me today? Nothing medical, I'm guessing, or Rachel would have come herself instead of sending you."

"No."

Gideon would know how to talk to the boy he'd grown up with, but John Kile was English now. There was pride in him, Gideon would guess—pride in his education and his position. That might make it more difficult to gain his agreement.

John raised an eyebrow. "Well?"

No choice but to plunge into it and trust to the gut Lord that he was doing the right thing.

"You maybe know that I've been helping Rachel out some."

John nodded, his face softening at the mention of his twin. "She told me you were building that greenhouse she wanted so much. That was good of you."

He shrugged that off. "She's been working with her plants a lot—taking things to sell at market, at my brother Aaron's stand."

"She always did have a green thumb, didn't she?"

John smiled, and all of a sudden that made him look like the boy he'd been. The antagonism Gideon had felt at first disappeared once John mentioned Rachel. Those two had always been as close as two halves of a heart.

"Ja, she did. She still does." He took a breath. He was skirting the issue, and that wasn't helping either of them. He'd best get to the point. "But she needs help."

John seemed to stiffen, his hands pressing hard against the railing, his face shuttered. "What business is that of yours? Did Rachel send you here, or is this your idea?"

Looked like he'd said something wrong, but there was nothing for it but to push ahead now. "Rachel didn't send me." He felt a twinge at the thought. No, Rachel hadn't asked him to do anything for her.

"Then what are you doing here?" John's tone made it a demand.

"I guess I'm interfering." He shrugged. "Somebody has to. And Ezra was my friend. I feel like I owe it to him to do what I can."

"You two always did hang together, didn't you?" John seemed to take a cautious glance at the past they'd shared. "All right. So tell me what it is that's so serious you have to butt in to it."

Gideon's tension eased a hair. Johnny would listen, anyway. That was progress.

"Rachel maybe told you that she's thinking of expanding what she's doing with her plantings, maybe even turn it into a regular nursery. She could make enough money from it that she wouldn't have to sell the farm."

"I knew money was tight. And that she doesn't want to let go of the farm. I guess that's as good a solution as any. So where does the problem come in? Does she need financing to get started?"

Gideon hesitated. Isaac's role in this wasn't his story to tell.

"The water supply from the well isn't always reliable. Putting in a windmill would solve it, and I'd be glad to do it. But she won't let me unless she can pay." He shrugged. "Your sister can be a stubborn woman at times."

John's jaw clenched. "I've already offered her money. And been turned down. You can guess why." His very tone was a challenge.

"That's so," Gideon said slowly, his gaze on John's face. "But it seems to me that a smart, educated man like you could figure out a way around that, if you really set your mind to it."

For an instant anger flared in that set face, and Gideon thought he'd failed. Then slowly, maybe reluctantly, John nodded. "You have an idea how we could accomplish that?"

Relief moved through him. This was going to work. "Not exactly. But I know who will help us, because I've already asked him. Bishop Mose."

# CHAPTER TEN

"I just can't believe this is happening so quickly already." Rachel stared from her kitchen window at the windmill that had risen almost overnight, it seemed, in the field beside the barn.

"The children aren't getting in the way of Gideon and the workers, are they?" Leah grasped the kitchen table, as if she was about to heave herself to her feet. "Maybe I should check on mine."

Rachel got to her in two quick steps and nudged her gently back into her chair. "You'll do no such thing," she chided. "It's a wonder to me Daniel let you come over here today. If you overdo, he'll never let me hear the end of it."

"But the children . . ."

"Are playing in the barn, well out of the way. Did you think Gideon would let them climb the windmill tower?"

Leah chuckled, subsiding. "I guess you're right." She smoothed her hand down over her bulging belly. "Seems like the closer this little one comes to being born, the more I fuss and fidget. Please tell me that's natural and not just me."

"Definitely not just you." Rachel sat down opposite her and stirred her own cooling tea. "I remember driving Ezra and the oldest two crazy with my fussing the month before Mary was born."

Funny, now that she thought about it, that she could talk about Ezra so naturally now. It felt gut—bittersweet, maybe, but gut.

Leah stroked her belly. She wore that looking-inward expression that pregnant women seemed to get, as if communicating with the babe inside them was far more important than anything that happened outside.

"The midwife says I've probably three weeks to go, but I keep feeling as if this little one won't wait so long." Her lips curved in a soft smile. "How much I want to hold him. Or her."

Rachel had to blink back tears. She remembered that feeling, too. "That will come soon enough. But hopefully not before the quilting bee at your house."

Leah nodded. "If everyone comes, there will be enough to finish two baby quilts that afternoon. People are being so kind—it's almost overwhelming."

"You were our schoolteacher for nearly ten years," Rachel reminded her. "Lots of folks have reason to be grateful to you. They want to share your happiness."

Despite her pleasure in having Leah here for a visit again, she couldn't prevent herself from taking another quick glance at the windmill, rising raw and new against the sky. That was Gideon on the top level now, working steadily and without hurry, as he always did.

And how she could recognize him at this distance in a group similarly garbed, she didn't want to think about.

"Enough about the baby," Leah said, putting her cup down on the table. "I want to hear all about the windmill. How did this come about? I didn't even know you were thinking about building one."

"It's not so surprising, really. You know we often had trouble with our water supply in the summer."

Leah nodded, not saying the obvious—that Ezra and Rachel had always been able to count on pumping their water over from Isaac's. But she was probably thinking it, wondering about it.

"Anyway, I needed to do something." She hurried on past the difficult patch. "Gideon suggested that the windmill would let me be . . . would increase the amount I could pump. Ezra had talked about that several times, but it seemed like there was always something else to spend the money on."

"Now Gideon is doing it for you."

If there was a double meaning in the words, Rachel decided to ignore it. "Not for free. I couldn't let him do that. And the truth was that I didn't see how I'd ever pay for it."

"Your parents . . ."

Rachel shook her head. "I didn't feel right about asking them. They're so eager for me and the children to move back in with them. They see this as just another thing holding me here. No, this help came from Bishop Mose."

"Bishop Mose gave you the money?" Leah leaned forward, face alive with interest.

"Not gave. It's a loan, and I'll pay him back." Rachel hesitated, the longing to talk this over with Leah strong. "I'm not even sure how Bishop Mose knew about it to begin with. It wasn't as if I was going around talking about it."

"Gideon must have told him." Leah glanced toward the window in her turn.

"I suppose so. Of course I told Bishop Mose no, but—have you ever tried to tell him no about something?"

Leah's lips twitched. "I can't say I have."

"For every argument I had, he had an answer. First he was rational. It was a gut investment and it would increase the value of the farm, so that even if I sell sometime, I'll get more."

"He's probably right about that. But if I know you, you didn't give in that easily."

"Well, no." Rachel fiddled with her teaspoon, balancing it on her fingers. "But he questioned my pridefulness, saying that's all that was keeping me from accepting help from one of the brothers when I needed it."

The spoon dropped from Rachel's finger, landing on the wooden table with a tiny *clink*.

"If the bishop tells you that you're falling into sin, you sit up and take notice. Thing was, I could see how he had it right. I *was* being prideful, thinking that I was the only one who could take care of my children, and not trusting others to help me."

Leah leaned across the table and put her hand over Rachel's, her grip warm and firm. "I'm glad."

"Are you?" Rachel flushed. "I mean—I know you don't think I can succeed at this nursery business, and that's mostly why I need the windmill—"

"Not think you can succeed?" Leah interrupted her, her fingers tightening on Rachel's. "Rachel, where did you get an idea like that?"

"That Sunday, after worship, when I told you about my idea. You . . . Well, you discouraged me. As if you didn't think I had it in me to make a success of it."

"Ach, Rachel, that isn't what I meant at all." Leah's face crinkled with such distress that Rachel had to believe her. "I was just worried about you, that's all. I was afraid you'd work yourself to death, not accepting any help and thinking you had to do it all on your own. That's what I was thinking. Goodness, I know you'll do anything you set your mind to."

Rachel flushed, this time with pleasure. "I thought—well, never mind. I'm just glad you feel that way."

Leah's eyes were bright with unshed tears. "I've felt, lately, as if there was something between us. I didn't like the feeling. Are we all right now?"

Rachel nodded, her own throat thick. There had been something between them, thanks to her own misunderstanding.

"Ser gut," Rachel murmured.

Before she could say another word, a ruckus erupted outside. Men's voices, shouting—something had happened.

She and Leah exchanged one quick, frightened look, and then she was rushing to the door, with Leah following more slowly.

She burst out onto the back porch and took the steps in a jump. Men were running toward the barn, Gideon in the lead. Rachel's heart thudded against her ribs.

Something was wrong—something bad.

*Please, Lord, please, Lord.* She didn't know what to pray, only that prayer was needed.

Elizabeth raced to them and clutched Rachel's apron with both hands, her face tearstained and frightened.

"Elizabeth, what is it? Tell me!" She grasped the child's shoulders.

"Becky." The word came out on a sob. "Becky climbed up into the barn rafters. She can't get down. She's going to fall."

*Becky . . . please, God, protect Becky.*

"Go to your mamm," she ordered, and she set off running toward the barn, fear clawing at her heart, breath coming in terrified gasps.

*Please, Father. Please.*

. . .

*Gideon's* leg throbbed as he reached the barn seconds ahead of the other men. He thrust the door wide and plunged in, blinking, trying to adjust his vision to the gloom after the bright sunshine outside.

He spotted the two boys standing in the middle of the barn floor, their heads tilted back, faces pale, shocked ovals as they stared upward. He followed the direction of their gazes, and his heart seemed to stop.

Becky. High in the rafters, thirty or forty feet up, Becky teetered on a beam, hands outstretched to clutch nothing but air.

For a second he couldn't move—couldn't do anything but utter a wordless prayer. Then the others rushed in, and his mind started working. Be calm, be rational, think only of what must be done, and not of what was at stake.

"Get a rope," he ordered. "And a tarp, a canvas, anything you can use to stretch out in case—"

He didn't finish. He didn't need to. They understood. In case she fell.

Murmurs of agreement. He grasped the ladder that led up to the loft level. "I'm going up."

"No, I will."

He hadn't seen William come in, but he was often around the farm. His round, beardless face was pale, and his voice had shaken on the words.

Gideon didn't stop his scramble up the ladder, but he threw the words over his shoulder. "I'm more used to working at heights. Stay with Rachel."

Not waiting to see if the lad agreed, he scaled the ladder to the loft and then paused to assess the situation. A rough ladder nailed to the wall led upward into the angled timbers that braced the roof. Becky must have gone that way, but how she'd gotten that far out on the crossbeam, he couldn't imagine.

"Gid, here." Aaron, who'd been helping with the windmill, tossed a coil of rope up to him.

Gideon caught it and slipped it over his head, then thrust his arm through the middle so that it crossed his body.

"What else?" Aaron said the words softly, as if afraid of disturbing Becky on her precarious perch.

Gideon measured the angle at which he'd have to bring the child down if he reached her. *When* he reached her. "Stay here on the loft. I might need to lower her down to you."

He wouldn't consider any other conclusion to this. He couldn't.

Aaron nodded, seeming to understand all that he didn't say. "Da Herr sei mit du," he murmured.

The words seemed to follow Gideon as he started up the ladder. *The Lord be with you.*

Gideon's gaze was fixed on Becky. He could see her better now that he was higher. Her face was as white as her kapp, her arms stretched out in an effort to balance herself.

Below, he heard the rush of running feet. Rachel. It had to be. She'd look up; she'd see her child in danger. Pray God she didn't cry out. The slightest thing could disturb Becky's delicate balancing act.

Straining his ears, his body tense, he heard a faint gasp—that was all. Rachel would see, would understand. She'd be strong, no matter how afraid she was.

And he—he couldn't look down, couldn't let himself be

distracted by the pain he knew she was suffering. All his attention had to be on Becky.

He reached the top of the ladder. Not close enough to reach her yet, but at least he could probably talk to her without causing her to move.

"I'm coming to get you, Becky." He kept his tone low and easy. "Got yourself in a bit of a pickle, I'm afraid."

She didn't speak, but her head moved in the faintest of nods.

A diagonal beam crossed beneath her. That must be how she'd gotten up there, but he couldn't imagine it. Still, if she had done it, then he could.

He eyed the beam she stood on. If he could loop the rope over it, that would help to stabilize him as he worked his way up the diagonal toward her. But he'd never do it from here. He'd have to edge his way up closer first.

Meanwhile, Becky was visibly tiring, and that increased the danger. He risked a glance down. If she fell from where she was now, she'd miss the loft edge where Aaron stood. The other men were already positioned below with a canvas stretched between them, their eyes and their prayers fixed on the child.

"Becky, can you sit down on the beam instead of standing, do you think?"

Frowning, she bent her knees slightly. Her arms waved, and someone below them gasped.

Then she caught her balance again, shaking her head slightly.

"That's all right." He edged upward along the beam. "You're fine just where you are. That beam is nice and wide. I'd guess you could stand there all day if you had to."

She seemed to straighten a little, as if she were trying to prove him right.

He edged a foot closer and grasped the beam with one hand while he lifted the rope free with the other. He would not let himself imagine the day Ezra had been above him in another barn. He would not think about Rachel, far below, watching in terror. He would only concentrate on the child.

"Becky, I'm going to throw my rope up around your beam. I don't want you to move or reach for it, okay? I'm just going to use it to help me balance."

Seeing that she understood, he loosened the loop, measuring the distance to the beam with his gaze. He knotted the end of the rope to give it a little more weight, swinging it several times to get the feel of it. Then he swung it upward.

It missed, falling back toward him. The momentum of his swing threw his body off balance. He lurched, stumbling on the beam, clawing at thin air, nothing beneath him but the canvas, which wouldn't hold his weight. He was going to fall—

His left hand brushed the beam, caught, held, and his body slammed into it, his legs dangling.

Hug the beam, don't look down, don't think about the pain, he thought, as his bad leg took all the weight when he dragged himself back onto the beam . . .

Gripping it, he looked up, shaking off the red haze that clouded his vision. Bless the child, she still held her position, though every muscle must be trembling with the effort it took.

"Missed, but I'll get it this time." He forced his voice to be calm. "Hold on, Becky. Only a few more minutes now."

Slowly, painfully, he inched back up along the beam. It was harder this time, his strength waning. He readied the rope again. Breathed a prayer. Threw it. This time it swung around the beam, the knotted end dropping almost into his hands.

Gripping the ends, he wrapped them around his left arm, leaving his right free to grab Becky. With the stability the rope gave him, he moved up the beam.

Then he was as close as he could get, and he still wasn't quite close enough.

"Becky, I need you to help me, okay? I need you to bend just a little, so that you can reach for my hand."

"I can't." Her lips barely moved. "I'll fall."

Be honest with her. "Maybe," he conceded. "But if you do, I'll catch you." *Please, Lord. Please.* "It's the only way to get you back down to your mammi. All right?"

She pressed her lips together firmly. Then she gave a slight nod.

"Wait until I give you the word." He strained toward her, stretching until his muscles screamed. Sweat poured into his eyes, and he blinked it away. "Okay, Becky. Now."

She wavered. Her small body bent slightly—her hand neared his, still a painful few inches away, but he couldn't quite reach. *Please, God—*

Then, as her body tumbled from the beam, he got a glimpse of her white, terrified face, heard a cry from below, grabbed, held, and pulled her tight against him.

He couldn't move. He could only balance there, clinging to the rope, holding her close against him, feeling the frightened beating of her heart, so quick, so light, like a little bird in his arms.

*Thank you, Lord.*

He could breathe again, move again. He edged back down the beam, aware of the sounds below him, the others scrambling up the ladder to the loft.

Finally he reached the relative safety of the crossbeam.

Becky's arms were tight around his neck, her tears wet on his shirt.

"Almost there," he said. "You have to be brave a little longer, all right?"

She nodded, and he felt the movement against his shoulder.

He edged his way to the rough ladder nailed to the barn wall, his strength nearly gone. Would his leg hold them both to get down the rest of the way?

But he didn't have to find out. There was Aaron, already halfway up the ladder, reaching toward him.

"Becky, I'm going to hand you down to my brother Aaron. But you have to let go of my neck. Can you do that? Just hang on to my arm instead. We won't let you fall."

For an instant longer she clung to him, her cheek pressed against his. Then she let go. Grasping her firmly with his arm across her chest, he lowered her into Aaron's waiting arms.

Aaron carried her quickly down. He could hear the murmurs of those below, the muffled sobs that must come from Rachel.

He should climb down, but he couldn't seem to move. He could only lean against the rough, warm wood, his heart hurting as if the Lord had taken a chisel to it and wrenched it open.

*By* the time supper was over, it seemed to Rachel that everyone in the community had heard about Becky's mishap, and half of them had stopped by to marvel and praise God over her rescue. Much as she appreciated their prayers and concern, she'd begun to wish that they would leave the subject alone for a while, for Becky's sake if not for hers.

Her parents had come, too, and stayed to eat supper, with Mamm taking over the kitchen the moment she walked in the door. Although Daad had yet to say anything to her about it, Rachel suspected that his somber expression meant he found this incident just one more reason why she and the children should move home.

"Ach, Becky, you don't have to dry the dishes." Mamm patted Becky's cheek. "You deserve a reward for being such a brave girl."

"Don't say that." The words spurted out of Rachel's mouth before she could stop them. "Don't give Becky the idea that she's done something brave. She was naughty. She did something she knew was wrong, and she caused a lot of trouble."

Becky's eyes widened at her tone, and her lower lip trembled.

"Rachel, Rachel," her mother chided. "You should be praising God that she is safe."

Taking a deep breath helped, just a little. "I'm sorry, Mamm." She pulled her daughter close against her. "I am praising God you are safe, Rebecca. We owe our thanks to the quick work of Gideon and the others who helped." She tilted her daughter's face up gently. "But that doesn't change the fact that you did wrong, does it?"

"No, Mammi." Becky's lips quivered, and she pressed them together for a second. "I'm sorry."

"Ser gut. Now I think you will help finish up the dishes, won't you?"

Becky nodded and turned back to her work.

Rachel glanced at her mother. Mamm's lips were pressed together much as Becky's had been. Obviously Rachel hadn't heard the end of this, but at least maybe her mother would wait until the children were in bed to discuss it.

By then, she'd have to find some measure of calm to deal with her parents' concerns, and she wasn't sure where that was going to come from.

"I'm going out to check the animals before it gets any darker." She dried her hands quickly on a dish towel. "I'll be back in a few minutes."

She escaped out the back door before her father could offer to do it for her.

Dusk had drawn in while they were in the kitchen, and the lilac hedge cast a long shadow on the lawn. There was still enough light to see, though, once her vision adjusted, so she didn't go back inside for a flashlight.

She walked quickly past the greenhouse. Then, knowing she was out of sight if her mother watched from the kitchen window, she stopped, putting her hands over her face.

*I'm sorry, Father. I'm sorry. I was wrong to speak that way to my mother. But that is what it would be like if we moved in with them. With the best intentions in the world, my parents would begin to take over with the children. As dearly as I love Mamm and Daadi, these children were given by You for me to raise.*

She blotted the tears that spilled over onto her cheeks. Even here, she shouldn't let herself cry, because the signs would be there on her face when she went back inside.

She glanced at the darkening sky. The children were the most important thing in her life. Was she doing right by them? She'd tried to continue handling them as she had when Ezra was alive. Maybe that wasn't enough. What if Becky's foolish act today was a sign that her parents were right?

Shadows deepened by the moment. She'd best get this finished before she couldn't see at all. She started for the barn, and then stopped again.

A buggy stood next to the barn, and a horse was still in the paddock. Gideon's buggy. Gideon's horse. Had he ridden home with his brother, or was he still here?

Her steps quickened. She slid the barn door back and grasped the torch that always hung just inside, switching it on.

The barn's interior sprang to life in the flashlight's beam, and her stomach clenched with the memory of what had happened here earlier. But Becky was safe, thanks to Gideon. She couldn't let the memory control her actions.

She took a step. "Is someone here? Gideon?"

A rustle answered her, and she swung the beam in the direction of the sound. Gideon sat slumped on a bale of straw, his bad leg stretched out. He lifted a hand to shield his face from the light, but not before she saw that it was wracked with pain.

Lowering the light, she hurried to him. "Gideon, was ist letz? Are you hurt?"

He shook his head, but she knelt next to him anyway, touching his bad leg gently.

"Your leg is paining you, ain't so?"

"It will heal." His voice was choked, alarming her still more.

"Daad is in the house. I'll get him to come and help . . ."

"No." He grasped her hand to keep her from moving. "I'm all right. I'll go now."

Bracing his hand on the stall behind him, he attempted to lever himself to his feet. A spasm of pain crossed his face, and his leg seemed to buckle under his weight.

"No, no." Sliding her arm around him and dragging his arm across her shoulder, she helped him sit back down. "I'm so sorry. Becky's foolishness has ended up with your leg getting hurt."

He leaned back, seeming spent, but he shook his head. "The leg will be better in a few days." He closed his eyes. "My heart will take longer."

She saw, then, and wondered why she hadn't realized it sooner. "This is about Ezra. When you saw Becky—it was just like Ezra."

His hand clenched spasmodically on hers. "I can't talk about it. Not to you, of all people."

She took a breath, reaching inside for calm. *Please, Father. I didn't see that he was hurting so much. Please, give me the words to help him.*

"You're wrong." She saw it now, if only she could make him understand. "It is hard to talk about. Hard to hear about. But maybe we two are the only ones who can really understand. Really help each other. Because we both loved him."

He shook his head again, but she sensed the need inside him to get it out.

"I know," she said softly. "When I saw Becky on that beam, I saw Ezra, too."

"I should have stopped him." His voice was harsh with pain. "I should have kept him from going up. If I hadn't been so slow, if I'd moved more quickly, maybe I could have stopped him."

"Gideon—"

"I shut it away. Tried not to think about it. But it didn't work. And seeing Becky today just tore it open."

His head moved again, and he was like an animal in pain seeking relief. Her own heart seemed clutched in a vise that tightened with every word. Somehow she had to ignore that so that she could ease his grief.

"You're not thinking straight. How could you have stopped him? You know what Ezra was like."

Even as she said the words, she realized that she was seeing Ezra more clearly than she had since the day he died. For the first time, she thought of that day without seeing him falling. Instead she saw him laughing, climbing higher just as Becky had, probably chiding Gideon for taking his time.

"He was daring, too daring sometimes. You know that better than anyone else." The hand that clutched hers feverishly seemed to relax just a little. He was listening to her, and for his sake she had to get this all said, just this once. "I know he teased you about being slow, but that was just his way."

"If I had—"

"No." She snapped out the word. "Don't you think I've been down that road a thousand times myself? If I had done something differently, maybe he wouldn't have gone. If I hadn't told him to hurry home, maybe he'd have been more careful."

"It wasn't your fault." He leaned toward her, and she knew her words had jolted him out of his absorption with his own imagined guilt. "Nothing you did caused Ezra to fall."

"No. And nothing you did caused it either." She gripped his arm with both hands, wanting to force him to understand. "Gideon, think about it. Ezra asked you to go and check out that barn for soundness because he knew that you would do it thoroughly, the way you do everything. He knew you would be careful and methodical—that's why he valued your opinion, isn't it?"

He nodded slowly, almost reluctantly.

"Ezra was a gut man, and I loved him with all my heart. But he wasn't perfect." She saw him with such precision now, as if he stood in front of her, with no need for a photograph to prompt her memory. "He was always daring, and Becky is too much like him in that. He was quick and impatient, and that day—" Her throat tightened, but she had to say the rest of it. "That day he should have been more cautious. But he wasn't, because that was who he was."

Something that had been tied up in knots inside her seemed to ease, and she could think of him without pain. "It was an accident, that's all. We both know that, don't we?"

His gaze fixed on hers, and her heart seemed to lurch. Then he nodded. "Ja. I guess we do."

# Chapter Eleven

Rachel misted the snapdragon seedlings, pausing to touch the creamy edge of a blossom that had begun to show already. These plants would be a beautiful addition to someone's garden.

Maybe hers. If she was going to sell plants from her home eventually, she'd have to have an overflowing flower garden herself. That would be what buyers expected.

William had painted a neat sign for the end of the driveway last year, advertising the strawberries she'd had for sale. Maybe he'd do another one for her plants.

She turned, movement drawing her eye, and her breath seemed to catch in her throat. Gideon was back to work on the windmill. Even as she watched, he pulled his wagon up close to the site, which probably meant he had supplies in it.

Or maybe that his leg was still bothering him and he didn't want to walk. If so, he shouldn't be here at all, although he wouldn't welcome her saying so.

They hadn't talked in several days—not since Saturday evening, when she'd found him in the barn. She'd seen him at worship on Sunday, moving cautiously, his brother or one of his nephews always close to lend him an arm. He hadn't come near her after the service, and she'd tried to respect his obvious wish to avoid talking with her.

He was embarrassed, she supposed, over having revealed so much of his inner feelings to her. He wasn't a man who did that easily in any event, and especially not when it came to something bound to be so painful to both of them.

She put down the mister and tried to focus on thinning out a tray of marigolds. Without her willing it, her gaze kept straying back to Gideon. He was starting up the structure now, making her hold her breath until she saw that he was wearing a safety harness.

Mostly the Amish didn't do that, and she'd seen enough of Gideon at work to know that it was unusual for him. Was he doing it because his leg was still paining him?

What happened on Saturday had been painful both physically and emotionally. And yet, for her at least, that encounter had been healing, too. She could see Ezra more clearly now, as if the fog of grief and guilt was lifting. She could only hope that was true for Gideon as well.

She finished the tray of seedlings before she let herself look again. And jumped to find someone staring in through the glass at her. William.

Smiling, she went to the door. "William. I didn't see you. Will you come in and look at my greenhouse?"

He took a step forward and then paused. "I—I—maybe I shouldn't. I mean, b-b-bother you."

"It's not a bother. I want to show you what I've been doing with the flowers."

She held the door wide in invitation, but still William hesitated, standing a few steps away and surveying the building as if it were a skittish colt about to buck.

"William? Do you disapprove of the greenhouse so much that you won't even come in?"

"No, no. F-f-for sure it's not that." Clutching his straw hat in his hands, he stepped inside, ducking his head to avoid the hanging pots of plants.

She stepped back, giving him as much space as she could in the confines of the greenhouse that was really made for one. "I thought maybe you agreed with Isaac—that I should forget this foolishness and sell the farm to Caleb."

He didn't respond, and she immediately regretted putting him on the spot. Hadn't she just been telling herself that she couldn't contribute to a family quarrel?

"I'm sorry, William. I shouldn't have said that to you."

He shook his head. "N-n-no, it's okay. I'm g-glad for you, that you have the greenhouse Ezra w-wanted to give you." His big hands tightened on the hat's brim. "J-j-just sorry G-Gideon was the one to build it for you."

She paused, not sure what to say to that but knowing she had to say something. "William, you're not blaming Gideon for Ezra's death, are you?"

"You d-d-did."

Her throat tightened, making it difficult to speak. "I didn't blame him. Not that. I just couldn't seem to forgive him for living through the accident when Ezra didn't."

"Now you d-d-don't f-f-feel that way." He said it almost accusingly.

"I think I see things more clearly now." She tried to marshal her thoughts. If only she could help William take the step that she seemed to be taking, it would be a comfort to him, she was sure. "You remember how Ezra was—always a little more daring than everyone else, always needing to go first, even to take chances."

"You th-th-think it was his fault." He threw the words at her.

"No, not at all. I mean that we both know what he was like. It was part of what we both loved about him, wasn't it?"

William jerked a nod.

She was talking out of hard-won insight, and her assurance grew as she formed the words. "It was in Ezra's nature to go first, just as it was in Gideon's nature to move more slowly, to check things out methodically, just as Ezra wanted him to." She found herself smiling. "Maybe that was why they were such gut friends. They each had something the other one needed."

William was frowning, but he seemed to be listening, even understanding.

"For a long time, when I thought about that last day, I could only see Ezra falling." Her throat tightened, but she forced herself to go on. "Now I can see him the way I know he would have been—climbing higher, enjoying it, maybe laughing at Gideon for taking his time. I can see how his eyes would sparkle when he did something daring." She touched William's hand. "It's better to see him that way. It is. Don't blame anyone else. All right?"

He jerked a reluctant nod. "Ja." He hesitated. "But I still wish I—w-w-we were the ones helping you."

She patted his hand, relieved at his acceptance. "Isaac wouldn't want you to be helping me with something he doesn't approve of. He hasn't said anything to me yet about the windmill, but I can guess what his opinion is."

"He says you are w-w-willful. I don't think that."

"Gut. I'm glad you understand." She wouldn't let herself dwell on what Isaac thought. "I just have to take care of the children the best I can. I wish everyone could see that."

"I—I do." He gripped her hand suddenly, his fingers tight on hers. "I'm on your s-s-side. Always."

"Denke, William." But she didn't feel comfortable with the intense expression on his face. Better to change the subject, if she could. "In that case, come with me and see the new windmill. Once it's finished, this farm will have plenty of its own water. Bishop Mose says that will make the farm more valuable, so that's gut, isn't it?"

She moved around him as she spoke, gently loosening the grip of his hand. She stepped outside, feeling as if she were stepping out of a situation that was getting increasingly uncomfortable.

William followed, ducking his head to get through the door. Funny. She always saw him as Ezra's little brother, but he was growing into a man now, and no one in the family seemed to notice.

She led the way toward the windmill. "The children have been fascinated to see it go up so fast. Isn't it amazing?"

"I d-d-don't know m-much about those things." William sounded sulky, but he followed her.

Gideon spotted them coming and began to descend more quickly than he had gone up. In contrast, William's pace seemed to slow when he saw Gideon.

"What do you think?" She turned toward William, but he was already stepping back.

"Ser g-gut. I—I have to g-g-go." And he strode off before Gideon could reach them.

*Gideon* unbuckled his safety harness, watching as William Brand strode off toward the barn. What ailed the boy? He'd always been a bit shy because of his stammer, but he seemed more distant than ever since Ezra's death.

But Rachel was standing there, giving him a tentative smile, and he tried to return it, tried to think of something ordinary and commonplace to say that wouldn't remind either of them of what had happened Saturday night.

"Have I scared young William off?"

Rachel glanced after the boy, a wrinkle forming between her brows. "William's not so young."

"I suppose not." What was there about William to bring that worried look to her face? "I guess I always think of him as Ezra's baby brother."

"His family treats him like a child." She bit off the words. "They don't see him as he really is."

"How do you see him, Rachel?"

And what troubled her about him? He couldn't ask that, but he found that he was losing the constraint he'd expected to feel with her. After what happened Saturday, after showing her all his weaknesses, he'd thought he wouldn't be able to talk comfortably with her.

Now, he just wanted to wipe away that anxious expression on her face.

She met his gaze, concern still filling her blue eyes. "I'm not sure. I just know that he's turning into a man now, and no one seems to recognize that. They continue to treat him like a child, just because he doesn't speak normally."

Rachel's concern seemed to be catching. He looked in the direction William had gone, but he'd disappeared into the barn.

"That's not a gut thing, to be holding someone back from growing. Ezra cared a great deal for him." Even when they were boys, Ezra had been remarkably patient with his little brother, quick to protect him if anyone should think of teasing.

"He was a buffer between Isaac and William, I think," Rachel said. "I'm just beginning to see that. I'd like to help William, but I don't know what I can do."

She probably had enough to worry about with her own situation, but he figured Rachel could no more keep from being concerned about other people than the sun could keep from rising.

"Just listen to him." The words were out before he realized how close they came to the very subject he wanted most to avoid. But it was true. That was what Rachel did so well. "That will help him more than any advice, I'd guess."

She nodded, but now she switched the concerned look to him. "About Saturday—"

"You were kind to listen to me, especially when I—when it—"

He was beginning to sound like William, and he understood how frustrating that must be. He couldn't take back what he'd told her on Saturday, and maybe that was a gut thing. But he didn't want it to stand as a barrier between them, either.

"I'm glad you told me." Her voice went soft on the words, but there were no tears.

"It hurt you. I shouldn't—"

She grasped his hand, silencing him. "Maybe it did hurt to

talk about when Ezra died. It hurt you, too. But since we talked, it's been better."

She paused, shaking her head, as if frustrated in her turn at the inability of words to show what she was feeling.

"You don't need to say anything more—"

"I want to." She took a breath, seeming to calm herself. "Since we talked, I can see Ezra more clearly now. I'd been so busy blaming you and blaming myself for the fact that he was gone that I risked losing him twice over. I don't know why, but talking to you about it helped me to see him clearly again. That's what I was just saying to William. Ezra wasn't perfect." She stopped, as if surprised she'd said that.

"No, he wasn't perfect." Gideon actually managed to smile a little. "If he were here, he'd be the first one to laugh at that, for sure."

"He would, wouldn't he?" Her face lit with a smile in return, and she seemed to have forgotten that she was holding his hand.

"Ezra was always one for a joke, and he laughed at himself more easily than anyone." He seemed to hear Ezra's hearty laugh.

Rachel was right, he realized. Just saying the words gave him such a vivid picture of Ezra in his mind, and there was no sorrow with it. No sorrow—just joy in remembering Ezra as he had been.

"Ja, he did." The smile clung to Rachel's lips a moment longer.

Then she seemed to notice that she was still holding on to him. She let go of his hand.

"Are we friends?" There wasn't a hint of embarrassment in her words or her expression, and he was glad of it.

"Friends," he agreed.

"Ser gut." She gave a quick little nod.

He glanced over her shoulder. "It looks as if your little scholars are home from school already."

"Ach, where has the time gone? I forget it when I get working in the greenhouse, that's for sure." She turned away. "I'll send Becky out with a cold drink for you."

She walked briskly across the lawn toward the children, the light breeze tossing her kapp strings and apron, and held out her arms to them.

He turned back to his toolbox, his heart lightened. Rachel had made things all right between them, and he was glad.

He was still organizing the tools he needed when Becky came trotting across the yard toward him, a thermos swinging from her hand. She stopped a few feet from him and held it out.

"Mammi sent this for you."

"Denke, Becky." He took it, tilting it up for a long drink of lemonade. "That tastes gut."

She nodded. "I'll have some with the brownies my grossmutter made for my snack."

"That was nice of her." He put the thermos down and began buckling on the safety harness. "She must know you like them."

"Ja." Her gaze was fixed on the leather straps. "You didn't wear a harness before."

"No, I didn't." He paused, and the memory of Rachel's words made it easier to say what was in his mind. "I thought maybe you got the wrong idea about it when I didn't wear a harness."

Her blue eyes went round with surprise. "You're wearing the harness now because of me?" Her voice went up in a little squeak.

"Ja." He fastened the buckle and adjusted the straps. "Working up high can be dangerous, like climbing up high for no gut reason."

Her gaze slid away from his, and she kicked at a clod of mud. "Mammi says I should thank you for helping me on Saturday."

He studied what he could see of her averted face, but couldn't make out what she was thinking. "You don't have to thank me if you don't feel it. It's better to be honest with people, I think."

"Elizabeth told on me."

He hesitated, thinking this conversation should be between Becky and her mamm. But she had said it to him, and he owed her an honest answer or he'd be running counter to what he'd just said.

"Elizabeth is your friend, ja?"

She nodded, her lower lip coming out. It made her look like Ezra as a little boy. His bottom lip would come out like that when he was told he couldn't do something. His grossmutter had teased him, saying that a bird would come and perch on his lip if he weren't careful. Funny, how fresh that memory was after all this time.

"A friend has a duty to see that you're safe." His heart twisted. He hadn't kept Ezra safe, had he? "She thought you were going to fall, so I think she did the right thing in getting help. Wouldn't you have gone for help if it had been Elizabeth up on that beam?"

"Elizabeth wouldn't climb up high. She's scared of that."

The words shot back at him, almost defiantly.

"It's sensible to be scared of some things." *Father, give me the right words to say to this child.* "I was scared when I climbed up after you."

"You were?" Now her gaze met his. Now she was listening.

"Ja, sure. It's gut to be scared, so long as it makes you careful. If I hadn't been careful, I might not have made it all the way up to you. Then what would you have done?"

"I . . . Maybe I could have got down by myself."

He looked at her, not speaking. She needed to face the truth of this one herself.

"I guess I couldn't have." She pressed her lips together, as if she wanted to say more but wouldn't let herself.

"No. You couldn't." What would Ezra have said to her in this situation? Gideon didn't know. He could only offer what he felt in his heart was the right answer. "It can be gut to dare enough to try new things. But it's foolish to risk your life doing it."

She didn't look convinced. Probably Ezra wouldn't have been at her age, either.

"Your daadi was my friend from the time we were younger than you." He hadn't spoken of Ezra to her before, and maybe it was a mistake now, but he had to try. "I wonder what he would say if he'd been the one to climb up in the barn to get you."

Becky stared at him for a long moment. Tears sparkled, beginning to spill over onto her cheeks. Then, without speaking, she turned and ran back to the house.

He'd hurt her, maybe. But it was worthwhile, wasn't it, if it kept her from taking foolish chances? He wasn't sure, and not knowing made him feel like he'd failed.

*Rachel* glanced into the living room once the stew she'd decided on for supper was well under way. All three children were there, instead of outside as they usually were at this time of day. She'd called them in when she realized that dark clouds were massing over the hills to the west. Rain was coming, and they were better off inside.

Joseph and Mary stacked blocks into a tower, which Mary was certain sure to knock down sometime soon. Becky sat in the rocking chair with a book, her gaze pinned to the page.

Was she actually reading? Or was she thinking about whatever it was that had brought her into the house earlier, trying not to cry?

Becky had been talking to Gideon. She'd come into the house upset. And that was all Rachel knew. Becky had shaken her head to questions, saying nothing was wrong.

But something was. And it was something Becky didn't want to tell her. Rachel's heart clutched. Her daughter was keeping secrets from her already. What had happened to the little one who'd leaned on her so confidingly? She'd changed in so many ways in the past year.

Rachel walked back to the kitchen, pausing automatically to check the heat under the stew. Maybe she should have asked Gideon what was wrong, but that seemed like interfering. She pressed her hands on the edge of the stove, staring at the pot without really seeing it. If something had happened that she should know about, Gideon would tell her, wouldn't he?

A few fat raindrops patted against the windowpane, and she went to lean on the sink to peer out. Gideon, ignoring the rain, was stowing his tools with steady movements.

At least he was off the windmill tower. She was developing a dislike for seeing anyone working up high, no matter what the circumstances. She'd have to conquer that feeling before the next barn raising.

If she talked to Gideon—

"Mammi, Mammi." Joseph rushed into the kitchen. "I didn't feed Dolly yet. I have to go back outside."

He was headed for the door when she grabbed him by the suspenders that crossed his back.

"It's starting to rain outside. Dolly can wait until later."

"But she's hungry. And she's going to have her babies soon, so she needs to eat."

"It won't hurt her any to wait a bit."

"Daadi always said the animals have to come first, 'cause they depend on us. And I won't melt in the rain. Remember how he used to say that?"

She heard Ezra's voice for a brief second. "I remember." She managed to smile at him. "But you go back and watch Mary for me. I'll take care of Dolly."

"Dolly's my job, Mammi." He pressed his lips together, for a moment his expression very like his father's.

"Well, you're my job, ain't so?" She ruffled his hair. "And I don't want you getting wet. I'll do it. Now scoot." She turned him toward the living room and gave him a little shove.

Fortunately the rain wasn't heavy yet. She swung her shawl around her as she went out the back door and started toward the barn. Sure enough, Dolly was bawling in her pen, used to having Joseph show up promptly with her dinner.

"Hush, now, you spoiled creature. I'll get your feed for you." She picked up the grain bucket and headed for the shed where the chicken and goat feed was stored, hunching her shoulders as the rain began pelting down.

Lifting the latch, she stepped inside. Then stopped and stared, dismay building. The lid to the large metal can where she stored the goat's mixture lay on the floor, and even as she watched, a mouse scurried out of sight.

Worse, water dripped from the roof, directly into the barrel. She blinked back frustrated tears. If the grain spoiled—

A sudden gust of wind tore the door from her hand, slamming it back against the shed wall and driving cold rain into her face.

"R-Rachel! What are you d-d-doing?" William was behind her, reaching out to grasp the edge of the door and pull it so that it shielded her from the worst of the wind. "Go in. I'll t-t-take care of the g-g-goat."

"The feed." She grasped the edge of the barrel and tried to drag it out from under the drip, which was rapidly becoming a steady stream.

William, seeing what was wrong, ducked his head and stepped into the shed. In an instant, he had wrestled the container out from under the leak.

Rachel put her hand on the surface of the grain. It felt as if only a small amount of the top layer was wet, thank the gut Lord.

"H-h-here." William picked up the bucket and began scooping out the damp grain. "It's not t-t-too bad."

"Be sure to get it all." Seeing how quick he was, she stepped back out of his way. "I'd rather throw away some that might be all right rather than risk mold spoiling the whole barrel."

"Ja." He focused on the grain. "Gut thing you c-c-came when you did to find it."

"The lid was off." She stared at it, as if the circle of metal could answer the questions that buzzed in her mind. "I can't believe that Joseph would be so careless."

William didn't answer, but he shrugged, as if to say anything was possible.

The door swung wider, and Gideon peered in, water dripping from the brim of his hat. "Was ist letz? What's wrong?"

She gestured mutely toward the barrel. "When I came to feed the goat, I found the lid off. And it was right under that leak in the roof." She frowned up at it. "I don't understand. How could it get so bad so fast? It was fine and dry in here during that heavy rain we had last week."

Gideon reached up, exploring the roof with his fingers. "I'll have a look and . . ."

"I—I—I'll fix it." William slammed the lid back on the can. His voice was determined, almost angry.

For a moment the two men stared at each other, and animosity seemed to sizzle in the close confines of the shed. Finally Gideon shrugged.

"Gut. I'll help you do a quick patch so Rachel doesn't get any more water in here today."

"Denke," she said quickly, before William could reply. "You're both very kind."

"Why don't you go inside? The children will be worried when you don't come back."

Gideon's tone was persuasive. It was clear he and William wouldn't be content until she'd gotten out of their way. And he was right, as well. She didn't want Becky or Joseph to come looking for her.

"I'll feed the goat on my way in." She grabbed a dry pail and scooped up the grain mixture, putting the lid back firmly.

As she edged past Gideon on her way out the door, she sent a worried glance toward the shed roof. Surely that was odd for such a bad leak to develop so quickly. She glanced at Gideon, to find that he was staring at the roof, too, a frown deepening on his face.

Drawing her shawl tightly around her, she hurried to Dolly's pen and dumped the feed in. The goat's complaints ceased abruptly, and Rachel ran for the house, wishing she could outrun her worries as easily.

"Mammi?" Joseph was waiting on the porch. "Was ist letz?"

She shepherded him inside the kitchen and shook out her wet shawl, draping it over the drying rack beside the stove. Then she turned to look at him.

"Joseph, are you sure you put the lid on the grain barrel the last time you fed Dolly?"

His mouth formed an O. "I did. Really. I wouldn't forget that. Honest."

She didn't think he would, either, but the fact was that the lid had been off. "The lid was lying on the floor beside the barrel. Are you sure you didn't do it in a hurry and forget?"

"No, Mammi. Anyway, I don't ever put the lid on the floor. I put it on top of the chicken feed when I get Dolly's meal out."

True enough. She'd seen him do that numerous times. "Maybe a raccoon got in and took it off. They can get into all kinds of things. I'll have Onkel William check for any hole where they might get in." She patted his cheek, wanting to chase the worry from his small face. "We won't worry about it. All right?"

He nodded.

"You go and watch Mary for me while I finish supper."

"Ja, Mammi." He ran toward the living room, his worry disappearing.

Getting out a bowl, she began mixing up dumplings for the stew. She did it at the counter where she could look out the window, staring through the rain at the men moving around the shed.

By the time the dumplings were ready, Gideon was approaching the back door. Setting the bowl aside, she went to meet him.

"Come in." She gestured. "You must be drenched. Do you want some coffee?"

He shook his head. "I'm too wet to come into your clean kitchen, and I'd best get along home anyway. I just thought I should tell you what we found."

She stared at him, dread pooling in her stomach. "What is it?"

"That hole in the roof." His voice went hard. "It didn't get there naturally. Someone took a pry bar and pulled the boards loose. It was done deliberately."

# Chapter Twelve

The sky was clear and cloudless. The only sign Gideon could spot of yesterday's rainstorm was the refreshed green of the pasture grass and the plants in Rachel's garden. The storm had been swept away, but the worry it left behind lingered like a stain on the crystal-clear sunshine of the day.

He studied the shed from his perch on the windmill. Seen from above, the shed roof was plainly visible. If he'd been up here when someone had taken a pry bar to the tar paper, he'd know who'd done it.

There was no doubt in his mind that the action had been deliberate. Someone, or more than one person, had set out to cause harm to Rachel's property.

Teenagers, intent on vandalism? That sort of thing was known to happen. English kids, even Amish ones sometimes, didn't always use common sense when they were out for mischief.

Still, he couldn't imagine any Amish teenager, knowing Rachel, who would pick a struggling widow to play a trick on. As for the Englischers—well, he didn't understand them well enough to say, maybe, but it seemed to him they'd do something more obvious than this. Splashing paint around, knocking over an outhouse—those were more the kinds of tricks you heard of from them.

One thing kept pushing its way back into his thoughts, as annoying as a protruding nail. That story Joseph had told him about the draft horse getting out of his stall one night—did that connect with the damage to the shed roof? Or was he imagining a pattern where none existed?

The screen door slammed, and Rachel came out of the house carrying a load of laundry she must intend to hang on the clothesline. She reached the line, paused for a moment, and then seemed to make up her mind about something. She dropped the basket in the grass and started toward the windmill.

He came down from the tower nearly as fast as she crossed the yard, reaching the ground seconds behind her.

She hesitated again, looking at him, the breeze blowing strands of fine blond hair across her face. He could read the doubt in her eyes. Whatever brought her here, she hadn't made up her mind to it.

"I shouldn't have brought you down from your work."

He shrugged, loosening the harness. "It makes no matter. I wanted to talk to you anyway. I see William got the shed roof finished, ain't so?"

"Ja. He worked on it this morning, soon as he finished with the herd. He made a gut job of it."

She said that as if she were trying to convince herself.

"I'm sure he would." He waited, knowing that something more had set that wrinkle between her eyebrows.

"I told William what you said." Her hands gripped each other so tightly that the knuckles were white. "That you believe it was done deliberately."

He wanted to hold those straining hands in his, but he couldn't. Instead he leaned against the windmill upright, taking the pressure off his leg.

"What did he have to say about that?"

"At first he said it must be just an accident. But finally he agreed that you were right. That someone had damaged the roof on purpose."

"Anyone who saw it would say the same."

Odd, that William would even try to deny it. Wouldn't he want Rachel to know the truth?

"He struggled with admitting it so much." Her hands pulled against each other, as if she fought to say the words. "It made me think . . . made me wonder, anyway . . ." Her lips pressed together, trying to keep the words in. Then she shook her head. "Maybe William suspects Isaac of doing it."

"Isaac." He said the name slowly, turning the thought over in his mind.

"I shouldn't think that!" The words burst out of her. "It's wicked, even to think that about Ezra's brother."

"Not wicked, no." Finally Gideon couldn't resist the impulse to touch those anguished hands, stilling them as he'd gentle a frightened animal. "Of course you don't want to think that of Isaac. Or of anyone you know."

"Am I imagining things?" She threw the words at him, demanding an answer.

He had to be honest with her. But . . .

"Tell me something first. Joseph told me about the night the draft horse got out. Did you ever figure out how that happened?"

Three vertical lines formed between her brows as she considered the meaning behind the question. "No. No, I didn't see how it could happen. Any more than I can see how the shed roof got damaged with the grain barrel left open right under it. You think the same person did both things?"

"I wouldn't go that far." His native caution asserted itself. "But it's two odd things happening without any reason we can see. They didn't happen by themselves. Somebody had to do them."

She nodded slowly. "Isaac—would he do something like that to show me that I can't manage the farm on my own? I don't want to believe that of him. I don't."

"You asked what I think." He gazed down at her hands, still held loosely in his. "I'd say that Isaac always wants things to go his way. If he sets his mind on something, he figures other people will fall in line."

"Ja. That is Isaac."

"It's hard to picture him doing something like this. But if he convinced himself it was for your own gut, he might be able to justify it in his mind."

She let out a long breath. "That's what I fear, too. I don't want to, but I do."

"There's someone else you haven't considered, though." He hated to add to her worries, but it needed to be said. "What about Caleb?"

"Caleb." She repeated the name, and he could almost hear her mind working. "I can't believe Caleb would want the farm badly enough to do something like that."

He shrugged. "I'd say that about both of them. Still, neither incident was really costly or dangerous."

"Not dangerous!" Sudden fury blazed in her eyes. "If someone let the horse out, they risked Joseph's life. How can you say that's not dangerous?"

He didn't want her anger turned on him. "Maybe whoever it was didn't think about Joseph being the one to open the door."

"Maybe so, but it was. If something happened to one of the children—" Her voice choked.

His fingers tightened on hers, and the need to take care of her was so strong that it nearly overwhelmed him. "Rachel, I don't want you to have to carry this burden by yourself. I wish—"

Now he had to stop. What did he wish? Where exactly were these feelings leading him?

"I know." Her chin firmed, as if she were determined not to show weakness. "You're a gut friend, Gideon."

A gut friend. Ezra's friend. That was how she saw him. That was who he was.

"Ja. Well, if there is anything I can do—anything—you must ask me, all right?"

She nodded. Seeming to become aware that he still held her hands, she drew them free.

She would be embarrassed, would walk away from him. He cast around for anything to regain a safe footing between them. "I've been thinking about Becky. How is she doing after her mishap?"

"I wish I knew." Rachel pressed her lips together, her worry seeming to deepen. "I'm afraid—" She pleated her apron between her fingers, then smoothed it down again. "Do you think she might have done that because she was trying to be like Ezra?"

The question hit him like a blow to the stomach, taking his breath away for an instant. "I . . . I don't know. She is like him in temperament, I'd say. Did you ask her?"

"No. But I wondered—William was talking to the children one day about how daring Ezra was as a boy. He didn't mean anything by it—just remembering. He always looked up to Ezra so much, you know."

"Ja. And the children did, too. But would Becky go that far?"

Rachel chewed on her lower lip. "She won't talk about it. And she won't tell me why she came in the house almost crying after talking to you, either."

That took him by surprise. After everything else that had happened yesterday he'd almost forgotten that troubling exchange with Rachel's daughter.

"I'm sorry. I didn't realize she was that upset."

That wasn't true, and he knew it as soon as he said the words. He'd known that the child was close to tears over his words. He'd just hoped that what he'd said was sufficient to keep her from trying something so dangerous again.

Rachel was waiting, and he knew he had to tell her.

"Becky said you had told her she had to thank me for coming to her rescue. It was pretty clear that she didn't want to. She claimed she could have gotten down by herself."

Rachel made a small sound of distress.

"I couldn't let it go at that." He could only hope she'd understand. "I had to help her realize how dangerous it had been. So I asked her what her father would have thought if he'd been the one to climb up after her."

Rachel sucked in a sharp breath. "You—that was hurtful. You shouldn't have taken it upon yourself."

"Maybe not." He had to be fair. "But she came to me, Rachel. I had to answer her, and I said the one thing I thought might keep her from doing something so dangerous again."

Rachel's lips pressed firmly together, but tears sparkled on her lashes, as Becky's had. Then, like her daughter, she turned and hurried away.

Rachel strode across the lawn, not sure where she was going, only that it had to be away from Gideon, at least for a while. How could he have said that to Becky? He didn't have the right. No wonder the poor child had been on the verge of tears.

Dolly bawled plaintively at the sight of her, so she changed course and walked toward the pen, glad of the distraction. Joseph had been as nervous as a first-time expectant father as the time neared for Dolly's twins to arrive, insisting that his mother had to check on the goat often while he was at school.

Rachel knelt in the grass beside the pen, reaching through the wire to scratch Dolly's muzzle. "Was ist letz? You just want some company, don't you?"

That reminded her of Leah, who no doubt wanted some company even more than the little goat did. It seemed Rachel was failing there, too.

"I wish I knew what to do," she murmured as the goat nuzzled her hand.

She wanted to hang on to her anger against Gideon, but she couldn't, not after he'd risked his life to save Becky. And if what he'd said kept Becky off any more high beams, maybe it was worth it.

She leaned her forehead against the pen's upright. Daadi had used Becky's misdeed as an argument to again urge her to sell the farm and move home. It had been hard to maintain her position that she could handle the farm and the children by herself when Becky had just risked her life that way.

"You're lucky, Dolly." She patted the little Nubian's side,

feeling the life that moved within. "Your babies will be content with milk and loving. They won't worry you and make you doubt yourself."

Dolly just gazed at her, seeming happy to hear her voice no matter what she said.

Once, her babies had been like that. No longer. Now every day they seemed to give her fresh reason to wonder if she knew what she was doing.

She stood slowly, her hand resting on the pen. She should get the clothes hung. She turned, but a sound from the barn brought her up short. A sound—like a footstep—in the barn she knew to be empty at this time of day.

She paused for a moment, staring at the barn door. She could go and call Gideon. She glanced his way. He was up on the windmill again, hard at work.

Calling him down was foolish. She was just scaring herself with this talk of someone causing accidents.

Besides, hadn't she been trying to reassure herself that she could manage things herself? Well, here was a chance to prove it.

The barn door stood slightly ajar. She went to it quickly, before she could change her mind, grasped the handle and shoved it open, letting sunlight pour inside. Not a creature moved. Dust motes swam in the shaft of light.

But she'd heard something. Or someone. She took a step forward. "Who's here?"

For a moment her voice echoed in the stillness. Then someone moved, coming from the shadows into the light. She blinked in surprise. Thomas Carver. The dairy owner. What was he doing here?

"Mr. Carver." She found her voice. "I'm surprised to see you. Were you looking for me?"

"Yes, well, not exactly." He gave an unconvincing smile. "Truth is, Mrs. Brand, I wanted to have a look around before I talked to you about my offer again. Sorry. I guess I should have asked permission before coming into your barn."

There was nothing she could say to that but yes, and he knew it, so she said nothing.

He came toward her, still smiling. "Well, anyway, I hope you've had a chance to think about my offer. Seemed to me that maybe you'd have come up with some questions about it."

If he'd come for that reason, he should have come to the house. "I really don't have any questions."

"You sure? Anything at all, I'd be happy to explain it to you. That's only fair. You can ask anyone you like to go over the paperwork for the lease."

"I'm not ready to go into it just now, Mr. Carver. I thank you for your interest, but I haven't decided yet what I'm going to do."

"You shouldn't wait too long, you know." He moved closer, almost uncomfortably so. "The offer won't stay on the table indefinitely. I'm ready to invest now, but if your place isn't available, there are some others in the valley I could make an offer on. I just thought of you first, because I knew how hard it must be for you, trying to stay on here with your husband gone and all."

She took a step back. "I will just have to risk your finding another property that suits you, I'm afraid."

"Now, you ought to think this through." Again he moved closer to her. "I know how you Amish like to deal with each other, but you won't get a better offer than mine."

He was so near that the scent of him filled her nostrils. She stepped back again, tension like ants crawling on her skin.

"Rachel?" A tall shadow bisected the shaft of sunlight. Gideon stood in the barn doorway. "Is there a problem?"

"Everything is all right." Now. She hoped her relief didn't show in her voice. "Gideon, you remember Mr. Carver."

"It is gut to see you," Gideon said politely, although he didn't sound happy.

"Zook." Mr. Carver gave a short nod. "I have some business with Mrs. Brand, so if you'll excuse us—"

"We are finished, I think." She moved quickly to the doorway, and Gideon stood aside while she passed through and out into the sunshine. "I appreciate your coming, Mr. Carver."

The man had no choice but to follow her out of the barn. He stood for a moment in the doorway, hands on his hips, and then stepped outside.

Gideon moved out behind him and stood quietly, his gaze not leaving the other man.

"I can bring those papers over sometime this week, Mrs. Brand. Just give them a look-see."

"I will let you know if I want to talk about it any further." She turned to Gideon. "Mr. Carver is interested in buying or leasing some of the land and the dairy herd."

The Englischer nodded. "Just stopped by to have a look around today. See if Mrs. Brand had any questions."

"I did not see your car, Mr. Carver."

Gideon made the observation quietly, but as he said it, Rachel realized how odd it was. Carver didn't seem the type of man to go anywhere on foot.

"Yeah, well, I wanted to have a walk along some of the boundary lines. Just checking things out. I left my car down the road." He gave Gideon a speculative look. "I see you're here to build a windmill for Mrs. Brand."

"He is also here as a friend." Rachel said the words firmly. Perhaps it was best that the man see that she was not without people to advise her.

"Well, you consider my offer, now. Remember, it won't stay on the table forever. You'd better decide pretty soon if you don't want to be left stranded."

"Thank you, Mr. Carver." She kept her tone polite. She didn't want to encourage the man to haunt the farm pestering her for an answer, but she didn't want to discourage him entirely, either. "I will think about what you have said."

"Good." He nodded to her, ignoring Gideon. "I'll hope to hear from you soon, then."

He walked off down the lane. Gideon made no effort to go back to his work, but stood watching until Carver disappeared around the bend in the lane. They heard the sound of an engine, and a moment later a pickup truck pulled out onto the road and sped away.

Rachel turned to Gideon. "Why did you come to the barn? Didn't you think I could handle Mr. Carver on my own?"

That came out more sharply than it should have. She had a feeling she was snapping at him just because she'd been so relieved to see him there.

Gideon leaned against the barn door, probably to ease his leg after climbing and standing so much. Because of her. "I did not know that Mr. Carver was here, Rachel."

"Of course not." She took a breath, consciously trying to relax her tense shoulders, unclench her hands. "I'm sorry. That wasn't kind of me."

"No need to be sorry. I wasn't trying to pry into your business." He gestured toward the windmill tower. "From up there, I couldn't help but see you staring at the barn. You stiffened as if—well, as if something wasn't right. When you went in and didn't come back out right away, I thought I should check."

That was natural. She should be grateful, instead of feeling that Gideon, like everyone else in her life, was trying too hard to manage things for her.

"Denke. I appreciate your kindness." She frowned. "It was odd, I think. Carver not letting me know he was here."

"He's made you an offer, you said?"

She nodded. She'd avoided telling Gideon about it once before, and the same reason held now. Gideon was so intent on doing what Ezra would want. She already knew what he'd say about the possibility of her making such a drastic change.

Still, their relationship had changed since that day. Gideon was already too involved in what went on here to keep him in the dark about this.

"This offer he talked about—he wants to buy the dairy herd outright, and then rent the barn and the pastures from me. That way, I could keep the house and as much land as I need for my own use, and the rest would be bringing in money for me and the children without the worry of the animals."

"And you are thinking about doing this?"

Something about his even tone raised her hackles. "I know what you will say, Gideon. You want everything to stay just as it was when Ezra was here, but—"

"No, Rachel, that is not what I would say."

"It's not?" Her voice lifted with surprise. "But I thought—"

"Maybe once I would have said that." He seemed to be looking inward. "All I could think was that I had to make amends to Ezra. I couldn't seem to see any further than that. Now—well, now maybe I am seeing him a little more clearly."

He was quoting her own words back to her, she realized.

Maybe that meant he was moving out from under the suffocating cloud of guilt that had burdened him. If so, she was glad.

"Ezra would never have imagined a situation in which you'd be going on without him." His voice was flat. "We both know that."

He was right. She did know that. "Ezra never let himself worry over what might happen. That's not a bad thing."

"I didn't mean that it was. I'm just saying that trying to think that he would want this or that is fruitless. All we can really be sure of is that he would want what is best for you and the children."

"Ja." She felt lighter, as if something had lifted from her, too. "You think that I should take Carver up on his offer?"

"I would not go that far." Gideon was cautious, as always. "Maybe just that you might consider it. If you're going to go ahead with the nursery business, you need to keep enough land for that. This might be better than taking Isaac's offer and selling out entirely."

"The People would not look on it favorably, if I did business with an Englischer instead of one of us." Carver had been right about that, if nothing else.

"Then one of our people should make you the same offer, before they judge your actions."

"Isaac would never understand. Or forgive."

The word dropped between them. *Forgive*. They both struggled with that, didn't they? Forgiving each other, forgiving themselves.

Forgiveness was never easy. Maybe that was why it was so important.

"I don't know the answer to that, Rachel. It may be that Isaac will not forgive any choice but the one he wants."

"Ja." That was certain sure, but wasn't doing what was right for her family more important?

"One thing that I think about Carver's offer— " Gideon paused, his gaze focused on the lane where the man had disappeared. "He is yet another person who might want you to decide that the farm is too much for you. And who might do something to force you to that decision."

# Chapter Thirteen

Mary put one block too many on top of the huge tower William had been constructing with the children, and it collapsed with a satisfying clatter. Mary giggled, not a bit sorry, while William groaned nearly as loudly as Joseph did.

William grabbed Mary, tickling her. "Schnickelfritz," he exclaimed. "You did that on purpose, ain't so?"

She just giggled all the more, clutching him around the neck.

Joseph's lower lip came out. "Mammi, Mary did that on purpose. Onkel William said so."

William exchanged glances with Rachel as he set Mary back on her feet, and he seemed to sober with an effort.

"I was teasing, that's all. Komm, let's pick up the blocks."

Rachel suppressed a smile. William went from playing as if he were one of the young ones to being the serious adult, but she suspected he didn't do it easily. Playing with them was more to his taste than enforcing any rules, much as he might try.

"It is time to clear up anyway," she said. "Becky and I will finish up the supper dishes while you do that."

"Not so soon, please, Mammi," Joseph protested. "I want to play with Onkel William some more."

"Not now," William said. "Now you must do as your mamm says. And I must get home to bed myself, so I can be back here early to tend the cows."

Amazing, that William could talk to the children without stammering at all, but could barely get out a sentence among adults. When he finally fell in love, would he find that with his special girl there would be no stammering either?

Rachel paused in the doorway long enough to be sure there'd be no more grumbling from Joseph. Then she and Becky headed back to the kitchen sink.

"Onkel William likes to play games," Becky observed as she picked up the dish towel.

"I was just thinking that myself." Rachel plunged her hands into the warm, soapy water. "Ach, he is not so very older than you, ain't so?"

Becky nodded, wiping a plate with careful circles of the towel. "He is not very much like Onkel Isaac."

"No, I guess not." Was there disapproval of either of her uncles in that? Rachel hoped not. "Brothers and sisters are sometimes alike and sometimes very different from each other."

"Onkel William is more like Daadi, I think." Becky set the plate on the counter and took a cup from the rack. "Daadi liked to play with us, too."

The towel might as well be tightening around her throat. "Ja, he did."

William came in from the living room, silencing whatever else Becky might have said about her father. Would she ever know? Did she want to?

She wiped her hands on a dish towel as she turned to William.

"Denke, William, for playing with the little ones. You are a gut onkel."

He colored, ducking his head. "S-s-supper was a fine meal. You were kind to invite me."

She'd probably said too often how much they owed him, so she just patted his sleeve. "We'll see you tomorrow."

"Ja." For a moment he hesitated, as if he'd say more. Then, perhaps thinking better of it, he went out, the door banging behind him.

The house was quiet when he'd gone, with only the soft voices of Joseph and Mary from the other room to make a sound. Rachel turned back to the dishes.

Or maybe it just seemed quiet because she was the only adult in the house now. Once, she'd have been looking forward to Ezra coming back in from the evening round he'd always made to check on the animals. She'd have been thinking of the things she wanted to tell him after the little ones were in bed—the small details of her life that interested no one but him.

And now interested no one at all.

She washed a plate with conscious care. The gloomy thoughts could gather too quickly in the evening if she weren't careful. She would not let them take control.

"My mamm and I used to do the dishes together always. Course, I was the only girl. Soon we'll have Mary to help, too."

Becky's nose crinkled. "She'd break things, Mammi."

"Well, and you did when you started, too. Breaking things is part of learning to do them right."

Becky made a small sound that indicated doubt. "Did you know that English people have a machine that washes and dries the dishes? That would save a lot of time."

"I guess so. But if we'd had a machine to wash the dishes, my mamm and I would have missed out on a lot of talking with each other. And I'd surely miss talking to you. So I'd rather do things our way."

Becky considered that for a moment. "I guess maybe I do, too."

"Gut," she said softly.

"I brought a new book home from school," Becky said, with the air of one veering away from an emotional moment. "Teacher Mary said that since I liked the Little House books so much, I might like this one."

"Maybe we can read together for a bit after the younger ones are in bed. Would you like that?"

Becky nodded.

It was tempting, so tempting, to be content with the fact that things seemed easy between them again. To believe that everything was all right.

But it wasn't. Becky had done a dangerous thing in climbing up in the barn, and Rachel still didn't really know why she'd done it. She'd hoped Becky would bring it up herself, given a little time, but she hadn't.

As Becky's mother, she must push it, no matter how easy it would be to let it slide. That had been Ezra's way with the children, not hers.

Her hand stilled on the casserole dish she was washing. That thought had been almost critical of him. She hadn't meant it that way, had she?

She set the casserole dish in the drainer and took Becky's hand when she would have reached for it.

"Just let that drain. I'll put it away later. Now I want to talk to you."

Becky's small face tightened. Natural enough, wasn't it?

Every child knew that the talk probably wasn't going to be a happy one.

"I have to understand, Becky. Why did you climb up in the barn?"

Becky shrugged, turning her face away. "I just did."

"That's not an answer." She took Becky's chin in her hand, turning her face gently. "Tell me."

Something that might have been rebellion flared in Becky's eyes. She shook her head, pressing her lips together in denial.

Rachel would not show the pain that squeezed her heart. "Komm." She drew Becky to the rocker. Sitting down, she pulled her daughter onto her lap.

Becky came, limp as a faceless doll and betraying just about as much emotion.

*Please, Father. Show me. Give me the words.* There was more than a little desperation in the prayer. How had she and her daughter gotten so far apart?

She set the rocking chair moving almost automatically, closing her arms around the unresisting, unresponsive child.

"I am your mamm, and you are my dear daughter." Through a shimmer of tears, she stared at the part in Becky's hair. It was almost, but not quite, straight—a sign that she had done it herself.

Pain tightened its grip on Rachel's heart. How had they slipped away, those days when her child depended upon her for everything? Not that she wanted to keep Becky a boppli forever—no, not that. But somehow, in the past year, preoccupied with grief and the struggle just to keep going, she hadn't even noticed the steps of her daughter's growth.

She pressed a kiss to the crooked part. "It has been too long since I've rocked you like this."

"I'm too big for rocking." But she didn't pull away.

"I hope you will never be too big for Mammi to love you." She smoothed her hand down Becky's back, feeling the sharp little angles of her shoulder blades. "Or to worry about you. Did you climb up because you remember Daadi doing that?"

Becky made a convulsive movement, and Rachel hugged her close.

"Daadi was a gut climber," Rachel suggested. "Were you trying to do what he would have done?"

For a moment Becky was still in her arms. Then her small face turned into the curve between Rachel's shoulder and neck, snuggling into place, gentle as an infant at the end of a feeding.

"I don't know," she whispered. "Maybe. We were playing in the barn, and Elizabeth said how high it was, and the next thing I knew, I was saying I could climb up."

Rachel's breath seemed stuck. Whatever she said now could mean the difference between learning and rebellion.

"I expect you had a picture in your mind of Daadi climbing up in the barn." She fought to keep her voice calm. "I do, too. Daadi liked to do things that were a little daring. But—"

"He wouldn't want me to do it." Becky muttered the words against her collarbone, so that she seemed to feel them as well as hear them. "If he'd had to climb up and get me, would he have been angry with me?"

Becky was echoing the question Gideon had asked her. So he had made her think. That was more than Rachel had been able to do, it seemed.

"Not angry, no. He'd have been afraid for you, first of all. And then—well, I think he might have been a little bit disappointed that you'd do something—"

"Foolish," Becky finished for her.

"Yes." She wouldn't gloss it over by calling it anything else. "But he would hug you very tight and love you just the same. You know that, don't you?"

Becky nodded, her face rubbing against Rachel's dress. "I guess so." Her voice was very soft. "Mammi—do you ever think you're forgetting Daadi?"

The question pierced her heart. Forget? Did her children think she was forgetting him when she talked so much, thought so much, about the things she did now that she'd never done with him?

Was she? How often in the past few days had she thought about him, not wondering what he'd think of her struggles with Isaac or her worries about the children, but just thought of him, pictured his dear face, imagined the feel of his arms around her?

". . . talking to Gideon."

Preoccupied with her own self-doubt, she'd missed the beginning of what Becky said, and the words were like a blow to her heart. Was Becky thinking that her mother was turning to Gideon in the way she'd once turned to her daadi?

"He remembers when Daadi was a little boy," Becky added. "I like to hear about that."

Rachel could breathe again. Becky was talking about herself, not her mamm.

"It's nice to hear other people's stories about Daadi," Rachel said. "We can see him through their eyes then, can't we?"

Becky nodded. She leaned against Rachel's shoulder, as relaxed as the babe Rachel had imagined moments ago. She snuggled her face closer to Rachel's.

"I'm glad we talked, Mammi," she murmured.

"I'm glad, too." A barrier that had been separating her from

Becky dissolved as simply as a patch of snow in the spring sunshine.

*Thank You, Father.*

But another worry had sprung up in its place. Would she have jumped to that conclusion about Gideon if the thought hadn't been in her mind to begin with? Was she talking to him too much? Confiding in him too much?

If she was, what did that say about her feelings for him?

"I said, are you going to hold this board straight or not?" Aaron's exasperated tone penetrated Gideon's thoughts.

"I am." He leveled the top stall board by a fraction of an inch. "It's fine. There's nothing wrong with my eye."

"Not when you're paying attention, there's not." Aaron's tone was that of every older brother who'd ever lived, Gideon suspected. And the truth was that he had been wool-gathering.

"Mahlon and Esther Beiler will be back from their wedding trip tomorrow, I hear. We didn't get this work frolic scheduled any too soon."

Aaron drove a nail home with a single swift stroke. "I hear tell they were going to stay out in Illinois a bit longer, but decided to come back early. The Beilers will have been missing Mahlon, him being the youngest boy."

"Ja." Not that any son wouldn't be missed, having been away for months on an extended visit to kinfolk out in the Midwest.

But Leah's parents had lost her little sister, Anna, their youngest, to the English world a year ago. No doubt they were still grieving that. They'd be glad to have the newlywed couple to fuss over.

And the community was made stronger when they gathered for a work frolic, getting the couple's new home ready for them.

Rachel was here somewhere, he had no doubt—maybe working with some of the other women in the house.

"Rachel Brand will be here today, ain't so?" Aaron's words, echoing his thoughts, made Gideon blink.

"Guess so." Gideon turned the question over in his mind. Aaron wasn't one to say something for the sake of hearing his own voice. If he asked about Rachel, there was a reason.

Aaron was frowning down at his toolbox, face turned away.

Gideon planted his hands on the stall bar, giving it a shake to be sure it was secure. "Why the interest in Rachel?"

Aaron shrugged. "No reason. I was just thinking—well, you're spending a lot of time over there. Lovina will have it that you're courting her. Are you?"

"No." He bit off the word. "I'm being a friend. If a man can't help out a neighbor without folks thinking he's courting—"

Aaron raised his hand to stop him. He clamped his mouth shut. Not because of Aaron, but because of what he might give away if he responded too strongly.

"I wouldn't think anything about it. But the thing is—well, Isaac Brand's been to see me about Rachel. And you."

Gideon wouldn't have been more surprised if Aaron had swung a two-by-four at him. "Isaac?" He forced back the angry words that sprang to his lips. "What has Isaac to say about my doings? Or Rachel's, for that matter?"

Aaron shrugged heavy shoulders. "Nothing to yours, I'd say. As for Rachel—well, as her brother-in-law, I guess he feels he has a duty to be concerned about what she's doing."

There were a lot of things Gideon would like to say to that, but only one that really made a difference. "Why did he come to you?"

"I had a little trouble figuring that out myself." His eyes crinkled. "Talked around and around about how worried he was about Rachel and those children and how he wanted what was best for everyone. But when he finally got to the point, it seemed he doesn't like our taking Rachel to market. 'Encouraging her to be willful' was what he said."

Gideon could only stare at him. "What is willful about earning money to support her children?"

The twinkle in Aaron's eyes brightened. "I expect Isaac thinks anyone's being willful who doesn't do exactly what he says."

Gideon found the twinkle reassuring. "And what did you tell him?"

"That I appreciated his concern, but that decision was up to Rachel."

Gideon blew out a breath. "That's what I'd expect from you. So why did you look so worried when you asked about me and Rachel? Just because Lovina's not happy unless she's matching folks up in pairs—"

"It's not that." Aaron leaned his elbow on the railing, turning toward him. The pose was casual, but his expression wasn't. "Rachel Brand is a fine woman, and nothing would make me happier than to see you settled with a wife and children."

Gideon started to speak, but Aaron was clearly not finished, so he held his tongue.

"We'd be happy if you and Rachel made a match of it, that's certain sure. But if you were doing it out of a debt to Ezra, that wouldn't be right for either of you."

He couldn't be angry with his brother, not when Aaron was looking at him with such caring in his eyes. But he also couldn't tell Aaron what he felt, when he didn't know himself.

"Don't worry," he said finally. "I promise you, that wouldn't be the reason if ever I did ask Rachel Brand to be my wife."

He shoved himself away from the stall and headed for the door.

"We're not finished in here. Where are you going?"

"To find Rachel. To tell her what Isaac is trying to do."

Aaron moved quickly. He put an arm the size and strength of a young tree trunk across the doorway. "Just hold on a minute. You go find Rachel looking like a thundercloud, do you think people aren't going to notice?"

"Let them notice."

"And then there will be more folks thinking the same way Lovina is." Aaron clapped him on the shoulder. "Komm, simmer down a bit first. You can talk to her more natural-like over lunch."

Gideon itched to push his way past his brother—to find Rachel and tell her exactly what Aaron had told him.

But maybe Aaron had a point. If people were already talking about them, speculating about them—well, did he really want to stoke that fire any hotter?

And then there was the fact that this would hurt Rachel. She was so sensitive to Isaac's feelings, even if he didn't seem to return the favor.

Gideon's jaw clenched. Probably the real reason that he wanted to put his fist through the board they'd just put up was that this was going to make Rachel's decisions even more difficult, and there wasn't a thing he could do about that.

*It* was wrong to be angry with a brother. Rachel kept reminding herself of that as she worked her way toward Isaac. It was against the teaching of the Bible, and against the beliefs of the church.

She should not tell herself that Isaac had been wrong to try to control her actions by intervening with Aaron that way. One sin did not excuse another.

She would talk to him calmly. She would make it clear to him that she had no intention of giving up the market with the Zooks. That she needed the income it provided to support her children.

Around her, the work frolic was coming to an end. Some buggies had already moved off down the lane, mostly women who were headed home to fix supper for their families. Small groups of people still clustered here and there—the women chatting as they packed up boxes of cleaning supplies or food left over from the lunch; the men catching up on the latest news now that the work was finished.

Isaac was at the center of one such group. He leaned back against the split-rail fence, elbows resting on it as he talked, looking relaxed and expansive, the center of attention.

Rachel halted a few feet from the group. What she had to say wasn't for everyone else to know. If she waited until later—

Isaac caught her gaze, just for a second. Then he turned back to his conversation.

He was keeping her waiting deliberately. A fresh spark of anger ignited and had to be extinguished. She'd been fighting that battle since Gideon spoke to her.

Gideon had been reluctant to tell her, she suspected, but he'd been right to do so. If Isaac was going to people behind her back, she needed to know that. As for what she was going to do about it—

The men's conversation ended on a rumble of laughter, and Isaac turned toward her. "Do you need something, Rachel?"

His tone seemed to imply that of course she did and that it was natural for her to come to him with her needs. Fortunately no one could see how tense her hands were under the concealment of her apron.

When she didn't speak right away, he raised heavy brows. Then his gaze shifted to someone behind her, and his features rearranged themselves into a smile.

"Isaac. Daughter." Her father came to a stop next to her, surveying Isaac with an expression she didn't understand. "You wouldn't be talking business, would you?"

Isaac straightened, as if reminding himself that his casual pose was disrespectful to the older man. "Not on my account. Rachel's the one who wants to see me."

The men's gazes swiveled toward her, pinning her to the spot. Was it going to be easier or more difficult to bring this up in front of her father? She wasn't sure. She simply knew that she couldn't keep silent. Isaac had gone too far.

"Perhaps we could talk more privately," she suggested.

Isaac stared at her for a moment, then shrugged and moved a few feet off to the side. It was hardly out of earshot of the other men, but they drifted off, leaving her alone with her father and her brother-in-law.

She took a breath, willing herself to calm. "I understand you had a conversation with Aaron Zook about me. About the fact that I've been going to market with him and Lovina."

"I might have done. Hard to remember everybody I've talked to." But his gaze slid away from hers, denying the casual tone of his words.

"According to Aaron, you want him to stop taking me to the market."

"I suppose Gideon told you that." Isaac's voice snapped the words, and she could sense her father turn to look at her.

"Does it matter how I learned of it? Aaron would have no reason to make up a story about it."

"No, he would not." The low rumble of Daad's voice startled her. "Is this true, Isaac?"

Isaac's jaw clenched until he looked as stubborn as the mules he used to pull his plow. "It seems to me that Rachel would be better off staying home with her children than leaving them to spend the day at the market, talking to outsiders, taking advice from folks who aren't even her kin."

She was ready to defend herself, but before she could speak, her father beat her to it.

"Are you saying that Rachel's children are being neglected because they spend her market days with their grossmutter and me?"

"Now, now, I didn't mean that." Isaac backpedaled away from the implication she was sure he'd intended. "But a young widow has to be careful about the appearance she creates."

Words pressed at her lips, demanding to be let out. "A young widow who is earning money to support her three young children is surely creating the right impression, don't you think?"

"You wouldn't have to earn money at all if you'd just listen to me." Goaded, Isaac's temper, always a little uncertain, slid from his control, his face flushing and his hands closing. "You're just being stubborn, clinging to the farm instead of taking my offer for it, as Ezra surely would want."

There it was again—that idea that he, and he alone, knew what Ezra would have wanted. Rachel had to clamp her lips shut to keep from flaring out at him. They were dangerously close to an open breach, and she would shrink back from that, whether Isaac did or not.

"We none of us know what Ezra would want." Her father

said the words that she was thinking. "The farm belongs to Rachel and her children now, and it's for Rachel to decide about selling."

Given how her father felt about the subject, that statement astonished her. If Isaac had gone about this in a different way, he'd have probably been able to get Daad lined up firmly on his side. Maybe she was fortunate that Isaac didn't have a lot of tact.

Isaac glared. "You can't think that Rachel can make a go of the dairy farm herself. It's nonsense. And who is she going to sell to, if not to me? That Englischer who's been hanging around?"

Daad swung to stare at her, and she could feel the warmth mounting her cheeks. Isaac had done that deliberately, but how had he even known about the man?

"Rachel?" Her father was looking at her with doubt and questioning in his eyes.

"I suppose you're talking about Mr. Carver from the dairy. He has been to see me twice."

"About dairy business?" Daad looked a little reassured at that. After all, most of the Amish dairy farms in the valley did business with Carver.

"In a way." She wasn't ready to talk about this yet, but she was being pushed irrevocably toward a decision she wasn't sure she wanted to make.

Isaac snorted. "He wants to buy the farm, ain't so? Everyone knows he's trying to expand. I'd never believe that my own brother's wife would think of selling his farm to an Englischer instead of to his own family."

"It's not like that at all." She pressed her fists hard against her skirt, trying to hang on to the calm that was rapidly deserting her. "He's not trying to buy the farm."

"Then what does he want?"

Daad's question demanded an answer. She was going to have to come out with the man's offer and why it mattered to her. She'd have to find out if the dream that had been drifting through her mind more and more lately would stand the light of day.

She fixed her gaze on her father's face, praying he'd understand. "He offered to buy the dairy herd. He'd lease the barn and the pastures, paying me rent for them. That way, I could keep the farm for the children's future, and I'd still have the house and enough land for my needs."

That was hurt in his face now—hurt that she was considering this without talking to him first and embarrassment that he was hearing about it in public.

"You might as well break up the farm completely as do that." Isaac had found his voice, and it exploded with fury. "The idea that you'd deal with him—and what do you need land for, anyway?"

There was the question. She had to answer it. Ready or not, as the children called when they played at hide-and-seek in the twilight.

"I need it for the flowers and shrubs I'm growing. I'm going to start a nursery business of my own."

Silence greeted her words. She looked at her father, praying she'd see support, or at least understanding, in his face.

He stared at her. Everyone within earshot stared at her. And no one spoke.

She had never felt so alone in her life.

# Chapter Fourteen

Rachel could almost tally the opinions of her community by counting up the number of people who'd come to call the next day. It was an off-Sunday, when they didn't meet for worship, so it was given over to visiting family and friends.

Her parents had been notable by their absence today. Even the children had noticed it, wondering aloud where Grossmutter and Grossdaadi were. She hadn't had an answer.

She gave the counter a last wipe, knowing she was making work simply to avoid the moment when she'd have to sit down alone in the silent living room.

Enough. She stalked through to the room, sat down in her favorite rocking chair, and picked up the basket of mending that sat near at hand on the table.

Moments later the dress of Becky's that she was shortening for Mary lay in her lap, the needle stuck through the hem, while her mind was caught in the now-familiar groove of worrying about her relationship with her parents.

Leah had sent Daniel over with the children for a short visit, a mute gesture of support. Aaron and Lovina had stopped by, Lovina's merry chatter filling up the silent corners of the old house. But Mamm and Daadi hadn't come, their absence clearly proclaiming their disapproval for all to see.

Johnny had been strong enough, or willful enough, to pursue his dream without their consent or support. She didn't think she was. How could she keep insisting that her way was right, if those who loved her best thought it wrong?

A tear dropped on the light blue cotton of the child's dress, and she blotted it away.

Lights crossed the front windows, and tires crunched on the gravel lane. She put the mending basket on the floor, her movement jerky. What if it was Carver, come to press her for a decision again?

She crossed to the window and peered out. Relief swept through her, gentling every frazzled nerve. It was Johnny.

By the time he reached the porch, she had the door open.

"I didn't expect you tonight." She hugged him, pressing her cheek against his clean-shaven one, aware as she always was of the sense of oddness about that. "How gut it is to see you."

"Good to see you, too." He gave her an extra squeeze, his gaze sweeping the room. "It's okay?"

She nodded. "No one else is here." She turned away, busying herself with taking his jacket and hanging it on the back of a chair. "It's been quiet today."

"I heard."

She swung toward him, staring into the blue eyes that were so like her own. "Heard what?"

"That you announced at the work frolic that you were starting your business. That the folks weren't exactly supportive."

"But . . ." Her mouth was probably gaping. "How did you find out about that?"

He shrugged, the movement fluid under the fine knit of the shirt he wore—blue, to match his eyes. "I have my sources."

"I don't understand what you mean." Who among the Plain People in the valley had a relationship with Johnny, other than herself? "Did Leah tell you?"

His gaze slid away from hers. "Never mind that." He set the bag he carried on the round table where the children had played a board game earlier. "I know you're disappointed about Daad, but you can't let it get you down."

"That's not so easy." Her hands gripped each other. "I'm not like you. I can't go against them."

"You won't have to." He clasped her tense hands in his, and his strong grip warmed her. "Daad will come around. You'll see. Give Mamm a chance to work on him."

"He didn't come around for you." Her fingers tightened on his. How much Mamm would give to be here right now, touching him, even just looking at him.

"Think a minute." Johnny's tone was brisk, as if he'd willed all emotion away. "The two things aren't the same at all. What you want to do isn't against the Ordnung. It isn't anything that dozens of other Amish right here in Pleasant Valley aren't doing. Starting a business, especially one that you can run right out of your home, is perfectly acceptable."

"Those other dozens aren't young widows whose family thinks she ought to do something else." But even as she said the words, she felt heartened by Johnny's support.

"Daad will come around," he repeated. "You know he wants what's best for you and the children, and once he sees this is it, he'll be there for you."

"Maybe." She wanted to believe that. "And will Isaac come around, too?"

"You worry too much about what people think." He pulled out a chair and sat down at the table, unzipping the bag he'd carried in. "Who cares what Isaac thinks? I want you to take a look at this instead." He slid a folder onto the table.

She cared, although it seemed her brother had moved so far from the Amish way of thinking that he wouldn't understand that. She cared about the opinions of every member of her church family, and especially about those of Ezra's brother.

Still, did that caring mean she should give up something she felt was right for her?

She pressed her fingers against her temple, wishing that would still the argument that raged in her mind.

*Please, Father. Please guide me, because I don't know what to do. I want to follow Your will, but I must understand what it is.*

"Okay, here it is." Johnny spread out a sheaf of papers. "Tell me what you think of this."

She looked. Blinked. And looked again. It seemed to be—it was—an advertisement, like one that might appear in the newspaper.

*Rachel's Garden,* it read. *Perennials, annuals, shrubs—40 Black Creek Road. No Sunday sales.*

She touched the page with her fingertips, marveling that seeing the simple words in black and white should make her dream seem so close to reality.

"It's beautiful." She blinked back the tears that filled her eyes. "But I can't—it's not appropriate—"

"Sure it is." Johnny flipped open another folder. "You think I didn't do my homework on this? Look, here are the ads put in by other Amish businesspeople. If they can do it, why can't you?"

She leaned over his shoulder to look. That was true enough. No one objected, so far as she knew. Even Bishop Mose's harness shop had an advertisement.

"Most people put small box ads in the local shopping paper. And in the booklets put out by the tourist association. You can put this up on the bulletin boards in stores, too." He swung around to face her, his gaze intent. "I'm not urging you to do anything that would cause problems with the church. I wouldn't do that."

The concern in his voice touched her. Johnny, who had seemed so impatient with her need to follow the rules, was now going out of his way to do so for her.

She touched his shoulder lightly. "You've done all this for me?"

Johnny put his hand over hers. "You've done more than that for me." His fingers tightened. "Just seeing me—making me a part of your life again—"

He stopped, his voice choking, and ducked his head. The light from the lantern above the table reflected from the gold of his hair, cut short over his ears.

"Johnny—" A mix of love and loss wrapped tightly around her throat. "I didn't see that it mattered so much to you. I thought you were happy in your new life."

His shoulders shrugged, the movement jerky under her hand. "Happy? I don't know if *happy* is the right word. I'm satisfied, I guess." His fingers tightened on hers so hard she nearly gasped. "I wouldn't give it up, Rachel. Understand that. I couldn't. I'll never come back. But it still feels as if a part of me is missing. It still hurts."

She wrapped her arms around him, pressing her cheek against his hair. He was her brother, her twin, the other half of herself, she'd always thought. "I wish I could make it better."

"I know." For just a moment he leaned into her. Then he straightened. "I made my choice, and I don't regret it. But I can't forget about you, or stop trying to help you. When Gid told me about it . . ."

He stopped, his voice trailing off.

"Gideon? You were talking to Gideon Zook?"

"Yeah, well, I ran into him." He rustled the papers into order, needlessly, it seemed. "Just happened to see him, and we got to talking. Anyway, I should have heard about it from you, shouldn't I? Why didn't you let me know what was going on?"

"I . . . I wasn't sure how you'd feel about it. The last time I saw you—"

He grimaced, as if that memory was still sore. "Guess that wasn't one of the good times, was it? Well, it doesn't change anything between us. You're still my sister. I still love you."

"Ser gut." She smiled, touching his face lightly. "I love you, too."

But even as she sat down next to him and listened to his ideas for her business, she wondered if starting it was really possible.

And she wondered even more how and why her brother had been talking to Gideon Zook.

*"Why* did you talk to my brother about me?"

Gideon's gaze jerked to the doorway of his shop, the metal piece he'd been working on clattering to the table.

Rachel stood there, her slender shape dwarfed by the giant doors of what had been one of the earliest barns built in the valley.

"Rachel?"

He walked toward her, his mind trying to process her words.

Had she found out about his arrangement with Johnny? How could she have?

"I'm sorry—I'm just surprised to see you." Playing for time, he gestured her in. "You've never been in my shop before, have you? Komm. Welcome."

She stalked into the barn with quick, determined strides, very unlike the way she usually moved. Waves of irritation, if not outright anger, swept toward him, and she shook her head, either to say that she hadn't been there before or to shake off his question.

"I need to talk to you. You didn't come today."

"I have to finish the blades for the windmill before I go any further." He motioned toward the worktable behind him. "Would you like to see?"

She gave the work area a cursory glance. "I want to know about you and Johnny."

Maybe it was a gut thing to have the reputation of taking things slow and steady. At least he didn't have to rush an answer to that. He leaned against the worktable. "What about Johnny?"

She made a short, chopping gesture with her right hand. "Johnny said that you'd told him about—about what happened at the work frolic. About Daad . . ."

Her voice faded. The annoyance in her face faded, too, as if a lamp had been extinguished. Pain took its place, so strong that it punched him in the heart.

He longed to protect her. Comfort her. He couldn't, but he also couldn't resist touching her shoulder.

"I'm sorry," he said softly.

She leaned against him. It startled him, the feel of her head against his shoulder. He held her, not letting himself think of the past or the future, just cherishing the moment.

It was over too soon. She straightened, pulling away, giving a shaky laugh.

"I'm sorry. I didn't mean to be so foolish. I just . . . I just need to know what's happening."

"I see." He did. But if he told her everything, how would she react? "I saw Johnny, ja."

She swung toward him. "But why? I mean—you know he's under the bann. Why did you talk to him—tell him?"

"Ja, I know, but it seemed to me he had a right to know." Memory painted an image in his mind, and he smiled. "I remember how you two were as children. Like two peas in a pod, you were, and just as close, ain't so?"

Her lips curved, almost reluctantly, her face softening so that for an instant she was that child he remembered. "Ja. We were that."

"Well, so, I thought you could use some family support. He's family, for all he looks and sounds like an Englischer."

"He is family." She looked stronger, just saying the words. Taking a deep breath, she seemed to shed some of the tension that had been driving her. "But your talking to him without telling me—that I didn't like."

"I'm sorry." If she didn't like his speaking to Johnny, he could just imagine how she'd feel about his plotting with Johnny behind her back.

"But I guess you did it for the best." She reached toward him in a movement that seemed impulsive. "Denke, Gideon."

He clasped her hand gently in his, nodding.

For a moment they stood there, hands clasped. And then she moved away.

Now it was his turn to take a deep breath. He needed it. But apparently the storm was over.

She was looking around the shop, seeming to see it for the first time since she'd walked in the door. "You said you had to work in the shop today?"

"Ja." Relief at the change of subject washed through him. He swung his hand toward the work table. "Once I finish the blades, I'll be back up on the tower again."

She moved between the table and the workbench, glancing around at the workbenches, the generator for his power tools, the wooden partitions against the back wall that held lumber. The corner nearest him was fitted up as his office, with his always-cluttered desk and his filing cabinets.

He perched on the corner of the desk, watching her. What did she see when she looked around? He always saw the work that had saved his life when he hadn't wanted to go on.

"It's a gut big space for your work."

"Believe me, Aaron hated to give up this old barn, even though he has a fine new one. Lovina says he'd have filled it up with more goats if she hadn't jumped in and convinced him I needed it for my shop."

"Lovina is a determined woman."

"Ja, she is." Interfering, some might say, but he appreciated her. She'd known what he needed. He patted the gray metal file cabinets. "If not for her, I'd probably keep my records in a shoe box."

Rachel stared at the cabinets for a moment, her expression unreadable. "Tell me something. If I looked at those records, would I find that you charged me the same amount for the windmill that you charged other people?"

The swing back into dangerous territory took him off guard. He cleared his throat. If he were the kind of man who could think quickly on his feet, he might come up with an answer for her. Instead he could only sit there, feeling like a dumb animal.

Rachel's eyebrows lifted in a mute repeat of the question. He couldn't evade an answer.

"No. You wouldn't."

She made a pushing away motion with her hands and started to turn. And he knew that he couldn't let her reject this.

He slid from the desk and caught her arm, turning her back to face him, trying to ignore the fact that he could feel the warmth of her skin through the fabric of her sleeve.

"Stop, Rachel. Think this through. If I had been building the windmill for Ezra, like I offered to do several times, would I have expected to charge him the same as I'd charge a stranger?"

She kept her gaze stubbornly averted from his. "We're not talking about Ezra."

He stifled the urge to give her a gentle shake. "Answer the question. Would I?"

"No." She glared at him. "But that's different."

"How is it different?" He would not repeat all the things he'd already said. If she didn't understand the reason behind his need to help her by now, she probably never would.

"It . . . it just is." For a moment confusion clouded the clear blue of her eyes. "You're trying to put me in the wrong. That I don't like. It *is* different, and you know it. Ezra was able to help you out with things, just as you helped him. I can't."

Anger flicked him. "Are you saying that my friendship with him was some kind of business arrangement? That we'd do for each other only because we'd get paid back?"

That got through to her. "No. Of course I'm not saying that. It's just that . . ." Her voice trailed off. For once, it seemed, Rachel could think of no argument to make.

"Bear one another's burdens," he quoted softly. "If Ezra had come away from the accident injured, I would have done his work gladly. Since he didn't come away at all, how much more must I want to help? Would you deprive me of that?"

"You are right. I know that." But still, her gaze was troubled. "But building the windmills is your business. You're probably losing someone else's business while you're building mine, ain't so?"

"Ach, I'm sure I'm losing a wonderful heap of business." Relief that she seemed to be accepting his words brought a smile to his face.

"Well, you might be."

"Listen to me, Rachel Brand. I would do it anyway. You know that. But it's a gut thing that I can work on your windmill at my own pace." He slapped his bad leg. "This still isn't as strong as it should be. Anyone else might expect me to be going full speed. You don't seem to mind if I take a day off now and again."

"No." She returned the smile. "No, I don't mind."

"Are we all right now about this?"

"Maybe I overreacted a little bit." She shook her head. "I don't know. I just don't like the feeling that other people are making plans for me behind my back. Talking about my business, like you and Johnny did."

"I explained about that." Would she never let it go? "I just ran into him at—"

His mind went blank. Where might Johnny have said they'd run into each other, when they'd actually met at the home of one of her brother's friends?

Suspicion tightened Rachel's lips. "Were you lying to me about meeting my brother then, Gideon Zook? Because if you were, you'd best tell me the truth of it right now."

"I . . . Maybe you should ask Johnny that." That was a feeble answer, and he knew it. How had he managed to get himself into such a pickle, anyway? Because Rachel was one stubborn woman, that was how.

"I will ask my brother." The anger that flared in her eyes didn't bode well for John. "Right now I'm asking you, and I'm expecting a truthful answer."

"All right. The truth of it is that I have seen Johnny. Several times over the past month. Sometimes at the clinic, sometimes at the home of a friend of his."

Was it only his imagination that she'd paled? He didn't think so, and he blamed himself for it.

"Why?" Her breath seemed to catch on the word. "Why, Gideon? Why have you been meeting with my brother behind my back? Why didn't you come right out and tell me, whatever it is?"

"Because you're too stubborn, that's why." It was a relief to feel a bit of anger at her. "You didn't want to let me help you, even when you needed it. You wouldn't accept help from your brother, either."

She was definitely paler. "You know the reason for that, just as well as I do. Johnny is under the bann."

"I know." His voice gentled. This wasn't easy for her, and probably Johnny, with that stubborn streak that matched hers, hadn't made it any easier. "But Johnny's not coming back, no matter what. And he had to find a way to help you. There has to be a way to help those we love."

Her lips trembled, and she pressed them together. "What did you do, the two of you?"

"Johnny wanted to help. I wanted to help. Bishop Mose

wanted to help. So I was the go-between for Johnny and Bishop Mose."

She looked horrified. "You don't mean—that money that Bishop Mose insisted on lending me for the windmill—he never took it from Johnny. He wouldn't."

"No, no, he wouldn't." That had been a tricky negotiation, and he had no intention of telling her just how tricky, trying to satisfy Johnny's pride and Bishop Mose's need to stay on the right side of the Ordnung. "Bishop Mose wanted to put up all the money himself. But Johnny—"

Rachel gave the slightest nod. Well, she had to know how stubborn and prideful her twin could be.

"The end of it was that the clinic threw some extra work Bishop Mose's way." He put up a hand to block her protest. "I don't know anything about the arrangement between Johnny and the folks at the clinic, and I'm not planning to ask. If the bishop is satisfied, I am. And so should you be, if you have any sense."

She opened her mouth and then shut it again. "You've left me without anything to say."

"That's a relief." He tried a smile. "You shouldn't be angry with kindness, Rachel. Be angry with us for not telling you, if you want, but don't be angry because people love you and want to help you."

"All right." Her giving-in was hardly more than a whisper. "I won't be."

*"I'm* here." Rachel maneuvered the folded-up quilting frame through the back door at Leah and Daniel's farmhouse. "Leah? I've brought the quilting frame."

Leah came through from the living room, skirting carefully around the kitchen table. "I'll help you with that."

"No, you will not." She pulled the frame away from Leah's hands. "Tell me where to put this. And then tell me how you're feeling. Are there any signs that this babe plans to arrive before tomorrow's quilting?"

"I wish there were." Leah crinkled her nose, half-laughing, half-serious. "Well, not really, I suppose. Everyone is looking forward to the quilting, and I wouldn't want to disappoint them."

"We'd all understand how that feels, having been through those last weeks of being pregnant ourselves." Rachel followed her into the living room and set the frame where she indicated.

Leah grasped one side, helping her to snap the legs into place. "This is such a nice frame. I love how it folds up. If I actually did as much quilting as my mamm, I'd want one like it."

"It is nice." Rachel ran her hand along the side pole nearest her. "Ezra put it together from a kit, he did." He'd been so pleased with how it turned out that she seemed to see his smile each time she used it. "I shortened the poles to sixty inches for the crib quilt."

"Ser gut. Using two frames will be faster and easier, I think." Leah lowered herself into a rocking chair. At nine months' pregnant, she was ready to sit every chance she got.

Several feet away, another frame occupied one corner of the room. "I see you have your mamm's frame up already, ja?"

Leah nodded, rocking a little. "Daniel and Daadi set it up last night. They're willing enough to help get things ready for the quilting, but they're both planning to make themselves scarce while the work is going on."

"Gut. We don't want them listening in on our conversation.

They might blush." Rachel brushed her hands together, not that there had been any dust on the quilt frame. "I'll just go and bring in the food I brought for tomorrow."

"I'll help—"

"You'll sit still." Rachel bent to press her cheek against Leah's. "You're supposed to be staying off your feet, remember?"

Leah's lips curled upward. "How can I forget, the way everyone keeps reminding me? Anyway, the midwife says it's not so crucial, now that I'm about full-term."

"Rest anyway. I'll put things in the kitchen, and then we can set up the quilts and get ready for tomorrow."

"Gut. We'll have a chance to talk while we do that."

The wistful note in Leah's voice registered, and guilt trickled through Rachel. She hadn't spent near enough time with Leah this past week. And even now, when she was here, her mind skittered off like a waterbug to all the other things she had to do.

"As much talk as you have energy for." She gave Leah a quick hug. "I'll be right back."

Two more trips to the buggy, and she'd brought in everything she'd prepared for the quilting—the pieced tops for the baby quilts, several loaves of banana nut bread, a huge tin of jumble cookies that her mamm had made, and a couple jars of strawberry preserves.

Plenty more food would arrive tomorrow. Every woman who came would bring something, so there'd be lots left for Leah's family to enjoy, for sure.

She carried the quilt tops, wrapped in clean sheets to protect them, into the living room and laid them on the table, then got out the backing pieces and her pincushion.

"You have to let me help with this, at least." Leah levered

herself out of the chair with her arms, sighing a little. "I feel as if I need a crane to get me up and down these days."

"Give it a little time, and you'll be feeling as if you need one to pry your eyes open." Rachel spread the backing piece for one quilt carefully over the frame, stretching it firm, and then began to pin.

Leah took a handful of pins and started on the opposite side. "We've done a lot of things together over the years, but I never thought we'd be doing this for a babe of mine."

Heart full, Rachel touched Leah's hand. "It's wonderful gut to share the excitement of the boppli coming along."

"You never expected it to happen either." Teasing filled Leah's voice. "Admit it, now. You thought I was destined to be a maidal forever."

"That's not true." Although it had seemed, at times, as if Leah had been almost too content with her single life. "I'm the one who pushed you toward Daniel, remember?"

"You and the rest of the church." Leah ran her hand down over her belly in a caressing movement. "I don't regret it now, but there were certainly times when I wished everyone would mind their own business instead of mine."

"I know just what you mean." The words had brought Rachel's concerns about Gideon and Johnny back to the fore, not that they were ever far from her mind. "There's something—"

She hesitated. But if she couldn't talk to Leah about this or anything else, then the world had turned upside-down already.

"Something that's worrying you?" Leah caught her mood instantly. "Tell me."

"I'm maybe being foolish about it."

She unfolded the batting piece and spread it over the backing. Was she? She just couldn't decide. She'd told Gideon she wouldn't argue with him about it, but it seemed she couldn't stop arguing with herself.

"You'll feel the better for talking, then." Leah slid a pin through the batting. "Out with it."

Rachel nodded, concentrating on lining the batting edge up perfectly. "You know about Bishop Mose lending me the money to pay Gideon for the new windmill, already. Well, for one thing, I got Gideon to admit that he's not charging me full price for it."

"I wouldn't expect anything else." Leah's voice was firm. "Rachel Brand, if that's what's bothering you, you're foolish indeed. Gideon was Ezra's closest friend. Naturally he wouldn't expect the same amount from you as he would someone he doesn't even know."

"That's what he said."

"Well, he's right."

"But he told me something else—" She sent Leah a troubled look. "You must agree not to say anything of this to anyone."

The laughter faded from Leah's face. "Of course."

"Somehow Gideon got together with Johnny. I don't know how, exactly. And they hatched a . . . a plot, that's what it was. And Bishop Mose went in on it." She still found that hard to believe. "Gideon says that Johnny's clinic is throwing extra work to the harness shop. It's all a way of letting Johnny help out, even though they won't admit that."

"What did Gideon say when you told him that?"

"That he didn't know what the arrangements were, and that if Bishop Mose was satisfied, then I should be, as well."

Leah was quiet for a moment, as if absorbing it all. "Gideon gave you gut advice. I think you should take it."

"But—"

Leah shook her head, lines crinkling around her green eyes. "Rachel, no buts about it. Bishop Mose would not do anything wrong. And besides, we both know that's not what you're fussed about anyway."

"What do you mean?"

"I mean that you're annoyed at all of them for going behind your back and trying to help you. That you're so bent on providing for the children yourself that you think no one else can do anything."

"If it was you—"

"If it was me, I'd maybe make the same mistake. But I hope I could count on a gut friend who'd point it out to me."

Rachel was still for a moment, absorbing Leah's words. Was she being prideful, holding back from accepting the love and help others wanted to share?

"You should accept all the support you're offered," Leah said. "All of it."

Something—some note in Leah's familiar voice—sounded an alarm in her. She knew Leah so well. She knew when something was being left unsaid.

"What, Leah?" She reached across the frame to catch Leah's hand and hold it tightly. "You're thinking of something beyond this. I can tell."

Leah's lips pressed together tightly, as if she'd hold the words back. "I wasn't sure whether I'd tell you this or not. It's just gossip, when it comes right down to it, and maybe nothing behind it at all except someone's imagination embroidering what was said."

A cold compress seemed to press against the back of Rachel's neck, dripping its chill down her spine. "I'd still rather hear it, whatever it is."

"Daniel heard it when he went to the farrier's to have the horses reshod this morning. Some of the men were talking. You know how they linger there and gossip, even though they insist that it's only women who do that."

Rachel could picture the scene well enough, the men leaning against wagons, watching the shoeing, exchanging all the news of the day. She'd never expected that she'd be the subject of their talk.

"Just tell me, Leah."

"It maybe means nothing at all." Reluctance dragged at Leah's words. "But they were saying that Isaac is furious about the idea that you might be leasing the farm to an Englischer, instead of selling it to him for Caleb."

Rachel's tension eased. If that was all it was— "I already knew Isaac was angry about that, but I haven't made a decision yet. I'm thinking on what Mr. Carver said, that's all."

"The talk is that Isaac isn't willing to wait for your decision." Leah took a breath, seeming to push the words out. "They're saying that he's going to the bishop and the ministers with a complaint about your conduct."

# Chapter Fifteen

Rachel worried at it all the way back to her parents' place to pick up Mary. Leah had continued to reassure her, repeating that it was rumor, nothing more. And even if Isaac had said that in a fit of temper, he might easily have changed his mind once he'd calmed down. And even if he did complain about her . . .

Rachel's mind refused to go there. Leah could say that she should present her own argument to the elders. That they would understand if she explained it to them.

Leah was braver than she was, for sure. Leah, with her years of teaching behind her, had a self-possession and ability to express herself that Rachel would never achieve, no matter how she tried.

If it came to an open conflict, Rachel knew perfectly well what would happen. She'd give in, restoring peace and harmony to the church.

The English world wouldn't understand that. It seemed to be built on competition, and even Johnny had been influenced by that, talking about doing better than a colleague to compete for a position.

Things were not like that among the Leit, the Amish people. Cooperation was valued, not competition. She would give up what she wanted rather than cause a rift in the family that was the church.

She turned into the lane and slowed the horse to a walk as they approached the house. Daadi was at the edge of the garden, in conversation with Jacob Esh, the son of his second cousin. Jacob, just a year out of school, was working the farm with Daad, learning as he earned a bit of money. At the moment he was plowing the garden, and he looked as if Daad was giving him a bit more advice than he thought he needed.

Fortunately for Jacob, Daadi saw her. He waved and headed across the lawn toward her.

He reached her as she mounted the porch steps.

"You're putting the garden in already, I see."

"Ja." He sent a glance toward Jacob, toiling across the length of the garden. "Jacob thought we should wait another week for the soil to dry more, but I'm ready to get peas and spinach in the ground."

"How is Jacob shaping up?" She'd be happy to keep the conversation on someone other than herself for as long as possible.

Daadi gave a snort, but his eyes held a twinkle. "Like most young folks. Thinks he knows more than his elders. He's a gut boy, though, and does what I ask, I will say that."

"He'll learn a lot from you." She studied her father's face as she spoke. She'd have said that he never seemed to age, but something—worry or tension, maybe—was exaggerating the lines around his eyes.

"Ja, well, he'll turn into a gut farmer, I have no doubt. Maybe he'll be taking this place over one day." He gazed across the field toward the orchard, shielding his eyes with his hand.

Her breath caught. That was the first time her father had spoken of the future he envisioned for the farm, now that Johnny was gone.

She didn't know what to say to that, so maybe it was best to say nothing. "I'd best get Mary ready to go home."

Before she could reach for the door, Daad stopped her with a quick gesture. "She's still napping, I think, judging by the quiet. Walk down to the pond with me, ja? Komm."

He turned, not waiting for an answer, and she fell into step with him.

He didn't speak as they walked side by side across the lawn. When she was young, she'd trailed him everywhere around the farm. Most of the time he'd been silent, but that hadn't bothered her. It had been a comfortable, accepting kind of silence, and she'd learned much even from the things he didn't say.

She waved at Jacob as they passed the garden. Both hands gripping the plow, he couldn't wave back, but he gave her a nod and a smile.

The day was warming, even though the grass dampened her shoes as they started through the grove of trees to the pond. She and Johnny had come this way together more times than she could count, on their way to catch tadpoles in the pond, most likely, or to grasp at fireflies in the dusk.

A pang of longing pierced her heart. If she had those days back again, she would cherish her moments with him, knowing that the time would come when they'd be few and far between.

Daadi stopped at the bench he'd built on the edge of the pond, so Mamm could enjoy sitting there in the evenings. He sat down, patting the space next to him.

Rachel sat, too, bracing herself. A private conversation with Daad would undoubtedly be on the subject of her stubbornness.

"Never heard the spring peepers as loud as they are this year." He leaned his elbows on his knees, gazing out over the still water of the pond. "You should bring the kinder down here in the evening sometime soon."

"I will," she said. She leaned back, staring as he did at the pond.

Maybe she was wrong. Maybe he hadn't brought her here to lecture her. The still surface of the pond reflected the drooping willow tree, already dressed in its pale green, and the puffy white clouds that drifted across the sky.

In the marshy area around the pond, the tan heads of cinnamon ferns lifted above the vibrant green of the unfurling fans of skunk cabbage. It was quiet, and peaceful, and as familiar to her as her own body.

Daadi spoke without turning to look at her. "Have you any new answer for me about moving back here with your children, Daughter?"

Well, she had known that was what was in his mind, hadn't she?

"No, Daadi." Best to come right out with it. "You know how I feel about that. I appreciate that you want us, but . . ."

"Don't say that." He turned toward her, his face tight with a tension she hadn't recognized. "Think about it, child. Don't tell me that you appreciate it. You need help, and we're your parents. You're a parent yourself, now. If one of your children needs, don't you have to go to the rescue?"

"Ja, I do." She took a breath, despairing of ever making him understand. With Daad against her plans and Isaac threatening to complain to the elders, was there any hope for her?

"Well, then," Daad said.

"Please, try to understand." She put her hand on his, willing him to listen to her. "Of course I would run to the rescue, but my children are hardly more than babes."

"The love doesn't change, no matter how old the child becomes. Your mamm and I want nothing so much as to help you raise those children. We don't want to see you wearing yourself down to nothing trying to run the farm and take care of them."

"I'm not. You know that I'm not doing any of the work with the dairy herd now."

"And what will you do if Isaac withdraws his help? He could do that, and then where would you be? I heard . . ." He let that trail off, but she knew what he'd intended to say.

"You've heard that he's talking of complaining to the elders about me." Surprising that she was able to say the words so calmly.

"Ja, I've heard that." He gave a heavy sigh. "It's a bad thing, having conflict in the family."

Anger flared up like a candle in the dark. "And isn't it a bad thing for Isaac to try to force his brother's widow to sell out to him?"

"Isaac is as headstrong as he ever was. Maybe worse, since his father died."

"Then you understand." Hope blossomed for a moment.

"I know that he's difficult to deal with." Her father shook his head. "But to think of selling to an Englischer rather than your husband's kin . . ."

"But that's the point. I wouldn't have to sell if I accepted Carver's offer." Everyone seemed to have a different version of what the man had offered. "He wants to buy the herd, yes, but he would only lease the barn and the land."

"Is it so important to you, to hold on to the farm in the hopes that the children will want to farm it? What if they don't?"

He hadn't let bitterness into his voice on the words, or sorrow, but she knew he must feel both. She never talked to him about Johnny. Maybe she should.

"Daadi, you know what I'm feeling. You've kept the farm, hoping that Johnny would come back, even though . . ." She stopped, not wanting to finish that.

"Even though you know he never will." Her father finished it for her.

"Ja," she said softly. "That is what I believe."

Daadi closed his eyes briefly, as if he could shut out the pain. "I don't want to see you work yourself to death to hold on to the farm for the children," he said again. "I believe you'd be better off to sell, to Isaac or the Englischer, I don't care which, and move back home with us."

Nothing changed. No matter how hard she tried to explain, everyone around her stayed firm in his own belief that he knew what was best for her. The weight of all that disapproval was almost too much to bear.

Her father's fingers tightened on hers. "But I have already lost one child. I will not drive another away."

It took a moment for his words to penetrate. She looked at him, her heart lifting.

"Whatever you decide, Rachel, your mamm and I will support you. If you must go before the elders, we will stand with you."

"Denke, Daadi." Her throat choked with tears.

He put his arm around her and drew her close. She buried her face in his shoulder, feeling the fabric of his shirt against her cheek, inhaling the familiar scent that had always meant safety and comfort.

Daadi might not believe in her dreams, but he would stand with her anyway. Maybe that would be enough.

*Gideon* tightened a last bolt and glanced at the sky. He'd stayed longer than he'd intended at Rachel's today. Before the accident, he'd have been able to finish this part of the job in a few hours. Looked as if he wasn't up to his normal speed yet.

It will come. *Please, God, let my strength return so that I can do my work.*

He started to climb down, his bad leg protesting from the effort. Halfway down, he paused to give it a rest.

Movement from the ground caught his eye. Joseph, it was, over at the goat's pen as usual. That boy was certainly devoted to his pet.

Even as Gideon thought that, Joseph took a quick step backward, away from the pen, arms pressing rigid against his sides. He whirled, racing toward the house.

"Mammi! Mammi, komm! Schnell!"

Something was wrong, or he'd not be crying for his mother that way. Gideon made quick work of the rest of the trip and unhooked the harness. By the time Rachel and Joseph had rushed to the pen, he'd reached it, too.

Joseph grabbed his hand. "Something's wrong with Dolly. Look at her."

"Let us see," Rachel said, exchanging a glance with him. She moved Joseph away from the pen door and opened it. She paused, hand on the door. "Gideon?" There was a question in her voice. "You know more about goats than either of us does."

He pried the boy's fingers from his hand and knelt beside her at the pen door. "I couldn't live on Aaron's farm without picking up a bit. Let's have a look."

The little Nubian lay on her side near the pen opening, panting. He expected her to rise when he reached for her, but she just looked at him with what almost seemed like confidence in her eyes.

"There, now." He stroked his hand down her side. "What's going on here?"

The answer came as soon as the words were out of his mouth. A shudder rippled through her under the pressure of his palm—an unmistakable contraction.

He kept his hand there until the contraction eased off. He patted the little goat. "Well, Joseph, I think Dolly is about to become a mammi. That's what you've been waiting for, isn't it?"

The boy nodded, eyes wide. "The twins are coming. Ain't so, Gideon?"

"They are for sure."

Rachel rested her hand on Joseph's shoulder. "You have the box stall all ready for her. Let's move her into the barn now."

Joseph started to reach for the goat. He stopped, seeming not to know how to move her, and gave Gideon a pleading look.

"Won't she walk if you lead her?" Rachel said, holding the pen door wide.

Joseph took hold of the thin collar the goat wore, that looked, for all the world, like a pet dog's. "Komm, Dolly. Komm."

The goat struggled, legs waving, seeming unable to get to her feet.

"Suppose I carry her," Gideon said quickly. He didn't like the look of that, but no sense in alarming the boy if it wasn't necessary.

Joseph nodded, his breath coming out in a whoosh of relief. He stepped back so that Gideon could reach into the pen.

He slid his hands under the goat, moving gently so as not to frighten her, and lifted her out. His leg grumbled a bit as he rose, cradling the goat against his body.

"Lead the way, Joseph."

The boy rushed to the barn door, knocking his straw hat off in his hurry to slide it open. He scooped up the hat and raced to open the door to one of the box stalls.

The stall had been cleaned, he'd guess, to the last inch, and a fresh bed of straw covered the wooden planks. Gideon knelt, depositing the goat on the straw that Joseph fluffed up. The boy promptly sat down next to her.

"Joseph, she can probably do this part without you. Komm. Supper is ready."

Joseph's face crumpled at his mamm's words. "I can't leave her. She needs me." He reached toward Gideon, tugging on his pant leg. "You'll stay, won't you, Gideon?"

"I'm sure Gideon has much to do—" Rachel began, but he interrupted her.

"It's fine. I'm glad to stay." He sat down on the floor next to Joseph and leaned back against the side of the stall.

Rachel's face lit with gratitude. A man would do a lot for a smile like that, not that he wouldn't have stayed anyway, since Joseph seemed to need him.

"Well, if you won't come in for supper, I'll bring something out for the two of you." Her gaze met his. "Denke, Gideon," she said.

When she'd left, the barn seemed steeped in stillness. The big draft horses, who were the only other occupants, watched them curiously for a few minutes and then turned back to their feed buckets.

Joseph stroked Dolly's head. "What do we do now, Gideon?"

"Now we wait." He settled himself as comfortably as he could. "First births can take a while, and there's nothing to do for Dolly but let nature take its course."

An hour later, he'd begun to wonder if nature was going to be enough. He lit a lantern to chase away the gathering shadows so that he could get a better look at Dolly.

The little goat seemed to be struggling, and this wasn't progressing nearly as fast as the other births he'd seen working with Aaron's herd.

Rachel came in again while he was trying to urge Dolly to her feet. She studied his face, seeming to look past the facade he kept up for the boy.

She took Joseph by the shoulders. "I want you to go into the house now."

"But Mammi, Dolly needs me." His hand lingered on the little goat's head.

She hesitated a moment, and then knelt beside him. "You may come back out again. But I want you to say good night to Mary. Then go to the shed and get some of the empty feed bags that are on the shelf. We might need them when the kids come."

Joseph's small face lit with the prospect of something helpful to do. "I'll do it, Mammi. Schnell." He scrambled to his feet and raced for the door.

Rachel swung toward him as soon as Joseph was gone. "Something is wrong."

"I'm not sure." He gave up the effort and let the little doe rest on her side again. "I thought standing might help things along, but she doesn't seem to have the strength for it."

"Is there anything we can do?"

He spread his hands, hating feeling helpless. "Once she starts pushing, we may be able to help. I've done that often enough with Aaron's herd. Until then—I don't think there's anything."

"If we were to lose her, Joseph would take it so hard." Her lips twisted, as if she fought not to cry. "I can't bear for him to lose something else he loves."

"It's not come to that." Gideon reached out his hand and she took it, fingers twining tightly. "Goats are like people, I guess. Sometimes the first babe is a long time in coming." His thoughts flickered to his wife, his babe, and he yanked them away.

"Yes, of course." She took a breath, straightening. "I shouldn't be so foolish. But—do you think I'm right in letting him stay out here?"

She'd never asked his advice on anything to do with her children before. He'd best have the right answer.

"What would he do if you sent him inside?"

"Wait. Worry. Fret." She gave a slight shrug. "You're right. That would be worse than letting him feel he's helping."

"That's how you'd feel, ain't so?"

She nodded, bending to stroke the little doe's side. "Be strong, Dolly," she murmured.

"Here I am." Joseph burst in, burdened with a flashlight and an armload of feed bags. "Did anything happen?"

"Not yet." Rachel brushed his hair from his eyes. "It'll be a little while yet. You do as Gideon says. I'll be back out after I get Mary to bed."

Joseph nodded solemnly and came to sit next to Gideon.

Once Rachel had gone, the barn seemed too quiet, too lonely. Was he right in encouraging the boy to stay? Joseph had certainly seen animals give birth before. He wouldn't be frightened by what was normal.

"Gideon?" Joseph rested his head against Gideon's sleeve. "Dolly isn't going to die, is she?"

"I hope not."

"But it shouldn't take this long, should it?"

"It does seem like a long time." He wouldn't lie to the boy. "But things may start to happen very fast. Kidding goes that way sometimes."

Joseph's face moved against his sleeve. "I love her," he whispered. "I loved Daadi lots, lots more, but I love her, too. I don't want her to die like Daadi did."

"I know." Gideon put his arm around the boy. He was skinny, like Ezra had been at that age, with sharp little bones that seemed fragile under Gideon's touch. A wave of protectiveness swept through him, so strong it scared him.

What was he doing, feeling this powerful a caring for another man's son? He'd set out to help Ezra's wife and children, thinking only of the debt he owed to Ezra.

He'd never imagined they'd become so dear to him. Too dear. How would he live with himself if he failed them, too?

Rachel paused before she reached the barn on her return, lifting her face toward the sky. Pinpoints of light clustered thick as clover in the meadow. The nearly full moon seemed fat with promise. Was it true, then, the old idea that the full moon brought on birth?

*Please, Father. I don't know what Your will is for this little creature, but I ask Your guidance for helping Joseph to deal with whatever happens tonight. Thank You, that you've provided Gideon to aid us.*

A few more steps brought her to the door. Again she hesitated, this time caught by what she could see inside. The glow of the lantern echoed the glow of the moon, illuminating the stall. Gideon sat, his back against the rough boards, and Joseph leaned against him, his head snuggled into Gideon's broad chest. The man's arm curved protectively around his shoulders.

Her throat constricted. Gideon was doing what Ezra would have in this situation. Did he even realize how wonderful gut he was with the children?

Gideon's attention seemed to sharpen on something out of her line of vision—no doubt Dolly. He moved, Joseph moving with him. As if it had been a signal, she scurried inside.

"Was ist letz? What's the matter?"

"Time to help her push." Gideon squatted next to the goat. "Will you?"

She nodded, kneeling in the straw next to him. "Show me what to do."

"I want to do something." Joseph's voice wobbled a little. "Let me."

"You will hold her head. Your mammi will put her hands here." He took her hands in his and positioned them against the goat's warm, smooth side. "When you feel her push, only then, you press along with her. I'll try to ease the kid out."

She nodded, breathing a silent, wordless prayer.

Gideon gave Joseph an encouraging smile. "We'll do our best for her. The rest is in the Lord's hands."

Even as he spoke, the goat's muscles contracted under her

hands. Rachel sucked in a breath as if she were in labor as well and began to push.

"That's it, gut. The kid is in the right position. It won't be long now." Gideon had rolled up his sleeves, and he leaned over the animal. "Talk to her, Joseph. Tell her to push."

"Push, Dolly, push." Some of the fear eased from Joseph's face as he concentrated on the goat. "You can do it. I know you can."

"Come on, Dolly. Come on." Rachel pressed with her palms, feeling the progress of the contraction. "It's working."

"Ja." Gideon's glance at Dolly held concern. "Ease off, now. Wait for the next one."

Did he fear the little goat didn't have the strength in her to finish the job?

Rachel longed to ask, but didn't want Joseph to hear the answer. Before she could think of how to phrase it, the next contraction hit, and she was too busy to say anything.

"It's coming," Gideon exclaimed, and in a moment the tiny kid, front hooves first, came sliding out onto the feed bag, squirming and messy.

"She did it." Joseph hugged Dolly's head. "You did it, Dolly."

Gideon lifted the baby away a foot or so. "Ja, but I think she has one more to push out. You come and dry this one off, Joseph, while your mammi and I help her."

The worry in his voice was plain, but fortunately Joseph was too enraptured by the brand-new kid to hear it. He dried the baby off, crooning to it.

Dolly stiffened under her hands, and in what seemed little more than a moment, the second kid arrived. The doe lay back, eyes closing, side heaving with strain.

"Do you think—" Rachel began, studying Gideon's expression.

Grasping her arm, he turned her toward Joseph and the kids. "You help him with the babies. I'll tend to Dolly."

Gideon looked so grave that she feared Joseph could hardly fail to pick up on it, but he didn't seem to. So Rachel helped him dry the kids, marveling with him at them. It wasn't hard to keep his attention fixed on the babies instead of the mother.

"We should name them." Joseph stifled a yawn. "What do you think, Mammi?"

"I think you've been up far too long. Say good night to them, now, and get into bed." She stilled his protest with a gentle touch. "They need to rest, too, and so does Dolly. Go now. I'll come and check on you when I come in."

He hugged her and sidled over to Gideon. "Denke, Gideon." He hesitated a moment, then flung his arms around Gideon's neck in a throttling hug. "Denke."

Gideon patted him. "Sleep well."

Rachel handed him a flashlight. Standing in the barn doorway, she watched the light bob across the lawn, staying there until Joseph was safely into the house. Then she turned back to Gideon.

"Is she going to make it?"

"I don't know." He moved one of the kids to Dolly's head, but she closed her eyes and ignored it. "She's letting them nurse all right, but she should be cleaning them off and taking a bit of notice of them by now."

Rachel knelt next to Dolly's head. "Poor little thing. She's exhausted. Isn't there anything we can do?"

"Just wait. Pray."

"That I've been doing already."

Gideon moved fresh straw around mother and babies. He was limping, she realized as he straightened.

"You've been here all day. You should go home and get some rest yourself already."

"I'll stay." He sat down, leaning against the wall again. "You might need me."

"You've already done so much. I don't know how to thank you."

"You don't, that's all. Joseph is a fine bu, and you should be happy with him. He did a wonderful-gut job tonight."

"As did you. You would have been a gut father."

The moment the words were out of her mouth, she remembered, and she wished them back. But it was too late. "I'm sorry. I—"

He touched her arm. "It's all right. I hope I would have."

There seemed nothing to say to that. She just hoped he could sense her sympathy.

He drew his knees up, wrapping his arms around them. "When I think about that night, it's most often the boppli that I think of. He should have had his chance at life."

Her breath seemed strangled in her throat. Ezra had said that Gideon never spoke of it, not even to him.

"He lives in Heaven," she whispered.

"Ja." He stared at the goats, quiet now, but she didn't think he was seeing them. "It was raining that night. So hard that I could barely see to keep the buggy on the road." His hands tightened to fists against his legs. "We should have stayed at home and waited for the midwife, but Naomi wouldn't hear of it. She was so sure something was wrong, so sure that I had to take her to the hospital. If I'd insisted, maybe—"

He stopped, his voice choking.

Rachel's throat was tight with unshed tears. She knew the rest of the story. The truck, speeding in the driving rain, hitting the buggy, smashing it to pieces. Naomi and the baby dead, Gideon so badly injured that most had thought he'd never recover.

She put her hand tentatively on his shoulder. "Don't, Gideon. It wasn't your fault. You only did what Naomi wanted."

He turned, grabbing her hand in a fierce grip. "I knew it was a bad idea. I should have followed my instincts."

"Anyone in that situation would have done the same."

"Would they?" His eyes were dark with pain. "I don't know that. I just know that they died, and I survived."

And then Ezra had died, and he had survived again. The pain in Gideon's soul went so deep—what could Rachel possibly say that would be a balm for that?

Straw rustled. Gideon seemed to choke back a sob as he let her go and turned to the goats. One of the babies was nuzzling at Dolly's head, pushing her muzzle with an almost angry persistence.

"Ach, let her be." She reached toward the kid, but Gideon intercepted her, grasping her hand.

"Wait."

She held her breath, watching. Waiting. The kid bumped Dolly's muzzle again. The little doe opened her eyes. Wearily, slowly, she moved her head. Looked at her baby. And began to lick him.

"They're bonding," she breathed.

"Ja." Gideon moved the other kid up close, and Dolly licked her, too, seeming to gain strength even as they watched. "I think they're going to be all right."

He looked at Rachel then, and she realized that she wasn't the only one blinking back tears. Gideon's hand clasped hers again, warm and gentle. Emotion flooded through her.

She cared for him, more than she'd dreamed possible. He meant so much to her.

But the wound he'd revealed to her tonight—perhaps that would never heal. And if it didn't, how would he ever be able to care again?

# Chapter Sixteen

*You* look half-asleep today," her mother scolded gently the moment she walked in Rachel's kitchen door the next day. "Were the kinder up sick last night and you all by yourself here?"

Rachel hugged her. "No, nothing like that. Joseph's goat kidded, and we feared for a time she might not make it. But it ended well, with twin kids to show for a long night."

"You never should have let Joseph know that pet of his was in danger. The poor boy must have been worried out of his mind."

Mamm hung her bonnet on the peg and set a container of what looked like whoopie pies on the table.

"I don't think he realized how bad she was," Rachel assured her.

Mamm's eyebrows lifted in a question. "You said 'we.' I thought you meant you and Joseph."

"Gideon Zook was here." She tucked her packet of pins and her grossmutter's silver thimble into her bag for the quilting. "Thank the Lord he was. He knew just what to do."

The questioning look lingered in her mother's eyes. "He's a gut man, he is."

"Ja." Rachel was afraid to say anything more, afraid of betraying feelings that she didn't want to examine too closely in herself. "It's kind of you to watch the little ones while Becky and I go to the quilting."

Her mother seemed to accept the change in subject. "Ach, you know it's a pleasure."

"You'll probably be chasing them away from the goats all day."

"Well, and I want to see these little twins, too, so that will be chust fine. Is that where they are now?"

"Joseph and Mary are. Becky is supposed to be getting ready, but it's taking her a long while." She went to the hallway and peered up the stairwell, but there was no sign of her daughter. "Becky, come along now. It's time we were leaving."

No response, but she heard a drawer close in the girls' bedroom. Exasperated, she started up the stairs. "Becky, do you hear me?"

She reached the bedroom door to find Becky sitting on the bed, one shoe in her hand, the other on the floor. She had obviously been changing, but she'd come to a standstill.

"Becky, komm. I can't be late."

Becky didn't look up. "Maybe I should stay home today. I could help Grossmammi with the little ones."

That was so out of character for Becky, who always wanted to be on the go, that Rachel could only stand and stare at her for a moment. What was going through the child's mind?

"I'm sure your grossmutter can manage without you. I thought you'd been looking forward to going. Maybe you can put some stitches in the quilt for Leah's new baby."

Becky stared down at the log cabin design that covered her bed, picking at it with her fingers. "I don't want to go, Mammi. Can't I stay home?"

"You can't—"

She caught herself, stopped, and went to sit down on the bed next to her daughter. Something was wrong, and she wouldn't find out what by giving orders. She schooled herself to patience and tried not to think about being late.

"Komm, tell me what is going on. You always like to go to Daniel and Leah's."

Becky hunched her shoulders, not looking at her. "I just don't feel like it today."

"Is it because you might be expected to sew? You don't have to, you know. I just thought you might want to."

Becky didn't respond, but her lower lip jutted out.

Rachel caught her daughter's chin and turned her face so that she could see the expression. Pouting, definitely pouting. Becky's stubborn streak was making itself known.

"Rebecca, I want an answer now."

The pout became more pronounced. "I don't want to play with Elizabeth."

Rachel blinked. "Not play with Elizabeth? Why ever not? Did the two of you have a spat?"

Becky shook her head, the mulish look intensifying.

"What then?"

For an instant Becky clung to her silence, pressing her lips together. Then she shrugged. "I don't want to be her friend. She told on me."

Rachel's mind produced nothing but a blank slate. Then she realized what the child was talking about. So much had happened since Becky's misadventure in the barn that it had slid to the back of her mind.

"Let me get this straight. You're angry with Elizabeth because she ran for help when you were stuck up in the barn."

Becky flushed, as if she knew how ferhoodled that sounded but wouldn't admit it. "Ja. She told. Friends shouldn't tell on you."

"Becky, you needed help. You couldn't get down by yourself. If Elizabeth hadn't gone for help when she did, you might have fallen."

Rachel stared at her recalcitrant child with dismay. This had been preying on Becky's mind, and she hadn't known it.

*Father, I should have known. Forgive me, and please give me wisdom now. I must have answers for my children, and I can't seem to find them on my own.*

She put her arm around Becky. Her daughter stiffened, not giving in to the embrace.

"Sometimes it is right to tell. Sometimes that is what a true friend does." She sucked in a breath, praying that wisdom came with it. "What if Elizabeth had done what you wanted, and you'd fallen? She would have had to live with that for the rest of her life."

Becky did react to that—a tiny, almost undetectable wince.

"You are holding on to a grudge. You are not forgiving her, even though you know in your heart that she did the right thing."

The rigid little figure shook suddenly. "I can't help it! I know I shouldn't feel this way, Mammi. I don't want to. Why do I?"

Rachel hugged her, longing to make it better even while she knew there wasn't an easy solution. Every problem with raising children seemed to come back, in the end, to the teaching of faith.

"Forgiving can be hard. Maybe the hardest thing of all. That's why it's so important, and why we have to keep learning that lesson over and over again. Jesus forgives us, and He expects us to forgive others."

"I want to." Becky turned her face against Rachel's sleeve, wetting it with her tears, her voice muffled. "How can I?"

Rachel stroked her hair, knowing that she had the answer but hating to reveal so much of her own failure. But maybe that was part of the lesson God had to teach her.

"You know, for a long time after your daadi died, I had trouble forgiving." Her throat tightened, not wanting to let the words out. But she had to speak them. "I knew it wasn't Gideon's fault that he lived when Daadi died, but I was angry, and I blamed him for it."

Becky didn't speak, but Rachel knew she was listening with all her heart.

"It was wrong, that not forgiving, and it hurt me even more than it hurt Gideon. I had to find a way to forgive and let go of the hurt."

"How, Mammi? How did you do it?" Becky tilted her face back, looking up into Rachel's eyes, her whole body seeming to yearn for an answer.

"I talked to Bishop Mose. And you know what he told me? He said that I had to act as if I'd forgiven, no matter what I was feeling. He said I should think of what I would do if I had forgiven, and do that. He said the feelings would follow. And he was right."

Becky's forehead knotted as she struggled to understand.

Rachel stroked the wrinkles gently with her finger. She had to concentrate on teaching forgiveness now, and leave the difficult lesson of when it was right to tell on a friend for another day.

"What would you do if you really had forgiven Elizabeth for telling on you?"

"I would go to the quilting and play with her." That answer was obvious.

"Then that is what you must do."

Becky hesitated for a long moment. Then she gave a nod, slid off the bed, and fished for her shoe.

*Have I said the right things, Father? More important, have I shown her forgiveness by my actions?*

Forgiving others wasn't easy. Gideon's painful confession, never absent from her thoughts, demanded her attention. Gideon had to master an even more difficult task. He had to learn to forgive himself.

*The* living room at Leah's seemed about to burst from the sheer volume of conversation as the women gathered around the quilting frames. Leah's mamm was there, of course, and one of her aunts. Two of her sisters-in-law, also—Barbara, plump and cheerful, had her six-month-old on a blanket at her feet, while Myra divided her attention between the quilting frame and the boppli who slept in a cradle near her chair.

Leah had placed herself and Rachel at the second quilting frame with her other sister-in-law, Esther, newly returned from her wedding trip, and one of their running-around friends from school, Naomi Miller.

Was Leah thinking about the person who wasn't there as she handed round spools of white thread? Rachel knew how much Leah grieved over her baby sister, Anna, lost to the English world. How happy it would make her if Anna walked in the door right now, to take her proper place around the quilting frame. But it wouldn't happen, not today.

Rachel thought of Johnny. Maybe never.

She was not nearly as accomplished a quilter as some of the others were, so maybe she'd best focus on her work.

Esther glanced toward the other frame. "They are going to have theirs done long before we do, that's sure."

"The fastest quilters are all on one quilt." Leah sent a teasing look at her mamm's frame. "Maybe we should make them send one over to us."

"Or tie one of Barbara's hands behind her back," Naomi said.

"Ach, I have one hand occupied with the boppli as it is." Barbara chuckled, her good nature unimpaired by the teasing. "Wait until you all have babes to deal with."

Since both she and Naomi had children, that comment was obviously aimed at Leah and Esther. Leah ignored it, her hand swooping smoothly over the surface of the quilt, while Esther's rosy cheeks grew even pinker. Had Esther come back from her wedding trip pregnant? If so, she didn't seem inclined to announce it with her mother-in-law sitting at the other frame.

The chatter proceeded as quickly, as the tiny, almost invisible stitches traced their pattern across the quilt. No one would admit it, but each one wanted her stitches to be as perfect as possible. Not a matter of pride, Rachel hoped. Probably the others felt, as she did, that this baby quilt was a precious gift for the child Leah had never expected to have.

Rachel caught Leah's gaze across the frame, the delicate pattern stretched between them. Leah smiled, her eyes glowing with a kind of inward light, and Rachel's heart lifted. It wouldn't be long until Leah held that babe in her arms instead of beneath her heart.

By the time Rachel rose to follow Leah into the kitchen to set out the midmorning snack, the other group, for all their talking, had predictably made more progress than they had.

"They're showing us up," she murmured to Leah as they reached the kitchen.

"Let them." Leah glanced back fondly at the women around the frame. "It will give Barbara something wonderful gut to brag about."

Anything that kept Barbara focused on her own business instead of everyone else's was just fine. They both knew that, though they'd try not to say it. Leah exhibited endless patience with her tactless sister-in-law—far more than Rachel would be able to manage, she feared.

Leah lifted the coffeepot from the stove. "I'm so glad to see Becky and Elizabeth playing happily together again."

Rachel's fingers tightened, crumbling a piece of cinnamon-walnut streusel cake. "Leah, I am so sorry. I didn't even realize that Becky was holding a foolish grudge until today. I should have known. I should have seen."

"How could you if she didn't want you to?" Leah was calmly reassuring. "Now, don't start blaming yourself for that. Think of all the things we kept from our mamms when we were their age."

"I suppose so, but still." She couldn't dismiss her sense of guilt that easily. "Sometimes I think that Ezra was much better with the children than I am. I don't remember having these kinds of problems when he was with us."

Leah set the coffeepot on a hot pad and snitched a corner of the coffee cake Rachel had broken, popping it in her mouth. "Of course not. They were smaller then, and their problems were smaller. The bigger they get, the bigger the problems. My mamm always says that, and I'm beginning to think she's right about a lot of things."

"Maybe when we're as old as our mothers, we'll be as wise."

"You're already a wise mother." Leah patted her hand. "Never think that you're not. You're just not perfect yet, is all."

"That's certain sure." Rachel smiled, feeling some of the burden slip away just from sharing it. It was always that way with her and Leah. She hoped their girls would be as fortunate in their friendship. "Will I tell the others to come in now?"

At Leah's nod, Rachel went to the doorway to announce that the food was ready. The quilters flowed into the kitchen on a current of talk and laughter.

Rachel found herself next to Naomi as she took a slice of rhubarb coffee cake.

"How are the children doing?" she asked in an undertone. Two of Naomi's three children had the Crigler-Najjar syndrome that affected too many of the Amish, and it was always possible that Naomi didn't want to talk about it today.

"Doing well, denke." Naomi's smile blossomed. "We are wonderful lucky to have the clinic where your brother works. They are saving lives, I know, and one day perhaps they will find a cure."

Rachel's heart warmed to hear Johnny spoken of so naturally. Before she could respond to Naomi, Barbara said her name.

"Rachel, I hear you and Isaac are on the outs these days." Barbara's smile was as cheerful as if she were talking about the weather. "He can be a stubborn one, can't he?"

Several women sent sidelong glances toward Barbara and then looked studiously at their plates.

Rachel shrugged, hoping Barbara would take the hint.

"Your raspberry cake is delicious, Barbara," Naomi interrupted forcefully. "You must let us have the recipe."

"Ja," Leah's mother said. "It's wonderful gut."

Barbara flushed with pleasure. "I will. But I was talking to Rachel about Isaac."

"I don't think Rachel wants to talk about that." Leah's mamm tried to rein in her daughter-in-law, and Rachel shot her a look of gratitude.

"Ach, I'm just saying what everyone is thinking," Barbara insisted. "Naturally Isaac feels he has a right to interfere as head of the family. But if Rachel were to marry again, then it would be none of his business."

She stopped, finally, smiling as if pleased that she'd come up with the solution to all of Rachel's difficulties.

Several people tried to say something, anything, to cover the moment. If she'd been dipped into a pot of boiling apple butter, Rachel couldn't have felt hotter.

The spatula Leah was holding clattered to the table, startling everyone to silence. "That's enough." Leah's voice snapped in the tone she had used in the schoolroom on the rare occasions when her students had gotten out of line. "Barbara, whether it is Isaac's business or not, it is certainly not yours!"

Silence. Stillness. No one moved, no one spoke. Impossible to tell what they were thinking. Shocked, most probably. For Leah, calm, patient Leah, to lose her temper—Rachel could not have been more surprised if the table had cracked under the weight of all those dishes.

Barbara laughed. An unconvincing sound, but at least she made the effort. "Ach, I'm sorry. I'm talking out of turn again, I guess. Levi's always telling me to think before I speak, but I can't get in the way of doing it."

"Just keep trying," Naomi said, surprising them and reducing the tension in the kitchen by a few degrees. "Maybe it'll take."

To give Barbara credit, tactless as she was, she took the rebukes gracefully. "Forgive me, Rachel." She looked as if she wanted to say more but firmly closed her mouth on the temptation.

"Of course," Rachel murmured, grateful that the others had begun chatting, maybe a little desperately, on whatever popped into their heads.

The moment was over. She could forget it, couldn't she?

Perhaps not. Because if Barbara was saying it, that meant other people were thinking it, and she couldn't doubt that the person most of them had in mind for her future husband was Gideon. And aside from her own confused feelings, one thing was clear. Gideon would never risk loving again.

*If* he could have gotten out of it, Gideon would not be helping to set up for a singing at the Miller barn. He'd have been taking refuge from his scrambled thoughts by working, as hard and fast as his body would let him.

But getting out of it wasn't an option. He'd agreed to help chaperone the singing, and that's what he would do. Aaron had come along, ostensibly to help, although he was more likely to enjoy a nice long chat with Nathan Miller instead of looking after a barn full of young people.

"Watch out." He swung his end of a plank out of the way of several running kinder who were as excited by the singing as their older brothers and sisters were.

Aaron grunted, taking a firmer grip on the long board as he headed for the barn. "Time those young ones were in bed."

"Too excited."

Gideon paused just inside the barn doors. The barn had been scrubbed as clean for the singing as it would be for worship. But instead of the backless benches they'd have for worship, Nathan and a couple of boys were creating long tables with planks set on sawhorses in the middle of the barn floor. More sawhorses waited along one side, where they'd need tables for the food.

"Come on, let's get this done with," Aaron grumbled.

"Anyone would think you'd never gone to a singing. Never kept your eyes peeled for that special girl you were hoping to see. Hoping she was looking for you, too."

His brother grinned, hefting one end of the plank onto a sawhorse. "You're sounding like a youngster yourself tonight. Ja, I remember my rumspringa. But I wouldn't go back and live those days over again for anything. Too much time spent worrying about what the girls were thinking, that's certain sure."

"You didn't have to worry. Lovina was set on you from the first grade, as I recall."

"Maybe. But she led me a merry dance along the way, I'll tell you that."

Nathan finished the table he was working on and came over to them. "Denke." He rapped the board with his knuckles. "We can use more tables, if everyone comes we're expecting."

"More planks in the wagon," Aaron said. He nudged Gideon's shoulder. "Komm, Gid. Let's get the work done."

"I'll send the boys to do that." Nathan beckoned to the teenage boys who were helping him. "Here, you two. Go and fetch the rest of the planks from Aaron's wagon. Schnell."

Jostling each other, the two of them set off at a run.

"Better for you to do the setup," Nathan said. "They're so

ferhoodled over the singing that any tables they knocked together would probably collapse halfway through. Glad you came, both of you."

"Gideon's a favorite of the younger crowd when it comes to chaperones. They must figure he's more likely to let them get away with things than us old folks with families."

Aaron didn't mean anything by his careless words. Gideon knew that. Still, they stung with the reminder. He didn't think he gave any outward sign, but his brother's face changed.

"Gid, I didn't mean—"

"It's okay. Let's get on with the work."

"Right." Aaron slid a long bench into place alongside the table Nathan had completed. "So, how is young Joseph's doe? Did she kid yet?"

Gut thing he was bent over to pick up one of the hay bales that Nathan was setting around the edges of the singing area. By the time he straightened, he made sure his expression didn't give anything away.

"Ja, she came through it fine. Twins, she had."

Fortunately a wave of boys came in just then, all of them helping to carry the planks. Pressed into service by their friends, no doubt. The barn was suddenly noisy enough and busy enough that Aaron wouldn't be asking Gideon any more questions.

Not that he'd been keeping it from Aaron. The trouble was that talking about the kidding brought that night back too vividly. Made him too aware of everything he'd thought and felt and said.

He'd told Rachel things he'd never confessed to a living soul. Was it the circumstances that had loosened his tongue? Or was it Rachel herself, with her caring eyes and her stubborn chin?

It didn't matter. He tossed a bale into place with unnecessary vigor. What he felt for her didn't count next to what had happened to him. He'd twice survived when he'd gladly have died in place of others. Even if he could forgive himself, he wouldn't risk living through that again.

And yet . . .

The yearning was there, deep in his heart. He had to find some way to deal with that.

The level of noise in the barn had steadily risen. Abruptly, it lowered—not ceasing, but changing in quality. Gideon glanced toward the door. The girls were coming in. Demurely, for the most part, in pairs or in giggling groups, they filed into the barn, stealing glances at this boy or that.

For a few minutes neither boys nor girls made a move. Then they began to drift toward the tables, the girls' dresses like flowers in the lantern light. The boys moved, too, in an awkward surge, as if in silent argument over who would go first. The girls took their places along one side of the table; the boys filed in opposite them.

A moment of silence, and then the high, clear notes of a familiar hymn soared toward the rafters. The boys, a little slower, joined in, and the sound grew richer, fuller.

Gideon realized he was holding his breath, and he let it out. Foolish, he supposed, to be so touched by the moment. They would spend the next couple of hours singing, with a lot of covert flirting thrown in. Then it would be time for the food, which was already appearing on the tables against the wall—eating, talking, maybe some discreet smooching in dark corners.

Some of them, the older ones, would pair off, with the boy driving the girl home if he was lucky enough to have a courting buggy. And in the fall, it might be that marriages would be announced.

Some of these very young folks, Gideon had no doubt, were engaging in riskier rumspringa behavior. Their parents, indeed their whole community, would turn their eyes aside and pray, trusting that God would bring them back to the fold in time. And mostly, it worked.

He stretched, tired. Aaron had already disappeared. Nathan, too, most likely. Duty said he should stay, but he could at least get something to drink and pull up a hay bale, while he was at it.

Cold jugs of cider, homemade root beer, and lemonade had already been placed on the table, along with trays of cookies. The rest of the food, tons of it, would be brought out from the kitchen before too long. He poured a glass of cider, snagged a couple of snickerdoodles, and headed for the nearest hay bale.

He rounded the end of the table and nearly collided with the woman carrying a tray full of moon pies. "Rachel." He steadied her quickly, dropping the cookies as he did. "I didn't know you were coming tonight."

She looked equally surprised to see him. "Naomi talked me into it." The tray wobbled a little, and he helped her set it down. "I must be clumsy tonight. I've knocked your snickerdoodles to the floor. Let me get you more."

"Leave it. I really just wanted a drink anyway." He lifted the cup and drained it quickly, the cider tart and cold on his tongue.

"You were helping to set up, I guess."

He nodded, reminding himself that he needed to deal with these foolish fancies he had where Rachel was concerned. If he had any brains, he'd make an excuse and walk off.

But Rachel's eyes glowed in the lantern light, and her head was tilted back to look at him, as if she really was glad she'd walked into him tonight.

She nodded toward the singers. "Remember when we were the ones sitting at those tables?" Her eyes went soft with the remembering. "We'd pretend we were concentrating on the songs, when instead all we could think of was each other."

His throat tightened. He did not want to remember, but he couldn't hurt her by saying so.

"You and Ezra were paired off right from the start, I remember." He hesitated. "Does that bother you, to think of how you were then?"

She tilted her head to the side, considering. Several other women came through the door with trays, and he guided her a step or two back, where they were out of the way of traffic. Out of the light, too, it seemed, but he could still make out her features.

"A few months ago it would have," she said. "But now—well, now it seems I can think of those happy times with joy, not pain." She put one hand on his arm as if eager to make him understand. "I've made my peace with Ezra's dying, maybe. Seems as if that's opened my heart to remember and cherish."

"I'm glad." He muttered the words. Did she really feel that? Or was she trying to fool herself into thinking that was true?

"Gideon." She said his name softly, her fingers insistent on his arm, so that it seemed he could feel her touch to his very bones. "Don't you see? You can't fight the pain. You have to walk through it and reach for the other side."

She was looking up at him, her tilted face very close to his, her eyes pleading. She wanted, so much, to heal his pain. And he wanted . . .

Without letting himself think, he lowered his face to hers and claimed her lips. He felt the sudden intake of her breath, inhaled the scent of her skin. Only their lips and their hands touched, but he was on fire with longing to hold her, protect her, love her—

The word jolted him back a step. He stared at her. Then, before he could say or do anything to make it worse, he spun and walked out the open door into the dark.

# Chapter Seventeen

*Worship* had ended, and folks were gathering to talk over the week's events, as always. How many of them were talking about her?

Rachel shepherded the children toward the picnic tables that were set up under the trees at Aaron and Lovina's farm. Prideful, that's what it was, to imagine that she was the topic of people's conversations. They had more important things on their minds than her little problems, didn't they?

"Rachel, over here," Mamm called, and she veered thankfully in her direction.

What if the rumors were true, and Isaac had talked to Bishop Mose and the ministers about her? That didn't necessarily mean they'd agree with him. At least that was what Daad said, and the strength of his support warmed her like the sun on her back.

"Can we go and play until the meal is ready, Mammi?" Becky tugged at her apron. "I want to see Elizabeth."

"Go, then, but mind you come straight back when it's time to eat." At least Becky's relationship with Elizabeth was mended, and that was certainly something to be thankful for. "Mary and I will be with Grossmutter."

Mary went running to her grandmother, and Rachel followed quickly.

"I'll just go and see if Lovina needs any help in the kitchen, if you don't mind watching the little ones."

"Ja, go." Mamm scooped Mary up onto her lap, tickling her. "We'll be fine, ain't so, Mary?"

Before she could let herself glance at Gideon, who stood talking with his brother, she hurried toward the kitchen. Surely she had enough things worrying her to make it easy to avoid thinking about those moments at the singing with Gideon. Not so.

The kitchen swirled with activity as women grabbed filled trays and carried them outside, and fortunately the busyness made it possible to join the parade without getting caught up in conversation with Lovina. Lovina's quick curiosity might easily lead her to detect that something was different, just through an unwary word or expression.

No one must know what had happened between her and Gideon. Rachel could only pray no one had seen. Probably the young folks had been far too wrapped up in each other to notice anything about their elders. And surely, if anyone had seen, she'd have intercepted some knowing glances by this time.

She put the tray down, narrowly avoiding a collision with two running children. When she looked up, Gideon was standing a few feet away.

Her heart thudded against her ribs. He was going to speak to her, and she'd have to reply without reliving that moment when his lips had touched hers.

He gave her a curt, unsmiling nod, and walked away, joining

a group of men who seemed to be discussing Aaron's goats, to judge from their gestures.

Carefully she straightened the tray she'd set on the table, as if the success of the meal depended on its alignment. Gideon's actions had made it only too clear that he regretted that kiss, regretted it so much, in fact, that he couldn't even come and greet her properly.

While as for her—she pressed her fingers hard against the wooden tabletop. For her it had been an awakening. It had brought to life feelings she'd never thought to have again. And now what was she to do with them?

"Daughter?" Her father touched her arm, and she hadn't even seen him approaching. "Bishop Mose is coming to speak with us."

A taut cord twisted inside her. Never would she expect to dread a conversation with the man she loved so dearly. At least Daadi stood at her elbow, waiting with her.

"Amos, Rachel," he greeted them. "A fine day. Everyone is grateful once we can have our meal outside, ain't so?"

Rachel opened her lips to reply, but her father spoke first.

"It might be that you should come to the house to talk to our Rachel." He stood very stiffly, his lean face seeming drawn against the bones.

Bishop Mose, on the other hand, looked as relaxed as if there was nothing on his mind but the weather. "Come now, Amos. A call from the bishop is just what I'm trying to avoid. If Rachel and Isaac have a bit of a disagreement, seems to me it's best to settle it quietly among ourselves, rather than dealing with it in church."

To stand in front of the congregation with Isaac, to confess that she was at odds with a brother—anything was better than that.

"If Isaac Brand thinks—" Daad began, but she put her hand on his arm to quiet him.

"I agree with Bishop Mose. Much better to settle things quiet-like if we can." *If.*

"That's gut, that is." Bishop Mose chuckled a little. "No need for everyone to know what we're talking about, is there? Now, you just tell me what you have to say. Isaac seems to have a whole list of complaints, but the only one I can see that affects the brotherhood is the idea that you'd sell to an Englischer, instead of one of us."

She took a deep breath, trying to compose her mind. "I'm not wanting to sell at all. That's the thing that has Isaac upset. He feels I can't run the farm. He wants me to sell it to him for Caleb."

For an instant she thought of telling Bishop Mose about the accidents—accidents that could be aimed at convincing her she couldn't manage the farm. But that would come dangerously close to accusing a brother. She couldn't. It would be a failure of faith to do so.

A small frown puckered the bishop's white eyebrows. "Where does the Englischer come in, then?"

"Thomas Carver, the dairy owner, offered to buy the herd. He wants only to lease the barn and pastures, not buy." How many times had she explained this now? "He's pushing me for an answer."

"And do you have one for him?"

"No." She met Bishop Mose's gaze. "It's not what I want. You know that. But I have to think what will be best for the children."

Relief filled his eyes behind the wire-rimmed glasses. "Gut, gut. If you haven't committed to Mr. Carver, let me see what I can do. I'll talk to Isaac, try to get him to think, see if there's not some other solution. See that it's a bad thing, straining the bonds of family over a farm. All right?"

"Ja." Her lips trembled, and she pressed them together.

He patted her hand. "Don't worry so much. As for your nursery business—well, seems like I've invested in that already, ain't so?" His eyes twinkled. "No one can object when your family is supporting you." He glanced toward her father.

For an instant Daad didn't say anything. Then he took a step closer to Rachel. "Ja. We do."

"Well, then." Bishop Mose studied her face, his callused hand resting on hers. "See if you can make peace with Isaac, child. It's not gut for brothers and sisters to disagree."

"I'll try." She would, because she agreed with everything the bishop had said.

But knowing Isaac, she feared there might be no compromise he'd be willing to consider. Then what? Did she give up her dream to keep the peace?

*Gideon* came back to work on the windmill the next day as calmly as if nothing at all had happened between them. Rachel was hanging laundry on the line when his buggy pulled in. He slid down, and if he hesitated when he saw that she was outside, he didn't let it show.

He started toward her, and Joseph came running from the barn, throwing himself against Gideon's legs. He used to do that with Ezra, and the memory squeezed her heart.

"And what are you doing home from school today? Did

Teacher Mary kick you out for misbehaving?" Gideon took off Joseph's hat, ruffled his hair, and clapped the hat back on his head again.

Joseph giggled. "Teacher Mary wouldn't do that. She had a meeting today with teachers from all the other schools in the district, so we're staying home to help Mammi."

"Most of the helping so far has involved those goats." At least the goats made for a safe topic of conversation, and they were eased past the difficult spot.

"The kids are growing like weeds. They want to eat all the time." Joseph babbled on about the goats, giving her a moment to catch her breath.

It didn't seem to do her much good. She was still staring at Gideon, loving the way he gave Joseph all his attention, and then handing out equal shares to Becky and little Mary, when they came running over.

Gideon's quiet stability had always been a counterpoint to Ezra's livelier nature. Maybe he'd been a bit eclipsed by him. Now she seemed to notice his gentle strength more every day.

Not that it mattered. Gideon had made it clear that he regretted kissing her. He'd pulled away, and he'd clearly never talk about it.

Unless she did. The very thought embarrassed her. If she couldn't think about it without feeling her cheeks grow hot, she'd certainly never do it.

"Go on now." She made shooing motions at her children. "Gideon has work to do, and so do you."

"You'll visit Dolly and the kids before you go home, won't you?" Joseph had to get in one last question.

"They're beautiful," Becky added.

"Ja, I will." Gideon slung his tool belt around his waist and fastened it. "Before I go."

They ran off, satisfied. Rachel turned back to her sheets, picking one up by the corners and shaking it before starting to peg it to the line. Gideon headed for the windmill, his shoulders maybe a little stiffer than normal.

The sheet seemed to be wrinkling in her hands, and she shook it out again. She couldn't. Her cheeks burned again. But she was going to.

Quickly, before she could change her mind, she dropped the sheet back into the basket and strode across the grass to the base of the windmill.

Gideon snapped the harness into place before he looked at her. "Is there something wrong, Rachel?"

"No. Ja." She stopped, took a breath, tried again. "We should talk about what happened between us at the singing."

His fingers gripped the harness for an instant, and then he went on with his preparation to go up the windmill tower, avoiding her eyes. "Best to forget it."

"I don't want to forget it." A sharp little edge of anger caught at her.

"It shouldn't have happened." His tone roughened. "That's all."

"No, that's not all."

He didn't respond, just went on preparing to climb the tower. No doubt thinking that he'd be safe from her harping if he did that.

"Gideon, listen to me." Her fingers tingled with the desire to grab his arm and shake him. "It's one thing if you regret—" She had to stop, swallow. "—if you regret kissing me because you don't care about me."

He jerked as if he'd been hit, and somehow that gave her courage. If what she said could have an effect on him, it was worth saying.

"But it's another thing if it's because of Ezra. We're both free, and—"

He swung to face her, and the bleakness in his eyes stole her breath. "I'm not free, Rachel. I'm not."

He turned away just as quickly, scaling the windmill tower as if a pack of wolves snarled at his heels.

She watched him, her nails biting into her hands. He was not free. He was right about that.

Gideon was imprisoned by his grief and guilt as surely as those early martyrs had been imprisoned by godless governments. It hurt her heart, as much for him as for herself. Unless God worked a miracle in Gideon's soul, he would never be free.

*Walk away. Get back to work. Don't let anyone see you watching him with tears in your eyes.*

But even when she'd returned to her wet clothes, she couldn't keep her rebellious gaze from going back to him.

He'd reached the platform at the top of the windmill now. He stood there as easily as if he stood on the ground, silhouetted against the sky.

A violent crack sounded. Almost faster than she could comprehend, the platform crumbled beneath his feet, his body plummeting toward the ground.

She was frozen, caught as if ice encased her feet, unable to help, to cry out . . .

The harness caught him, stopping the mad plunge, slamming

his body against the windmill frame. He dangled there, limp and very still.

Had she screamed? Her throat hurt as if she had, and she was running across the damp grass, heart pounding so loud in her ears that she couldn't hear, couldn't think . . .

She reached the windmill tower and clung to it, looking up, shielding her eyes to try to see him against the sun. He wasn't moving. She couldn't see his face.

"Gideon! Are you hurt? Can you hear me?"

Nothing. She grabbed the first crossbar. Gideon climbed up so easily, it seemed, but could she do it?

Becky barreled into her, her breath catching on sobs. Joseph came behind her, tears streaming down his face, and then Mary, not understanding what was happening but crying anyway.

Rachel's fists clenched. She had to get control of herself, for Gideon's sake, for the children's, too. This was not the time to fall apart.

"Stop the crying, now." Her voice was so sharp that the children were startled into silence.

"We must work together now to help Gideon." Calmly, calmly, don't frighten them any more. "Becky, you're the fastest. Run to Onkel Isaac's and get help. Schnell!"

Becky nodded and took off across the lawn, her feet flying.

"What must I do to help Gideon, Mammi?" Joseph stood tall, awaiting her orders.

"You will help me put the ladder up." Pray God they were strong enough to raise it. "Mary, you must go back five steps and sit on the ground."

Mary sniffled a little, but she did as she was told. Joseph rushed to help her with the ladder. Fortunately the men had left it lying on the ground next to the windmill tower.

Together they grabbed it. Heavy, it was so heavy. How would they ever get it up?

*Please, God, please, God, give us Your strength.*

Joseph strained, his small face pale. Rachel's arms screamed with pain as she struggled to raise the ladder. They forced it against the first crossbar.

"Stop a second. Rest." She tilted her head back. Was it her imagination, or had Gideon moved? "We're coming, Gideon. Hang on!"

"I'm ready, Mammi." Joseph took his position, hands braced against the side of the ladder. "We'll get it this time."

*Please, God.*

She grabbed, pulled, muscles crying. The ladder lifted, swung, and slammed into place against the tower.

"Gut." She shook it, making sure it was stable, and started up.

"Let me come, Mammi," Joseph cried.

"Stay where you are. You must be ready, in case I need you to run for anything."

Knowing he would obey, she climbed, pressing down the queasiness that cramped her stomach. Gideon needed her.

A few more rungs brought her within arm's reach of him. "Gideon." She reached out, grabbed his arm, and was relieved to feel it warm against her hand. "Answer me."

Slowly, very slowly, he turned his head. "What . . ."

"Hush, now. You're going to be all right. Just stay still."

He blinked, shaking his head and wincing with pain. A huge lump rose on his forehead, and he moved his hand, as if to touch it. His whole body swung at the movement, and awareness and alarm dawned in his eyes.

"Easy." How long could the harness hold his weight? *Please,*

*please, don't let it give way.* "The platform broke, but the harness is holding you."

He moved, as if to assess the situation, and something above them creaked ominously. She didn't dare take her eyes off him long enough to see what it was.

"Can you grab hold of the frame with your right hand?"

He tried to move it and a spasm of pain went through him. "Don't think so."

"It's all right."

She drew him a little closer, so that his left hand could touch the ladder. He fumbled for a moment and then gripped it. She could reach him better now, and she anchored her arm around his waist.

He tried to pull free. "Don't want to take you with me."

If he fell, he meant. But he wouldn't. He wouldn't.

"Be still." She spoke as if he were one of the children. "Just be still. Everything will be all right."

*Let my words be true, Father. Protect us.*

And even as she prayed, she recognized the truth. She didn't just care about Gideon. She loved him with all her heart.

"Mammi, they're coming!" Joseph's shout was triumphant. "They're almost here!"

*If* everyone would stop poking and prodding him, he'd feel a lot better. Gideon tried to evade the light that the paramedic kept shining in his eyes, but the man held his face as if he were a child.

"I am fine." His voice sounded husky and uncertain, even to himself. "Just bumps and bruises is all," he added, putting more force to the words.

"Let the man examine you."

Rachel stood next to the porch steps where he sat. A stranger might think her perfectly possessed, but her eyes bore lines of strain around them, and her hands were knotted under the protective cover of her apron.

"Ja, that's right." Isaac, who'd come racing across the fields, his wagon hastily loaded with a ladder and extra timbers, planted his hand against the porch railing. "You didn't look but half-alive when we got you down."

Fortunately the paramedic didn't understand Pennsylvania Dutch, so he didn't know Isaac's opinion of his condition.

"Did you lose consciousness at all?" The man tucked the penlight into the pocket of his jacket.

"I don't think—" he began.

"He was out for several minutes." Rachel cut him off. "As long as it took Joseph and me to get the ladder up. He was starting to come round when I reached him."

"How you and the boy managed to put that heavy ladder up, I'll never understand."

Isaac actually sounded admiring. Apparently he'd forgotten his quarrel with Rachel in the excitement. Too bad he wouldn't stay that way—it would save Rachel some heartache.

"God gave us strength," she murmured softly.

By the time the paramedic was finished, a sizable crowd had gathered around—Isaac, William, and Isaac's two oldest boys had been the first to rush to help, of course. Someone must have sent for Aaron, because he was even now checking out the wreckage of the platform. Lovina had come with him, and she'd gathered up the children and swept them into the house for cookies and milk.

Every other minute, it seemed someone else turned up, demonstrating the amazing power of the Amish grapevine. Much as Gideon appreciated the love they showed, he'd just as soon be left alone. But he didn't figure that would happen anytime soon.

"Bruises, you're going to have plenty of those." The paramedic finished writing something on a clipboard. "Suppose you let us take you in to the hospital to have that head looked at. Just in case it's a concussion."

He shook his head and instantly regretted it. "No need. I'm fine. Nothing is broken." He flexed his right hand, wrapped in an elastic bandage. It was swollen already, and he wouldn't be doing any carpentry work for a while. "I'd rather go home."

"If they think you should go . . ." Rachel's voice died away. She'd be thinking that she didn't have the right to insist.

"We'll keep a gut watch on him tonight." Aaron joined the group. "If anything seems not right, we'll get someone to drive us in to the hospital."

The man nodded and thrust the clipboard at him. "Sign here."

Gideon scribbled his name, barely listening to the rest of the instructions. Instead he watched his brother's face, but Aaron wasn't giving anything away.

When the paramedics began gathering up their equipment, folks moved back to give them room. Aaron leaned in next to him.

"You know that platform . . ."

"I know." He kept his voice low. "Knew the instant I put my weight on it, but don't say anything."

"Don't say anything about what?" Rachel demanded.

"Ach, it's nothing." Aaron tried to turn her concern away.

"It's the platform, isn't it?" she demanded, her voice ringing out above the sound of the departing van. "That's why you were up there looking at it for so long. Someone did this."

Isaac put his hand on her arm. "Rachel, you're imagining things. No one would do a thing like that."

She shook the hand away. "Wouldn't they? And I suppose no one would let the draft horse out at night, or damage the roof of the grain shed. No one would do any of those things."

"Rachel, don't—" Gideon saw where she was headed and tried to stop her.

"Except someone who wanted to convince me to sell the farm."

Isaac's mouth sagged. He took a step away from her. "You . . . think about what you're saying. I couldn't—"

"He didn't!" The voice was so shrill that for a moment he didn't recognize it. Then William pushed his way to the front of the group, his face white, his eyes tormented. "It was my f-f-fault. I did it, n-n-no one else."

"William—" Rachel whirled toward the boy. "No! What are you saying?"

"I'm s-s-sorry, I'm so sorry." Tears welled over in his eyes, so that he looked more Joseph's age than nearly a man grown.

Isaac caught him by the shoulder. "You don't know what you're saying. You couldn't do such a thing."

"I did." He scrubbed his face with his knuckles, as if trying to force back the tears.

"Why, William?" Rachel's lips trembled. "Why would you hurt me that way?"

"N-n-not—" He stopped, shook his head in frustration. "Not hurt you." He seemed to force the words out. "I w-wanted you to n-n-need me. Depend on m-m-me. Not Gid."

Shocked, grieved faces looked from William to Gideon. When one hurt, they all hurt.

"I d-d-didn't mean you to get hurt so bad. I'm s-s-sorry. I'll do anything t-to make amends."

Gideon couldn't seem to speak. Rachel was the one who needed help and comforting right now. She was stiff, rigid, looking as if she'd shatter to pieces if anyone touched her.

Isaac reached toward her, but then drew his hand back. Maybe he saw in her what Gideon did. "I'm sorry, Rachel. I don't know what to say. I hope you and Gideon can forgive this."

Bishop Mose cleared his throat. "This will have to go before the church, William. You understand that, don't you?"

William bobbed his head. He would kneel before the church, confess his fault, and bear the punishment they agreed upon. Then it would be over.

But not for Rachel. Gideon needed to do something—something that would help to heal this breach, something that would take away the pain Rachel felt at this betrayal by the boy she loved.

"William." The boy swung toward him at the sound of his voice, but he kept his gaze on the ground. "You say you want to make amends, ain't so?"

He nodded, managing to lift his gaze to Gideon's feet, it seemed.

"Ser gut." He gestured with his bandaged hand. "I'm going to need a right hand if Rachel's windmill is to be finished. What do you say?"

Now the boy looked at him, hope dawning in his face. "Y-y-you'll let me help?"

"Ja." He deliberately stared at Isaac. Seemed as if Isaac, in his stubborn determination to get his own way, had contributed to all this mess. "If Isaac agrees."

"I agree," Isaac said. "That is only what's right."

Murmurs of agreement came from the others. The frozen chill began to leave Rachel's face.

"Ser gut," she murmured.

# Chapter Eighteen

Rachel patted Brownie as she slipped the harness into place on the mare. Brownie, with the ease of long practice, stepped back between the buggy shafts and waited patiently. If the mare had hands instead of hooves, she'd do it all herself, no doubt.

Rachel let her gaze slide cautiously to the windmill tower. In the days since Gideon's accident, she had struggled to accept the truth, and in some ways, it still felt impossible.

How could William, the little brother Ezra had loved and nurtured, the boy she'd treated as her brother, too, have done such a thing? Try as she might, she couldn't even picture him doing something to hurt her or the children.

*I wanted you to need me,* he'd cried. Her cheeks burned at the implication. That foolish proposal, which she turned away so lightly—he'd actually meant it. The poor boy thought himself in love with her.

She hadn't seen him or spoken to him since then. But today he was working on the windmill, attempting to be Gideon's right hand. It would be easy, so easy, to climb into the buggy and drive off to Leah's with no more than a wave. Easy, but not right. She should speak to him. Somehow, she had to find a way to deal with him.

And with Gideon. Could she talk to him without letting the love she felt show in her face? Or did he already guess?

She patted Brownie again. Then she turned and walked toward the tower.

Both men stood at the base. Gideon seemed to be demonstrating something to William. She'd face both of them at once.

But as she approached, William turned and hurried off toward the barn, ducking his head. Obviously she wasn't the only one dreading this meeting.

"I hoped to get things back to . . ." She let that die out. Gideon must know as well as she did that her relationship with William would change. "I wanted to express my forgiveness."

"You'll have to give him time. He's too embarrassed to talk to you right now, I'd say." Gideon put down the bolt and screw he was holding in his left hand. His right still wore the elastic bandage.

"Your hand—how is it?" She fought to keep too much emotion from coloring the words, but she couldn't look at him without seeing him dangling from the tower, dark and motionless against the sky.

"Better. I maybe could do this myself in another day, but it will do the boy gut to make amends."

He was the kind of man who would think that, even of someone who'd done him harm. How had it taken her so long to see what a gut man Gideon was?

"Ja, I think it will." Her voice had gone husky in spite of

herself. "He seems able to face you, and it was you he harmed the most, not me."

"William doesn't love me," he said.

The words, gently spoken as they were, stabbed her to the heart.

"William has been hurting all this time. I talked to him every day, and yet I didn't understand that. How could I have been so blind? I should have seen, should have talked to him about it."

"I doubt you could talk him out of loving you, Rachel." Gideon paused, seeming to weigh something in his mind. "You should know something that William confessed to me." He stared down at his bandaged hand. "William saw us, the night of the singing. He saw us kiss. That's why he damaged the windmill platform."

She couldn't speak, but she could feel the tide of embarrassment sweep through her.

Maybe misinterpreting her silence, Gideon hurried into speech again. "Understand, Rachel, he's miserable about it. Seeing me get hurt was enough to bring him to his senses."

She cleared her throat. "Gut." It was all she could manage.

"It will be better once he confesses at the next worship. Better for him, better for all of us."

The act of public confession was difficult, doubly so for William, with his stammer, to have to kneel and confess his fault before the church. If Bishop Mose thought the bann was justified for a time, all who were present would have to agree.

*Ich bin einig,* I am agreed, each one would say, with varying degrees of pain and sympathy.

And then, when it was over, William's sin would be as if it had never been.

"I should confess, too." The words burst out on a wave of pain. "I didn't see."

"That is foolish, Rachel. Yours is not the sin. You couldn't have known."

But she still felt it.

Gideon cleared his throat, maybe feeling that they'd waded into water that was too deep. "Are you better now? No one has seen you for the past few days, I hear."

"Ja." She forced a smile. "I must be all right. The advertisements are already in the paper about the nursery opening on Saturday, and there is much to do."

He nodded toward the buggy. "You're going to pick something up for the opening, then?"

"Not now. I'm on my way to Leah's. The family is going to a farm sale over near Fostertown, and I told Daniel I'd stay with her. And I must be off, or she'll be wondering where I am."

She turned away, but he stopped her with a hand on her arm. His touch seemed to heat her skin right through the fabric of her sleeve. He snatched his hand away. Did he feel it, too?

"One thing—I'll be finished up here in another day's work, probably, depending on the weather." He shot a glance at the clouds that were massing along the western horizon. "I start a new job next week, putting in windmills for Elias Bender."

She turned her face away on the words, hoping he couldn't see her expression. Well, what had she expected? He would finish the job for her and move on.

Her smile seemed to stretch her face. "We will not see so much of you then."

"No."

And that was it. They would be friends, and she must be content with that. Gideon didn't want anything more.

. . .

*"Are* you sure another batch of pretzels is really necessary?" Rachel paused before adding the butter to the pan of scalded milk. "Haven't we already made enough?"

They had been baking all afternoon, it seemed, and still Leah wasn't satisfied.

"We may as well do another while we're making them." Leah sprinkled coarse salt over a tray of pretzels and slid it into the oven, glancing at the clock to note the time. "I want to have a nice treat for Daniel and the children when they get home. And you must take some for your family, too."

"We'll have enough for most of Pleasant Valley, it seems to me." Rachel set the pan aside to cool a bit before adding the yeast. "Not that I don't enjoy making pretzels with you, but I think you're overdoing it already."

Leah touched the batch of pretzels that was cooling on a rack. "I have to be doing something. I've been cooped up too long. Every time I move, someone tells me to rest. The children are as bad as Daniel is."

"They love you," Rachel reminded her. "That's not a bad thing, having people who want to take care of you."

"I know." Leah's mouth curved in the smile that Rachel had come to think of as her "mother" look. "I just feel so restless today." She grabbed a cloth and began to wipe the table with quick, hard strokes.

"You know what I think, Leah Glick? I think this baby is going to arrive soon. I remember the day before Mary was born. Ezra found me in the cellar, rearranging all the canned food alphabetically."

That brought on the laughter she'd hoped for. Leah sank into a kitchen chair, chuckling. "Ach, I can just see you doing it. Well, if it is a sign, I'm glad of it. I'm ready to meet him or her." She patted her belly.

"At the risk of getting hit with a pretzel, I'm going to suggest you sit awhile. Have something to drink. Eat a pretzel."

"I am thirsty."

"I'll get it—" she began, but Leah had already gotten up again.

She poured a glass of tea from the pitcher on the counter and added a sprig of mint from the bowl on the windowsill. Rachel watched her, torn between amusement and frustration.

"Now will you sit down?"

"I will." Leah made her way back to the chair and took a sip. "I think we've talked about everything imaginable this afternoon except about the situation with William. Would you rather not?"

"It's all right." Rachel dried her hands slowly, staring out the window absently. The rain that had begun shortly after she arrived continued without pause. Her plants could use it. "It's just all so sad. Poor William. I should have seen he was getting too attached to me."

"I wondered how long it would take for you to start feeling that it was your fault," Leah said. "You are not responsible for William's emotional needs."

"I suppose not, but I wish I could help him. He's too embarrassed even to talk with me about it now."

"Isaac is embarrassed, too, according to what Daniel has heard. Has he come to talk with you?"

"No. I wouldn't expect him to."

"Maybe not." Leah considered that, frowning a little. "Still, I hear he's dropped his complaint to the bishop."

"He has? Are you sure? No one has said anything to me."

"Maybe no one wanted to bring it up, but I'm sure as can be. Daniel heard it direct from Bishop Mose."

"Well, that is a relief." Rachel sank down in the chair opposite Leah. "I haven't slept easy since I heard about it."

Leah patted her hand. "Now you can. Unless you've found something else to worry about."

"William, of course." She sighed. "I wish I could help him find a girl to love, but he wouldn't welcome my help."

"Much as we all like to matchmake, some things are better left to the Lord. William is still smarting from his jealousy of Gideon."

"Gideon is being so kind to him. I just wish he could be as forgiving to himself as he is to other people."

She bit her lip. She shouldn't have said that. It was Gideon's private business.

"You love him, don't you?" Leah's voice was gentle, filled with the love she shared so freely.

There was no use trying to pretend. Leah knew her too well.

"Ja, I do. But it's no use."

"Don't say that." Leah gripped her fingers. "You don't know that. Maybe Gideon thinks it's too soon after Ezra to say anything to you."

Rachel shook her head, her eyes filling with the tears she was determined not to shed. "It's not that. It's something deeper in himself that keeps him from loving again. All he wants from me is friendship. That's all he'll let himself want."

"Rachel—"

"No, don't." She managed a watery smile. "I know you want to encourage me, but this time it's no use. I know that now, and the best thing I can do is get over these feelings. So you see I really do know how William feels."

"I'm sorry." Only two words, but they bore a world of caring and sympathy.

"It will be all right." She glanced at the clock. "I'd best check on those pretzels."

"I'll do it," Leah said, predictably.

"Sit. I have it." Rachel pulled the tray out with a hot pad, glad of something to do that would change the subject. She set the tray on the waiting rack. "They're just perfect."

"Gut." Leah started to get up, one hand on the back of her chair. "I think—"

The chair rocked. Heartbeat rushing, Rachel reached toward her friend, but she was too late. Her hand grasped empty air, and Leah fell heavily to the floor.

"Leah!" Rachel rushed to kneel beside her. "Are you all right? Does it hurt anywhere?"

Leah shook her head, grimacing a little. "Only my pride is hurt, that's all. You'd think I could at least get up from a chair. I told you I was going to need a crane pretty soon."

"Take it easy." Rachel got one arm around her. "Slowly. Don't rush. I'll help you."

"I'm all—" Leah bit off the words with a gasp. She clutched her belly, eyes wide and frightened as she looked at Rachel. "The pain—Rachel—"

"It's going to be fine." She could only hope her words sounded more confident than she felt. "Is it a labor pain?"

Instead of answering, Leah grabbed Rachel's hand and put it on her belly. She felt the contraction, hard against her palm.

She forced a smile. "I guess so. I told you this baby would be coming soon."

"But—it shouldn't start this hard, should it?"

The contraction eased, and Rachel glanced automatically at

the clock. Keep her calm, that's what she had to do. Time the pains, and hope that nothing bad had happened when she fell. And pray that Daniel would come home soon.

"Everyone's different." She hoped she sounded reassuring. "Haven't you had any contractions at all today?"

"No."

"Now, stop thinking about all those descriptions in your books of how childbirth is supposed to happen. Remember, the baby didn't read any of them."

That brought a smile to Leah's face. "I guess not. Maybe I should try to get up, and we can start timing the contractions."

"I already have." Rachel slid her arm around Leah again. Hopefully she had enough time to get Leah comfortably situated before another contraction came. "Let's get you up and—"

She felt the contraction almost as soon as Leah did. Leah's face contorted as she struggled to remember her breathing exercises. "It's too fast," she gasped. "Rachel, why is it so fast?"

"You'll be fine," she soothed, stroking Leah's cheek. "You'll be fine, don't worry."

All very well to say don't worry, when her heart twisted with anxiety. Why was it this fast? In all the tales women told about their babies' births, she'd never heard of someone starting in labor with contractions so hard and so close together.

The contraction eased at last. Leah lay back, panting.

"Do you want to try to make it to a chair or the bed?"

Leah shook her head. "I'm afraid. Something is wrong."

"We don't know that." Rachel scrambled to her feet and grabbed a cushion from the rocker, returning to ease it under Leah's head. "But we need to tell someone what's happening. I'll help you through the next one, and then I'll run across the field to your parents' house . . ."

Leah was shaking her head. "No one's there. They all went to the sale, too." She grabbed Rachel's hand in an anguished grip. "What are we going to do?"

"We're going to be calm." Although she felt anything but calm inside. "Where is the nearest phone shanty? I'll have to go and call for help."

"My midwife's number is on the counter."

"Ja, I'll take it, but I think this babe is coming so fast that we can't wait for a midwife. Paramedics can get here quicker."

"I don't—" Another contraction cut off whatever Leah was going to say, and she clung to Rachel and breathed.

Murmuring nonsense, anything soothing that came into her mind, Rachel held her, stroking her while she watched the clock.

Leah lay back again, white and exhausted, and shook her head. "The phone is clear at the far side of my father's back pasture. It will take too long—Rachel, don't leave me. What if the baby came while you were gone?"

"I know, I know. But we need help—"

"Daniel will come soon. I know he will. The rain probably slowed him down. He'll go for help."

"Yes, yes." Anything to calm the panic in Leah's face.

*Father, guide me, please, guide me. If I make the wrong decision, I could put Leah and the baby in danger. Hold them in Your hands, Father. Keep them safe.*

"Pray for my baby," Leah whispered.

"I am."

"Out loud, so I can hear."

Rachel nodded. She stroked Leah's belly gently. "Our Father, we come to You now. We reach out for Your hand. We're afraid, and we need to feel Your presence. Be with us now, and protect Leah and her baby. Keep them safe and well."

*And show me what to do,* she added silently. *Please, Father, show me what to do.*

"You're going to be fine—" she began, and then stopped.

"A buggy!" Leah started up and then sank back. "Daniel—run and tell him."

Rachel scrambled to her feet and raced for the door. She plunged outside, to be hit by a shower of water as the wind blew the rain toward the porch.

"Rachel!" A man slid down from the buggy. But it wasn't Daniel. It was Gideon.

"*Your* mamm was worried. Asked me to check—" He stopped, registering the expression on Rachel's face. "What is it?"

Rachel grabbed his arm and tugged him to the door. "Leah's in labor."

He drew back instinctively. But that was foolish. He had to do what he could. "I'll go for help."

"Ja, you must. Her folks aren't home, so best to go to the nearest phone and call the paramedics." Still she pulled him into the kitchen. "First help me with Leah."

"Better I should go—"

Leah lay on the floor of the kitchen, her face contorting with pain. But he didn't see her—he saw Naomi, lying in the road . . .

Rachel rushed to Leah, grasping her hand. In another moment Leah sank back on a pillow, her face easing.

"Gideon is here. He'll call 911, but first he can help me get you onto the bed, so you'll be more comfortable." She glanced back at him, looking surprised, maybe at the fact that he'd backed himself flat against the door. "Komm."

That was a command, not a request. Forcing himself to focus, he strode to them and squatted down. "Show me what to do."

"We'll wait until after the next contraction. Then just slide your arms under her and lift her." She jerked a nod toward what he thought was a storage room next to the kitchen. "That's all ready for the delivery and the first day or two, so Leah won't have to go up the stairs."

Leah inhaled, eyes widening, and all Rachel's attention went back to her. "Here it comes."

He would have retreated, but Leah had grabbed his hand, squeezing it, and all he could do was hold on and send up wordless, incoherent prayers.

When the contraction finally eased, he felt as if he'd been put through a wringer.

"Now," Rachel said.

He slid his arms around Leah, half-afraid to touch her, and cradled her against him as he rose.

"In here." Rachel pushed the door open, moving swiftly to turn down the covers on the single bed that took up much of the small room. "This will be much better. You'll see."

She continued to talk, soothing Leah, he supposed, until she was settled on the bed. Leah sank back against the piled pillows, sighing.

"That's better."

"Ja." Rachel stroked her forehead. "You rest while I get a lamp. We'll need more light, since your boppli decided to come on such a gray day."

She caught Gideon's elbow and guided him back into the

kitchen. He had the sense that she barely knew it was him. Anybody would do in this situation.

"I'll go right away."

She didn't let go of him. "Be sure they understand that it's an emergency." She'd lowered her voice with an anxious glance at the door. "She fell, and the labor came on sudden and hard. Pains are only two minutes apart already. They must come at once."

*Something's wrong, Gideon.* Naomi's panicked voice sounded in his head. *Something's wrong. I'm going to lose the baby—I just know it. You have to get me to the hospital.*

"I'll make sure they understand." He clasped her hand in a quick, firm grip, but he couldn't find the right words. "Da Herr sei mit du," he murmured, and headed for the door. *The Lord be with you.*

He hit the steps at a run, crossed the yard, and threw himself into the buggy. Joss seemed to recognize the urgency, starting off instantly at a quick pace.

*Concentrate. Think about what you must do, not about the past. Never about the past.*

They reached the road and turned left, into the driving rain. Thank the gut Lord there weren't cars on the road, though if there had been, he might have flagged someone down, asked to use a cell phone.

Too much time explaining, probably. Get to the phone shanty, make the call. He knew just where it was, at the far end of Leah's parents' pasture, accessible by another narrow lane. After this, Daniel Glick would probably be putting one in considerably closer.

Unless he was mourning—

No. Don't think that, not now. Leah would be all right, her baby, too.

Rachel had been frightened. No one else would guess that, masked as it was behind the brisk command she'd taken of the situation. But he had known—had felt it in the grip of her hand, as if they were connected at a place deeper than words.

The rain drove in his face, stinging like ice. Joss plunged sturdily on.

Gideon narrowed his eyes. They'd passed the lane that led to the Beiler farmhouse. The one to the phone shanty would be coming up pretty quick.

With a blare of a horn, a car swept past him, sending up a sheet of water that nearly blinded him. He clenched his jaw to keep from saying something he shouldn't.

It had been raining that night, too. The road had been a black ribbon against the blacker fields, almost invisible in the downpour. Naomi had huddled, crying, on the seat, ducked down under the blanket. She wouldn't have seen the car coming at them, known it was going to hit them, known they were going to die—

His hands tightened on the lines, and Joss slowed. There was the lane. Do what he had to do. Forget the time when he'd done nothing but live.

The buggy jolted along the narrow lane, hardly more than a track in the field. Joss halted automatically at the shed, and Gideon jumped down and raced for it. Grabbed the phone, punched in 911. The operator answered immediately.

He stammered out the words, remembering what Rachel had said.

"We're sending a unit at once. If you stay on the line until they arrive—"

"I can't. I'm at a phone down the road. I must get back to them."

The words surprised him as he heard them come out of his mouth. He didn't want to go back.

But he would. Of course he would. Rachel and Leah and her baby needed him.

*Once* Gideon had gone, Rachel felt more alone than she ever had, even in the dark days after Ezra's death. Alone—with Leah and her unborn child depending on her.

She took a deep breath, giving herself a shake. Foolish, so foolish she was being. They weren't alone. God was with them. Leah and the baby were in His hands, not just hers.

"Now, then." She bent over Leah, trying to sound calm. "This baby is going to be fine, and you, too."

Leah's head moved restlessly on the pillow. "Are you sure? What if . . ."

She couldn't let Leah's mind travel down the path of all the things that could go wrong. "Trust, Leah. Just trust."

"I do, but—" Leah shook her head, managing a slight smile. "You're sure you know what to do?"

"Well, I did have three babies." She stroked her friend's belly. "That was a bit different from delivering someone else's, for sure, but at least I know what to expect."

Again she felt the contraction almost as soon as Leah did. Again they rode it out together.

When the contraction receded, Leah sank back against the pillow, face white.

"Rest now, just rest while I get things ready."

Thank the gut Lord Leah had planned on a home birth. Everything the midwife might need was ready at hand. Rachel moved quickly between the bed and the chest, busying her hands while trying to calm her mind. She'd told Leah she knew what to expect, but she didn't.

She stood still for a moment, a folded sheet in her hands, picturing herself at this point when Mary was born. Of course she'd had the midwife there and her own mother, too.

Gideon would bring help. She focused on that. He would.

And if the boppli arrived before the help did? *The Lord is my strength and stay.* Her heart spoke the words, and it seemed to fill with peace. *A very present help in time of trouble.*

Leah gasped, and Rachel hurried to help her through the contraction. Somehow, the peace didn't leave. She could feel it steadying her hands, calming her voice. God's peace flowed through her on a tide of love to Leah and the boppli, and she knew God would give her whatever strength she needed.

# Chapter Nineteen

It seemed an eternity until Rachel heard the thud of boots on the back porch and knew that Gideon was back. The back door swung open.

"Rachel?" He called her name, his voice strained. "The paramedics are on their way."

"Gut." She smiled down at Leah, cradling her babe in her arms, and went to the door so she could see his face when she said the news. "They will be just in time to check out Leah's baby girl."

"The babe . . . it's here already?"

"A beautiful little girl." Joy filled her heart, bubbling through her until she wanted to laugh with the sheer happiness of it. "She and Leah are both fine, thank the gut Lord. Do you want to see them?"

"I'd best go down to the end of the lane. Tell the emergency crew where to turn in." He swung around and bolted back out the door.

Was he uncomfortable about being with a woman who'd just

given birth? Was this too vivid a reminder of the way his wife had died?

Rachel hadn't even thought of that when she'd pressed him into service. She'd needed someone, and he was there. Even if she had remembered, there would have been no other solution.

"Rachel? Is there any sign of Daniel yet?"

Leah's voice sounded stronger by the minute. She was eager to show off her daughter, obviously.

As for Rachel—well, she'd rather see the paramedics at this point. She thought the birth had gone well, and everything seemed as it should be, but she wasn't a midwife. Having three babies of her own didn't make her an expert on all the things that could go wrong.

She went to peer through the kitchen window at the lane, but saw no one except Gideon. She hurried back to Leah, carrying the towels she'd had warming next to the stove.

"Not yet, but I'm sure he'll be along soon. Let's wrap this around your little girl to be sure she's snug enough." She tucked the soft, warm towel around the tiny bundle in Leah's arms.

"She's so perfect," Leah crooned, touching one small pink hand. "I can't take my eyes off her."

"I know." She remembered those first moments of bonding—that sense of absolute wonderment that so perfect a creature could have come from her.

Leah's mouth crumpled suddenly.

"What is it? Are you in pain?" If something went wrong . . .

"No." Leah wiped tears away with the back of her hand, laughing shakily. "I'm being silly. Just—I'm so glad you were here today. If you hadn't been—"

"But I was, so don't think that. And I'm glad, too."

She wrapped her arms around Leah in a loving hug. They had

gone through so much together, she and Leah. And now she'd been here to experience the wondrous gift of helping Leah give birth to her first child. As terrifying as it had been at times, she would never forget this as long as she lived.

"Did Gideon leave?" Leah brushed a strand of hair off her face.

Rachel smoothed the hair back and secured it with a hairpin. "He's watching for the paramedics." Even as she said the words, she heard the sound of tires on the gravel. "Here they are. I'll go and let them in."

In minutes the house seemed overly full of the emergency workers—three of them, but one a woman, to Leah's obvious relief. She checked out Leah while another looked over the baby and the third filled in forms.

Pushed out of the room where she'd been indispensable, Rachel had busied herself with making coffee. She could use a cup herself, and she didn't doubt that someone else would. She glanced up to see Gideon lingering on the threshold.

"Is everything all right? Leah and the baby?"

"They seem to be fine, as far as I can tell. The emergency workers are with them now. They'll know better. I—"

Without warning, her knees seemed to buckle. She sat down abruptly in the nearest chair.

Gideon was with her in two quick strides. "Was ist letz?" He knelt next to her.

"Nothing. I mean, I'm all right." She pressed her hand against her cheek and blinked to keep the tears away. "I'm being silly, that's what. Anyone would think I had that baby."

He reached toward her and then seemed to change his mind. Instead he filled a mug with coffee, added sugar, and brought it to her.

"Drink this." He wrapped her hands around the warm mug. "You delivered the boppli. Seems to me you have a right to be a little shaky after that."

"Ja. Shaky is right." She sipped cautiously at the scalding brew, feeling its heat all the way to her stomach. "I was too busy to think about what could go wrong. Now that it's over—"

"Now that it's over, it would be ferhoodled to fret about things that didn't happen."

"Or things that happened in the past?"

She studied his face, so dear to her now. It was a dangerous question, but somehow the events of the last hour had pushed her beyond her usual caution. Gideon could be angry with her if he wanted, but this once she would try to probe past the guilt he kept like armor around him.

He took a step back, his face tightening. "Some things you can't help but remember."

"Remember, ja. But you didn't let the memories keep you from doing what had to be done." That was important. She sensed it but didn't have the words to explain why.

He grasped the back of a chair, his big hands dwarfing the slat. "Leave it, Rachel."

"I can't." Her throat was tight, but she forced herself to go on. "I can't let you hide yourself away behind guilt that wasn't yours to begin with. You didn't choose to have an accident."

"No." His face twisted. "But that doesn't matter. At least today Leah and her baby lived. I'm glad of that, but if you imagine it evens things up, you're wrong."

"Of course I don't think that." She'd get up, but she didn't trust her legs to hold her. "There's nothing to even up, nothing to repay, don't you see that?"

He didn't. That was written in the tense lines of his face. And before she could find any other words, footsteps thudded on the back porch and Daniel burst into the room, his eyes wide with fear.

"Leah . . ."

"Leah is fine." Strength surged through Rachel, and she went to him, clasping his hands in hers. "You have a beautiful daughter."

The fear dissolved into incredible joy. "A little girl? You're sure they're all right?"

"Go and see for yourself." She pushed him toward the door. "They're waiting for you."

He paused for an instant on the threshold, and she doubted that he even saw the three Englischers in the room. Then he ran toward his wife and baby.

She was crying again. She mopped at her face with her hands. This was a day for tears as well as joy, it seemed.

She turned to say something of the kind to Gideon, but it was too late. He was gone.

*Much* as she might want to, Rachel had no time to think about Gideon. Drawn by the emergency vehicle, Leah's parents hurried in with the children, who'd apparently gone home from the sale with them.

"Leah? The baby?" Mattie Beiler clutched Elizabeth's shoulders, keeping her from rushing into the room.

"All well." Rachel's eyes filled again at the words. "The paramedics are still in there. Maybe best if only Leah's mamm goes in at the moment."

"Ja, that's right." Elias, Leah's father, caught young Jonah and put his hand on Matthew's shoulder. "We will wait a moment."

Elizabeth came to Rachel as soon as her grossmutter disappeared, seeming to need the security of another woman. "The boppli is all right? You're sure?"

"I'm sure." Rachel hugged her. "A little sister for you."

"A girl?" Elizabeth's face lit, the anxiety vanishing from her eyes. "I'm glad. I mean, a boy would have been nice, too," she added, always eager to do and say the right thing. "But I already have a little brother."

"Becky is going to be jealous of you, I'm afraid. She would love to have another baby around to help with and to hold."

Rachel's heart seemed to wince as she said the words. She would love that, too, but it was unlikely ever to happen now.

The paramedics came out, ready to leave after failing to convince Leah to go to the hospital. She would stay at home, she insisted, just as they had planned.

People started arriving, worried and eager to help. Some were satisfied with a brief explanation and headed off home to prepare food to bring. Others started for the barn to take over Daniel's chores, needing no explanation of what had to be done. One of Leah's brothers went to contact the midwife. It was her community at its best, but Rachel could have done with a little more quiet.

Probably Leah, in the room adjoining the kitchen, felt the same. When she'd planned to stay downstairs for a few days with the new boppli, maybe she hadn't anticipated the noise problem.

When the rush finally died down, Rachel tiptoed to the doorway to take a peek inside. Leah slept, the babe dozing in her arms. Daniel sat on the edge of the bed, one hand over hers, the other touching his new child.

Blinking back tears, Rachel beckoned to the children. They

slipped out quietly. "We should let your mamm sleep now, ain't so?"

They nodded, maybe a little reluctant. Then Matthew clapped Jonah on the shoulder. "We'll go do our chores. No sense letting other folks do what we should do."

The boys went out, and Elizabeth tugged at Rachel's sleeve. "About what you said before—about Becky, I mean." Her small face was very serious. "Tell her that she can love my new baby sister, too. All right?"

"Ja. Ser gut." Rachel hugged the child, touched by her thoughtfulness. "I think your grossmutter went upstairs to get some blankets and diapers for the boppli. Maybe you can help her."

Elizabeth nodded and scurried off toward the steps, skipping a little in her happiness.

Everyone was happy, it seemed. Everyone but Gideon.

Rachel's heart ached so much that she put her hand on her chest. Gideon was a prisoner of his own guilt, and he wasn't the only person who hurt as a result.

She loved him. The feeling had crept up so gradually that she hadn't even noticed it until it was too late to stop it. Not like she'd loved Ezra—not more or less. Just different. This love wasn't the same, but it still could be full and complete. They could have been happy together.

Gideon had helped her in so many ways, even with things they hadn't spoken of. He'd helped her heal from her grief. He'd helped her gain the confidence that she could manage on her own. And now, with God's help, she'd do exactly that.

But they could have been happy.

Daniel came into the kitchen, a contented smile still lurking in his eyes. "I know you must be getting back to your own family, but Leah is awake and wants to see you before you go."

"Gut. Then I can see that sweet babe again."

She started into the room, and as she passed him, he touched her arm lightly.

"Denke, Rachel," he whispered. "Denke."

She nodded, heart full, and went to Leah.

Leah leaned back on pillows propped against the headboard, still cradling her sleeping daughter in her arms. Rachel sat down gingerly on the bed, careful not to jostle them.

"You know, you really can put her down in her bassinet."

Leah's lips curved. "No, I can't. Not yet." She traced her finger along the baby's soft cheek. "I'm too busy marveling at her."

"I know." Rachel said the words softly, content just to watch Leah with her babe.

Their friendship had lasted for her entire life, but it wasn't the same as it had been. That was gut. With each new challenge met, with each grief they endured, they grew, and so did their bond.

She didn't have to say that to Leah. Some things went too deep for words.

"Daniel and I have been talking for months about the name for the boppli. Funny, but we could never decide on a girl's name." Leah dropped a feather-light kiss on the baby's head. "Now that we have seen her, we know exactly what it should be."

"And what is it?" A family name, most likely.

Leah smiled, but it was tinged with just a little sorrow. "I want you to meet Rachel Anna Glick. Named for the sister I lost, and for the friend who is closer than a sister."

Tears filled Rachel's eyes again. For a moment she couldn't speak. Then she managed a whisper.

"Denke, Leah." She touched her friend's hand. "Perhaps one day Anna will return."

"I never stop praying for that. I never will."

"I, too," she whispered, her heart full.

*Gideon* tightened the screw and stood back to study his handiwork. It was odd. This idea had been in his mind for a long time. Today, he felt driven to turn it into reality.

The model windmill was an exact copy of the real thing, but it stood only five feet high. Just the right size, he'd think, to go into someone's garden.

He picked up the next crosspiece. Maybe he'd been figuring that working on something new would keep his mind off Rachel. If so, he'd been wrong. She drifted through his thoughts, distracting him, making him feel things he'd put away long ago.

"What do you have there, Gideon? Something new to sell?"

The voice startled him. He turned to see Bishop Mose pausing in the doorway as if waiting for an invitation to enter.

"Komm in." He put down his tools. "What brings you out our way today?"

"Ach, if I'd use my head, I wouldn't have to put so many miles on my buggy." The bishop rounded the worktable and stood surveying the miniature windmill. "I had to speak to Aaron about trading his date for the worship schedule. So I thought I'd step out here to see what you are working on."

"Something new. You're right about that." An object that was just "for pretty" as the people said. Would the bishop question that? "As for selling—well, I haven't got that far yet."

Mose walked all around the windmill. "Just like a real one, ain't so?"

Gideon nodded, waiting.

Mose stroked his beard, seeming to consider. "A gut idea, I'd say. Englischers will want one of those to put in their gardens. Some of our own people, too, I don't doubt. You should put one on display."

"Maybe."

He'd said once, half-joking, that he'd make them for Rachel to sell alongside her plants. But going into partnership with Rachel suddenly seemed a dangerous business—dangerous to both his heart and his peace of mind.

Mose didn't prompt him for more of an answer. That wasn't his way. He just looked at him for a long moment, wise eyes seeming to see further into a person's heart than was comfortable.

"I stopped by the Glick farm on my way here. Baby and Mammi are both doing fine. Thanks to you."

Gideon picked up the crosspiece and began fitting it into place. "Not me. I did nothing but make a phone call. Rachel is the one who did the hard part."

"Ja. Leah and Daniel are mighty thankful that she was there. But you arrived at just the right time, I hear. The gut Lord's doing, no doubt. Rachel and Leah both would have been frightened if they hadn't known they could count on you to get help."

"It was only what anyone would do." He tapped the screw to start it and began to screw it in. "I'm thankful Leah and the boppli are both doing well."

And he'd be even more thankful if he could stop talking about it. Thinking about it. Remembering Rachel's courage and her confidence in him.

Bishop Mose showed no inclination to leave. He propped himself against the workbench as if he had all day to talk. "Did you hear what they named the boppli?"

"No."

"Rachel Anna."

Gideon had to swallow the lump in his throat. "That's fitting, isn't it? Since Rachel brought her into this world."

"Ja. She's a fine woman, Rachel is."

"Nobody knows that better than I do." Where was this going?

"I guess that's true enough. You've spent plenty of time over at Rachel's place this spring. I don't know how she'd have gotten along without you."

Bishop Mose was clearly hinting, and maybe he'd best deflect him from his matchmaking.

"Just doing the work I promised is all. Guess I won't be seeing as much of her and the kinder now that it's done. I'll be starting on a new job next week."

"I see." Bishop Mose blew out a long breath. "So you made gut on your promise to Ezra and that's an end of it, is it?"

Gideon focused on the work so he didn't have to look at the bishop's face. "I'll still help as they need me. I'm not going to leave Ezra's family on their own."

Mose took a step forward, so that he stood next to Gideon. He touched the blade of the model. "I'll be honest with you. I had hoped for more than friendship for you and Rachel."

Gideon's fingers tightened on the crosspiece. If he gripped it any harder, he'd probably break it right off.

"I know what you're saying, but I'm not the man for her. She deserves more than I can give."

"Ach, that's nonsense, that is. You'd be a fine husband to her, and a fine father to those children. Why does everyone see it but you?"

He swung to face the bishop, feeling the dark emotions roil like thunderclouds. "You're wrong. They're wrong. I can't."

"Gideon, Gideon." Mose's voice was gently chiding. "What happened to Naomi and the babe was tragic, but it was a long time ago. You can't mourn forever."

"I can feel guilty forever." His voice cracked. "I can't forgive myself."

"That is wrong, Gideon, and I speak as your bishop as well as your friend." The old man's eyes turned to steel, and the steel filled his voice, too. "Failing to forgive yourself is failing to accept God's forgiveness. You're saying you know more than your Creator. You're wrong, and it's time you faced the truth. You are turning away from God's plan for your life, and that's the most tragic thing anyone can do."

He turned and walked out of the workshop, leaving Gideon stunned and speechless.

# Chapter Twenty

She was always up early, even on Saturday, but Rachel didn't remember a time when she'd felt so nervous about what the day would bring. The eastern sky had begun to brighten when she heard the *clop-clop* of horse's hooves in the lane. She peeked out the kitchen window to see Daad helping Mamm down from the buggy seat. Her mother started toward the house, while he drove the buggy on toward the barn.

She hurried to open the door. Her mother's hug dispelled some of the jitters.

"I'm happy to see you. I didn't expect you to be here this early."

Mamm set a pan of still-warm sticky buns on the counter next to the coffeepot and hung up her bonnet. "Ach, you know how your daadi is. He's not happy unless he gets places before everyone else."

"That's if anyone else comes." Rachel poured a mug of coffee for her mother.

"Of course folks will come. Your ad looked real nice in the

paper. Georgia Randall from down the road brought it to us. She'll be coming by, I know. Said she wanted to get some snapdragons in. I told her you'd put some back for her."

"I'll be glad to." Rachel didn't expect that much of a rush on any of her flowers, but Mamm would worry she'd run out before her English neighbor arrived. "I'll be glad to sell even a few things today. Hopefully then folks will tell others, and I'll get some steady business from it."

Her father appeared at the door just then, stomping his feet on the mat.

"Ready for some coffee, Daad?"

"Ready for you to tell me what needs doing," he answered. "Got to be set for business when the customers get here."

She couldn't help it—her eyes filled with tears. "Denke. It means so much that you came."

Her father brushed that away with a sweep of his hand. The thunder of children's feet on the stairs said that the young ones had heard their grandparents' voices, and Rachel banished the emotional response. This was her day to behave like a businesswoman, and that didn't include any crying.

"I'll see to the children's breakfast," Mamm said. "You go on out with your daad and get organized."

"Ja, I will." She gave the children a smile. "You be wonderful gut for your grossmutter, now. It will be a busy day."

She hoped.

"What first?" Daad said the moment they were outside. "You're wanting to put some tables up so you can have plants outside the greenhouse, aren't you?"

"Ja." But she didn't want her father to be doing any heavy lifting. "Let's check on the number of seedlings I have potted, first. See if you think it's enough to start with." She headed for the greenhouse. "Komm."

If she waited until the children came out, she could enlist them to help carry the planks for the tables. Daad would insist he could do it, as he always did. He hated admitting that the doctor had cautioned him to slow down.

By the time they emerged from the greenhouse, the sun had struggled above the trees, and a wagon came lumbering down the lane. Rachel stared, holding her breath. It wasn't—ja, it was. Isaac and William sat side by side on the wagon seat.

Isaac drew to a stop near her, inclining his head to her and to her father. Daad nodded in return, not speaking. Was he holding on to a grudge against Isaac? She prayed not. It would be far better to let go. Whether or not Isaac had done wrong in going to the elders about her was of less importance than restoring family relationships.

"We brought some sawhorses and planks to set up tables for your plants. Just tell us where you want them."

"That's wonderful gut of you both." She smiled at William, but he was carefully avoiding her gaze. "Right here near the drive will be perfect. Denke."

"About the farm—" Isaac looked as if he were shoving the words out. "We'll keep going the way we have been. No need to make any changes that I can see, ain't so?"

It was as close to an apology as Isaac was ever likely to come. She nodded, thankful. "Ser gut."

Isaac slid down, and in a moment William followed suit. They began unloading the materials for tables. Daad watched, frowning a bit. Finally his face eased, and he caught the end of a plank as Isaac slid it off the wagon.

Now, if only she could get William to speak to her, perhaps one of the thorns would be removed from her heart.

The tables began to take shape. She carried a flat of snapdragons out, veering so that her path led her close to William.

"William, will you put these on the table for me?"

He started like a deer at the sound of her voice. Nodding, his eyes still not meeting hers, he reached for the flat.

She seized the moment to pat his hand. "Denke, William. It's kind of you."

Color flooded his face. "I—I'm sorry. I'm s-s-so ashamed."

"It's over," she said quietly. "You'll confess. God and the people will forgive."

"But I— "

"No, William." Her fingers tightened on his. "Forgiveness is a precious gift. Don't push it away with your guilt." Pain gripped her heart at the reminder of Gideon. "That hurts too many people. Promise me."

His eyes were dark with questions, but he nodded. "I promise."

"Gut." She turned away, trying to quell the memories of Gideon that flooded her. For today, at least, she must keep reminders of him at bay so that she could do the work that was before her. She'd have plenty of time to think of him. To regret.

Another buggy appeared in the lane. She started toward it. Surely everyone she'd expect to help was here already.

The buggy pulled to a halt. She could not, after all, keep away from reminders of Gideon, since it was Lovina, his sister-in-law, who smiled at her a little uncertainly.

"Lovina, it's so gut of you to come." She would not let Lovina feel that anything that happened between her and Gideon affected their friendship.

"I wouldn't miss your opening. I brought some things." She gestured to the floor of the buggy, stacked with trays. Several gallon jugs of lemonade nestled against the seat.

"What is all this? You didn't need to bring food."

Lovina slid down from the seat and began pulling trays out, handing them to Rachel. They were filled with dozens of cookies. "I noticed that whenever stores have their grand openings, they always have refreshments for folks. So I thought you could, too."

Rachel's throat tightened. Lovina's expression suggested that she was trying to make up for something. It could only be that she knew or guessed what had happened between Rachel and Gideon and was trying, in her own way, to express sympathy.

"You are so kind. If Gideon— " She stopped. That sentence couldn't go anywhere happy. "Denke."

"Gideon is an idiot, and I'd like to tell him so." Lovina snorted, grabbing a jug of lemonade. "But Aaron says we must be patient. Patient! What do men know about it anyway?"

Rachel actually managed a weak laugh at Lovina's words. "I'm not upset." Grieved and pained, but not upset. "It is in God's hands."

Lovina looked as if she thought the Lord could use a little help, but she kept the words in. "Let's get these inside until opening time, ja?"

"Ja." Rachel led the way toward the kitchen. Odd, to feel so heartened by Lovina's support.

She'd like to believe that patience was the answer, but she couldn't. She feared all the patience in the world wouldn't bring Gideon to the place where he could love again.

. . .

*There* was still a half hour to go before the opening time, but a car came down the lane already. Rachel assessed the situation, nerves jumping. Were they ready?

The refreshments weren't out yet. Everything else looked fine. The potted marigolds glowed yellow and orange along one end of the table, while snapdragons formed a rainbow at the other end. Between them were waves of cosmos and zinnias, ready to take off in someone's garden.

A second long table held the perennials Rachel had potted up. Not so many of those, but she could always do more if there was a demand. They were ready.

She took a deep breath and turned to greet her first customer. But it wasn't a customer. It was Johnny.

Any concern she felt at having him come when so many Amish were around was supplanted by pure gratitude. He'd supported her throughout, believing in her idea when others didn't. Without his help and encouragement, her dream might not have become a reality.

"Johnny. You're here." She hugged him hard. "I'm so glad."

"I'd have come earlier, but I stopped to put up a few directional signs. Wouldn't want your customers getting lost on these back roads, would we?"

Probably no one else would notice the nervousness shown by the way he shifted his weight and ran his hand through his hair. But she knew him too well to be fooled by the casual expression he'd put on.

"You are so kind. I'd never have thought of that." She squeezed his arm. "I just hope I have some customers to follow the signs."

"That's a sure thing." He patted her arm. His gaze wandered past her, scanning the display of flowers ready for sale. Then he froze.

"Guess I should have known Daad would be here." He moved back a step, his jaw hardening. "I don't want to cause trouble, Rach. I'll leave."

"No." Sharp and hard as an axe, the word stopped him. "Don't you dare go."

"I'm thinking of you . . ."

"If you are, then think of this—I can't stand to keep losing people I love. You and Daad are just alike. Do you know that? You're both letting your stubbornness keep you apart."

Emotions warred on his face. She could almost feel the desire to leave, but to his credit he fought it.

"I don't want to hurt you." He stopped, as if he struggled to get the words out. "But if Daad won't change, there's nothing I can do."

"There's always something you can do." She said the words fiercely, unable to keep Gideon out of her mind. "You don't just give up."

"But—"

"You don't have to apologize for what you believe. Don't expect Daad to apologize for what he believes, either. Just take a step toward him. Give him a chance."

Johnny stood there a moment longer, fists clenched. Slowly, as if he were wading through a muddy field, he started across the lawn to where William was helping Daad set up a table for the refreshments.

A step sounded on the porch behind her. Mamm stood close, hands folded under her apron.

"You heard?" Rachel whispered.

"Ja." Mamm's hands seemed to grip tighter, and Rachel knew she was praying.

*Please, Father. Please. Don't let them shut each other out.*

Johnny reached, grabbing the end of the board Daad was trying to put onto the sawhorses. Daad froze. They stared at each other, the length of the board between them.

Daad gave the smallest of nods. Together, they put the board into place. Together, they lifted the next one.

*Thank You, Father.* Rachel felt the tears Mamm was stifling, felt her own eyes prick. *Thank You.*

A few hours later, Rachel knew that her opening was a success. She'd been steadily busy, selling to English and Amish alike.

She knew, well enough, that the Amish had turned out to support her and might not prove to be continuing customers, but that didn't matter. Plenty of English had come, praised the quality of her offerings, and promised to tell others.

Everyone had come—everyone except Gideon. Rachel tried telling herself that she was foolish. She had every reason to be happy today. Her business was booming, her friends had turned out to support her, the breach with Isaac and William was well on its way to being healed.

Best of all, her father and brother were working their way toward a new relationship. God had answered her prayers in an amazing way, and she was truly grateful.

Yet each time she looked at the greenhouse, overflowing with plants, each time she saw the windmill, its blades circling gracefully, each time she let her mind stray to Gideon, her heart grew heavier.

Nodding and smiling as she waited on a customer, she tried

to be sensible. Gideon had done what he'd set out to do. He'd fulfilled his promise to Ezra, and thanks to him, she would become self-sufficient.

She still had to make a decision about the farm, but with Isaac no longer pressuring her and some money coming in, she could take her time. She would listen for God's leading and trust that He would show her the right decision at the right time.

And then she saw him. Gideon worked his way through the crowd toward her. He carried a windmill—the model windmill he'd shown her the plans for, that day when she'd begun to feel she knew him.

She took a deep breath and forced a smile. "You've made the model windmill you talked about. It turned out so well. You must be pleased with it."

"Ja." He set it at the edge of her flowerbed, twisting it to settle it firmly into the damp soil. "I made it for you. For the business, I mean." He was staring at the windmill instead of her. "Maybe folks will want to buy them for garden ornaments."

"Maybe they will." Was that the only reason he'd come? To try to give Ezra's widow another small source of income? She swallowed, trying to relieve the tension in her throat. "You're very kind."

For an instant something flared in his eyes at her words. It was gone so quickly that she couldn't identify the emotion.

He cleared his throat, as if his was as constricted as hers. "I wonder—" He glanced around, seeming to register the other people for the first time. "Could we—there's something in the greenhouse I want you to see. Can someone else take over here?"

Before Rachel could speak, someone bumped her elbow. Lovina had slipped behind the table where she kept the cash box.

"Let me handle the sales for a bit. You've been working all day."

"Denke, Lovina."

She wouldn't let herself imagine what this might mean. Instead, she walked steadily across the lawn to the greenhouse. Gideon came beside and a little behind her, not touching. He ducked his head to follow her into the greenhouse and closed the door behind him.

She'd forgotten how much he filled up the greenhouse when they were inside together. With plants hanging all around and filtering the sunlight, it was as if they'd sheltered inside a quiet cave.

Gideon took a breath so deep that his chest heaved. "This is not a gut time. Your opening— " He stopped, shook his head. "I know how William feels when he can't get the words out."

Somehow his awkwardness gave her courage. "Just say it, Gideon. Whatever it is. You can tell me anything. We're friends, ain't so?"

"Can I tell you that I love you?" His hands clenched. "Ach, I'm making a mess of it, but I want, I need for you to know my heart."

*Love.* She heard the word, and her own heart seemed to swell to meet his. She reached out her hands to him, hardly knowing that she was doing it, and he clasped them in his.

"I think I've loved you for a long time, but I couldn't accept it. How could I love you when Ezra was gone? How could I love you when Naomi was gone?"

"Having loved before shouldn't keep us from loving again."

"No. It shouldn't." His fingers moved caressingly on the backs of her hands, and the touch went straight to her heart. "But I was blind to that, tied up inside myself."

"What changed you?" She wanted to put her hands to his face

but held back, almost afraid to believe this was happening. "At Leah's, you said— "

"I was stupid." His mouth curved just a little. "Lovina has been aching to tell me so. I don't know why she hasn't."

A bubble of happiness was rising in Rachel, filling her with warmth and light. "Because Aaron told her to be patient."

Gideon's chuckle was soft and deep. "Bishop Mose ran out of patience with me."

"Bishop Mose? What did he—how did he know— "

"He knows everything, I think. Especially the things we don't say." His eyes darkened. "He told me that not forgiving myself was a sin. That it was refusing to accept God's forgiveness, thinking that I knew better than God."

"Gideon, I'm sorry." She wanted to comfort him, but she didn't know how.

"Don't be. At first I felt as if he'd hit me between the eyes with a two-by-four. It knocked me to my knees. And then I knew it was true. I'd shut myself away from the Lord with my stubbornness, and shut my heart away from loving, too."

"We make mistakes. It's only human." And how often those mistakes came down to forgiveness—forgiving yourself, forgiving others, even forgiving God for taking away someone you loved.

"Can you love someone so stubborn and foolish, Rachel?" He raised her hands to his lips, and his breath crossed her skin in a promise.

She seemed to see Ezra's face in her heart. He would always be there, but he wouldn't regret the happiness she and the children would find with Gideon.

"I can," she whispered, lifting her face for his kiss. God had brought them both through the darkness to new life. They would cherish every day, in His name.

# Glossary of Pennsylvania Dutch Words and Phrases

**ach.** oh; used as an exclamation
**agasinish.** stubborn; self-willed
**ain't so.** A phrase commonly used at the end of a sentence to invite agreement.
**alter.** old man
**anymore.** Used as a substitute for "nowadays."
**Ausbund.** Amish hymnal. Used in the worship services, it contains traditional hymns, words only, to be sung without accompaniment. Many of the hymns date from the sixteenth century.
**befuddled.** mixed up
**blabbermaul.** talkative one
**blaid.** bashful
**boppli.** baby
**bruder.** brother
**bu.** boy
**buwe.** boys
**daadi.** daddy

**Da Herr sei mit du.** The Lord be with you.
**denke.** thanks (or *danki*)
**Englischer.** one who is not Plain
**ferhoodled.** upset; distracted
**ferleicht.** perhaps
**frau.** wife
**fress.** eat
**gross.** big
**grossdaadi.** grandfather
**grossdaadi haus.** An addition to the farmhouse, built for the grandparents to live in once they've "retired" from actively running the farm.
**grossmutter.** grandmother
**gut.** good
**hatt.** hard; difficult
**haus.** house
**hinnersich.** backward
**ich.** I
**ja.** yes
**kapp.** Prayer covering, worn in obedience to the Biblical injunction that women should pray with their heads covered. Kapps are made of Swiss organdy and are white. (In some Amish communities, unmarried girls thirteen and older wear black kapps during worship service.)
**kinder.** kids (or *kinner*)
**komm.** come
**komm schnell.** come quick
**Leit.** the people; the Amish
**lippy.** sassy
**maidal.** old maid; spinster
**mamm.** mother

**meddaagesse.** lunch
**mind.** remember
**onkel.** uncle
**Ordnung.** The agreed-upon rules by which the Amish community lives. When new practices become an issue, they are discussed at length among the leadership. The decision for or against innovation is generally made on the basis of maintaining the home and family as separate from the world. For instance, a telephone might be necessary in a shop in order to conduct business but would be banned from the home because it would intrude on family time.
**Pennsylvania Dutch.** The language is actually German in origin and is primarily a spoken language. Most Amish write in English, which results in many variations in spelling when the dialect is put into writing! The language probably originated in the south of Germany but is common also among the Swiss Mennonite and French Huguenot immigrants to Pennsylvania. The language was brought to America prior to the Revolution and is still in use today. High German is used for Scripture and church documents, while English is the language of commerce.
**rumspringa.** Running-around time. The late teen years when Amish youth taste some aspects of the outside world before deciding to be baptized into the church.
**schnickelfritz.** mischievous child
**ser gut.** very good
**tastes like more.** delicious
**Was ist letz?** What's the matter?
**Wie bist du heit.** It's nice to meet you.
**wilkom.** welcome
**Wo bist du?** Where are you?

*Dear Reader,*

*I hope you've enjoyed meeting the people of Pleasant Valley. If this is your second visit, welcome back. Although the place doesn't actually exist, it seems very real to me, as it is based on the Amish settlements here in my area of central Pennsylvania.*

*Rachel's journey from devastating grief to the joy of loving again made me cry more than a few times while writing it. I hope that it has touched your heart as well.*

*I would love to hear your thoughts on my book. If you'd care to write to me, I'd be happy to reply with a signed bookmark or bookplate and my brochure of Pennsylvania Dutch recipes. You can find me on the Web at www.martaperry.com, e-mail me at marta@martaperry.com, or write to me in care of Berkley Publicity Department, Penguin Group (USA) Inc., 375 Hudson Street, New York, NY 10014.*

*Blessings,*
*Marta Perry*

An Excerpt from

# Anna's Return

*Pleasant Valley*

BOOK THREE

by Marta Perry

Coming in June 2010
from Berkley Books

She was beginning to fear that the prodigal daughter wouldn't make it home after all. Anna Beiler pressed on the gas pedal. "Come on, you can do it." The old car responded with nothing more than a shudder.

Daad would probably say that this was what she got for depending on something so English as a car to get her home, and maybe he'd be right. Just the thought of seeing her father made her stomach queasy. How would he, how would any of the family, react to Anna's turning up at her Amish home three years after she'd given up all they believed in to disappear into the English world?

The car gave an ominous sputter. It might be her prized possession, but she didn't know much about its inner workings. Still, that noise and the shaking couldn't be good signs.

She gripped the steering wheel tighter, biting her lip, and faced the truth. She wasn't going to make it to the Beiler farm, the place where she'd been born, the place she'd left in rebellion and disgrace. She'd been nineteen then, sure she knew all about the world. Now, at twenty-two, she felt a decade older than the girl she'd been.

But there, just ahead, she spotted the turnoff to Mill Race Road. Two miles down Mill Race was the home of her brother and sister-in-law. Joseph and Myra would welcome her, wouldn't they?

Forced into a decision, she'd have to take that chance. She turned onto the narrow road, earning another protesting groan from the car. Her fingers tensed so much that she'd have to peel them from the steering wheel. Worse, now that she was so close, all the arguments for and against coming here pummeled her mind.

Was this the right choice? Her stomach clenched again. She didn't know. She just knew returning was her only option.

It was strange that things looked the same after three years. Pleasant Valley, Pennsylvania, didn't change, or at least not quickly. Maybe there'd been a little more traffic on the main road, but now that she was off that, not a car was in sight.

The fields on either side of the road overflowed with pumpkins, cabbage, and field corn that had yet to be cut. Neat barns and silos, farmhouse gardens filled with chrysanthemums, sumac topped with the dark red plumes that made them look like flaming torches—this was September in Pennsylvania Dutch country, and she was coming home.

Maybe she should have written, but when had there been time? There'd been no time for anything but to get out of Chicago as quickly as possible. And there was no way she could explain the unexplainable.

She glanced into the backseat, and her heart expanded with love. Gracie slept in her car seat, good as gold, just as she'd been throughout the long trip. At not quite a year old, she could hardly have understood her mother's fear, but she'd cooperated.

The neat white sign for Joseph's machine shop stood where it always had. Anna turned into the narrow gravel lane, determination settling over her. It was far too late to worry if her decision would work. She had to make it work, for Gracie's sake.

Joseph and Myra's place was a hundred-year-old white frame farmhouse, identifiable as Amish only by the fact that no electric lines ran to the house. They owned only a few acres, not enough to farm but plenty for the machine shop that her mechanically minded brother ran.

In the pasture to the right of the lane a bay horse lifted his head, eyeing her curiously, probably wondering what a car was doing here. Tossing his mane, he trotted a few feet beside her along the fence.

If Gracie were awake, she would point out the horsey, something that up until now Gracie had seen only in her picture books. Everything about this place would be strange and new to her.

Not to Anna. For her, it all had an almost heartless familiarity. The very sameness made it seem to her that Pleasant Valley had gotten along quite nicely without her, thank you very much, and could continue to do so.

Joseph's shop was in the large outbuilding at the end of the lane, while off to the left beyond it stood the horse barn. Surely there'd be room in one of them to store the car.

Get it out of sight—that was all she could think. Get the car out of sight, and then they'd be safe.

Maybe she ought to drive straight to the shop. She could park behind it, if nothing else. As if it had read her mind, the car gave one last sputter, a cough, and died, just short of the house.

"No, don't do this," she muttered. She switched the key off and then turned it on again, touching the gas pedal gently.

Nothing. The car seemed to sink down on its wheels, like a horse sagging into clean straw after a hard day's work.

She pounded the steering wheel with the heel of her hand. Still, at least she was here. Joseph would help her, wouldn't he? He'd always had a tender spot for his baby sister.

Mindful that Gracie still slept, Anna slid out of the car, leaving the door open for air, and straightened, groaning a little. Her muscles protested after all those hours in the car, to say nothing of the tension that had ridden with her.

She glanced down at the faded blue jeans, sneakers, and wrinkled shirt she wore. It might be less harrowing for Joseph and Myra if she'd arrived in conventional Amish clothes, but she'd certainly have drawn attention to herself driving a car that way.

Not giving herself time to think about their reaction, she walked quickly to the back door.

She knocked on the screen door, paused, and then knocked again, louder. Nothing. The inner door was closed—odd on a pleasant September day. She opened the screen door, tried the knob, and the realization seeped into her. The luck that had gotten her all the way here from Chicago had run out. No one was home.

She stood on the back step, biting her lip, frowning at the car. The dark blue compact, liberally streaked with rust, had been her friend Jannie's, and now it was hers, the only car she'd ever owned. Pete knew it well, too well. If he'd followed her—

That was ridiculous. Pete couldn't possibly have known where she was going. She had to stop jumping at shadows.

But her common sense seemed to have fled. All she could think was to get the car out of sight and submerge herself and Gracie in the protective camouflage of the Amish community as quickly as possible.

Joseph and Myra were away, but one of their horses might still be in the barn. If she could hitch it to the car, she could tow the vehicle out of sight. Hurrying, she checked the sleeping baby. Gracie still slept soundly, her head turned to one side in the car seat, a small hand unfurling like a leaf next to her face.

Gracie was all right. She just had to keep her that way. Anna turned and jogged toward the barn, urged on by the fear that had pursued her all the way from Chicago.

She slid the heavy door open and blinked at the dimness, inhaling the familiar scents of fresh straw, hay, and animals. From one of the stalls came a soft snort and the thud of hooves as the animal moved. *Thank Heaven.* If the horse had been turned out in the field for the day, she might never have caught it.

The bay mare came willingly to her, nosing over the stall boards. It was Myra's buggy horse, most likely. Wherever they were today, they'd taken the one Joseph drove. Did he still have that big roan?

Lifting a lead line from the hook, Anna started to open the stall door.

A board creaked behind her, and she whirled toward the sound, her breath catching.

"What are you doing with that horse?"

A man stood in the open doorway, silhouetted against the light behind him. Not Joseph, for sure, but Amish, to judge by the outline of him and the cadence of the words he'd spoken in English.

Well, of course he'd spoken English. That was what he thought she was, standing there in her jeans and T-shirt—an English woman. A horse thief, maybe.

He moved toward her before she could find the words for an explanation, and she could see him better. Could recognize him.

"It's . . . Samuel Fisher, ain't so?" The Amish phrase she hadn't used in three years came readily to her lips. Samuel was her sister-in-law Myra's brother. Maybe Joseph and Myra had asked him to look after things while they were gone today.

He stopped a few feet from her, assessing her with a slow, steady gaze. Slow, she thought. Yes, that was Samuel. Maybe *deliberate* would be a kinder word. Samuel had never been one to rush into anything.

"So. Anna Beiler. You've come home, then."

He'd switched to Pennsylvania Dutch, and it took her a moment to make the mental change. After so much time away, she even thought in English.

"As you can see."

"It's been a long time."

"Three years." She shifted her weight impatiently from one foot to the other. She didn't have time to stand here chatting with Samuel. The baby could wake—someone could spot the car. "Do you know where Joseph and Myra are?"

He took his time about the answer, seeming to register every detail of her appearance as he did. "They've gone over to Fostertown for the day. Joseph didn't say anything to me about you coming."

"Why should he?" The words snapped out before she could moderate them.

Samuel's strong, stolid face didn't register much change—but then, it never had. His already-square jaw might have gotten a little squarer, his hazel eyes might have turned a bit cold, but that was all.

As for the rest—black suspenders crossed strong shoulders over a light blue work shirt, and a summer straw hat sat squarely on sun-streaked brown hair. He seemed taller and broader than he had when she'd last seen him. Well, they were both older. He'd be twenty-six, now, the same as Joseph.

"Joseph and I are partners in the business, besides him being my brother-in-law," Samuel said, voice mild. "Usually he tells me if he expects somebody, 'specially if he's going to be away."

"Sorry," she muttered. "I didn't mean to be rude. Joseph didn't know I was coming."

"Ja, I see. And you thought you'd take Betsy to go and look for them?"

"No, of course not." Her fingers tightened on the lead rope. "Look, Samuel, I need . . ." How to explain? There wasn't any way. "I need to put my car in the barn or the shop, but the engine died. I thought I could pull it with Betsy. Will you help me?"

He kept her waiting again, studying her with that unhurried stare. Her nerves twitched.

"Well?" she demanded.

Samuel's firm mouth softened in a slow grin. "I see you're as impatient as ever, Anna Beiler. Ja, I will help you." He took the rope from her, his callused fingers brushing hers. "But I wish I knew what you are up to, I do."

She stepped out of his way as he opened the stall door, talking softly to the animal. He didn't seem to expect any answer to his comment, and she couldn't give one.

What could she say? She could hardly tell him that she'd come home because she had no place else to go—and that she was only staying as long as she had to. Little though she wanted to deceive anyone, she had no choice. Gracie's future depended on it.